Duckett
Delivered

Where's Elvis?

Book one

Kim Lemen

Published by Yawn's Publishing
2555 Marietta Hwy, Ste 103
Canton, GA 30114
www.yawnspublishing.com

Library of Congress Control Number: 2016942792

ISBN: 978-1-943529-54-4 paperback
        978-1-943529-55-1 eBook

Cover art:
Front Cover: Concept - Nicholas Worcester
                    Execution - Debbie Byrd
Rear cover concept and execution: Nicholas Worcester

Printed in the United States

Dedicated to Richard, my husband and the bravest guy I know, and to my son, Tyler, the other bravest guy I know.

And also my wonderful parents, Harold and Jean Varner, for their unwavering love and support.

A list of characters can be found
at the back of this book.

Chapter One
Elvis Who?

Sheriff Todd "Fearless" McPherson ducked into his office, plopped down in his creaky wooden swivel chair, and running a hand over his neat blond hair, he regarded the mound of paperwork piled on his desk. Diving in, he signed a dozen reports, not bothering to read them, then shoved them in the appropriate files—at least in his best estimation. After assembling the files in a messy stack, he swiveled his wooden old-fashioned chair around to the row of half-sized filing cabinets that served as his credenza. What he saw displeased him. A sloppy mountain of moldering files was begging for attention. He horse-sighed as he hastily gathered up a number of them.

Before turning back to his desk, he leaned back, stretched out his long, muscular legs and gazed through the picture window at the ancient, softly rounded North Georgia Mountains that embraced Duckett County. Surprisingly, an unexpected disdain for his beloved stomping grounds washed over him. Though the presence of the mountains kept the county's inhabitants safe from outside invasion, they also guaranteed that said inhabitants would remain isolated and backward. The strange feeling vanished as abruptly as it had appeared, and Todd entertained the idea of going hunting in the morning. He was a young sheriff, and sometimes he envied the more carefree lives of his peers. Anyway, the Indian summer had lingered even into this late October, making the idea of traipsing around Duckett Forest in hunting garb unappealing. He glanced at the unadorned clock on the wall. Its ticking always seemed to slow down during the late afternoon. Maybe he could slip out before the mayor arrived for his usual Friday afternoon chinwag. Lately, the old windbag had become increasingly tedious. Todd reached for the aged leather satchel that his father, a farmer, had inherited from his father and grandfather, also farmers. After stuffing

1

some moldering files into it, he stood up to leave.

Right on cue, he heard the tottering footsteps of His Corpulence himself, Mayor Sonny Davis, who reigned over the 945 ½ persons living in the metropolis of Duckettville, the only town in the whole county. Sonny said something to the 911 operator/secretary/ receptionist, LeeLee that made her chortle. Groaning, Todd slumped down in his chair. He was about to become a cornered animal in his own man-cave.

If only Sonny had been held up by a customer at his Moonshine Runners Gently Used Auto lot, which was located on Main Street just up the road from Todd's office. Of course, customers were few and far between in these parts. It only took a few minutes for Sonny to totter up "Main Street" to Todd's antique office, which stood catty-corner to the old red brick county courthouse. What folks called "Main Street" was a few blocks of a lonely two lane highway going east and west. The county courthouse sat on a patch of weedy grass where Main Street met up with another quiet two-lane highway going north and south.

Sonny liked to have his fingers in a lot of pies, so some years ago had asked the county commissioners to appoint him the Chief Operating Officer of the county. It was not an unusual request, given that Duckett County politics were known to be horribly incestuous. As COO, Sonny was Todd's supervisor. That fact rankled Todd at times because the middle-aged politician didn't know shit from shinola about law enforcement. Todd grabbed a file from the satchel and placed it on the desk. May as well look like I'm accomplishing something.

Sonny tottered into the room with a Coca-Cola that he had swiped from the office fridge. He settled his considerable bulk in the guest chair, rubbed his shiny pate, and stacked his feet on Todd's desk. He commenced the usual pre-chinwag pleasantries, though they weren't reciprocated by Todd, who pointedly pulled a file out from under the mayor's feet, which were surprisingly small for a man of his height. Hence the tottering. Todd remarked testily that he'd be a might bit better off if Sonny removed his feet from his desk. Sonny complied then attempted unsuccessfully to cross his elephantine legs while keeping up the obligatory "How's Your Momma?' niceties.

Once the politeness was over, Todd expected Sonny to ask for this week's departmental briefing, but instead the old mayor enthusiastically plowed into his all-too-familiar speech on the bright future of Duckett County.

"Fearless," Sonny said, referring to Todd's old high school football nickname, "You gotta know that the expansion of this county's economic base is—"

"Vital to the well-being of our citizens," rattled off Todd, "especially for the young folk, who are leavin' us in droves." With a barely disguised yawn, he added, "I've been hearin' this same discourse from you for months now."

Sonny watched Todd for a few beats then arranged his features in his trademark used-car-salesman's confident grin. "My, my, ain't we full of spit and vinegar today," he said affably. Todd only shrugged. Sonny drew a long breath. "You gotta know, Fearless, that my mission while in this slightly too heavy earthly body is to bring home jobs—as many jobs as this county can hold." He exhaled and said, "Les and me grew up—"

"In a singlewide in Foggy Bottom with a boozy momma and a series of questionable uncles. And if nothin' ain't done about the lack of development in this county, it will soon be covered over with the kudzu vine run amok." Todd opened the file on his desk, and with a flourish, signed the top paper. Looking at Sonny pointedly, he snapped the folder shut, hoping that the mayor would get the message that it was time to pack it in for the week.

Sonny's smile evaporated. His normally ruddy checks grew a little ruddier. Todd glanced up and caught his boss's expression. He studied his pudgy face, with its Irish button nose and cupid's mouth, which at the moment was drawn in a tight downward bow. Todd ran a hand over his hair. I've done gone too far. He pulled out the container of sanitizing wet wipes and began his pre-departure desk-disinfecting routine.

Instead of lambasting him, Sonny once again composed his features. "Okay, okay, I reckon I've been a broken record lately." He pulled out his handkerchief and wiped perspiration off his forehead and bald pate. His right leg began to jitterbug.

Todd noticed that the frenetic movement of the mayor's appendage had an aggressive quality to it. He had never noticed Sonny to sport a twitchy appendage before. He regarded the stilted smile displayed on the face of this usually garrulous good ol' boy. He's hiding something. Smiling lopsidedly, Todd said, "Look, Sonny, all that growth and development business don't interest me. I'm just not strung that way."

Sonny managed to find his chair's armrests underneath his bulk. "That may be, but you gotta understand, Todd, that..."

As Sonny ran on, Todd's gaze wandered out the window. He daydreamed that the air had turned crisp and he was hunkered down high in a deer stand somewhere in Duckett Forest. A fifteen pointer wandered into range. Holding his breath, he raised his rifle then... "BANG!"

Todd jumped then realized that Sonny had pounded his fist down onto the desk. "Hey, blockhead, no daydreamin' in front of your superior," blurted Sonny, still managing a teasing tone. Todd yawned for the second time, and Sonny now was unable to hide his displeasure. He shook his head, causing his gelatinous chins to waggle. "You just don't get it, do you?"

"Like I want to?" Todd retorted a little too sarcastically.

Sonny's next words had a growly edge to them. "You gotta understand, Fearless, that your future is tied to the future of this—"

"County and as an elected official, I—I meaning me— need to be more pleasant and get out and talk to people, et cetera, et cetera..."

"Maybe I'm startin' to get through," said Sonny warily. "So does this mean you're goin' to the football game tonight?"

"Nope."

Sonny looked like he was sucking on rotten eggs. "You are beginnin' to get on my last nerve, Fearless."

"I gotta ride my fences. That was a nasty storm we had last night," returned Todd, and to himself he added, to be followed by an excessive amount of brooding in front of the TV with a bottle of Budweiser in each hand.

Sonny wiped his perspiring face and commenced to jitterbug his leg again. "Look," Todd said, "I have no idea where you're goin' with all this future of Duckett County talk."

"Lemme explain—agin. The key to a positive future for the county—and for you and me—is the upcomin' referendum on Liquor-by-the-Drink." Todd grimaced. Not the Liquor-by-the-Drink lecture. "If it passes," continued Sonny with his natural enthusiasm returning, "we can get some chain restaurants and—"

"Maybe even a Hooters!" interjected Todd with fake keenness.

Sonny didn't catch the sarcasm. A dreamy expression settled on his features. He was no doubt picturing a Hooters restaurant stuffed with curvy waitresses located just up Main Street across from his Moonshine Runners Gently Used Autos car lot. He gave his head a vigorous shake then went on to wax eloquently on the virtues of the patrons of the Bucking Bull being able to buy hard liquor instead of having to bring it in a brown paper lunch bag. Reeling in Todd's wandering gaze, he said, "This election is our last chance. If that referendum don't pass, this town—this whole county for that matter—is gonna roll over, hooves up."

Todd gave Sonny a deadpan look. "Again, that don't have nothin' to do with yours truly."

Sonny finally lost it. Pulsating with resentment, he stated curtly that he had managed Todd's campaign for sheriff and Todd shouldn't forget it. He added that Todd should especially remember that it was he who came up with the brilliant idea of bringing in Satellite News Network to cover the story of the youngest man in America running for county sheriff. Todd had hated the media's intrusion three years ago, but he had to admit that Sonny's idea had put him over the top at the ballot box.

"All of which means," summarized Sonny, "that you gotta learn how to dance with the one that brung ya."

"You'll step on my toes."

"Seems like lately all I hear from you is a bunch of smart remarks. I'm talkin' about the stuff that goes on in the backroom, Todd. You gotta know how the game is played. You—"

"What's with all the clichés?" Todd had by now gone from bored out of his mind to irritated consternation. Sonny pressed his poochy lips together, as if he were sealing in his words. Todd sat back and placed his hands behind his head. "Oh that backroom. Sorry, Sonny, but I'm allergic to cigar smoke." *Why do I behave this way?*

Sonny's face shaded toward reddish-purple. "Listen up, numbskull you gotta learn to roll some logs, or you ain't long for this job."

"Let's just hull this down." Todd leaned forward and peered into Sonny's beady blues. "What do you want from me?"

"I want a letter to the Duckettville Weekly stating that the roads would be safer if Liquor-by-the-Drink passes."

"No can do. The data don't support it."

"It's not a request."

"You know me better'n that. I ain't a gonna roll logs when it comes to misleadin' the civilians."

Sonny crumpled his empty Coca-Cola can then leaned over and slammed it into the wastebasket. For once in his life, he was speechless. Still glaring, he pried his bulk out of the chair, angrily tugged on the bottom of his sports coat, and stormed out of the office.

Todd stepped out of his office and watched his boss stomp across the lobby. When Sonny reached the front door, he turned back. "You think real hard about what I said." He passed through the doorway.

Todd muttered too loudly, "Yeah, yeah, don't let the door slam you in the butt."

6

Sonny stuck his head back in. "What'd you say?"

LeeLee, Todd's receptionist and 911 operator, had watched the scene from her desk. She quickly offered, "He said, 'Don't step in that mud out front.'" LeeLee was the mother of one of Todd's best friends growing up, and she could be quick to cover Todd's back when necessary. Sonny grunted then closed the door too loudly. LeeLee, wireless headset perched on her short, brown, bubble top hair, rolled her office chair around the corner to confront Todd. "Honestly, Fearless," she huffed, "you can be so ornery. If they throwed you in the river, you'd float upstream!"

"Didn't I tell you not to be rollin' that chair all around the office," snapped Todd. LeeLee gave him a look and crossed her arms. She was a petite woman, but she could look mighty big when worked up. As he rolled her back to her desk, Todd grumbled, "I'm beginnin' to think that Sonny Davis is the biggest pocket of untapped natural gas known to man." Todd crossed the lobby and locked the front door. "You need to keep your ear flaps folded in, Mrs. Lee Ann Lee," he said as he pulled down the shades.

LeeLee's clear periwinkle eyes narrowed. "And you're in sore need of a woman. You best get on up the street to the wart taker and get her to conjure you up one."

"And your tongue's a mile long." Todd returned to LeeLee's desk, spread his feet, and crossed his arms. He had discovered that body language was an aid to establishing authority over people who were decades older than him. He said, "Dispatch Dillon to come in from the field. He seems to have forgotten he has station duty for swing shift. Tawanda is pulling a double shift and she can't do everything by herself. Tell him that."

"Scratch will be takin' my dispatchin' duties in five minutes. Let him do it."

Todd gave LeeLee another no-nonsense look. She scrunched up her pixie features and stuck out her tongue. He growled low in his throat

7

then headed through the open door to "perp walk", the hall through the area where the prisoners were kept. There were only four jail cells on each side of the hall. The cells were old style, with bars across the front of each one. There was only a curtain in front of each cell to provide privacy for females. Todd's antiquated jailhouse provided for only short term accommodations for arrestees. The county had to contract out to a neighboring county for longer jail stays. Every time Todd walked up perp walk, he silently cursed the county commissioners. Instead of allocating tax dollars to build a new sheriff's office, they were planning to build a golf course, mostly for their own use. Few of the county's country folk could afford to pay for the privilege of swinging a stick at a little white ball when in their free time they could be putting food on the table by hunting game.

Todd stopped at the privacy curtain in front of his only prisoner. He peered through the viewing pane and saw that Tonya Wigglesworth was asleep on her bunk and snoring loudly. The night before she had gotten soused and aimed her Cadillac SUV at the nice hot tub that her husband, Dude, had built. She floored it and ended up with the front left tire submerged. Unfortunately, Dude's mother was in the hot tub at the time and that fact had been enough to get Tonya arrested. With mother and wife now separated, Dude was home, enjoying the peace and quiet so much that he was dragging his feet with respect to putting up Tonya's bail money.

As if a hard snore was not proof of life, Todd stepped in and shook Tonya's shoulder. She mumbled something then turned on her side. Satisfied, Todd made a notation on the checklist on the clipboard hanging outside her cell. He walked to the locker room and pulled his running clothes out of his locker. He exited through the back door, locked it, and then sat in his sheriff's Bronco and called his mother, letting her know that he was on his way home. He asked if Molly had gotten off the school bus okay. His daughter had entered kindergarten the previous month and Todd was having a tough time with the idea of her riding the bus. Kids going to middle and high school rode the same bus along with the elementary school students.

Just as he was about to roll out of the fissured asphalt lot, LeeLee flew down the back steps, waving her arms frantically. Though generally competent, she was a high maintenance dispatcher. Even the most minor call had the potential for unnerving her. The younger two of her three sons were Navy Seals and were involved in black-box anti-terrorist operations overseas, and this fact caused her anxiety to reach a new high every day. Right now, she was breathing like an accordion at a hoedown, and she was quaking from her hair down to her impeccably clean sneakers. Todd thought she must wash her sneakers in her washing machine every night. All these thoughts rushed through his mind in the time it took for LeeLee to dash down the steps.

As Todd stepped out of the Bronco, LeeLee said breathlessly, "A hiker has done found a body! Actually, she said it was a piece of a body!" She paused to gulp air. "She didn't say which piece," gulp, gulp, "and she ain't seen no more parts layin' around—leastwise, that's what she said!"

"Where?" Todd didn't wait for her answer, because he already knew where. Duckett Forest. In two steps he ascended the back stoop with LeeLee in tow. Inside, he passed the clumsy field kit to her, then threw a half-dozen pairs of binoculars and the same number of two-way radios into a cardboard box. Tawanda Berry, Todd's only black deputy and perennial office homebody, assisted Todd in tossing a number of orange vests, whistles, and flashlights into the box. Todd then hustled outside with a nervously yapping LeeLee at his heels. He stowed everything in the Bronco then bent down, placed his hands on LeeLee's shoulders, and said sternly, "Now focus. Exactly where in the Forest did the caller find the body part?"

By now LeeLee was close to passing out from hyperventilation, but she still managed to whine, "Oh, why do all those Atlanta murderers dump their dead folk in our nice wilderness?" She balled her petite fists.

"They should keep their bodies to themselves!"

"Come on, spit it out! Where in the Forest?"

LeeLee suddenly shrank back and in an I-don't-know-nothin'-about-birthin'-no-babies whine, she said, "I-I cain't remember. She was so scared. I heard how scared she was. I felt it…"

Growling like a perturbed bear, Todd straightened and ran a hand over his hair. Then, as if LeeLee were a tube of toothpaste, he bent down again and squeezed the small woman's upper arms in the hope that more information would issue forth. "LeeLeeeee!" He bored into her with his deep blue eyes.

Suddenly, she came to attention and blurted, "Off Boggs Road, two miles west of the Creepy Creek cut through. She said the body part's in a clearin' about a half mile up that old injun trail. Blaine's almost there already."

Todd knew that clearing. He was one of only a handful of men who could not get lost in the 19,468 acres that made up the Duckett County Wildlife Management Area, known colloquially as Duckett Forest.

LeeLee turned to run inside, but Todd spun her around. "Listen here, we need a search party. Rustle up the usual volunteers then send a dozen deputies to that sector. And call the State Patrol, we need boots on the ground." LeeLee turned toward the stoop, but Todd pulled her back again. "Call Scratch in early to take over dispatch. When he gets here, you drive to my place and pick up my bloodhound then meet me at the scene." He hurriedly stepped into the Bronco and slammed the door.

"I ain't goin' back up in there!" yelled LeeLee. As Todd peeled out, she stood on her tiptoes, cupped her mouth with her petite hands and yelled even louder, "Hound dog handlin' ain't in my job description!"

* * * * *

Todd pulled the Bronco over at the trail entrance. As he stepped out of the truck, he spied Deputy Virgil Pilch speeding towards him in

10

cruiser No. 2, its lights flashing and siren screaming, all of which was unnecessary on this road because just like many of the others in Duckett County, it was lightly traveled. The cruiser screeched to a halt. The veteran deputy threw open the door, unwound his long, spindly legs, and sprang out of the vehicle as quickly as a cat pouncing on a robin. Twitching with excitement, he combed his stringy, colorless hair with his boney fingers in anticipation of an impending media blitz from Atlanta. He pulled a shotgun out of the trunk. Todd shook his head. Virgil gave him the stink eye and reluctantly stowed the weapon. He grudgingly accepted the field kit. Cody zoomed in from the east in cruiser No. 10. Shawn raced in from the west in cruiser No. 7. Both vehicles sported flashing lights accompanied by wailing sirens. Each of the young deputies whipped his squealing vehicle into a three-sixty and landed on the side of the road behind Todd's Bronco. When they emerged, Todd growled, "That little stunt is gonna cost y'all." It was all he could think to say given the pressing situation. He told them how to get to the site, but that they needed to wait for the other deputies and the search-and-rescue volunteers to show up. Then he handed each of the disappointed deputies a box of supplies.

Todd spotted a tangle of bootprints entering and exiting the entrance to the trail. The trail headed into a dense copse of mountain laurel and rhododendron and thick underbrush. Todd carefully picked his way beside the path so as to avoid stepping on the bootprints. Virgil followed close on his heels like an eager coon dog. It had rained two days earlier, and the soft ground offered up some excellent medium for the prints, now hardened by the sun. Sheriff and deputy continued to shadow the trail until they came to a part where it widened temporarily. Here the trails of bootprints separated just enough to make some sense of them. One of the trails was made by a set of male-sized boots going up the path and then returning. Todd guessed that this person had come from the road, having returned from somewhere up the trail. It was probably where the suspected body part had been found. By the erratic nature of the prints, Todd guessed that the man had been stumbling.

There was also a trail of smaller bootprints belonging to a sub-adult male or a woman. A medium-sized dog had accompanied this person. They also appeared to have made the round trip. They had walked up the trail, but by the change in indention, Todd could tell that they had hustled back. The same person appeared to have returned up the trail with the dog, followed by the unmistakable print of a pair of the department's regulation shoes. Todd guessed that the responding deputy, his second cousin Blaine Hensley, had made these prints. The smaller bootprints belonged to the caller. That meant the depositor of the body part could have made the larger bootprints.

Every time Todd spotted a particularly distinct print made by the larger boots, he instructed Virgil to stick a flag beside it. In between his flag-planting duty, Virgil, impatient to get to the site, bobbed and weaved like a basketball player, pressing an annoyed Todd from behind. Eventually, the thickening underbrush forced the sheriff and the deputy onto the path, and they began to perform a leaping-fairy dance in an attempt to preserve the footprints. Finally, Todd fairy-leapt into a good-sized clearing, and what he saw brought him up short. Perched on a bent-over tree trunk was a lovely young woman sporting long, loose, dark-chocolate curls. Her locks were pulled back in a barrette, but much of it had escaped confinement and fell loosely about her shoulders, while wisps of it framed her finely boned face.

Her back was to Blaine, who was standing ten yards beyond. The fleshy young rookie had positioned himself beside a three-foot-tall rock, and he was excitedly motioning for Todd to hurry. Eyes on the trail, Virgil leapt into the clearing and crashed into Todd. To Todd's mighty embarrassment, he noticed the look on the girl's face said that she didn't suffer fools. As much as he wanted to hang his head, he couldn't take his eyes off of her. She was wearing a sleeveless tan shirt, tan shorts, and low-cut hiking boots. Though she was sitting, Todd estimated that she was around five-foot-eight or -nine and was in the possession of a fine figure. She was clutching a leash that was attached to a panting liver-spotted English setter lying at her feet.

"Afternoon," Todd nodded to the girl. "You the caller?"

She gave him a well-duh look that made him blush. "Yes, it was I, Jasmine Roseberry," she stated in a disciplined British accent.

Todd rubbed his forehead in an effort to anchor himself. Just looking into Jasmine Roseberry's doe-eyes, fringed with long, dark lashes, made him lightheaded. "You alright?" he asked. She responded by folding and cradling her arms and studying the ground. Todd said, "I'm Sheriff Todd McPherson, and this is my deputy, Virgil Pilch." He motioned with his head toward Virgil, who was flagging a print while keeping one eye on the female furriner. "I take it you've met Deputy Hensley." He motioned toward Blaine.

Jasmine leaned forward and said in a stage whisper, "Yes. He's a bit "puckish", if you ask me."

Todd didn't know what puckish meant, but he took a stab. "Oh, he's just gotta baby face." He was rewarded with a quizzical stare. Beyond Jasmine, Blaine was alternately fidgeting and pacing. He gave Todd a hard glare and gestured grandly to the rock.

Todd nodded toward the dog at Jasmine's feet. "Nice dog." He jerked up the waist of his pants and tucked in his shirt. (It was a habitual move made by all lawmen who wore the weighty duty belt from which hung a number of implements.) "I'll just go have a look-see." Then he turned back to the girl. "I need you to hang around for now, okay?" She nodded reluctantly then looked away.

Virgil began to fumble about, looking every bit like he'd suddenly lost his desire to see the body part. Todd impatiently motioned for him to follow, but Virgil pretended not to notice. Todd's sharp whistle brought the dawdling deputy to attention and he dutifully fell in behind Todd.

As Todd approached the rock, he saw that Blaine's khaki shirt displayed a dark smile underneath his man-boobs. "You're not gonna believe this," Blaine panted. He moved out of the way, and there on a three-foot high, flat, gray rock, laid out neat as a Jimmy Dean sausage, was a human penis.

Virgil bent over to inspect the specimen. He gulped and said, "Jesus, it's a ... a tallywhacker!" He snapped up and dropped the field kit on Todd's foot. Todd swore as he hopped on the other foot. Virgil covered his crotch. "It's just like that Loretta Blobbitt woman—the one that chopped off her philaderin' husband's willy. Only it's happenin' here in Duckett County!" His head swiveled around nervously, as if he expected some knife wielding Kamikaze female to leap out of the underbrush and castrate all of them on the spot.

"Damn it, focus, Virgil!" growled Todd as he shook his sore foot.

"We shoulda brought the rifle, Young Buck." Virgil attempted to force his attention back to the body part, but as if they had a will of their own, his eyes darted about the edge of the clearing. His squinty gaze shifted in the direction of Jasmine, who was reaching down to stroke her nervously panting dog. He muttered, "She ain't from around here."

"It was Lorena Blobbitt, you nitwit," said Blaine, who prided himself on being in possession of a greater number for brain cells than Virgil. Todd realized that Blaine was too young to realize that slugs commanded more brain cells than Virgil.

"Lorena Bobbitt," said Todd tersely. Even at their tender age, Todd and every other third-grade boy at Duckett Elementary somehow knew about the Bobbitt case. He knelt down, and dug the magnifying glass out of the field kit. The specimen was Caucasian and circumcised. There was some blood. Average size, he guessed. It hadn't been there long, due to the fact that a carnivorous critter had not yet made an afternoon snack of it. He rubbed his chin, stood up, and looked at Blaine. "You search the immediate area?"

"Gawd no," blurted Blaine, looking around nervously.

Todd gave him a look then turned to Virgil. "Get out the chalk and outline the ... ah ... victim—and don't look at me like that."

14

"But Fearless, nobody outlines bodies no more," whined Virgil.

Todd's radio crackled on. It was the county medical examiner. Todd briefed him on the situation then turned back to Virgil. "They don't outline bodies anymore, but this...thing needs to go in a sterile container ASAP, and that means before we finish processin' the scene." Virgil nodded grudgingly and dug into the crime-scene kit for an old piece of chalk.

Todd returned his attention to the tracks. "Lookee here, both sets of bootprints come right up to this rock." He looked back at Jasmine, who had once again turned her back to them as she stroked her dog. He eyeballed her boots, while trying to ignore her shapely calves. He jerked his head in her direction. "The dog's prints are shadowing this set of smaller prints. These are definitely from her."

"She could have dropped the package off first, then called us," stated Virgil, boring a hole into Jasmine's back with narrowed eyes.

Todd said, "She's actin' scared, but not guilty, and she doesn't have any blood on her hands." He pointed to one of the large footprints. "These are the prints made by the person who placed the penis on the rock. He hurried in from the road, left this specimen, and then hustled back to the road. Of course, just to be thorough, we'll have the search-and-rescue team comb the area."

"Looks like the prints were made by a Georgia Boot," offered Virgil.

Blaine snorted. "Ninety-nine percent of the households in Duckett County got at least one pair of Georgia Boots."

Todd ordered Virgil to get some molds of the tracks after he'd finished with the specimen. He instructed Blaine to set up a perimeter, and then told both of them to search the site thirty yards out upon completing their current tasks.

Blaine whined, "But Todd, the brush is as thick as—"

"Just find a way," growled Todd.

Virgil snapped on a pair of rubber gloves, and despite his trembling hands, accurately outlined the specimen. Blaine pulled a roll of yellow crime-scene tape from the crime bag. Todd radioed Scratch and told him to dispatch more deputies to the scene and to request outside help from neighboring counties and the State Patrol. He clicked off and said to Virgil, "Now, take the Q-tips and get a blood sample. Stroke the sides too. Maybe you can pick up some epithelial cells in case it had sex recently."

Virgil recoiled. "I cain't do that. Besides we ain't s'posed to touch a corpse before the ME gets here."

"That rule only applies to whole bodies," lied Todd. The truth was that he wanted his own samples because Doc Mahmondi occasionally misplaced the samples that he took before said samples could be transported to the state crime lab. It wasn't that the young doc wasn't competent; it was just that, having no enthusiasm for his part-time coroner's job, he tended to confine his competency to his living patients.

A shudder rifled down Virgil's spine. "I just cain't do it," he whined.

"Why the hell not? You help Doc take samples from bodies all the time." Todd was not a particularly patient man, and Virgil had a gift for pushing him right up to the edge.

"Yeah, but those bodies are dead - dead, and this thing is…sorta undead."

Blaine, who was wrapping yellow crime-scene tape around a tree, snickered. "Well, it's not like it's pulsatin' like an alien or somethin'."

Virgil succumbed to nervous laughter. "It's the alien from Planet Testosterone!" Blaine burst out laughing.

Todd grabbed the Q-tips from Virgil. "Step away from the penis." he ordered gruffly. The two deputies chortled. "You two need to get a hold of yourselves," growled Todd. "There's a female civilian back there." He looked at the girl and saw that she was staring back at them with a thoroughly disgusted look on her face.

Virgil and Blaine struggled to suppress their mirth, but after a few beats, they erupted in renewed gales of laughter. Blaine asked between outbreaks of high-pitched giggling, "If I have to tag it and bag it, which end do I tag and which do I bag?"

"Hey, Todd," said a cackling Virgil, "if you wanna make the ex-owner proud, wait 'til rigor mortis sets in to measure it." Blaine fell into a new round of hysterical giggling, punctuated by queer little hiccups.

Todd pointed in the direction of the highway. "If you two can't control yourselves, go to your vehicles! I mean it—now!"

Blaine and Virgil each propped themselves up by placing a hand on a tree and leaning into it. In a constricted voice, Virgil said, "We're good, Baby Chief, I mean Chief." Lest he start giggling again, Blaine remained mute, but came to attention and clicked his heels together.

As Todd gathered the samples, he said, "Be on the lookout for Vince. I expect him to be here any minute."

"Speak of the devil," said Blaine as he spied Vince Verona fairy-leaping into the clearing. The mid-forties owner of the Duckettville Weekly frequently served as a volunteer police photographer. Addicted to his police scanner, Vince often reached a crime scene before the deputies. He was a man whose height was just under what one would call tall, of Mediterranean complexion, and in possession of neatly trimmed, nondescript brown hair. As usual, a camera was swinging from his neck. He paused in front of the young lady, touched the brim of his old-time reporter's hat, then moved on toward the three lawmen.

Blaine pointed at the rock. "You're not gonna believe this."

Vince stepped forward and bent over to inspect the specimen. "Holy fuckoli, is that what I think it is?" he asked in his South-Side-Chicago accent (tempered by a self-financed college education).

Blaine snickered. "It ain't gonna be doin' no fuckoli no more!"

"Jesus wept!" Vince quickly crossed himself. "Who in the name of Peter, Paul, and Mary lost their fucking monkey leg?" His quick, fox-like eyes darted around the edge of the clearing.

Virgil pulled his waistband out and looked down his perennially loose pants. "It ain't mine." Blaine giggled, and both deputies received a glare from Todd.

Vince went about the business of taking photos, while Todd pulled a ruler from the field kit and placed it beside the specimen. Virgil and Blaine scrambled over to check out the thing's measurements for the sake of self-comparison. Todd rolled his eyes and ordered them to get on with their search. Grumbling, both men went about the business of attempting to pry open a space between the dense, low-slung mountain laurel trees. As they squeezed through, Todd called out, "If y'all see someone with a knife, holler."

Blaine's voice came back. "If we got throats left, that is."

From her perch on the bent-over tree, Jasmine called out, "Hellooo! Excuse me, Constable, but I'd rather like to take my leave." Todd walked back to her, noting that her face was very pale. She slid off the tree, but as soon as her feet touched the ground, she began to wobble.

"Whoa there!" said Todd as he took her elbow and helped her back on the tree trunk. He sat next to her. "You've had quite a shock." She didn't respond. He rubbed the thick, crusted bark of the ancient oak. "The Cherokees did this. They bent young, pliable trees to mark the best hunting trails. This tree grew bigger with time, but it stayed bent-over like this. Couple of hundred years later, it makes a pretty nice seat." *What am I babbling about?*

The woman must have been thinking the same thing, because she just stared at him out of those remarkable eyes. Todd thought she looked like some young countess in an antique painting with her porcelain skin, pouty lips, smooth, thoroughbred legs… *I'm mentally feeling up my caller and not ten yards away some man's disembodied ding-dong is on display. Jeez.*

"Might I take my leave now?" Jasmine asked again.

Todd rubbed his chin. "Well, I tell you what. I really should send you down to the office with a deputy and get a signed statement. But if you answer some questions now, I'll let you stop by in the mornin' and we'll do all the official paperwork then. How's that sound?"

Jasmine kicked at the dirt beneath her feet. "Tomorrow is Saturday."

To Todd, even the girl's scowl was sexy. "This is a special situation," he explained. "Some fella has lost his…ah … important part, and we need to figure out what happened. We're most likely lookin' at a homicide here," he said in his most authoritative voice. "So, we got a deal?"

She brushed a wisp of hair away from her face. "I don't really have a choice, do I?"

Todd pulled out his black memo book. "So what's your full name?"

The girl suddenly appeared contrite. "Forgive me. What I just said sounded quite insensitive. My given name is Jasmine Olivia Roseberry." She extended her hand.

Todd switched the memo book to the left hand and took hers. Immediately, its smoothness created a pleasant sensation that spread throughout his body. "Nice to meet you, Jasmine Olivia Roseberry. You can call me Todd. Can I call you Jasmine?" Todd held her gaze and smiled his warmest smile to put her at ease. It usually worked well with women.

Jasmine, however, appeared doubtful. "I suppose. But I shall need my hand back. I function better with two."

"Oh, sure." Todd surrendered her hand, then asked for her phone number and address and wrote it in his memo pad. He looked up, saw her studying him idly, and felt his face growing warm, "Ah, you ain't— are not—from around here, are ya?"

"I was born in Cambridge, Great Britain, but I attended Harvard University in Boston and have lived in Beantown for four years since graduating. I also received my master's degree from Brandeis while I was working at—"

"I have degrees in history and criminal justice," blurted Todd.

19

During his campaign for office, this fact had impressed the electorate, since more than half of them hadn't graduated from high school. But he realized that in this situation, he had made a major blunder. The girl gave him a quizzical, if not slightly annoyed look, as if to say, "What's does that have to do with anything?" Todd dug himself in further by saying, "I graduated from Young Harris College, which is just a few counties over." The girl's frown deepened. To hide his blush, Todd ducked his head and pretended to write something on the memo pad. "I bet Duckett County is sure a change of pace."

Jasmine exhaled deeply. "Oh, you have no idea. Anyway, I will bring you my passport and my green card tomorrow if you like."

"That's not necessary," Todd replied reassuringly. Non-citizens could be very touchy over police matters, even the ones that were here legally.

Jasmine swept her curls to one side. "I moved to Emerald Lake Resort a week ago. Today, I was hiking in this forest with my dog Tristan, here."

"Hey, fella," said Todd. Tristan sat up and Todd reached down and gave him a scratch behind the ears. "I like your dog." *If I like your dog, can I pet you too?* Todd had to bite his tongue to keep from blurting such a stupid thought out loud.

Jasmine fastened her eyes on his and said irritably, "Sheriff, twice you've complimented me on my dog. I'm quite delighted that you are fond of my pet, but can we get through this ordeal so I can get the bloody hell out of here?"

Todd would not allow her to draw him off the track. "Hiking in Duckett Forest ain't … isn't allowed durin' huntin' season, so you are real lucky that you haven't gotten shot."

"Frankly, I've heard only silence in all directions," she returned.

To Todd, Jasmine Olivia Roseberry talked like the long-gowned actresses who played across from Cary Grant in the old black-and-white movies that his widowed mother watched on cold, rainy nights. He said,

"Here's the thing. You and me are sittin' in this county's very own humongous huntin' park, which in itself is cradled by nearly a million acres that make up the Chattahoochee National Forest. And, as if that weren't enough unruliness for anybody, said forest is snuggled up to another half-million acres of federal wilderness along our border with North Carolina. That's a lot of game comin' our way. So, trust me when I say you can't swing a cat in this county without hittin' a hunter."

"But—"

"And a high-powered rifle can propel a shell a long, long way." Jasmine stared into the woods, visibly bristling at his chastisement, but she held her tongue. Todd added, "Back to the subject at hand." He looked Jasmine in the eye. "You have any idea who ... ?"

"None whatsoever," she snapped, emphasizing each syllable.

Todd abruptly changed directions. It was a tactic he often used. "You said you just moved to Emerald Lake. There are lots of hiking trails up there inside the resort and you'd be safer cuz no huntin' is allowed inside the resort. Of course, anywhere you hike this time of year you risk runnin' into a bear. They're out scarfin' down everything in sight to get ready for winter. And then there are the mountain rattlers and the copperheads... It'd be better if you hiked with a partner." Todd realized he was rambling. He couldn't remember what his point was. The girl's exquisiteness intoxicated him.

Her dark eyes flashed and she said stiffly, "I've already hiked a number of the trails at Emerald Lake. I can take care of myself. I was a Girl Guide in my youth." She was clearly miffed at his assumption that he thought she was a babe in the woods. "As for the bears," she continued, "that's why I wear this anklet of jingle bells." She lifted her smooth, shapely calf to show the suede band with attached bells loosely tied around her ankle. "It's to let them know I'm around so I don't scare them." She folded her arms and returned his frank gaze.

Todd had to look away to keep from laughing out loud. What notions these granola-munching, city slickers believed! She was definitely a furriner, which in Southern Appalachian terms meant anyone from above the Mason-Dixon Line and beyond, and that certainly included English people. Todd might be head over heels, but he still had to rule her out as a suspect. "Speakin' of ankles—I mean boots—I need you to bring in one of yours tomorrow." Jasmine gave him yet another confused frown. He pointed to the bootprints on the ground. "We're going to cast a few of these. I wanna verify that these smaller ones match 100 percent the sole of your boot. I need to eliminate any ambiguity that the other set of prints came from the person who deposited the ... ah ... body part. So if you don't mind, please bring your boot down to the office tomorrow." Jasmine shrugged her consent. Keeping his voice friendly, Todd asked, "So you just moved in. Don't you have like a million things to do? How do you have so much time to traipse around the woods?"

"Because," Jasmine proceeded as if she were an irritated teacher dressing down an errant second grader, "the bloody moving company shipped the totality of my belongings to Emerald Lake, Montana. It seems they had a computer glitch. I'm going to be working for the resort, but my new boss is out of town, and he didn't want me to begin until Monday when he will be back in the office. This was supposed to be my unpacking and settling-in week, but there was nothing to unpack." She pulled her hair off her shapely neck and continued in a bristly manner, "Now you know precisely why I've been traipsing around, as you so eloquently describe it." Jasmine crossed her arms again. "I'm quite offended that a total stranger would accuse me of fannying about."

Todd held up his hands in surrender. "Oh, no, no, no, neeew. I would never take you for the ah ... the fannying type." He quickly followed with, "So what kind of work will you do at Emerald Lake?"

"I'm the new Chief Financial Officer for the Property Owners Association. I'll be working for the General Manager, Mr. Les Davis. You can verify that on Monday—"

Todd thought that Jasmine Roseberry looked far too young to be the CFO of anything, but then a lot of people also thought he was too young for his job. He cleared his throat. "Let's get back on track. Did you see anyone while you were hikin'?"

"No."

"Hear anything out of the ordinary?"

"Absolutely not."

"Did you see any vehicles on the road?"

"This is a lonely spot of earth, this place."

Todd smiled crookedly and returned his black memo pad to his back pocket. "Yes Ma'am. This county is understocked with people and overstocked with raw land. May I look inside your pack?" He pointed to the old-fashioned canvas backpack lying against the tree trunk.

Jasmine's eyes widened. "You really think I…?" Todd just kept watching her. "Oh, how pervy," she said. She reached down to grab the pack.

"I'll take it," said Todd abruptly. "Excuse me." He reached over her to pick up the backpack. A bolt of electricity shot through him as his chest lightly touched her thighs. Jeez, it's like I'm thirteen again. Trying to sound as professional as possible, he asked, "Is there anything in here that I need to know about before I look inside?" Jasmine gave him a perplexed frown. Todd added, "Any guns, needles, grenades, or maybe Jimmy Hoffa's toes?"

Jasmine looked even more confused, but shook her head. Todd began to open the bag, and she blurted, "Watch out for the butcher knife!"

Todd hesitated, and then glanced at her. He stuck his hand in the bag and yelled, "Ouch!" He jerked it out and vigorously shook his finger.

Jasmine's eyes flew open, then she burst out with a bewitching laugh. Blushing, she covered her mouth with her hand and looked away. When she looked back, Todd gave her a bona fide Southern-boy grin, reached in the pack, and pulled out a cell phone, a bottle of water, an extra pair of socks, a map, keys, and a wallet. He checked the wallet to see if her driver's license matched the unusual name that she had given him. He stuffed the items back in the pack and handed it to her. He said in a conversational tone, "So, how'd you come across the…ah…item?"

Jasmine gestured toward the path. "We were walking through here and Tristan had run on ahead. My apologies, I suppose you have a county leash law."

Todd chuckled. "The only animals kept on leashes in this county are the married men. Go on."

"Tristan halted all of a sudden and commenced to whining and—"

Alarmed, Todd reached out and touched her on the arm. "He didn't fetch it, did he?"

"Oh, no. Tristan is an expertly trained English setter. He stood in perfect point position until I caught up with him."

"Good boy, Tristan." Todd reached down and scratched the canine behind the ears again, resulting in an appreciative tail-thumping. Todd looked up in time to see a tiny smile appear at the corners of the Jasmine's lovely lips. A breeze blew some wisps of hair across her face, and she reached up to brush them back. Inexplicably, all activity in the clearing seemed to cease. Suddenly, Todd and Jasmine were a young man and a young lady listening to the wind rustling through the tall Georgia pines. With soft, enquiring eyes, they tentatively explored each other, every glance heavily scented with a myriad of possibilities.

Then Shawn and Cody fairy-leapt into the clearing, and as quickly as a hummingbird's departure, the enchanted moment evaporated. The search-and-rescue volunteers began to trickle in. Todd stood to greet them. First up was Coach Flagg, who had hastily departed the high school football field, leaving his assistant in charge of whipping the team into preparedness for tonight's game. Wild horses couldn't drag the coach away from practice, but he would do anything for Todd. The rest of the volunteers were Todd's neighbors on Main Street. Tammy Flagg, daughter-in-law of Coach Flagg, was wearing her usual pissed-off expression. Her tight jeans were stretched over her generous thighs, and her favorite Dale Earnhardt Jr. T-shirt was stretched across her buxom bosom. It was the uniform that she wore at the restaurant she owned, the Checkered Flagg Grill and Poolroom. Next up was Todd's former father-in-law, Preacher Dodge, pastor of the Evangelical Church of the Last Hope, carrying a Bible in his left hand and a walking stick in his right, which he would use to probe the underbrush. He was followed by Sikes Freeman, a late-fiftyish African-American man. Sikes was the owner of Freeman's Gun Repair and Barbershop. Next up was the owner of Hair Haven, Bambi Davis. She was wearing her beauty-parlor smock and sporting a head full of foil wrappers. Todd thought that if he hooked her up to a shortwave radio, she could probably pick up a dozen channels. He decided that even with her fawn-colored hair in tinfoil, Bambi was cute as a dimpled ladybug, especially with that determined look she was wearing on her pretty face. Middle-aged Marvalena LeJuene, the local wart taker, brought up the rear. Oddly, her long, frizzy, gray hair abruptly turned blonde halfway down to the ends. Weird. Unruly strands of it danced spasmodically in the breeze. Todd noticed that Marvalena was carrying her magic wand, a divining rod that she usually used for finding water. He wondered how a divining rod was supposed to help find a body.

As the group gathered quietly around him, Todd breathed a sigh of relief. With grateful eyes, he sent each member of the team a silent, somber greeting. These people knew from experience how to comb through wilderness for bodies because they had done it too many times. Todd waved them towards the dismembered member, but he remained sitting the bent-over tree that held the Enchantress of the Forest. Just one more minute.

LeeLee burst into the clearing. She was doing her best to control Hooty, who upon spying Todd, began to bellow and pull hard on his lead, forcing her to stumble forward in order to keep from falling face-first. Her unsteady stride was only made worse by the fact that she was shielding her eyes with her spare hand so that she could only see the ground immediately in front of her. She stumbled up to the tree and handed Hooty's lead to Todd. Virgil appeared from out of the underbrush and reported that there was nothing in the nearby vicinity. Typically, he began to hover nervously. Todd handed off Hooty's lead to him.

LeeLee whined, "I done my duty. Can I go home now?"

Todd turned to his new love. "Jasmine, this is our day dispatcher, Ms. Lee Ann Lee. We call her LeeLee." Rising, he helped Jasmine off the tree trunk. "She is the one that answered your 911 call."

"Enchanted," said Jasmine. "I'm going back with you."

"Hey," muttered LeeLee. She lifted her hand from her eyes long enough to snatch a quick look at the bewildered furriner. "I'll walk you back to yer car - long as you don't tell me nothin' about what you seen."

"I shall endeavor to scare up the necessary self-control."

Todd pulled LeeLee aside. "When you get back…" He lowered her hand from her eyes. "When you get back, I need you to put out an all-points bulletin on anyone with a missing penis, and also contact all the emergency rooms in the area askin' if anyone minus a penis had been admitted."

LeeLee's over-plucked brows drew together. "Scratch is on duty now. Let him do it."

"Scratch will be busy with dispatchin'. Plus, he's too young to…ah…handle this situation."

"Well, I won't do it!"

Todd bent down, rested his hands on his knees and with his eyes bored down on LeeLee. "Yes, you will."

"No, I cain't! I cain't call it a p…you know. I won't!" She stomped her elfin foot, balled her hands, and looked for all the world like she was going to take on Todd, even though that he loomed over her and weighed twice as much.

Todd straightened and rubbed his forehead, then glared her down.

26

"Look, Stands With Fist, sometimes we all gotta do things we don't wanna do." He bent down again and locked on her eyes. "You figure out what the hell to call it, just make sure you know they know what you mean. You know what I mean?" LeeLee pressed her lips together so tightly that they turned ashen. Todd straightened up again and exhaled noisily. "What is this—uncooperative female day?" he muttered glancing at Jasmine, who was standing a few yards away with her arms folded and crossed. He bent down again and laid his hands on LeeLee's slender shoulders. "Come on, LeeLee, I'm countin' on you." He gave her a little shake and then pulled a twig from her hair. "You're still my gal ain't cha?"

LeeLee's features softened. "I reckon," LeeLee said on the wings of a sigh. Todd knew that in the end there was nothing LeeLee wouldn't do for him. She blurted, "But I know I'm gonna make a complete idjit of myself!" She turned on her heel and said to Jasmine, "Come on, Miss English Gal." She took Jasmine's arm. "Let's blow this scene." LeeLee gave Todd a withering look as she stomped off with Jasmine in tow. Skirting the trail, the mismatched pair threaded their way through a dozen leaping deputies.

The deputies wordlessly congregated around Todd, who motioned them towards the crime scene. They moved on and assembled themselves just outside the volunteers, who had arranged themselves outside the circle of crime-scene tape.

As Todd followed, it occurred to him that he was viewing the scene of a pagan ritual. He rubbed his eyes vigorously, fearing that if he couldn't rid himself of that vision, he would start giggling like Blaine. He kneeled down, and the team closed in around him while he drew a circle in the dirt with a stick. "Virgil and Blaine have searched the heavy brush, which extends ten yards out. After that visibility will be much better. The terrain is rough, so be care—"

"Hold on, Todd," interrupted Preacher Dodge, raising his Bible. "As head of the volunteers, I think we oughta take a moment to pray."

"With all due respect, Preacher," interjected Marvalena, "we can each say a prayer when we put our tired butts to bed tonight. Right now, we need to get out there and find the rest of this poor soul."

Todd growled under his breath. This was no time for an ecumenical argument between fundamentalist preacher and a witch.

Preacher Dodge gave Marvalena a stern look. "That divinin' rod you're carryin' ain't gonna help us none. We gotta rely upon Jesus right now."

"I vote for prayin'," said Bambi, her round doe-eyes darting around the clearing, the foils in her hair glistening in the sun.

Coach Flagg jumped in. "Bambi, we need you and everybody here out there on the field now. Let's get the job done. The clock's a tickin'." Coach lifted up his cap and wiped his forehead with his forearm. "Y'all know we're playin' Fannin County tonight, and I expect y'all all to be there to support the team. I gotta get back real soon, so let's save the prayin' for the locker room."

"This ain't no game, Daddy El," insisted Tammy. "I'm for prayin'. The kingdom has to come first in all thangs," she stated stubbornly.

Todd grabbed the Bible from Preacher Dodge. "Alright, we pray, but I'm leadin' it." He held up the Bible and closed his eyes. "Lord, help us all to find the rest of this poor, pitiful victim, if in fact there is more of him out there. And help the Duckett Bucks win the game against Fannin County tonight." Todd opened one eye and could see that Preacher Dodge's eyes were closed, but he wore a disapproving frown on his face. "In-Jesus-name-we-pray-amen," he added expeditiously. He handed the Bible back to the preacher, then knelt and resumed his drawing in the dirt. "Now, here's how we're gonna cover the area."

Just as Todd sent the team took off in search of whatever, Young Dr. Gorov Mahmondi showed up carrying a Coleman cooler in one hand and his lab kit in the other. Grumbling, he tugged on plastic gloves, picked a few insects off the specimen with a pair of tweezers, and performed some tests, while occasionally muttering quiet prayers or oaths in his native Hindi language. He carefully slipped the penis in a sterile plastic bag and placed the bag in the cooler.

Next, Todd accompanied Gorov back to his empty clinic. Gorov had hastily closed it when he received Todd's summons. Gorov removed the specimen, bathed it in a kind of marinating fluid, and then placed it back in the cooler. The cooler, in turn, was crammed into a crowded, stainless-steel refrigerator. Gorov slapped a padlock on the handle, and for extra measure, taped a big "KEEP OUT" sign on the door. Todd double-checked to make sure the lock on the back door was bolted. The two men crossed the lobby and stepped out the front door. Gorov bolted the lock on that door, and Todd double-checked it.

Todd returned to the site just as Marvalena and her divining rod were leaving. She was accompanied by Coach Flagg, who was antsy to get back to his football team. She declared that her spirit guides told her there was nothing else to be found - and that was that. The absence of the coach and psychic was offset by the arrival of a dozen deputies from neighboring counties. Oddly, no one from the Highway Patrol showed. Todd and the rest of the team searched until an hour past sunset, when he sounded the air horn. He returned to the office, picked up the phone, and assembled a new volunteer team to continue the search at dawn. After updating the alert on the computer, he scoured the missing person reports from the tri-state region. None were relevant to this crime, and there were no reports on recently discovered bodies or parts thereof.

* * * * *

It was close to midnight when Todd climbed the front-porch steps of the McPherson farmhouse, where he found his mother sleeping in her bed. Next to her lay his five-year-old daughter, Molly, whose thin, pale arm was draped protectively across her grandmother. Though Molly had a bedroom in Todd's apartment over the garage, she also had a bedroom in the farmhouse since she was a baby because Todd was randomly summoned in the middle of the night to supervise serious situations.

Despite having two bedrooms, however, Molly mostly slept with her grandmother, a habit of which Todd was trying to break her. As he brushed her long, pearlescent curls away from her face, he was struck with the familiar spasm of guilt over the fact that Molly was no taller than the average three-year-old. Sadly, his little sprite looked more like an animated toy doll than a real child, especially when she was with her much bigger peers.

His mother stirred. "Todd? That you? Don't tell me nothin', cuz I don't wanna know right now." Jessie McPherson's deep voice, partnered with her characteristic slow, deliberate manner of speaking, complemented her six-foot tall, rawboned frame.

Todd whispered, "Good, cuz I don't want to talk right now."

Because her glasses were on the bedside table, Jessie squinted as she peered up at him. "They's nasty people out thar."

"Well, knock me down." Todd bent down, kissed her on the forehead, then stretched over and kissed Molly, who scratched her nose and rolled over. Jessie rolled in Molly's direction. Todd straightened up. "Oh, Momma?"

"Hmm?"

"I met the girl I'm gonna marry."

"That's nice," Jessie mumbled, then lapsed into a light snore.

Todd left the farmhouse, walked across the compound, and climbed the long, steep stairs along the outside of the enormous garage that held the tractor, hay mower, round hay baler, cotton picker, his late father's old Dodge pickup, his momma's old Oldsmobile and her newer Olds, his Chevy pickup, a partially restored 1965 Mustang, a couple of four-wheelers, a four-stall horse trailer, and the golf cart that his mother used for driving to the mailbox.

Once inside his apartment, Todd discarded his duty belt, grabbed a bottle of Bud Light from the refrigerator and wiped it off with a germicidal wet wipe before opening it. He flopped on the sofa and took a long swig, even though he knew he'd be chasing the brew with black coffee. He drew in a deep breath and jabbed at his antique message machine.

"Todd, this is LeeLee. Well, I done what you told me to do, and let me tell you it weren't easy. First off, everbody I called thought I was playin' a practical joke on 'em. I could hear the emergency staff laughin' at me in the background on the other end of the line. It didn't help none that Sam was standin' behind me guffawin' his face off. I finally hadda lock Sam outta the room and—" [beep]. Todd chuckled and stabbed the forward button. "It's LeeLee again. Dang message machine run out on me. Anyway, wonst I got 'em to believe me, they all said the same thing: no one had come in with no such injury." She sighed loudly and added, "Well I'm goin' to wash my shoes. I'll come in and dispatch for you in the mornin' cuz Jalaine has the crud." The message machine clicked off.

Todd smiled. Once again LeeLee had risen to the occasion. Why hadn't she called his cell phone or the office? Because, he decided, she knew he wouldn't be home until late. Leaving a message would allow her to avoid talking to him directly, which could lead to another colorful assignment. Todd checked the machine for more messages and found that miraculously, there were none. He half-expected one from the mayor, thinking Sonny had heard about the whole affair from Coach Flagg at the game. But then Coach had been busy, and anyway, Elvin knew how to keep his trap shut and let Todd handle his job. Todd realized he should have briefed his boss earlier, but he'd been terribly busy and had wanted to wait until he had something to go on. Now it was too late to wake him up.

Todd decided it was time to broaden the investigation, although in his heart he felt that this was a local crime, given the freshness of the specimen. He radioed Savannah, the night shift dispatcher, to get Dillon, the deputy on station duty, on the radio. When a sleepy-sounding Dillon answered, Todd ordered him to check the computers for any hospital in the Southeastern United States reporting an emergency admission of a man sans penis. Savannah came back on the radio and

31

naively suggested an AMBER Alert. Shuddering, Todd had said "God, no," as he pictured a photo of Little Lost Johnson plastered on every TV screen in America. He leaned back, stacked his socked feet on the coffee table, then upended his beer bottle and pondered about the case. The State Patrol had never shown up to assist with the search. Todd guessed it was due to recent flippant remarks he had brashly made to the media about the current shortcomings of the outfit. He was learning the hard way that a hasty temper and sharp tongue can come back to haunt a sheriff.

Half an hour slipped by before Dillon radioed him, explaining that six severe groin incidents had been reported in the Southeastern United States. Only one incident had resulted in complete separation of man and friend. One involved a farmer who became entangled in the blades of a manure spreader. Todd had to snort at that image. When he was a youth, his father had warned him of the numerous possible injuries that could occur as a result of improper handling of the farm equipment. But, Hoyt McPherson had never mentioned this particular threat.

Todd clicked off and finished his beer. He wished he had years of experience under his belt like other sheriffs. And it wasn't like he had all kinds of support from his deputies. When he had been elected sheriff several years ago, the older deputies, save Virgil, had taken jobs in neighboring counties. All that he had now in the way of expertise was his thirty-year-old lieutenant, Rusty Moore, and of course, Virgil, whose usefulness was debatable.

Considering the publicity the Lorena Bobbitt case had received, Todd surmised that tomorrow could bring out the media leeches. He thought that the potential benefits of the inevitable media coverage outweighed the potential liabilities by only a smidgen. One fact was certain, Vince Verona, Duckett County's local media mogul, was not going to get the scoop of a lifetime because the Duckettville Weekly wouldn't be out until next Wednesday.

Chapter Two
Surreal Saturday

With dawn still two hours away, it was pitch dark at the clearing. Except, that is, for the brightly illuminated, professionally dressed lady reporter—blonde, petite, early-thirties—standing in relief beside a section of yellow crime-scene tape that circled the soon to be infamous clearing in Duckett Forest. When she received her cue, she said into the camera, "That's right, Dan, the severed penis was taken into custody yesterday, but a white-chalk outline of it remains on that rock." She pointed to the rock in the middle of the circle. The cameraman zoomed in and the camera's light fell on the outline of poor, pathetic John Dick. The reporter continued, "The recovery of this rather unusual body part is bound to elicit a flood of national attention." Ansley paused to look around. "Oddly, Sheriff McPherson hasn't posted any deputies to protect this site. In fact, the only deputy that we have seen was one droopy-lidded young man sitting in his cruiser at the road by the entrance to the trail. He simply waved us on without any questions." Ansley took a few steps away from the yellow tape. "With the help of my cameraman's lights, I'm going to return to the road. While I walk, I will attempt to contact Sheriff McPherson on my cell phone, and with the miracle of modern technology, you can listen in."

The ringing of the phone jarred Todd out of his sleep, and he cursed the darkness as he fumbled for the receiver. Through blurry eyes, he discerned that the clock said five.

"Sheriff McPherson?" The voice was female, youthful but businesslike, and vaguely familiar.

"Uh, yeah, this is him ... he."

"Sheriff McPherson, this is Ansley Mason from Satellite News

Network. What can you tell us about the severed penis found in Duckett Forest late yesterday afternoon?"

Todd bolted to a sitting position. A twenty-four-hour news station hadn't been up here since he had campaigned for sheriff. "Uh—"

"I'm walking toward the trail head," said the reporter, "and I'm wondering why you don't have more guards posted to protect the site."

"Uh—"

"Are you sure it's human? Have you found any more body parts?"

Todd muttered, "I'll be givin' a press briefin' at high noon on the steps of my office." *Did I just say "high noon"?* "Right now I've only had three hours of sheep—sleep." *Shit, I've been sacked in the backfield!* Todd chastised himself for not being prepared for the inevitable media onslaught. Why had Forrest, who tended to have more horse sense than the rest of the deputies, let this woman and crew hike right up to the site?

"Do you have any leads as to—"

"That's all I have to say right now," snapped Todd. He clicked off, and after a few seconds of sleepily staring into space, he unplugged the phone. Picking up the remote, he turned on the TV. The attractive reporter was talking into the camera as she walked, her identity surfaced in Todd's memory. Ansley Mason had covered the story of the inexperienced twenty-four-year-old former high school quarterback who was running for sheriff of the most rural county in Georgia. She and her crew had returned on the day he took office, which happened to be his twenty-fifth birthday. Ansley had repeated to the world a comment she'd heard from a local who had jokingly referred to him as "Baby Chief." Of all his nicknames, Baby Chief was one he despised, and it had proven to be one that he had not yet managed to shake. He warily returned his attention to the TV.

Ansley paused and looked around. "This is strange, Dan," Ansley said quizzically. "Though it is still dark, a few curious people are beginning to pass me as they walk in the direction of the clearing."

Indeed, just as she spoke, a hastily dressed couple hurried past her.

"Oh, how reeeediculous!" yelled Todd. He hit the bathroom light and lifted the toilet lid. (He kept it closed, as he didn't like to look at germy water whenever it was not necessary.) Starting his wiz, he shouted, "Jeeeesus, God, and the Holy Ghost! The damned prick ain't even there no more!"

Todd's mother was napping on the couch when she heard his bellow. A half-hour earlier she had crossed the compound, climbed the stairs to his apartment, and dozed off while she waited for him to waken. Rising, she turned on the light in the kitchen and called out, "You got time for coffee?"

Todd pulled on an undershirt, and grabbed a uniform from the closet. "My crime scene has been trampled!" He wrestled on his shirt. "As soon as I can find Forrest, I'm gonna kick his goddamned ass to Kentucky and back!"

"Language, Cotton."

Todd realized he had not yet called the mayor. He attempted to jerk on his pants at the same time that he juggled the phone, but ended up hopping on one foot around the bedroom as it flew out of his hand, ricocheted off the wall, and disappeared beyond the far side of the bed. Pants half-on, he launched himself across the bed, and dove for the slippery device. His head popped up when SNN returned after a commercial break. On the tube, the pleasant-faced Hispanic anchorman was continuing with what he knew about the case, which wasn't much. "Freakin' national news," Todd groused. "They're already out there with a story, and they don't know a freakin' thing!" He gave up on the phone, stood, jerked up his pants and angrily tucked in his shirt. "Hell, I don't know a goddamn thang, so what the hell goddamn thang do they know ... just a bunch of miserable ... Ouch! Goddammit!" In his haste, Todd had stuck his thumb as he pinned his sheriff's star.

"It's not necessary to take the Lord's name in vain," called out Jessie. Realizing the coffee would not be ready before Todd departed, she dropped some fruit and yogurt in the blender.

Todd cursed under his breath while he sucked blood from his wounded finger. As he buckled his belt, the TV again caught his eye, and what he saw made his jaw drop. Against a predawn background, Bambi Davis's half-painted back stoop filled the TV screen. She was holding the screen door open as an Asian-American male reporter held out a mic. Only Bambi didn't look like Bambi, who most of the time had shoulder length, fawn-colored hair. Right now she looked like someone had dumped a bowl of spaghetti on top of her head.

Like a lot of rural Georgians, Bambi's voice went up on the end of her statements as if she were asking a question. Todd had never even noticed this tendency in her, but it sounded weird on TV. Still, in real life or on TV, Bambi's dimples and luminous hazel eyes were captivating. She said, "I seen bodies before on account of they get dumped a lot out in Duckett Forest? I'm a search-and-rescue volunteer, but this was the worst thing I've ever seen? By the way, my hair usually don't look like this? Marla was in the middle of high-lightin' it when the sheriff's office called, and I ran right out the door with my foils on?" The reporter turned the mic on himself and began to translate Bambi's comments into standard English.

Todd rubbed his forehead vigorously in an effort to ward off an imminent headache. He growled, "I should have ordered them not to talk ... especially her!"

Jesse walked into the bedroom. "Wouldn't have done any good," she said in her deep, unruffled voice.

"But this is fu ... freakin' SNN!"

"When a woman's gonna blab, not even the Almighty himself can cork her."

Todd hurried into the bathroom and applied toothbrush to gleaming teeth. "I guess I shouldn't get so worked up," he said through toothpaste lather. "These people are my friends. They have integrity. All they will do is tell the truth." He stuck his head out of the bathroom when he heard

36

Bambi's voice again. Brushing distractedly, he sat at the end of the bed and stared at the television.

Bambi was completely engrossed in her own description of the events of yesterday and her role, sparse as it was. "And it was at least eighteen inches long!"

By now, Todd was (literally) foaming at the mouth. "Oh, Christ!" he shouted as he flopped back on the bed, his toothbrush clamped between his teeth.

On the television, the scene switched abruptly to the SNN anchorman. "I'm told," he said in a serious voice, "that Ansley is now standing on the road where the trail begins. Let's check in with her."

Todd's head shot up. The scene switched to Ansley, who said, "Dan, I'm standing at the trail head, and though it is still dark, I'm now seeing a steady stream of early risers flowing onto the trail." As if to punctuate her statement, a family of hastily dressed locals quickly shuffled past in front of her.

Todd's toothbrush fell out of his open mouth. "I've lost control," he muttered in a stangled voice.

"And just over here," said Ansley as she took several steps to the left, "is the sheriff's cruiser in which the exhausted deputy had been sitting earlier." Ansley looked up and down the road. "He seems to have disappeared." She stepped toward the cruiser and peered in. "Wait. This is astonishing, Dan. The deputy is in his cruiser alright, but he is passed out!" The cameraman shone his light on the tubby, dark-haired man, who was sprawled on his back in the rear seat and drooling on his tattooed arm.

"Blaine!" shouted Todd and Jessie together as they gaped at the deputy whose nametag read "Hensley."

"It's hard to believe," continued Ansley, "but this slumbering deputy seems to be the only person in charge."

"This is astounding," interjected Dan the Anchorman, whose face appeared in the corner.

Ansley shrugged. "And as you heard just a few minutes ago, I caught Sheriff McPherson, the clean-shaven young lawman who some call Baby Chief, completely off-guard." She rested a hand on the cruiser and said wryly, "Apparently, Deputy Hensley here is not the only Duckett County lawman sleeping on the job."

Fuming all the way, Todd sped to the site where he made a point of ignoring Ansley and the other gossip-grubbing reporters who were milling about under the fading stars. By now, some tired night-shift deputies had shown up. One of them must have warned Blaine because he and his cruiser were nowhere to be seen. A new group of search-and-rescue volunteers were arriving. These were Todd's early birds; they preferred hunting for bodies at the crack of dawn rather than feeling around for them in the dark. Todd organized the volunteers, and along with most of the deputies, he spent the next three hours combing the woods with them, stopping only long enough to check with the office for updates to the missing person reports or body recovered alerts. Still no bodies. Still no missing males. Todd thought that the owner of the lost willy might have been a homeless person who was in the wrong place at the wrong time. He decided to return to the office to coordinate the transfer of the wayward body part to the state lab in Atlanta.

Dogged by reporters, Todd drove into Duckettville. Knowing that he preferred the press as far from the office as possible, tiny Deputy Tiffany Youst and the size-worthy Deputy P.J. Johnson had roped off an area for the press across the street in front of the Evangelical Church of the Last Hope. Since only two deputies could be spared for the job, P.J. and Tiffany were desperately attempting to round up the news correspondents and return them to the makeshift corral. Todd drove around to the back parking lot, then fought his way past more reporters and bounded up the steps to the back door. Once inside, he promptly relocked the door. How could the blood suckers have gotten here this soon!?

As was his habit, he picked up the clipboard that held the booking summaries for both swing and night shift and began his stroll through perp walk. Dude Wigglesworth had finally bailed out his wife, Tonya, but three new prisoners had been checked into Chez McPherson overnight. Cell No. 8 held a repeat visitor, A.W. Crank. A.W. gripped the bars and stared at Todd beseechingly with a hung-over, hound-dog face. Todd skimmed the report and discovered that in the middle of the night, A.W. had driven his pickup through the Dairy Queen's front wall. He told the arresting deputies that he had a craving for a Dilly Bar. Todd gave him a severe look. This was the old drunk's worst crime yet. With breath that could knock over the Empire State Building, A.W. reached for Todd through the bars. "Sheriff, you gonna protect me from that mob out thar. They could hang me!"

"Relax, I am the protector of the innocent as well as the stupid."

Buddy Clump was standing at the bars in cell No. 4. Buddy was fortunate enough to sport wavy, shoulder-length, fair hair and prefect white teeth. His wife, Marla, stood at the bars of the cell across from him. She had not been blessed with Buddy's good looks. In twenty years of marriage, the Clumps hadn't figured out how to not pound on each other when they took to drinking. Last night, they had dueled with his-and-her curling irons, and now both had superficial burns on their arms and legs.

Marla narrowed her pea-sized Confederate gray eyes as Todd approached. "Those cameras better not be out thar when we git bailed out. We look a fright, and you've done confiscated our curlin' irons."

Buddy snickered. "What difference do it make, Marla? Yer face would make a maggot gag."

"Shut up, Buddy, or I'll slap the taste right outta yore mouth!"

Warming to his subject, Buddy proclaimed, "Well, yer so ugly, you'd make a train take a dirt road!"

A.W. called out, "Sheriff, I'm not feelin' safe!"

"Stop!" snapped Todd. He glared at Buddy, then Marla. "You two need to either quit drinkin' or get a divorce." He turned and walked quickly down the hall.

Marla caught Buddy's gaze. "I don't like him," she said through the bars. "I voted for Mumper."

Buddy's eyes followed Todd as he passed through the open door. "I bet he'd throw a drownin' man both ends of a rope."

Todd hung his jacket in his office, then stepped into the lobby where LeeLee, frazzled and green about the gills, was furtively hanging up on reporters. Todd realized that he didn't need LeeLee flaking out on him, so he mustered up a pleasant tone and asked, "You ready for another excitin' day of crime fightin,' Sparkle Plenty?" LeeLee just gave him the stink eye, so Todd retreated to his office.

In a few minutes, LeeLee rolled her chair around the corner so she could peer into Todd's lair and announced that his best buddy was here. Blaine shuffled into the office, looking anywhere but at Todd. He had gone home and finished his nap, then showered and dressed in a fresh uniform.

Todd indicated for him to sit. He squeezed his bulk into a chair and dropped his gaze to the linoleum. "Please don't fire me," he begged. "You cain't fire your own flesh-and-blood cousin. You don't want yore momma to end up havin' to feed me." Blaine risked a glance at Todd.

"You ain't my cousin," snarled Todd. "You're my cousin's retarded issue."

Blaine shrugged.

Sending Blaine a hostile glare, Todd drummed a pencil on his desk. "Tell me, retard, how did you come to be guardin' the site last night? I gave that job to Forrest."

"Well it was like this," said Blaine nervously, "Forrest met a girl at the Buckin' Bull, and he offered to pay me double to take his night shift spot, see?" Like Bambi, Blaine had a way of going up the scale on the end of his sentences.

"Just get to the reason for passin' out in your cruiser."

Blaine swallowed hard. "Last evenin' my buddy Grady had a keg party for finally gettin' his GED? I was the only one what showed up, so naturally we both had a might bit too much to drink? That's when Forrest called me to take over his shift?" His eyes wide with sincerity, Blaine shook his fleshy face. "I didn't drink on the job or nothin' like 'at, but I was a little soused when I had to go on duty?"

Through clenched teeth, Todd said, "Do you know - do you have any idea - how much you humiliated me and the department with your little beauty nap?" Blaine dropped his gaze to the floor. Todd rubbed his forehead vigorously and stared out the window where Tiffany was attempting to herd the reporters to the corral across the street. "I'm too angry to be angry right now. Get out of my sight before I kick your stupid fat ass down Main Street and give those leeches out there more reason to hang around." He heard the scrape of the metal chair's legs on the linoleum and the shuffle-shuffle of Blaine scuttling out of the room. Next, he heard LeeLee rolling back up the hall, then more foot-shuffling as Blaine dodged her. Todd slumped over and banged his forehead on his desk a few times, then just let it lie there. Head still down, he reached for the phone. He still had to coordinate with Gorov to escort the pitiful penis to the state lab.

From the open door, LeeLee said agitatedly, "That limey gal just called from her cell phone. She's comin' in the back."

Todd's head shot up. "Don't call her that," he snapped. He hurried up perp walk, unlocked and opened the back door, and saw Jasmine Roseberry wearing a Red Sox baseball cap pulled low over her face. She was on the second step of the stoop. With one hand, she was clutching a plastic bag containing her boot. Her other hand was clenched over her purse. She was making little headway through the pack of hungry reporters who obviously smelled suspect. And, as reporters were wont to do, they were pushing their microphones in her face, peppering her with embarrassing questions. Todd leaned out, reached down, and grabbed Jasmine under the arm. He hoisted her into the office and locked the door. Lifting the brim of her cap, he asked, "You okay?"

Jasmine looked up at him with luminous, almond-shaped orphan eyes that made his heart go thump. She removed her cap, thereby unleashing a breathtaking cascade of dark curls. As she stuffed the cap in her purse, she said emphatically, "I am quite alarmed that this situation has mushroomed into a media melee so rapidly." She handed him the plastic bag.

"Yep, it must have been a slow week in the 24-hour news game," commented Todd as he surreptitiously admired Jasmine's smooth legs and wished her jeans skirt was shorter. "Speakin' of the news, have you heard any of this mornin's coverage?" he asked while he led her toward perp walk.

"My stars, no," she said ardently.

Todd breathed a sigh of relief. *There's hope.* "I want you to know, Ms. Roseberry, that this county is usually a very peaceful and quiet place to live." Not including all the stiffs fished out of Duckett Forest.

Todd ushered Jasmine past the trio of detainees, praying they would keep quiet. Thankfully, all three of them were struck dumb at the site of the statuesque brunette. Jasmine, in turn, presented a pleasant - if nervous - smile, but she grimaced when the smell of A.W.'s moose breath hit her full on. Todd realized that even he, a hardened lawman, was holding his breath. Both he and Jasmine hastened to the lobby where they exhaled deeply. Todd slyly observed his reluctant visitor as she eyed the wanted posters and hunting/fishing regulations on one wall and then turn her gaze to the giant map that said in big letters, "Duckett County Wildlife Management Area." She raised her eyes to the stuffed head of a buck mounted above the front door and the roaring black bear head above the entrance to perp walk. Turning to Todd she said, "I prefer that my name be kept out of this…this beastly affair. Will that be possible?"

"I'll do my best," Todd assured her and gave her his most sincere smile, thinking that at this very moment the reporters outside most likely had already called in to their producers a request to run down her license plate number.

Todd showed Jasmine to a metal table and seated her at the spot where LeeLee had already laid out the witness/finder form. He placed his hand on the back of her chair and leaned over to show her the paperwork. Immediately, he became intoxicated with the scent of roses and fresh rain wafting off her body. "Ah…Please fill this out, and right here put down in your own words exactly how you came across the, ah, the item—"

"I'm sick of all this fannying about." Jasmine's dark eyes flashed. She looked up fiercely and pointed the back end of the pen at Todd. "Let's just call it what it is: a penis…PENIS!"

LeeLee gasped. "Hey! We don't talk like that 'round here!"

Todd kept his hand on the back of Jasmine's chair and, without straightening up, said, "No, LeeLee, Miz Roseberry is right." He sent LeeLee a no nonsense look. "Miz Roseberry will write a statement about how she found the ... ah ... penis." He looked into Jasmine's amazing eyes.

"That is correct," Jasmine said solemnly, still looking up at him.

"Okay," replied Todd, just as solemnly.

Jasmine suddenly broke into a self-conscious grin, then she giggled. Todd burst out with a laugh. He felt so silly he had to look away. He was drawn to this woman, but the lightheartedness he felt was short-lived when he remembered where she dwelled. Emerald Lake was a world where the well-heeled - mostly retired business people from Atlanta perpetually played genteel games of tennis and golf. Todd's world, on the other hand, was inhabited by stinky drunks and filthy meth-heads.

Someone banged on the locked front door. From outside, Mayor Sonny Davis yelled, "Todd, dammit, open up right now!" Todd slapped his forehead. He had forgotten to call the mayor, and now the barbarian himself was at the gate. He unlocked the door with trepidation. As soon as Sonny crossed the threshold, he began to rave. "How could you not call me when you found the damned thing? Or last night? Or, for Christ's sake, this freakin' mornin'?" Sonny tossed several green tummy tablets into his mouth.

Todd placed his hand over his heart. "Sonny, I apologize. I was plannin' on callin' you first thing this mornin', but there wasn't a phone signal in the woods and since I got back the phones have been ringin' off the hook and—"

Sonny stomped up so close to Todd that he bumped him with his enormous belly. "You apologize! It's way too late for that, you nin [bump] com [bump] poop [bump]!" Stunned, Todd stumbled backwards with each bump, but Sonny kept pace with him. Sonny's face was by now a mottled purplish color. As he bellowed on, he spit bits of green tummy-mint froth on Todd, who particularly loathed anyone showering him with spittle, green or otherwise.

Todd was mortified that he'd been belly bumped and called a nincompoop in front of Jasmine, even if he did deserve it. He glanced at the ladies. LeeLee and Jasmine were both staring openmouthed at Sonny. LeeLee's face had gone from puke-green to a white nearly as white as her tennis shoes. Bellowing tended to do her in. There was too much drama in her life already. Todd said, "If you would care to step into my office, Mayor, I'll bring you up to speed."

Sonny turned to LeeLee. "Six this mornin' I get a call from some she-male reporter from SNN askin' me about some wanderin' willy over at Duckett Forest. Hell, I figure it's a crank call, hang up on Miz Idjit, and go back to sleep. Then a little while ago, Alice come runnin' into the bedroom screamin' about Bambi bein' on the TV! My own ex-daughter-in-law's blabbin' to the world about some chopped-off dingdong, and I don't know crap because my shit-for-brains sheriff ain't informed me about squat!" LeeLee had slunk just about as low in her chair as she could go without it rolling backward out from under her. Sonny took little heed. "Of course, I couldn't even get a line into this

44

godforsaken nervous ward y'all call a sheriff's office!" He turned away from LeeLee, threw his hands in the air, and bellowed, "Would somebody please tell me what the gol-durned freak-face is goin' on?"

Todd said nervously, "Just what you heard on TV - except for the part about the thing bein' eighteen inches long. Bambi exaggerated that." Todd gestured again toward his office.

The enraged mayor bore down on him. "This situation is a kay-tas-tro-phee of mega proportions!" He shoved his face in Todd's face and bumped him with his belly again. Todd stumbled backward and fell against the wall, knocking down a dozen Most Wanted posters. The mayor continued to bellow. "And this is an a-number-one calamity for every man, woman, and child in Duckett County!"

"And especially for the former owner of the penis," interjected Jasmine.

The mayor spun around and looked at the female furriner as if he were noticing her for the first time. "And just whooo the hell are you!?" he asked dramatically.

Todd was squatting and picking up the posters. As he stood, he distractedly attempted to plop the posters on the table, but most fell off, much to Jasmine's amusement. Todd moved behind her chair so as to put something between him and the mayor's badass belly. "Sonny Davis, meet Jasmine Roseberry," he said. "She is the person who found the…ah—"

"Penis," Jasmine finished dryly.

Todd gestured toward his boss. "Jasmine, this is Duckettville's mayor, Sonny Davis."

Sonny immediately lost all interest in the love of Todd's life. Instead, he bore down on Todd and growled, "Fearless, you are on my last nerve, my very last G.D. nerve!"

Todd stepped away and held up his hands. "Okay, I believe you. Just don't belly bump me again!" Jasmine burst out laughing, then slapped a hand over her mouth, but her dancing eyes said it all. A hot, prickly blush scampered up Todd's spine and spread over his scalp.

A.W. yelled through the open door to perp walk, "What's goin' on, y'all? I need to know I'm safe!"

"You're safe!" Todd, Jasmine, and LeeLee yelled simultaneously.

Sonny suddenly deflated, plopped into a chair at the end of the table, and tossed a few more green tummy tablets into his mouth. Eyes unfocused, he chewed and muttered, "This is terrible timing ... terrible, terrible timing for the ... the ... " He nervously glanced at Todd.

"Excuse me, but is there any fortuitous time for one to lose a penis?" asked Jasmine with a facetious smile.

"Would people quit usin' that word?!" hissed LeeLee as she glared at Jasmine.

Sonny continued to stare into space and grumble to himself. "This is a bad day for Sonny Davis ... a very, very bad day," he muttered. Then his fury abruptly returned. He glared at Todd, pounded the table with his fist, and said, "I swear, Fearless, sometimes you don't have enough sense to spit downwind!" He wiped his perspiring pate with his handkerchief. "You best nip this whole thang in the bud!" He folded the handkerchief and asked in a disgusted voice, "Well, where is the sombitch thang now?"

Todd felt immense relief that the worst of Sonny's wrath seemed to be spent. "It's at Doc Mahmondi's," he said as he returned to the task of picking up the Most Wanted posters.

"He do some kinda autopsy on it or somethin'?"

"Gorov ran some tests last night, cleaned it up for reattachment, in case whoever it belongs to is still breathin' and wants it back."

"Wants it back? Great God Almighty!" gasped Sonny. "Of course he wants it back!" He added more thoughtfully, "Well no matter, the sucker's probably dead." He popped a few more green tummy tablets. "Well it sure as hell better be safe with the doc," he spat.

Todd noticed that Sonny's enormous chest looked like an overworked bellows. "Oh, I guarantee that it's safe," he said confidently, trying to allay Sonny's anxiety. He stuck his hands in his pockets and glanced at Jasmine, who quickly turned her attention to the witness form in front of her.

There was more banging on the front door. A voice from outside yelled, "Open up! It's P.J.!" Three hundred pound P.J. Jackson had been the center on Todd's high school football team, and had become a deputy, mainly because he still harbored a need to protect his former quarterback. Todd unlocked the door and saw that P.J. was trying to shake off a half-dozen reporters who were clinging to him like giant ticks. Once P.J. made it across the threshold, Todd noticed something under his enormous armpit. Like a mother hen, P.J. slowly lifted his wing and then gently pushed Dr. Gorov Mahmondi forward. With the package delivered, P.J. then turned and charged back outside.

Gorov looked even smaller than usual, and his crumpled white lab coat appeared to engulf him. His big brown eyes seemed to roll around the lenses of his round, wire-rimmed glasses, and his breath came in little spastic wheezes. Finally, in his crisp Hindi accent he gasped, "The specimen ... it is gone!"

The only sound in the lobby was the rhythmic rocking of the unbalanced ceiling fan. The stuffed buck stared blankly at the black bear, who in turn roared silently.

In a surprisingly nimble move, Sonny leapt to his feet. "What do you mean the specimen is gone?"

Gorov clutched the lapels of his lab coat and wheezed, "What do you mean, what do I mean? Elvis has left the building!" He pulled an inhaler from his pocket and gave himself a few hits.

Sonny shoved his face in the diminutive doctor's face. "Well, it didn't just hop up, jimmy open the fridge, and skip right on out of thar all by its lonesome, did it?"

Todd stepped between the corpulent mayor and the undone transplant from Mumbai. "Gorov, let's take this from the beginnin'. What happened when you arrived at your office this morning? Was the back door locked?"

"No, it was only pulled shut, and I'm sure I locked it last night. You were with me. As you saw, the door has a heavy-duty bolt lock. Anyway, I went in. I was pretty darn scared, I tell you. Everything was the same, except the refrigerator. The padlock had been cut. I looked with trepidation inside and ... " He paused, gave himself another hit from his inhaler, and cried, "The cooler was gone. GONE, I tell you!"

Todd was transported back to his high school quarterbacking days, feeling like he had just been sacked hard in the backfield. In a daze, he stepped slowly toward the dispatch desk and said rather distractedly, "LeeLee, ah, radio Virgil to come meet me over at the clinic to dust for prints." By now, LeeLee's face was a ghostly shade, but she picked up the mic and pressed on the lever at its base. She opened her mouth, but it took several attempts for her to summon up an audible voice. Out of the corner of his eye, Todd saw the mayor swaying. He turned and asked, "You alright, Sonny?" Since Sonny arrived, his face had turned from crimson to purple to crimson again, and now it was a sickening pale bluish shade. His mouth was moving, but nothing audible was forthcoming. That was unusual. Todd was used to ignoring what dribbled out of Sonny's poochy lips, but he'd never actually observed them flapping without some kind of verbal utterance issuing forth. Suddenly, the mayor collapsed onto the doctor, knocking him to the floor and obliterating him from sight.

Todd shouted, "LeeLee! Call for an ambulance! No, make that two ambulances." It took some tugging by Todd and Jasmine, but they managed to roll the mayor off the doctor, who was sprawled on his back and looked like a giant flipped-over, squished, albino cockroach with a smashed pair of wire-rimmed glasses laying askew on his flattened nose. Gorov's usually expressive eyes were vacant, and he did not appear to be breathing.

"Check his pulse!" ordered Todd, as he continued to administer to Sonny.

Just as Jasmine knelt beside the doctor, he gulped air and opened his eyes. "This one's breathing," she reported.

Todd probed for a heartbeat on Sonny's fleshy neck and felt nothing. He listened for breath sounds and heard nothing. He called for LeeLee to bring the defibrillator.

LeeLee croaked, "It's broke. Blaine was s'posed ..."

Todd swore then looked at Jasmine, "You know how to do two-man CPR?" Jasmine gave him a confidant nod, though her soft lips quivered. She repositioned herself on the other side of the mayor, and then she and Todd looked at each other and grimaced. Obviously, neither one wanted to do the mouth-to-mouth part of two-man CPR on Sonny, who was emitting a copious amount of green, foamy slobber. Jasmine blinked first. She wiped the mayor's mouth with the lapel of his sports coat, pinched off his piggy nose, and covered his poochy mouth with her lovely lips. Todd pushed on Sonny's fleshy chest, counting out, "One, two, three, four, five." LeeLee found her voice and managed to convey the situation to the fire department. She set the mic down then a small whimper escaped her as she slid slowly from her seat and disappeared beneath her desk.

* * * * *

Todd closed the door to his office, slumped in his chair and brooded over this morning's loathsome events. Doc Mahmondi had recovered before the ambulance arrived. He had been in such a daze, however, that he failed to register the intense efforts on the part of Todd and Jasmine to keep the mayor alive. He also didn't notice the small body under the dispatcher's desk. Instead, he wordlessly slipped his broken glasses into the pocket of his lab coat and stumbled up Main Street to his clinic.

Todd and Jasmine managed to get Sonny rebooted, and only noticed LeeLee's situation as the fire department arrived. While she was being wheeled outside, LeeLee had sworn to Todd that she wasn't coming back to work "unless them doctors load me up with gobs of them hormones and tranqs."

While Todd was dealing with the situation, Jasmine had hastily finished her report and departed without a word. Todd thought that she must have a very low opinion of him after she witnessed his boss belly-bumping him across the lobby. He thought it best to try and forget about her.

After things had calmed down, Todd had called in the dozen deputies involved in yesterday's operation and grilled them upside down and backwards. He came to the conclusion that none of them were likely to have been involved in the nabbing of the penis. He called the Fannin County sheriff's office and inquired about the dozen deputies that had been loaned out to augment his own search-and-rescue team. All of them had been on swing shift at least an hour before the penis had been deposited on that rock. There was only an infinitesimal chance that any of them could have been involved in either the depositing of the penis, or the subsequent stealing of it. Elvis. Gorov had dubbed it Elvis.

Todd had then questioned his deputies, and did turn up something fruitful. He came up with a short list of the half-dozen early onlookers, who had stopped their vehicles and stood on the road to watch. All of them were male. The person who deposited Elvis could very well have been amongst the curious. Not happy to see the doc getting into Todd's Bronco holding the cooler with Elvis inside, he might have decided he wanted him back.

Todd returned his attention to the task at hand. He glanced at the clock. Ten minutes to noon – ten minutes until the dreaded news conference that he had promised the annoying Ansley Mason. Ten minutes until he would have to stand on the courthouse steps and announce to the world that Elvis was AWOL. Ten minutes until he collapsed, face beet-red, into a puddle of wiggling, giggling green Jell-O in front of the world.

"Todd, Delray Hamilton's on line one," piped up scrawny Shawn, who had taken over LeeLee's job as dispatcher.

"Dammit, Shawn, use the intercom!" Todd shot back, not sure if he was relieved or annoyed that Duckett County's prosecutor had finally returned his call. Todd felt pessimistic that Delray would actually provide any support. In Todd's opinion, the slothful D.A. would be as apathetic to Todd's plight as a neutered bull would be toward his unneutered peers.

And it wasn't that Delray was incompetent. But, his assets in front of a jury were mainly superficial: his height of six-feet-one inch, his sparkling baby blues, and his devilish dimples. In addition, he sported a head of luxurious black hair, which he wore long on the sides and swept back. On anyone else, the style would look smarmy, but being movie-star handsome, Delray carried it off. And though at thirty-five he was starting to go ever-so-slightly fleshy under the chin, he still cut a vigorous figure.

Definitely one who enjoyed the leisurely life, he often spent weekends with his wife in North Carolina, lounging around his favorite comfy, upscale lodge while leaving the kids home in the care of the of the grandparents. No doubt about it, by nature, Delray Hamilton was a lodge lizard.

Todd picked up the phone. "How come you only return calls when you feel like it?"

"I'm supposed to be away this weekend. Somethin' you should try once in a blue moon," returned Delray good-naturedly. Normally, Delray's genteel Atlanta accent grated on Todd's nerves, but today the solicitor sounded as smooth and inviting as a slide trombone in a French Quarter speakeasy. "Well, guess what, Devilray, shit happens on the weekend - even here in Duckett County. All hell has broken loose." *And you don't know the half of it.*

Delray chuckled. "Yeah, I saw it on the idiot box."

Todd pictured the lazy lawyer relaxing in a comfy leather club chair, Cuban cigar in one hand, a glass of fine Kentucky bourbon in the other, and a big shit-eating grin on his face. "I'm askin' you," pleaded

Todd, "as one gentleman to another, will you please get down here and help me deal with this situation?"

"I can't just yet. Kathy and I picked up the gut rot. It's runnin' all through the resort." Delray produced a barely believable cough.

"Don't pee on my shoes and tell me it's rainin', Counselor."

"Now Hot Toddy, I'm offended that you would think I could ever be less than truthful with you," replied Delray with obvious feigned pathos. "As far as your dodgy ding-a-ling situation, we don't know if a crime has been committed. Could have been self-mutilation," he offered gamely.

Todd bolted upright in his seat. "I don't think so," he said with emphasis on each word. Out of spitefulness, he refrained from letting Delray in on the fact that Elvis had been stolen, even though the useless barrister would hear it on TV. in a few minutes at Todd's news conference.

Delray chuckled. "I bet ol' Fartbag has had a stroke."

"As a matter of fact, Sonny may be this minute standing outside the pearly gates, belly-bumping St. Peter to let him in - which is another reason why I need you down here to back me up." Todd realized that once Delray heard that the penis was missing, it was going to take an extra stick of dynamite to convince him to return. Though Delray was all-too-aware of the dazzling impression he made on TV, he wouldn't want to be associated with this mess, especially since his wife was standing for reelection to the Georgia General Assembly, and the vote was coming up in nine days.

Todd was reduced to appealing to the barrister's better nature, which was always a long shot. "It's not fair," he said, "that I gotta go out there and give a press briefin' without my almost dead-mayor and my darlin' D.A. ridin' gunshot."

"Now Toddy," chided Delray, "quit whinin' and accept the fact that you got the short end of the dick. Ha, ha! Get it?"

"Not funny," retorted Todd, though he had to admit to himself that it was a clever remark. Delray Hamilton was a clever man, no doubt about it.

"I'm not comin' back," stated Delray firmly, "until Kathy and I are over this flu. If you need a D.A., call ol' Fob Barker in Gilmer County. Now I know what you're thinkin', but he's been sober for a few months straight now." Todd heard Delray fake a groan. "Gotta make a dash to the can," he said abruptly. "I'll get back to you soon. Good luck, buddy." He hung up.

Todd gave the receiver the stink eye then slammed it down. He looked at the clock on the wall, which seemed to be ticking unusually loudly. It was high noon - time to face down the media mob alone. He was a know-nothing sheriff of a two-bit county, who had never traveled farther north than North Carolina or west than Alabama, yet he was going up against a gang of war-hardened, globetrotting, microphone-slinging news jockeys. Standing up, he exhaled on his badge, shined it with his shirttail, and stuffed his shirt back into his pants. He strapped on his sidearm, settled his hat on his head, squared his shoulders, and stepped out into the blinding sun.

Chapter Three
Saturday Afternoon Frivolity

As soon as the press conference was over, Todd retreated inside the office and locked the door. Shawn had been watching the reporter's wrap-ups on the portable TV that sat on the filing cabinet by the dispatcher's desk. When he saw Todd, he gaped at him.

Todd spied the dismay in Shawn's walnut-colored eyes. "Who you lookin' at?" he growled.

"Nobody."

"Turn that TV off. Get on that radio and see if the search team has found anything." Todd headed into his man-cave to marinate in self-pity. It had been humiliating having to admit to the world that Elvis had been stolen right out from under his nose, so to speak. After all, Doc Mahmondi's clinic was just three doors down from his office. Shawn called Todd back to the reception area and pointed to the window. Todd watched as the Georgia Bureau of Investigation crime-lab unit roared into the parking area. Todd hadn't requested help from the GBI, but here they were. The fact that the GBI was now in the game electrified the news correspondents, who had been wrapping up their analysis of the press briefing. While the agents rumbled about inside the van, P.J. and Tiffany rounded up the reporters and relocated the roped off area even farther back.

Three men exited the van. They were wearing identical dark sports coats and matching FBI sunglasses. To Todd's dismay, he immediately recognized the senior agent: Harwood Slaughter. He was flanked by his two clean-cut assistants – college boys, no doubt. "Well, here comes the Three Blind Mice," Todd muttered.

The reporters began firing questions at the GBI agents, but because

54

they were all shouting at once, their requests for information were garbled. Turning their backs on them, the GBI agents trotted up the steps, looking for all the world like vigorous super heroes arriving to save the planet since the ignoramus local sheriff had flubbed the job. Slaughter tried the doorknob, and finding it locked, banged on the doorframe. Todd reluctantly let them in and relocked the door.

Slaughter was in his mid-forties, but looked older, probably because he was a hard case. He sported a graying brown flattop, a touched-up bushy mustache, and a medium-sized beer belly. Todd had tangled with him three months earlier on case in which a woman's body had been found in the Forest. The GBI team had incorrectly focused on Duckett County as the scene of the murder, and with a most abrasive manner, Slaughter moved in on Todd's territory. He had slighted Todd in the press conferences, undermined him in front of his deputies, and worst of all - withheld evidence. Afterwards, Todd had written several letters to Slaughter's superiors requesting that they never send him back to Duckett County. Obviously, his request had gone unheeded. He decided that things were going to be different this time around.

"Jesus," exclaimed Slaughter, eyeing Todd up and down. "You're a goddammed prisoner in your own goddammed jailhouse." He laughed a wheezy laugh that turned into a smoker's guttural cough.

"This story has legs, as they say in the news business."

"It's a goddamned runaway centipede. That's why my boss sent me up here on my day off. Apparently, Baby Chief, somebody down at HQ was checking the alerts. Obviously, you're in way over your head and I'm gonna have to carry your water - again." He reached up to pat Todd on the cheek, but Todd blocked him with a swift arm movement.

"Try that again and it will be the last time you ... try that again," said Todd through clenched teeth.

"My, my, touchy, aren't we? I guess that's why you wrote those nasty letters to the powers that be back at headquarters," growled Slaughter, his mustache writhing like an irritated caterpillar. He pulled out a pack of cigarettes.

"This is a no-smoking jail," said Todd curtly. He assumed the traditional cop bearing by widening his stance slightly and crossing his arms.

Slaughter laughed gutturally and looked at his assistants. He stuck a cigarette in his mouth. Without taking his eyes off his adversary, Todd snatched the cigarette, crumpled it, and dropped it in the wastebasket that Shawn had simultaneously slid into position.

Startled, Slaughter looked at Todd with new eyes. "Enough with the fraternizing. I wanna see the site. At least I can smoke outside." He looked at his assistants and laughed dryly. "If Baby Chief lets me, that is."

Slaughter rode with Todd in the Bronco while the two junior agents followed in the crime-lab van. The senior agent joked crudely on his cell phone with his assistants. Todd realized that Slaughter's casual demeanor meant none of the three agents had knowledge of the latest development - that Elvis had flown the coop. The reporters outside Todd's office had collectively shouted questions at the GBI agents when they had exited their van, but Slaughter and company apparently hadn't understood the garbled questions. They had been too busy looking important to pay attention to the members of the press. Todd drew in a deep breath and informed his nemesis of this latest development. It was the most humiliating truth that he'd ever had to confess. Surprisingly, Slaughter didn't blow. Instead, he put the phone to his ear, called his team, and curtly informed them of the situation, then lapsed into a stony silence.

When they reached the trail head, Todd saw to his dismay that the crowd milling about on the side of the road had grown tenfold. It was as if the location were some kind of Mother Mary sighting. Several TV news vans were parked along the shoulders of the two-lane road, and reporters were interviewing the crowd.

After the Blaine debacle, Todd had personally called the State

Patrol, requesting assistance with securing the area since all his available deputies were combing the woods with the search-and-rescue team. In response, the State Patrol had sent a single smokey. The patrolman was sitting in his cruiser, which he had parked in front of the path to the crime scene. He was talking on his cell phone while curious people simply walked around his vehicle. Upon spying Todd, he stepped out of his cruiser and began shooing them away.

Slaughter's tongue thawed and he began to berate Todd for losing Elvis. Todd asserted that his team had retrieved the available evidence yesterday and had taken plenty of photos before the reporters and the snoops had descended on Elvis's rock. But none of his assertions appeased the snarling detective. In fact, Slaughter kept up a nonstop soliloquy during the hike from the highway to the clearing.

"Goddammit!" he ranted, "What's with all these crackers? Bunch of sexually repressed snake-handling, strychnine-swigging, dummy-dust-smoking hillbillies!" He heard rustling coming from the underbrush and spied a young couple making their way parallel to the trail. "Hey, get the fuck out of here!" Slaughter threw up his arms in disgust and angrily continued where he left off. "People don't stand and stare at the ground where a body's been dumped - not once it's been drug out! McPherson, can't you secure the site better?"

"This is a wilderness area," snapped Todd. "It's virtually impossible to seal off a site under these conditions. You know that."

The team reached the clearing where Cody was doing his best to disperse the curious. At least the yellow crime-scene tape was still intact. Also intact was the now famous chalk outline of Elvis on the now famous, nondescript rock.

Cursing under his breath, Slaughter examined the footprints around the rock. Some movement across the way caught his eye. "Look at that—JEEZUS!" He pointed at two teenage girls approaching from the north. "GET THE HELL OUT OF HERE... FUCKING TRAILER TRASH!" He picked up a rock and threw it in the direction of the two girls, who turned and ran toward the ridge, insuring that they would get hopelessly lost and possibly fired upon by an overly eager hunter. Todd sent Cody to fetch them.

Slaughter bent to pick up another rock, but when he stood up, Todd grabbed his wrist. "Drop ... the ... rock," he ordered, coming to a full stop after each word.

Slaughter attempted to jerk his arm away, but Todd's grip was ironclad. Slaughter muttered, "Alright, alright, don't wet your g-string." He gave Todd a counterfeit smile and dropped the rock. Todd let him go, but it only took a few minutes for Slaughter to build up another head of steam. "The prick's not even here anymore. You'd think it was still laying right out in front of Jesus, Joseph, and Mary ... and everyone else! But the fucking thing is gone thanks to you. You should have contacted us as soon as that limey girl called it in. We could have whisked it off to Atlanta. That was a dumbshit move leaving it with your raghead doc. Next time one of your redneck hunters stumbles onto a body, a pinky finger, or even a hangnail, you call the GBI as fast as you can punch in the goddamned numbers. You got that, Baby Chief?"

"Sorry, Harwood, I'm just a stupid county Mounty from the sticks," snarled Todd. "I don't even know how to use one of them new-fangled cell phones." By now, the two adversaries noses were only inches apart. Todd added, "From now on, I decide when this department needs outside help." His scowl deepened as he locked onto Slaughter's cold, mossy eyes.

Slaughter's men and Todd's deputies watched the pair of lawmen, each one wondering if it would be worth risking a limb to separate them if feuding foes came to blows. If they did, the older, chain-smoking Slaughter would be no match for the brawny young sheriff. On the other hand, getting in a physical brawl with a GBI agent would also likely mean the end of Todd's career in law enforcement.

Slaughter backed off. He lit a cigarette, inhaled deeply, and like a fire-breathing dragon, forcefully exhaled smoke through his nose. "We will take this up later. Now show me the fuck what you found before this site gets any more contaminated. It already looks like a pockmarked whore's butt."

"As I said before, we don't take to rudeness here," retorted Todd. He thought that while he had the advantage, he might as well press ahead.

Slaughter threw up his arms. The cigarette sticking out of his mouth became a dancing marionette as he declared, "Jesus, Mary, and Joseph, show me the fuck what you fucking found - please." He forced a ghoulish jack-o'-lantern grin around his cigarette.

Redheaded Rusty Moore, Todd's second in command, having just returned from the search team, stepped inside the yellow circle. Rusty had been on a Florida fishing trip when he had heard about the Elvis story last night over the scanner application on his phone. Though Todd hadn't asked him to, he dutifully drove most of the night back to Duckett County and joined the search party just before Todd had left the scene this morning. Rusty called the sheriff and detectives over to view one of the distinctive larger footprints that Todd had noticed yesterday.

"I noticed this one before I took off with the team," said Rusty in his usual tranquil manner. "I told Cody to keep the gawkers away from it."

Slaughter looked down at the footprint. "Baby Chief, I sincerely hope that you managed to take a cast of this."

Before Todd could think of a retort for being called Baby Chief again, Rusty offered, "Everything that's got a flag got its picture taken yesterday, and this particular print has been cast."

Todd, Rusty, and Slaughter squatted and examined the impression in the red Georgia clay while the GBI assistants looked over their shoulders. Both Todd and Harwood forgot their mutual animosity for the moment as they eyeballed their most promising piece of evidence thus far.

Georgia boot? asked Slaughter.

"I've determined that already," said Todd.

"It's a man's size - about an eleven," added Slaughter, raking his mustache.

"It's deeper in the heel than in the front." Todd silently chastised himself for not noticing this anomaly yesterday. "I think you know what that means: a kid, or more likely a petite woman, came walking through here in boots that were too big for them."

Slaughter stood and flicked his cigarette into the underbrush, and one of his assistants rushed over and rubbed it out with their foot. "Watch your dicks, boys." Slaughter proclaimed. "We got a Lorena Bobbitt on the loose." His gravelly laughter morphed into a spastic smoker's cough.

"Bobbitt threw her trophy right out of the car and into a field," said Todd. "This perp was a little more in control of herself. She nicely laid it out on that rock."

"She'll be harder to catch," muttered Slaughter.

The two assistant agents took their own molds of what was left of the flagged footprints, and performed some chemical tests on the tiny amount of dried blood on Elvis's rock. Rusty suggested that he return to the search team, but Todd gave him a list of the half-dozen bystanders who had shown up in time to see him and the doc walking out from the trail head with the cooler. Never one who enjoyed being switched abruptly from one task to another, Rusty frowned, then reluctantly accompanied Todd and the GBI team down the trail.

Slaughter returned to the Sheriff's office in the crime-lab, then the three GBI agents walked to Doctor Mahmondi's clinic. They dusted for fingerprints, even though Virgil had found no prints on the refrigerator. After that, the agents returned to the crime van with their evidence. The gaggle of news people, having broken free of their corral, surrounded the van. Whatever the two agents were doing in their lab-on-wheels made it rock and sway, which caused the reporters to snicker.

Slaughter emerged, and sloughing off the media, banged on the office door. After Todd let him in, he launched into a new tirade because he didn't have access to the tissue samples that Gorov had taken. The doc had informed him that Todd had ordered a deputy to drive the tissue samples to the state crime lab last night. Todd couldn't help but be amused over Slaughter's hissy fit. Slaughter always wanted the evidence in his hands, and his alone. Todd retreated to his office, closed the door, and began to return phone calls, leaving the frustrated GBI agent with nothing to do for the time being but to return to the portable crime lab.

A listless Gorov, wearing his bulky, black-framed, spare spectacles, wandered into Todd's office and flopped in the chair. He took on the hunched-over position of a big-time brooder. Being a brooder himself, Todd was familiar with the doc's body language. Every so often, Gorov would stand and pace the room for a minute, then take his chair again to resume his brood. Not wanting to summon a third ambulance today, Todd left the young doctor alone to decompress. Finally, Gorov looked up and mumbled, "I never lost a patient - at least not in my own clinic."

"Now come on, Gorov, Elvis wasn't exactly a patient."

"But I had it all prepared for reattachment in case ... in case you find the poor slob at the other end of the thing. There could be future children involved." Gorov wiped a tear away with the sleeve of his lab coat. Todd thought that Gorov was taking this whole thing very hard. Perhaps Gorov felt responsible for the fact that millions of wiggly sperm cells would never make their way through that particular vessel to have a shot at becoming people.

Todd reached the end of his patience and called for a deputy to drive the doc home. Cody, back from the site, appeared in the doorway and Gorov stood up as sluggishly as an eighty-year-old man and shuffled out of the room after him.

The GBI team reappeared. Before Slaughter spoke, Todd said, "The best way to handle this case will be to work it backwards." Slaughter reluctantly grunted his agreement. Anxious to show Slaughter that he'd learned a few things since their last case together, Todd added, "If we find the penis's thief, said thief is likely to lead us to the perp. They could be the same person."

Again Slaughter grunted his agreement. He asked Todd for a list of names of those persons who had volunteered to be on the search-and-rescue team the previous evening. He divided the list into three sections and gave a section to one of his assistants, and the second section to the other assistant. Todd paired up Shawn with assistant #1 and Tawanda with assistant #2, and then the foursome left to interview their "suspects." Personally, Todd didn't think any member of the search and rescue team could possibly be involved, but he had to go through the motions. Slaughter grabbed the last third of the names on the list and Todd left with the ill-mannered agent. It would not be a comfortable situation for Todd, because they would be interrogating friends with whom he had grown up, as well as men who had mentored him through the turbulence of adolescence and the challenges of early manhood.

The first stop was the house of Preacher Dodge. Todd had no idea why Slaughter thought a holy man like J.T. Dodge would lift a penis. Maybe he was just ruling out the least likely suspect of an already unlikely bunch. Out of politeness, Todd let the late Mrs. Dodge's sixteen-year-old, champagne-colored miniature poodle, "House Beautiful," sit on his lap during the interview. House Beautiful was oozing from all its facial orifices, making Todd worry about what was happening at the end that sat on his khaki-colored pants. His hands full with the pathetic creature, Todd let Slaughter ask the questions. The interview seemed to take forever because Preacher Dodge endeavored to answer each question with a sermon.

Next, Todd and Slaughter drove back to the Checkered Flagg Grill and Poolroom and sat down with Tammy Flagg. Todd again let Slaughter ask the questions. That way he could better observe the interviewees. Afterwards, the pair of lawmen walked up Main Street to "Curl Up and Dye," Bambi Davis's hair salon. They squirmed in cramped hairdryer chairs while Bambi, taking perm papers from slack-jawed Valinda Mills, recounted her activities from the time she had received the call from LeeLee to help on the search-and-rescue team until dawn this morning when the SNN reporter was interviewing her. Since Todd felt that Bambi was hardly a suspect, he found himself reconstructing Jasmine Roseberry's dazzling smile in his mind's eye.

After they finished with Bambi, Todd drove Slaughter to Duckett High School, where they found Coach Flagg sitting in his office working on next year's playbook. Slaughter asked to speak to Mrs. Flagg, so Coach Flagg punched in the number on his phone and handed it to Slaughter. After a few minutes of exchange, Slaughter hung up and said, "Your wife insists that you were in your rightful place all night." There was a suspicious note in his voice. "I'll be wanting to question her in person." Todd rolled his eyes. He was anxious to get back to the office to check the tips on the phone lines and the alerts on the computer. Slaughter was wasting his time with this bunch. These outsiders didn't know these people like Todd did.

Despite Mrs. Flagg's alibi, Slaughter launched into a line of questioning that in Todd's view was ludicrous. Slaughter had found out from Tammy that her husband, Jimmy, was Coach Flagg's only son, and that Jimmy was in the pen at Alto. Coach Flagg stayed calm throughout the interview until Slaughter began to question him about Jimmy. There was no reason as far as Todd could see for Jimmy or his father to be the slightest bit interested in lifting a penis. Presumably, Jimmy wasn't getting any use out of the one he already had.

"Did you talk to your son last night?" Slaughter asked gruffly.

"No," Coach Flagg replied. "Why are you bringing my boy into this mess?"

"When did you last see Jimmy?"

"One week ago on Saturday. My daughter-in-law Tammy, my wife, and me go visit twice a month."

Perhaps Slaughter had had a bad experience with a spiteful coach when he was a boy, because he pointedly picked on Coach Flagg. "Must be kind of weird, you coaching all those boys who turn out to be fine, strapping young men like Fearless McPherson here ... " He clapped a hand on Todd's muscular shoulder, while Todd looked away. "And your own son turns out to be a worthless dope trafficker."

Todd expected Coach Flagg to blow a gasket, but uncharacteristically, he appeared to deflate. In a small voice, he said, "I don't know what happened with my boy. He wasn't athletic, you know, so we didn't have much in common. Maybe he was jealous of the time I spent with boys like Todd." He nodded his head in the direction of his undefeated quarterback. His mouth melted into a sad frown.

Todd stood up. "I think we're done here."

Once they were back at the office, Slaughter headed next door to the Checkered Flagg, this time to grab something to eat. Todd received a call on his cell phone from his ever-diligent and remarkably efficient second-in-command, Rusty. Rusty reported the results of his interview with the onlookers. Todd hung up, and feeling the need to confide in a friend, he walked past the grill to Sikes Freeman's shop, where an old red and white barber's pole marked the entrance. A bell above the door tinkled as Todd opened the heavy, wooden door. The stained-glass inserts above the front windows lent a timeless, cathedral-like air to the room. Four old-fashioned barber's chairs sat in front of a long mirror. Across from them in front of the picture widow stood a row of unoccupied antique shoeshine chairs for waiting customers. Todd liked the musky smell of the dark, wormy wood paneling and the way the wide, pine floor planks complained when he walked across them. His father had spent many hours shooting the breeze in this manly refuge. Hoyt Todd, or H.T. as everybody called him, had been a true extrovert, a good ol' boy who stood firmly on the sunny side of life. Unfortunately, the optimistic farmer was diagnosed with melanoma at the age of forty-five and was dead by fifty-one.

Todd heard the rasping of metal being filed coming from the

backroom. Sikes was taking advantage of some down time between hair jobs. Todd heard him call out, "Come on back, Cotton." Todd realized that Sikes knew the sound of his footsteps by heart. The gibberish from a twenty-four-hour news channel turned down low became audible as Todd rounded a barber chair and entered through the opening to the workroom. "I wish you wouldn't call me Cotton," he muttered.

Sikes muted the volume on the small TV. "You know that's what we called you when you was a youngin' cuz your hair was so white." He was sitting at his workbench, wearing a pair of protective goggles and filing on the firing mechanism of an antique Colt 45. He specialized in finding parts for broken antique firearms brought in by customers and fitting the pieces together like they had been made for each other. Without taking his eyes off his work he said, "Seems like I been callin' you Cotton since forever."

Todd thought he had too many distasteful nicknames – Fearless, Cotton, and Virgil often called him Big Buck. Ugh. He grabbed a wooden chair, turned it around, and straddled it. "Speaking of forever, did you see the press briefin'?"

"Yup."

"And?"

Sikes swiveled his stool around to peer at Todd through his goggles. "I guess a half-assed performance is better than a full-assed performance."

"Thanks." Todd draped his arms over the back of the chair. "I feel so much better."

Sikes chuckled. "Just kiddin'. Let's just say no hillbilly sheriff is a match for Ansley Mason and the rest of that lynch mob they call the media." He returned to his filing while Todd studied the dark, fifty-something profile which stood in contrast to the faded-white wall. Without looking up, Sikes asked, "Any news about your worked-to-death dispatcher and the mayor?"

"I talked to LeeLee. She's been released and sent home to rest up over the weekend. They gave her hormones to take in the mornin' and tranquilizers to take at night. Looks like Sonny's gonna be okay, too. They're gonna keep him a few days for observation cuz they can't figure out why he quit breathin' like that. Of course, he released a statement that he'll give an interview as soon as the doctor will let him."

"An interview about the bright economic future of Duckett County, no doubt." Sikes's words slid out on a good-natured chuckle.

Todd rubbed the smooth back of the old oak chair with the palms of his hands. He looked down and saw that, amazingly, even after four years, there was still a slight indention on his ring finger. He looked up at Sikes. "In a few minutes GBI Agent Harwood Slaughter - I reckon you remember him - is gonna come in here and ask you a lot of embarrassin' questions about your past."

Sikes raised the goggles to his forehead and peered at Todd. "No foolin'?"

"Questions that—"

"Questions that you always wondered about." Todd shrugged his response, so Sikes changed the subject. "You gotta bead on who pinched the weenie?"

Frowning, Todd rubbed his dry, sleep-deprived eyes. "I've eliminated Coach Flagg, who was snuggled up to Mrs. Flagg all night; and Preacher Dodge cuz he is, well, Preacher Dodge." He exhaled loudly. "I've grilled the deputies upside and backwards. They were all cuddled up to their love bunnies last night, except for two who were at the Buckin' Bull tryin' to pick up a couple of warm bodies with which to snuggle."

Sikes snorted and Todd continued, "Rusty has already managed to question the onlookers and their wives. The wives said they were entwined all night with their honeypots."

Sikes shrugged. "Maybe they were coverin' for their men."

"Rusty is fairly good at tellin' when a person's lyin'."

"Not as good as you, Cotton."

66

Todd hid his smile by studying the cracked linoleum. The rare compliment from Sikes never failed to warm his heart. "One notable fact has arisen," Todd said. "All the Main Street merchants are on the search-and-rescue team and none of them, like me, has a cuddle partner to get them through the night. Which means, Mister Watson, they don't have an alibi."

"That would be Tammy, Gorov, Vince, Bambi, and the wart taker - Marvalena." Sikes chuckled. "And me." He shook his head, "Come on, Cotton, none of us would do somethin' like that. You know us. We're all your friends," he smiled slightly, "save Marvalena, who you're scared of."

"I ain't scared of ... to get back to the point, some members of the search team could have a motive."

Sikes gave Todd a "get-real" look. "What possible motive could any of us have for stealin' the wazzit?"

Todd shrugged. "Meanness ... Tammy could get back at me for sendin' her louse of a spouse down river. Attention ... Bambi got herself on TV, even if her hair made her look like somethin' out of Dawn of the Dead. Publicity ... Vince, the Ambitious may still get some kind of inside scoop out of the whole mess. Sympathy ... Doc Mahmondi resents bein' pressed into performin' the county's medical examiner duties. By stealin' a body part, he would bring attention to the fact that the county needs get on with hirin' a full-time ME with his own more secure office at the hospital."

Sikes threw his head back and laughed at the inanity of Todd's theories. "And what about me?" he asked around the edges of a big chuckle.

"Maybe you're just flat-out bored and wanna spice things up around here."

Sikes rolled his eyes. "Come on Cotton, those are the most sorry-ass motives I ever heard. In fact, you sound downright ridiculous."

Todd lifted his hands in surrender. "Believe me, I know. But I can't rule y'all out neither."

"Lots of other deputies from neighboring counties, and also more bystanders, showed up at the trail head eventually," asserted Sikes. "They didn't see Gorov leave with the thing in his little cooler, but they could have put two and two together and figured out where it had been stored for the night. I heard that some of those bystanders that came later were strangers. A stranger probably took it."

Todd rubbed his chin. "According to Tammy, there were several strangers hangin' around the grill last night."

Sikes pointed the end of his metal file at Todd. "There you go. Maybe Tammy mentioned where the wazzit had been put to bed, and the strangers swiped it as a prank."

"Tammy doesn't talk to strangers. Tammy doesn't talk to nobody, so there's no way in hell she'd blab to an outsider about Elvis."

Sikes smiled out of one corner of his mouth. "You callin' it Elvis?"

"Doc named it."

"I s'pose Big Elvis is dead. Right?"

"Well, no hospital within two-hundred miles of here has reported an admission of someone with an unaccounted for dingaling. So if Big Elvis ain't dead, he's in a world of hurt cuz he ain't had no official medical attention."

Sikes switched back to Little Elvis's current predicament. "You find any fingerprints at the clinic?"

"The refrigerator was wiped clean, and neither Virgil nor the GBI could find any latent prints on it or on the doorknobs."

"Maybe the thief was the person who did the crime in the first place. He laid Elvis on the rock then hid in the brush when he saw the cavalry drive up. He saw the doc carry the cooler out of the woods, followed the two of you to see where you stowed it, then waited until the middle of the—"

"We didn't see anyone hiding in the brush." Todd sighed and grasped the sides of the chair back. "Still, I hope it was a stranger that took it; but right now, I have to stick with the people who knew about the operation because they were part of the operation: the Main Street proprietors."

"Back to us? Well, I think it's ridiculous of you to even think that one of your friends could possibly have anything to do with swiping Elvis, not to mention play a part in a murder."

Throwing up his arms, Todd said, "I agree, and, like you said, all y'all's possible motives for lifting Elvis are too trite to bother with. But in the absence of any computer alerts or credible phone tips, y'all are the only leads I have. Hell, maybe y'all are all in it together."

Sikes had to chortle at that. When he brought himself under control, a thoughtful expression crossed his brow. "But there could be a hidden motive for one of the Main-streeters to take Elvis. And when you uncover said motive, you'll find the thief who stole Elvis - and maybe the body of Big Elvis too."

Todd tsk-tsked him. "Hidden motive, my eye. I think you have been spendin' too much time watchin' your old black-and-white detective DVDs with my momma."

Sikes repositioned his goggles over his eyes and returned to shaping the Colt's hammer mechanism. "It do look like this case is turnin' out to be a whodunnit."

Todd sat up and said enthusiastically, "Maybe it was Mister Green in the conservatory with the candlestick!" Sikes chuckled and both men fell into a companionable silence for a moment as the older man attended to his work. Finally, Todd said, "The weird thing is, I can't get the girl out of my mind."

Sikes glanced up. "What girl?"

"The girl who found it." Todd idly spun the cylinder of the Colt 45 on the worktable. "My mind will be goin' a mile a minute on this ludicrous case, and then a vision of her lovely face pops up right in front o' me."

Sikes snatched the spinning cylinder from Todd. "Didn't your daddy teach you nothin' about guns?"

"I think I love her."

Sikes raised his goggles once again and peered at Todd. "Cotton, you big ignoramus, sometimes it seems like you got the brains of a garden hose. What you are experiencing is physical attraction. It's a fact of life that all men must lust."

Todd snorted. "Nope. This is somethin' way, way bigger. Crazy, ain't it?"

"The sooner you realize that life is crazy, that you're crazy, that I'm crazy, that even crazy people is crazy - the happier you'll be."

Todd sighed, draped himself over the back of the chair, and let his arms dangle. "She has the most beatific eyes."

"Oh boy, we've got trouble right here in River City." The bell on the front door jingled and Special Agent Harwood Slaughter walked in. "Well, here we go," said Sikes under his breath.

Slaughter found his way to the backroom and sat on the workbench, cutting off Todd's view of Sikes. Todd stood up, leaned against the wall, and crossed his arms. Slaughter immediately began firing questions. "How long have you lived in Duckett County, Mr. Freeman?"

Sikes said, "I've been here twenty years."

"Not much of your kind in these mountains. How'd you end up here?"

Sikes crossed his arms over his chest. "By my kind, I take it you mean the African-American kind."

Slaughter's look said, "Duh."

"Todd's daddy took me in on a prisoner-release program through their church," said Sikes evenly. "I wanted to work outside after all those years of bein' locked up. I worked on the McPherson's farm. Nursed every old, raggedy machine on the place, from the washin' machine to the combine. Tightfisted bunch they are. Anyway, I ended up workin' there from the time Todd here was about seven until he was nigh on fifteen. By then, I'd saved enough money to buy this shop."

"What were you in for?"

"Aggravated murder."

"Where did you commit the crime?"

"Atlanta."

"How long were you in for?"

"I spent twenty years in Arrendale state pen, from when I was eighteen to age thirty-eight."

Slaughter's marble-hard eyes bored into Sikes. "You ever rob anyone?"

"No. Yes, once when I was twelve, I took a Playboy magazine from a 7-Eleven." Sikes winked at Todd, who smiled and looked down.

Slaughter scowled. "You think this is funny?"

Sikes held up his hands. "No sir. Some poor sap's dingo has gone missin.' I reckon that's pretty serious."

Slaughter jotted down something down on his notepad. "You know how to pick a lock, Mr. Freeman?"

"A lock ain't a gun. A gun ain't a lock." Sikes's gaze flitted up to Todd, who was still leaning up against the wall with arms crossed, watching him carefully. Above Sikes's head, a little cuckoo bird burst out of its house, coo-cooed, and then repeated its routine two more times.

* * * * *

After the rather unproductive interview with Sikes, Todd decided to let Slaughter and his assistants interview the remaining members of the notorious Main Street gang. In his opinion, Slaughter was behaving like a bull in a china shop, a tactic that was doomed to fail in this county where no matter high how one's station in life, one was expected to treat others with politeness. Because of this, Todd decided instead to interview the remaining Main street proprietors who had been on the scene by himself at a later time without Slaughter. He returned to the site and checked in with Cody, who held up his radio and said that the team hadn't found anything so far. Todd asked Cody if Virgil and Blaine had called in confirming that they had made contact with the team. After Virgil had completed his fingerprinting duties, Todd had ordered him and Blaine to carry a second field kit to the team. That way, the team could be split into two sections.

Cody shrugged. "I ain't heard from them. Maybe they're lost."

Todd horse-snorted. "No maybe about it. They're lost." *Hopefully permanently.*

Just then, Virgil's voice crackled over the radio. He stated that they had failed to find the team, but that they had stumbled on something of interest in an illegal dumpsite. Grumbling under his breath, Todd hiked through the wilderness in the direction of the two lost deputies and found them in a clearing strewn with moldering couches and forlorn-looking rusted out appliances. Virgil jerked up the chronically loose waistband of his pants and rocked back and forth on his feet. "This is one deputy who knows when to keep vital info off the radio," he said and winked knowingly at his young boss.

"It better be Elvis," said Todd, scowling.

Blaine was standing by a chipped, claw-foot bathtub that was resting on its side. His puppy-dog eyes were looming large. "No Elvis but it's somethin' big. We pulled up one side of this ol' tub."

"And we just about broke our backs," Virgil added.

Blaine ran a hand over his sweat-dampened hair, the length of which was really not legal for a probie. "We was sure we was gonna find a den of copperheads, but instead we found this."

Todd walked around the bathtub and knelt down. There on the damp ground was a gray, weather-worn human skeleton, minus the skull and some of the smaller bones. Todd rubbed his chin and muttered, "Well, don't that knock the fleas right off a monkey."

Blaine snickered nervously. "This sure ain't the guy who owned Elvis, unless he had some powerful voodoo tallywhacker mojo for his Elvis to stay fresh all that time." The comment earned him a glare from

Todd.

"You think it's Billy Evans?" asked Virgil.

"Maybe, maybe not," Todd responded. Billy Evans was an insurance salesman who disappeared with his secretary one Friday night ten months earlier. He was supposedly taking her home after work, but they never arrived. It was rumored around town that Billy, who was married, had been having an affair with the much-younger Bonnie. The prevailing sentiment was that they had run off to Mexico to start a new life, but Todd had never believed that. For one thing, Billy was known as a devoted Christian. He was also a pillar of the community; in fact, he was serving as a county commissioner at the time of his disappearance. And as far as Bonnie was concerned, her bank account had showed no large withdrawals. Also, nothing had been missing from her house.

Todd realized that the search for Elvis had inadvertently led him to this huge discovery. Funny, he never thought he would feel any obligation to a penis other than his own. Maybe if he kept following Elvis, he would not only find Elvis's owner, but also the killer of this poor skeleton. Then he realized that had been a ridiculous thought. The odds were overwhelmingly against the two crimes being related.

He pulled a tape measure out of the field kit. "It's definitely a man's pelvis and the length of the femur suggests that he was from five-feet-nine to five-feet-eleven."

"Billy was five-feet-ten," said Blaine. The disappearance of Billy Evans and Bonnie Wells had happened a few weeks after he became a probie, and he remembered every detail. Todd had the deputies, the State Patrol, and dozens of volunteers tromping through Duckett Forest for two weeks. Of course, they managed to cover only a small fraction of the wilderness.

Standing, Todd brushed off his pants. "A lot of men are five-foot-ten. We're gonna hope that the state lab can get some DNA out of these bones."

"Alls I see is some very dead bones," said Virgil. "How are they gonna get DNA from them?"

Todd said, "Now days, those clever criminologists can extract a sample for DNA testing from ground-up bone. Of course, I'll need somebody to go over to the Evans's farm and get a DNA sample from one of Billy's kids for comparison's sake." *And tell Jeanie about the bones.* Todd grimaced. "I recon that someone will be me." He looked closely at the scratches in the dirt along the indentation of the tub's sides. "Looks like some animal got a hold of some of the smaller bones."

"That don't explain where the skull went," responded Virgil, as he nervously swiveled his head around. He returned his gaze to Todd. "I take it, Young Buck, that yer gonna switch the search-and-rescue team over here to look for it."

"Nope."

Both Virgil and Blaine looked quizzically at their boss and then at each other. Todd snooped around the dumpsite and then returned to the bones. "I'm callin' off the search team at dusk. Big Elvis just ain't in these woods. Those big bootprints back there on the trail prove that the person who dropped off Little Elvis came from the road, and then after depositing the poor, pitiful thing on that rock, he or she returned to the road."

Todd looked the two deputies in the eye. "Tomorrow at daybreak, I want you two to get back out here and look for more bones. If this was Billy, Bonnie's bones could be around here too. And try to locate the skull to this set." He pulled the magnifying glass out of the kit, and looked more closely at the remains of the day. "Also, bring some metal detectors to search for spent rounds and casings." He grinned broadly. "By the way, good work, guys! I knew pairing up my oldest and youngest deputy would pay off eventually."

Blaine suddenly looked uncomfortable. Then he grinned ghoulishly and sang, "Dem bones, dem bones, dem dry bones…" Virgil snickered and broke into a spasmodic skeleton dance.

Todd abruptly reversed his opinion that Blaine and Virgil were a good team. Blaine had brought out an annoyingly playful side to the normally jittery Virgil. In turn, Virgil hadn't helped Blaine to grow up. "Hey!" Todd shouted. "Have some respect, Boneheads!"

Blaine erupted in one of his famous high-pitched giggles. "You said boneheads!"

"Have some respect, dipshits. How's that?" Todd fixed on Blaine. "And you have to know that you are skatin' on skinny ice." Blaine gulped down a giggle, then dropped his gaze to the ground. Todd circled the bones once again. "Virg, get the camera out of the field kit and take pictures."

Blaine looked up. "No Vince?"

"I want to this kept quiet until I know for sure whether or not that's Billy layin' there."

"So no press briefin'?" quizzed Virgil. Todd didn't respond. Virgil scratched his head, while Blaine stared at his second cousin/boss.

"I've got my reasons," said Todd.

A sudden case of nerves hit Virgil. As if they had a life of their own, his eyes darted wildly about the clearing. "You know, Young Buck," he said, "the perp might could have seen on TV all the hal-la-ba-loo goin' on up on the road at the trailhead to Elvis's rock. He could have figured out that during the search, we'd stumble onto this dumpsite sooner or later and find the bones. He could be right out there in the woods right now, watchin' us."

Blaine shuddered. "So you gonna leave us alone to get kilt?"

"You two," chided Todd. "Even if the killer of these bones does live in these parts, he or she ain't gonna come near to this place right now with all this attention on the Forest."

Again, Virgil swiveled his head around, fearing that the killer of the bone man was about to attack. He stammered, "I don't know 'bout that. I still think—"

"I'll do the thinkin'. Y'all take care of the site."

Virgil's face relaxed. "I just remembered, Blaine and me are s'posed to switch to swing shift Monday night, so the rest of today and tomorrow are the only days we can do this here search." He smiled at Blaine, who let out an audible sigh of relief.

Todd rubbed his chin as he pondered. "Well then, I'll have Cody and Tiffany take over come Monday. I know I can count on them to play this close to the vest." He fixed Virgil and Blaine with a grappling hook of a stare. "Like I said, I want you ladies to keep this under your skirts, copy?"

Virgil stuck his thumbs in his duty belt and rocked on his feet. "Don't worry about me, Todd. This is one crime fighter who knows how to keep an investigation close to his bulletproof vest."

The late afternoon sun was heating up the clearing, and the dark twin smiles on the front of Blaine's khaki shirt indicated that he was sweating under his man-boobs. He wiped his damp face with his forearm. "Sure thang, cousin - I mean, Chief."

Todd pulled out his cell phone, checked to see if he had a signal, and made a call to Gorov. He hoped that by now the doc had recovered from the trauma of losing Elvis and would be up for another adventure. After he hung up, he poked around the site some more and discovered twin tire grooves in the forest floor. "Here is where people have been gettin' in to dump their junk. We'll use it to get the, ah, body out of here." Blaine pulled the yellow crime-scene tape out of the field kit. Since he was still a probie, he was always assigned this boring task. Todd shook his head and said, "No tape."

Blaine cocked his head. "Come again?"

"No tape for now. This is to be kept low key."

"I have to tell ya, Young Buck," said Virgil, "not stringin' tape around the scene of a crime is highly unorthodox."

Todd ignored him and turned to Blaine. "I want you to hike back to the clearing and call in the volunteers. Then go get in your truck and meet the doc at the beginning of this illegal road, which by my calculation comes out of these woods on Pirkle Road." He added emphatically, "and keep your sirens and overheads off."

Blaine drew his damp uniform shirt away from his chronically leaky torso and asked, "Since the county ain't got no coroner's wagon, you gonna call an ambulance? Cuz a skeleton on a gurney would look stupid." He began to snicker again.

Todd thought that Blaine was just as irritating today as he was the first time his cousin, Laurel, had brought her newborn to visit, and it had commenced to wail louder than all of Duckett County's patrol vehicles put together. But Blaine had a point. In Duckett County, the ME was the coroner, and the county didn't have a coroner's van. Instead, it relied on the EMT service. Hence, every dead body was required to be admitted into the emergency room and be banded with an ID bracelet - just like a living patient - before finally landing in the morgue. Todd looked at the bones again. He didn't know if he wanted to puke or guffaw at the image of this headless skeleton being wheeled out of the emergency room wearing a wristband.

He turned to Virgil. "After the doc is done, we'll carefully and respectfully load the bones into the back of Blaine's vehicle, and then you two will hightail it down to the state lab. That way we can avoid the whole ambulance thing."

"Jesus, Todd, that's a five-hour round trip," whined Blaine. "It'll put us nearbouts night shift by the time we get back."

Todd pulled the air horn out of the field kit and tossed it to Blaine. "Don't get lost."

* * * * *

After processing the scene and sending Blaine and Virgil on their un-merry way to Atlanta, Todd returned to his office to attack a stack of phone tips on the Elvis case that had been taken by Tawanda and Forrest. It seemed like everyone had a theory regarding the whereabouts of Elvis, but only a few tips were worthy of further attention. Just as

Todd was about to pick up the phone, Delray Hamilton called from his fancy guest lodge in North Carolina and asked if the search team had found any other body parts.

"Negative," said Todd.

"Not even any matching balls?" quipped the rascally solicitor.

"Nope. Looks like the set got broken up." Todd hung up, thinking there was no point in telling "Delray the Useless" about the bones yet. Suddenly restless, he stepped into the front room and looked out the window. Through the dusky light, he spied Harwood Slaughter returning from interviewing the last three Main Street establishment owners. Slaughter brushed off the few remaining reporters, climbed into the crime lab van, and slammed the door.

Todd followed-up on the more legitimate-sounding tips, but uncovered nothing worthwhile. By then it was long past sunset. All was quiet now that the media hounds had departed to rest up for another day of badgering. Todd locked the front door and was briefing Scratch, the dispatcher for swing shift, when one of Slaughter's junior agents came calling at the front door. Todd unlocked and opened the door, but didn't invite him inside. The agent said Slaughter wanted Jasmine's cell phone number. Guessing that Slaughter wanted to pay Jasmine a visit, Todd told the agent that it was no use trying to find her place tonight. He explained that she lived high on a mountain in Emerald Lake Resort; and since the weather was moving in, the roads would be even nastier up there than down here. The agent said in that case, Slaughter would set something up for the morning. Todd reluctantly pulled the memo book out of his back pocket and gave him Jasmine's cell number. He didn't want Harwood the Crude anywhere near the new object of his affection.

The agent asked, "Where is the nearest motel? Harwood said that the last time he was assigned a case in Duckett County, the state reserved him a room in a motel outside the county line, and it was a time consuming drive back and forth to Duckett Forest."

"Well, the huntin' lodge burned down last month," responded Todd. Repressing a naughty smile, he gave the agent directions to the Restful Forest Motel and Lodge, the only sleeping accommodations in the county outside of the picturesque Emerald Lake Inn, which required advance reservations and charged far more than a state-government stipend would pay. The charge for a bed at the Restful Forest, on the other hand, was more than reasonable. Thanks to the presence of legions of termites, human guests were able to entertain themselves by watching the walls of their room gradually disintegrate. According to Todd's mother, the nasty creatures had feasted on the motel ever since Porter Waggoner and a very young Dolly Parton had come to the county to play at the Moonshine Festival in the early sixties. Nowadays, the Restful Forest was held up mainly by chewing gum and dried boogers. When Todd was in high school, he had once been told by a teammate that the mattresses at Restful Forest harbored legions of itty-bitty stowaways. Todd couldn't have imagined a worse place to lose one's virginity.

His reverie was broken by the young agent's throat clearing. The agent said, "Harwood also wants to know where he can get…um…to put it in his words ... a rub and a tug.'"

"Tell him Duckett County ain't that hospitable," retorted Todd, slamming the door.

The three blind mice departed in their crime van, and Todd realized he could no longer put off visiting Billy Evans' wife and Bonnie Wells' mother. As he drove to the Evans farm, he rummaged amongst his thoughts for the right words to say. It occurred to him that maybe those folks who had voted for Mumper for sheriff instead of him knew what they were doing, because at this moment he felt far too inexperienced to deal with what he was about to attempt to deal with. Horse-snorting, he muttered, "You might have led me to those bones, Elvis, but the bones have led me here, which means that right now you most definitely are not my friend."

Where's Elvis?

Todd turned into the asphalt driveway of the Evans farm and spotted a couple of mares grazing in the front pasture. They were smart looking Paints, except for the fact that their white areas were the color of terra cotta as a result of rolling in the Georgia mud. Todd drove past the barn and spied a trio of Palominos waiting placidly by the door for their hay, oblivious to the human drama that had swirled around the Evans household for the past ten months. Todd thought how Jeanie had to be a steel magnolia to keep up with this farm and three teenagers, in addition to teaching his own daughter's kindergarten class.

Jeanie's eldest child, Shane, answered the door. Todd hadn't expected the teen to be home on a Saturday night. The handsome high-school senior was the quarterback for the Duckett High Fighting Bucks, and that fact alone guaranteed him a date anytime he wanted one.

Upon recognizing the visitor, Shane's face warped into a picture of fear and dread, and his solemn brown eyes turned morose. "Hey," said Todd softly. "Your momma home?"

Shane hesitated for a second, and then stepped back. Todd wiped his boots and followed him to the family room, where Jeanie was sitting at the far end of the couch, crocheting and listening to the TV. Shane walked over and turned it off. Jeanie looked up in surprise, then followed her son's eyes. When she read the expression on Todd's face, she dropped her crocheting and began to cry softly. She muttered, "You've found him, haven't you?"

Todd sat down on the tufted settee in front of her. He glanced at Shane. Jeanie pulled herself together and said, "He can stay. He's been the man of the house ever since ..."

Todd inhaled, exhaled, and then said, "Please keep this information to yourselves until I can make a positive ID." He paused and looked Jeanie in the eye. "A couple of the deputies found a skeleton in Duckett Forest."

Jeanie's hand flew to her mouth. When she could speak, she blurted, "I feel relieved to know for sure that Billy didn't run off with

80

Bonnie." Then a look of horror crossed her face. "I can't believe I just said that!" She cried quietly into a tissue. Shane, blinking back tears himself, sat on the arm of the couch and squeezed his mother's shoulder.

When Jeanie regained her composure, Todd continued, "The bones belong to a male who was about Billy's height, but we need to have the state lab test for a match between the DNA from the bones to the DNA of a biological relative." He looked at Shane. "I'll need a sample of your hair for comparison's sake." Todd realized he had already sent Virgil and Blaine to Atlanta with the bones, and now he was going to have to sacrifice another deputy to take Shane's hair sample. He attributed his lack of farsightedness to sleep deprivation.

Jeanie asked, "Why is a DNA test even necessary? I gave you Billy's dental records."

Todd gently picked up Jeanie's hand and held it in his own. "There was no skull." Jeanie's face paled and a moan escaped from her lips.

Shane wiped away a tear with his fist. "So, if it is Daddy, how do you think this went down?"

"I was thinkin' about that on the way over here, and I keep comin' back to one scenario: This is gonna sound crazy, but I think it was a professional hit."

Both mother and son gasped. Jeannie said, "But there's no reason - no reason at all for—"

"Daddy never did no one wrong," interjected Shane.

"And Bonnie was so innocent," added Jeanie.

"Here's what I think happened," said Todd. "The perp's accomplice drops him off at the office just before it closes. The perp - let's assume he's a he for now - he pulls a gun and orders Billy to get into the front seat of Billy's Taurus. He gets in the back seat with Bonnie and, holding the gun to her head, orders Billy to drive down Pirkle Road. Then the perp had Billy turn onto an old bootlegger's dirt track that leads to an illegal dumping site in the Forest. The accomplice met up with them there."

81

Jeanie looked at him quizzically. "I thought you said before that he had probably made himself scarce."

Todd wished for the world that he didn't have to say what he was about to say. "Now I'm thinkin' that after the killer shot Billy and Bonnie in the…head, he needed help…decapitating them ... and hiding their bodies." Jeanie once again buried her face in her hands and sobbed into Shane's arms. Horrible sounds, sounds that Todd had never heard from neither a human nor beast, came from Jeanie. He waited for them to subside. Finally, Jeanie lifted her head and Shane handed her a Kleenex. Softly, Todd continued, "The accomplice helped hide Billy's bones under a claw-foot bathtub. Then the killer probably assigned the job of ditchin' Billy's Taurus to the assistant, who did a good job, considerin' that neither it nor its plates have ever been recovered."

"Maybe you're wrong," said Shane despondently. "Maybe those bones ain't Daddy's."

Jeanie wiped a tear away and looked at Todd. "I don't know if I want those bones to be Billy's or not."

Todd took her hand and searched her eyes. "Me neither," he said with a hoarse catch in his voice.

Carrying a Ziploc bag with a sample of Shane's hair, Todd walked out to the Bronco. Shane joined him, and the two stood for a moment in darkness that was illuminated only by the partially cloaked moon. "How's the quarterbackin' goin'?" asked Todd, knowing that his conversational tone sounded stilted after what had just transpired in the living room.

Shane's square shoulders slipped into a defeated shrug. "If we had won last night, we would have went to the playoffs." He picked up a small rock and threw it as if he were trying to skim it over water. It bounced up against the gray asbestos siding of the seventy-year-old farmhouse. Finally he said, "Coach Flagg thinks you are the best QB that ever come out of Duckett High. He said you were gonna come out to the field on Thursday and give me tips so I could be prepared for the game last night."

Todd felt Shane's accusing eyes boring into him through the darkness. He sighed. "There was a note on my desk, but I got busy and forgot. I apologize." Shane wordlessly picked up another rock. Todd ran a hand over his hair and held it on the back of his neck. He didn't know how he was going to make the time, but he asked, "You wanna meet at the field tomorrow after the church potluck and toss around the ball?"

Shane said scornfully, "Don't you know, man? Don't you fuckin' realize? I'm a senior and I'm not good enough to play college ball. Friday was my last day to play football for the rest of my so-called life." Shane's bitter words cut through Todd like a light saber. Shane added, "Besides I gotta take care of Momma, my sisters, and the farm."

Todd flashed back to his own senior year when his father was diagnosed with melanoma. He had been offered football scholarships to several large state colleges. Given that Duckettville High hardly had enough students to be classified in the AA division, it was a great honor that the school's star quarterback had attracted attention from the big time scouts. Todd would have given all his teeth for a chance to test himself against the boys coming out of the big high schools, but he turned the offers down and chose to attend the nearest regional college so he could return home on weekends and help his ailing father around the farm. Young Harris College didn't field a football or basketball team; however, Todd was offered a baseball scholarship, which he accepted. But baseball wasn't football. It never would be. He laid a hand on the shoulder of the young athlete before him, half-expecting it to be shrugged off. "It will get better, Shane."

* * * *

Todd fought a howling, blustery wind on the drive home. The visit to Bonnie Wells' mother hadn't been any easier. Todd was surprised to find himself feeling irritated over the timing of this development - or possible development - in the Evans-Wells case. He didn't need to be zig-zagging between the bones and Elvis's case with his limited resources. Especially with the media and the GBI breathing down his back. The imperative, Todd concluded, was to find, as soon as possible, Elvis and the body of his former owner.

Todd ate the stew he had found in the Crock Pot in his mother's kitchen. Jessie and Molly had eaten dinner hours earlier. Later that evening when his mood had lifted somewhat, he sat at the kitchen table across from Molly, who was perched on her chair like a little monkey. Chin propped on hands, she studied the checkerboard between them. Jessie had loosely braided her long, satiny hair; and though she was only five, Todd had a fleeting vision of the beautiful young lady she would someday become. With her turned up-nose, she looked more and more like her mother, except that Molly didn't have Brandy's flaming red hair. And though she was short like Brandy, Molly's bone structure was much slighter, almost fragile. Molly did, however, share her mother's love of clothes. Tonight she was wearing her favorite pale-pink Barbie pajamas with chartreus faux-feather trim on the ends of the sleeves.

Jessie was at the stove, stirring cocoa into sweetened milk. In her characteristic deep voice she said, "I visited with LeeLee after she got home from the hospital. She says she can come back to work on Monday."

"What's wrong with Mrs. Lee?" asked Molly.

"Nothin' for you to be concerned about," said Todd. He moved one red checker. "She wasn't feelin' too well today, that's all." Molly moved a black checker and Todd jumped it. "Crown me," he ordered. He studied Molly as she jumped up and down on the chair, clapping and smiling with delight, celebrating the fact that her opponent had just been crowned. She hadn't yet learned about competition: that when the other person gained, you lost. Sadly, now that she was in school, she would soon lose that sweet innocence along with her still-intact baby teeth.

Jessie said, "I sure was hopin' this mess could be kept quiet."

Molly looked up at her father. "What mess?"

Todd grabbed her pixie nose between his knuckles. "Miss

84

Busybody, you are missin' a very big opportunity to jump me." Molly saw it, and with a flourish took three of Todd's red checkers.

Jessie asked, "So what'd you do when you wasn't at the site or gettin' on TV?"

"I followed that dip-shi…" He glanced at Molly. "I mean, I followed Agent Slaughter around like a puppy dog."

Molly threw her head back and laughed. "A puppy dog!" She jumped down from her chair and squealed. "Catch me if you can, puppy!"

"Oh, I can!" shouted Todd, and he and his squealing daughter commenced a wild game of cat and mouse around the kitchen.

Todd caught up to Molly and swept her up in his arms, turned her upside down, and tickled her. "I'm the King, I'm the King!" he teased.

"No, I am … I am!" she squealed, in between bouts of uncontrollable upside down giggling.

Todd said, "Okay, Missy, summersault out." Molly flipped through his arms and landed on her feet. Abruptly, Todd froze for a few beats, then picked up the phone and punched in a number he knew by heart. When the phone went to a recorded message, Todd hung up. He grabbed his jacket. "Go put on your house shoes, Molly." To his mother he said, "I need to go check on somethin'."

Molly groaned. "You promised that after I played you in checkers, you'd play somethin' I want to play."

"Don't break your promise, son," chided his mother as she poured the hot chocolate into three mugs. "She's seen so little of you lately."

Todd reluctantly removed his jacket. "Okay, okay, but I gotta get on the radio a sec." Molly skipped off to her room, and Todd yelled after her, "I'm not playin' with those nekkid Barbies!" For all the Barbie clothes that Molly owned, her numerous plastic glam girls were always lying around the house nude. Todd was constantly stepping on them with his bare feet.

He walked back to the kitchen, turned up the two-way radio, and called for a deputy in Zone 5. It turned out to be Blaine, back from Atlanta. Todd asked, "Jesus, Blaine, are you on a twenty-four hour marathon?"

The static quelled and Blaine said, "Bo offered me fifty dollars to finish his shift. He's line-dancin' at the Buckin' Bull with some girl."

"You in a truck?"

"Roger that," replied Blaine warily. A truck meant he was about to be sent off-road into the forest.

"What's your 20?"

"I'm on Route 72, nearbouts Bubba Creek cutoff."

"Good. Get on down to Alex Meriwether's place and check on them."

"Holy crap, Todd! You know their place is way back up in the woods. It'll be pitch-dark down there. Plus, all them turns leave me more confused than a nun on her honeymoon!"

"Go out there right now and get it over with. That's an order."

"Why in the hell—?"

"Their homestead is just across the boundary to the Forest, and it's not far from Elvis's rock."

"Jesus, Todd! The penis slasher could be there! You could be sending me to certain dismemberment!"

"Good. You don't need to be handin' down your faulty genes to nobody." Todd signed off and walked into the living room just as a plastic Barbie suitcase flew out of Molly's room. When it hit the wood floor, it sprang open and a load of little Barbie dresses and tiny plastic shoes exploded forth. Molly skipped out of her room with a big grin on her face and a naked Barbie doll in both hands.

Chapter Four
Sunday Go To Meetin'

Having worked the Elvis case deep into the night, Todd slept through the rooster's first crow, only to be roused shortly thereafter by the ringing telephone. He picked up the receiver with two fingers, expecting that the reporter, Ansley Mason, was perched on the other end of the line, sharpening her talons.

But it wasn't Mason on the line, it was Special Agent Harwood Slaughter. "This is your wake-up call, Baby Cop," Slaughter said in an irritatingly cheerful voice. "Time to get your hick ass out of bed and open up your office. We're over at some greasy pancake house on the other side of Duckett Mountain. I figure we'll be on your doorstep in forty-five minutes. You know where your office is don't ya? It's at the corner of Hog Fat Highway and Sheep Dip Drive."

Todd heard Slaughter's cronies guffawing in the background. "Excuse me, did you say you want to meet at my office?"

"You got a problem with that?"

"It's Sunday. My family goes to church on Sundays, and I'm going with them." *For a change.*

Harwood cackled. "You heathens hear that?" he said to his assistants. "It's Sunday and Pretty Boy has to kiss some God butt while he looks for a break in the case under the pews." There was more background guffawing. Slaughter turned back to the phone. "That's thinkin' with your dipstick, redneck."

Todd rested his elbows on his knees and sneezed loudly, hoping that he had blown out the cobwebs from his sleep deprived brain. Still, he was too drowsy to think up a clever comeback. Slaughter added, "By the way, thanks for that wonderful recommendation on the sleeping accommodations. I especially enjoyed the chariot races in the attic until the wee hours. Every time I rolled over on my back I got a mouthful of ceiling plaster."

"So, you met Ben Hur and the gang," Todd scratched his chest. Just thinking about the Restful Forest Motel made his skin itch. He pulled off his T-shirt. "Look, why don't you and your boys just go on home? You got all the physical evidence you're gonna get and you've interviewed everybody except Jesus. I pinky promise I'll alert you if any leads pop up today if you pinky promise you'll share any that come your way. Ain't that reasonable?"

"Wash that yellow gunk out of your ears and listen up, farm boy. We're not here at your fucking beck and call. It's the other way around."

"Well, don't that beat the titties off a milk cow. Show me that reg in writin'. Frankly, I'd prefer you and your little buddies exit my territory ASAP—and don't trip over the county line on your way out."

"Hold it, Baby Chief. We still gotta interview that dripping pussy—what's her name—"

"Call her that again," Todd growled, leaping to his feet, "and you will no longer be in possession of your fat, useless tongue."

Slaughter snickered. "Uh oh," he said to his men, "Farm boy has a crush on the suspect. Tsk, tsk, not very professional." More guffawing ensued before Slaughter turned back to the phone. "I just busted your chops again, Baby Chief. You make it so easy."

"It won't help to talk to Ms. Roseberry. There's nothing else she can—"

"I'll be the judge of that. Since you'll be in Sunday school where you belong, we'll pay the luscious little lass a long visit," retorted Slaughter. Todd heard him strike his lighter. "And I expect to see you after lunch." The lighter snapped shut, and then the line went dead. Running his hands repeatedly over his face, Todd growled low in his throat, then shook his head vigorously. He stepped into the bathroom and turned on the shower. While waiting for the water to warm up, he slipped off his boxers. He had switched to boxers as a deputy because they were cooler than briefs and more comfortable for climbing in and out of a cruiser all day. Just as he was about to step into the shower, the phone rang. It was Vince Verona.

"This is kinda early for you to be up on a Sunday, ain't it?" Todd asked.

"I've got a few questions for my newspaper, Kid. Are the bones Billy Evans's?"

"Whew! Sixteen hours—that's a record. I suppose that a certain loose-lipped medical examiner tenant of yours spilled the beans."

"What can I say?" Vince replied with his usual crafty voice. "Gorov can't handle the hooch."

Todd opened a fresh bar of soap with one hand. It smelled of cleanliness itself. "Vincent, I have an ambivalent feeling about you."

"That's what my mother always says. So what's the skinny? Are they Billy's bones or do they belong to some dumb luck meth head?"

"Jesus, Vince. I'm standing here nekkid gettin' ready to take a shower."

"Now that's information I don't need. I'll admit, you gotta hot bod, Kid, but I just ain't bent that way."

"I'll give you a statement when we know more."

"What about Elvis? Have you found—"

"Just like the bones thing, I will give you a statement when Elvis decides to sing."

"But as you well know, my deadline is tonight—"

"Goodbye, Vince." Todd clicked off and stepped into the shower.

* * * * *

Todd escorted Molly to her Sunday school class then slipped out the side door. He knew he could not sit through adult class where he would have to endure the inevitable ribbing over his thus far inept handling of Elvis. Not to mention Blaine's horizontal demonstration of how a hillbilly deputy slacks off on the job. Instead, he walked "Main Street," which was actually a two lane highway called State Road 77. It consisted of the two block "business district" that made up "downtown" Duckettville. It was a blink-and-you-will-miss-it town, one in which a portion of the roads branching off Main Street were still gravel. On the north side of the street, sat Sonny's Moonshine Runners Gently Used Autos, followed by the row of churches—the First Methodist Church of Duckettville (his family's church), the First Baptist Church of Duckettville, and lastly, the Evangelical Church of the Last Hope, which was led by Preacher Dodge. Lately, the churches had gotten into trying to outdo one another with the cleverness of their signs. First Methodist's read "Tired of Being a Loser? —Turn to God." First Baptist's proclaimed "The Rapture: Separation of Church and State." Last Hope's enticed, "Come in and Meet Preacher Dodge—He Loves Hurting People!" One week ago, First Baptist's slogan had been, "God's Favorite Word Is—Come!" But Sonny had intervened and Pastor Jeffords changed the sign to "Stop, Drop and Roll—It Won't Work in Hell!"

Todd walked past the churches and cut diagonally across the road to the courthouse, which sat at the crossroads of State Routes 77 and 92. The two-story red brick building, which Sonny swore leaned to the south, sat on three weedy acres. Its main function seemed to be to serve as a traffic control device since travelers coming from either direction had to stop and drive around the grounds in order to continue on their way. Of course, the courthouse really wasn't needed for that function because at any given time, the vehicles traveling Duckett County's roads were few and far between.

Atop the courthouse's white Georgia marble steps stood the bronze statue of the founder of Duckett County, Colonel Stewart R. Duckett, proudly sitting astride his horse, Eulalie. Duckett was gazing off to the vast wilderness that his peripatetic and not too fertile heirs would later donate to the county.

Todd angled over to the south side of Main Street and swiftly strode past his office lest anyone inside dash out and buttonhole him. The front parking area was devoid of reporters, and Todd guessed they were looking for crumbs of information at the site. Having learned his lesson, he had secured the site with six deputies. He resisted the impulse to go inside the office, where Shawn and Tawanda were hopefully teasing out the prank calls from legitimate leads. Instead, he stood on the sidewalk and called on his cell for a report. Tawanda said they'd salvaged no new promising leads. Disappointed, Todd clicked off and walked past Tammy's Checkered Flagg Grill and Pool Hall, which was closed on Sunday mornings. Then he passed Sike's Barber/Gun Repair shop, also closed. Dr. Mahmondi's clinic was not open for business either. Todd saw that the windows of the Duckettville Weekly office were darkened. Inside, Vince, lit up by his computer screen, was intently typing. Todd crossed a gravel road, then passed Bambi's "Curl Up and Dye." Since it was Sunday, the shop wouldn't open until after lunch. He halted just before the faded white clapboard house of the wart taker, which sat across the street from the Moonshine Runner's Gently Used Autos car lot. Sonny often complained about having to look out toward a soothsayer's house, with its confused mix of weedy perennials crowding the picket-fenced front yard. Todd thought that Marvalena probably didn't care much to look out at the mayor's jumbled used car lot either.

Some faint chanting emanated from the house, followed by the pulsating, crisp tones of a bell being struck. Todd didn't know what the heck to make of what was going on in there. Even so, he found it hard to believe that Marvalena would swipe a penis, just as it would be out of character for any of the Main Street merchants to suddenly become snatchers of body parts. He resolved to rule them out as suspects as quickly as possible so that Elvis's disappearance didn't degenerate into a silly inane drawn out who-done-it. There had to be some other explanation. But then, there was Sikes's hidden motive theory. Todd cursed him for dropping that stupid idea into his brain. What Sikes didn't know, thought Todd, was that hidden motives were a lot easier to dig up in the movies than they were in real life. He horse sighed,

91

vibrating air through his lips noisily. There was nothing to do but trudge on. Elvis had helped him out by leading him to the bones, now Todd needed to return the favor by finding Elvis's owner.

He continued his ruminations as he walked the Main Street circuit three times before crossing the street and returning to First Methodist. Sunday school was over and the service was just beginning. He spied Molly up front coloring away as she sat on the aisle in the "Quin" pew. The Quins were Todd's mother's people. Next to Molly sat Jessie, then Aunt Colleen and her husband, Uncle Monk. Uncle Monk had always been a quiet man, and now that he was a catatonic, he was one of the easier of the older relatives to manage in church. Granny Quin sat on the other side of Uncle Monk. She was wearing one of her satiny church-going bibs tied around her turkey neck. On Granny Quin's other side sat Todd's sister, brother-in-law, and their daughter, Kylie, a fellow kindergartner, who was not allowed to sit next to the more boisterous Molly. The McPherson pew, which had cradled the haunches of McPhersons for as long as anyone could remember, was rooted just behind the Quin pew. Since the two families had been so genetically intertwined over the generations, Todd thought that it was amazing he and Katie weren't born total mouth breathers.

On impulse, Todd sat in the last pew on the right between Tammy Flagg and Bambi Davis. Suddenly, he felt that he was reliving his high school days, except that Brandy, Todd's ex-wife, was not present. The four of them had been as thick as thieves in their teens. Todd noted that some of his other teammates who used to sit on the back pew with them were scattered about the congregation, sitting with their wives and children. Funny, back then he couldn't have imagined how things would end up a decade later, yet here he was, divorced from Brandy, sitting on the back pew between Bambi, also a divorcee, and Tammy, whose husband was in the pen. In fact, the three of them were in a kind of permanent free fall.

A spitball from the balcony dropped onto Todd's lap. So that's where the cut-ups of today hang out. Old Lady Hamm was sitting in the pew in front of him just like the old days. Todd tossed the spit wad into her Civil War-colored (blue and gray) hair, and Tammy and Bambi each gave him the stink eye and slapped him with their rolled up programs, just like old times. Then they covered their mouths and giggled, just like old times. And just like old times, Todd was shot a warning look from Coach Flagg, who was sitting in the Flagg pew, across the aisle and one row up. Suddenly, Todd was struck with a longing for Brandy to be here with them. She had been the biggest cut-up of them all, and he had loved her for it.

Pastor Ed finally said the benediction and the threesome shot out of the church's massive front doors. Indian summer had surrendered, at least for today, to a norther' that had blown in last night, and now a blustery, unforgiving sky was punishing the parishioners with a damp, stinging wind. Todd, Tammy, and Bambi scrambled past First Baptist and ran into the expansive fellowship hall of Last Hope. This was the third Sunday of the month, which meant Last Hope would be hosting a potluck. Tradition had it that the other two Main Street churches joined them on the Sunday before the Moonshine Festival, so today's feast promised to be a mother of a potluck.

Todd, Bambi, and Tammy filled their paper plates far beyond a safe load limit and claimed some folding metal chairs against the wall. Todd took perch in between the ladies and dove greedily into his helping of pulled pork, eating with all the gusto he could manage with the flimsy plastic fork and knife.

Except for breakfast, Bambi was a picky eater, so instead of eating, she just jabbered. "I thought I'd never get my hair put back to my usual fawn brown. To think that me, a professional hairdresser, was seen in Communist Red China with spaghetti hair!"

Tammy had already heard all about Bambi's Oriental hair horror. She ignored her flaky friend and turned to Todd. "I take it there's been no break in the Elvis case." Her use of the body part's code name

93

brought Todd up short. The public was not supposed to know the thing's nickname. But then, this was Duckett County, where nothing was secret. Tammy added, "If you get desperate you can try the Wart Taker."

"Marvalena? She'll have me swingin' dead chickens over my head or somethin'," Todd said through a mouthful of potato salad.

Tammy swept her deep chestnut bangs aside with the back of her chunky hand. "Well, I been goin' to Marvalena. I'm hopin' one of her spells will sway the parole board next time Jimmy comes up." For the first time this morning, a hostile expression crossed her face. "I still don't know why you couldn't have gave Jimmy a little gettin' away time."

Todd licked gravy off his fork. "Now, Tammy, the problem had to do with certain letter combinations—FBI, DEA, GBI and ATF, to be exact. When all those letters tell me to collar a suspect, I don't monkey around."

Bambi jumped in. "Do you realize, Tammy, that you'll be thirty-seven when Jimmy gets out of the pen? You think you'll even remember how to make love?" She giggled. "Maybe you should get you one of those vibrameters."

Todd choked on a mouthful of fried chicken. Bambi occasionally had a problem with pronouncing words. It was a trait Todd found endearing, but Tammy found it irritating. Tammy found everything irritating. She slapped him on the back while she glared at Bambi. "The word is vibrator," she chided as she glanced around. "And just cuz you were on international TV don't mean you can go around talkin' dirty in the House of the Lord."

Bambi waved a fried drumstick. "This is comin' from a gal who owns a pool hall."

"We have one pool table, that's all. Just one."

Bambi giggled, "And you're hidin' poor Elvis in one of its pockets."

His mouth stuffed with green bean casserole, Todd mumbled,

"Ladies, can we not get in a cat fight today? I'm too hungry to take the time to separate you two. In fact, I feel like I haven't eaten since twelfth grade." He wiped his mouth with his paper napkin then checked his tie, certain that he was seriously close to a mishap. "Besides, I gotta keep my strength up so I can keep a watch on all my suspects."

Tammy frowned. "So why ain't you out there lookin' for Elvis's owner right now?"

Between mouthfuls of mashed potatoes and gravy, Todd said, "I assigned my junior detectives to look after the phones this mornin' so as I could snoop around here and see if I could pick up any gossip that might lead to a lead."

Tammy picked up a fried chicken leg then abruptly dropped it, sat up straight, and stared at Todd. "Surely you don't really thank that I…"

Bambi gasped and pressed a hand to her bosom. "Or me?"

Todd finished stuffing a hunk of cornbread in his mouth and looked severely at Tammy, then Bambi. "Well did ya?" The two women looked at Todd as if his fetching features were melting off his face. Todd nudged Bambi, and then Tammy. "I tell ya what. I'm gonna deputize the two of ya on the spot so as y'all can meander about this here potluck and pick up any gossip about where Elvis's new home might be." His mock serious look deepened. "If you two find the Elvis snatcher, then y'all are off the hook." He nodded to each lady encouragingly then picked up a plump ear of yellow corn and fell to chomping. Tammy huffed, while Bambi's big eyes darted eagerly amongst the occupants of the fellowship hall in search of the worst gossips.

Three fifteen-year-old girls moved towards them in one unit. "Hey Bambi," Ashley Lee Morgan said, "we saw you on TV and thought you were awesome." She bent down to hug Bambi's neck lightly, careful not to crush the paper plate on her lap.

The other two girls squealed their agreement. The dark-haired one, Becca, gushed, "I thought your hair was way rad."

The third giggly girl, Rachel, piped up. "Yeah, you shouldn't have put it back."

Ashley Lee said, "I want you to do mine like that. Anyway, weren't you just grossed out—you know—at the thang?" She screwed up her pixie nose, suddenly resembling her Aunt LeeLee. "I mean, I'd just die if I saw somethin' like that." Becca and Rachel nodded their agreement and then vacillated between giggling and looking nauseous.

Todd's lips were still moose-smooching his ear of corn, but he abruptly stopped mid-gnaw and eyed the girls from behind his corn. Something was wrong. Usually the high school lasses idolized him because he was still young enough to be the local heartthrob. They often followed him around at community events, giggling and peppering him with questions. While he was careful not to return their flirting, he was friendly with them. Today, however, he was...he searched for the word...invisible. That was it, he was invisible; otherwise, these well-bred girls wouldn't be discussing Elvis in front of him. Invisible. Todd un-suctioned his lips from the corn, suddenly wishing that he were over with the guys debating the best trout lures or the latest changes to the NASCAR rules.

Bambi announced to the girls, "This ain't somethin' to talk about in mixed company," and rolled her eyes toward Todd. The girls seemed to notice the sheriff for the first time.

"Hey, Sheriff Todd," volunteered the trio unenthusiastically.

"Hey," said Todd, flicking a kernel of corn off his tie.

With a slightly sarcastic tone, Tammy said, "The sheriff here gave a press conference yesterday that was heard around the world." She smiled smugly. "And I'll lay odds that piece has been aired at least a hundred times ever since." Tammy's hard eyes deflected Todd's stink eye, and then she looked back at the girls. "Didn't y'all think he was awesome?"

The girls regarded Todd. "Oh yeah, you were great," said Ashley Lee unconvincingly. "You've got corn on your chin," she added, touching her own chin. The girls giggled in one unit, and in one unit moved on.

Todd wiped his chin with a paper napkin and glared at Tammy. He gathered up the paper plates, headed for the trashcan, and watched with Clint Eastwood eyes as Tammy followed the teens out of the fellowship hall. He decided that they were probably going to the bathroom to talk about him. He returned to Bambi with two cups of coffee, black for him and cream and sugar for her. They sat companionably and idly gazed around the crowded room.

As Bambi daintily blew on her coffee, Todd saw that her eyes were a dusty turquoise today. Noticing that he was noticing her, she said, "Wade's got the kids this weekend. We could do some sinnin'." She smiled coquettishly.

Todd pressed his shoulder into hers. "Aw now, Bambi, you know that was four years ago, back when you and me were new divorcees. You've been my pal since kindergarten, but as I recall, our little tryst almost wrecked our friendship." He pulled a tiny twig from her windblown hair. "But thanks for the offer." She looked disappointed, so he gave her a side-arm hug, carefully, so as not to slosh her coffee.

After a respectful minute, Todd told Bambi that it was time for him to do some scouting. He stood and took a few aimless steps into the horde of jabbering people. He suddenly had no clue as to which direction to go, and oddly, no one was moving aside to offer a space where he could squeeze into their conversational clutch. Just as he was taking a sip of coffee, he received his first backslap of the morning, which caused him to spill coffee on the lapel of his sports jacket. A giggle escaped from Bambi, who was watching from her seat. Preacher Dodge said, "Can I have a quick word with you alone, young man?" Todd brushed coffee off his jacket lapel and followed Last Hope's shepherd as he wove his way around the squealing kids who were sliding down the hall in their socks. Todd felt a hint of trepidation as the preacher held open the door and stood waiting for him to enter his office, home to so much confessed human pathos.

Todd sat down in the comfortable leather club chair in the corner of the cozy office, while the man of God claimed his desk. "I sure appreciate your help on the search team, Preacher Dodge," Todd said, hoping that jumping in with a compliment would ease whatever pain was coming next.

"Will you please call me J.T.?" The preacher sounded slightly annoyed. "I used to be your father-in-law, you know. And in the Lord's eyes, I'll always be your father-in-law."

"I'll try," responded Todd meekly.

Preacher Dodge leaned forward and his intelligent sepia-toned eyes probed Todd's own eyes. "By the way, have you got any leads on the Elvis case?"

"No. In fact, I decided to come to the potluck today in order to pick up some gossip that would provide me with a clue. Oftentimes a person with information is reluctant to call us or be seen comin' in to the office to talk, but they'll volunteer information in a more neutral setting." Todd shrugged. "If I sound desperate, it's cuz I am."

"I'm sure somethin' will break soon." The preacher ran his hand along the desktop, then looked out the deep casement window beside Todd's chair. "So how's Bethany?" Bethany was Todd's ex-wife's given name, but she had insisted on being called Brandy since third grade. She even changed her name legally when she came of age. Being lifelong abstainers, Preacher and Mrs. Dodge had strenuously objected to the alias; but, when Brandy wanted something, Brandy got something.

Todd measured his words carefully, knowing that the preacher appreciated precise communication, especially when it came to his only child. "She seems okay," he said. He shifted his position and added, "As you know, she's been exercisin' her visitation rights since Molly's fourth birthday, so I've seen her two weekends a month for over a year now. And she's appeared to be sober each time. Being a lawman, I've gotten good at spottin' when someone's took to the bottle." *Too bad I*

98

sucked at it when she was pregnant. Todd scrutinized his mirror-shined dress uniform shoes. "Why don't you give her a ring?"

"I've left many messages on her phone, but she doesn't return my calls." Preacher Dodge laid a finger on his Bible, which was well worn and endowed with dozens of colorful plastic page markers. "Anyway, that's not why I dragged you in here. I wanted to speak with you about the Liquor-by-the-Drink vote that's comin' up a week from Tuesday."

Todd exhaled loudly. "Oh now, Preacher Dodge - I mean J.T., sir - I've already been through this with the mayor. I'm just not—"

"Now, hold on a minute." The gray-headed theologian held up ten knotted fingers. "Just hear me out. My congregation is all riled up over the fact that this alcohol thing has even gotten on the ballot. Duckett has always been a dry county."

"Yes sir, but—"

"And it should stay a dry county. Shoot, I don't know why the First Methodists and the First Baptists have not gotten more riled about this. Well, I do know why you First Methodists haven't ... I guess it's cuz y'all are, well ... Methodists. But the First Baptists, they are surprisin' me with their apathy." Preacher Dodge laid his hands flat on the desk. "Well, that ain't none of my business. My congregation is my business, and they have asked me to ask you to put out a statement in the Duckettville Weekly sayin' how unsafe the roads would be if we pass Liquor-by-the-Drink. And by the way, the Weekly's deadline is midnight tonight."

Todd squirmed in the chair that just a minute ago had felt so comfortable. "Sir, I know you are in the morals business. But I'm in the public safety-business, and the research shows that as to whether this county goes wet or stays dry, it won't make a smidgen of difference to road safety. So I'm sittin' this one out. Now if you'll excuse me, I've got some snoopin' to do." Todd pushed himself out of the club chair.

"But, Todd—"

Just then a piecing shriek brought Preacher Dodge up short.

"I do believe we both know the originator of that squeal," Todd said through a lopsided smile. He opened the door and swept up Molly, who was sliding past in her socks. He turned to the preacher and extended her out horizontally. "Hug your Grandpa's neck," he ordered. Giggling, Molly wrapped her delicate arms around the preacher and he gave her a sweet peck on the cheek. Todd carried the wriggling girl out of the office and set her down. "Put your shoes on and go find your grandma. We gotta be hittin' the asphalt." Molly skipped off with jackrabbit speed.

Todd returned to the fellowship hall and saw that a few folks were beginning to leave. He stood by the row of front doors, hoping someone would signal that they wanted to talk as they exited. But no one seemed to notice him. Finally, his sister stepped up. Katie, tall and willowy, was crowned with shoulder-length hair, which was darker blond than Todd's own flaxen pelt. She did, however, possess Todd's intense blue eyes. She was carrying baby Will, who grabbed Todd's extended finger. "We're takin' off," she said, and gave him a peck on the cheek then headed out the door.

Todd's brother-in-law, Bobby, followed with his daughter, Kylie, in tow. He turned back and clasped Todd on the arm. "Don't worry about what they're sayin' about ya. Remember, you're the one and only Fearless McPherson." He squeezed the arm of his former high school football teammate, then he and Kylie disappeared through the door. He was the assistant high school football coach, and right now Todd envied Bobby for having such a wholesome occupation.

Todd glanced around the crowded fellowship hall and spotted LeeLee surrounded by Bambi, Tammy, and a gaggle of other women who were wearing buttons saying "Defeat Liquor-by-the-Drink" and "Re-elect Kathy Hamilton, Republican." LeeLee was apparently reenacting her role in the events of Friday afternoon. She placed a hand over her eyes and pretended to be clutching Hooty's lead as she took a few comical steps. The ladies cackled, then abruptly looked at Todd. He hastily shifted his gaze away, hoping none of them had seen the prickly

100

blush that spread up his face. Just as suddenly, the ladies returned to their conversation, chortling at something else LeeLee said. Todd crossed his arms and attempted to look unconcerned, but in truth, he was not used to people laughing at him behind his back.

Thinking it was best to look like he was preoccupied, he walked to a stainless steel urn and drew himself another cup of coffee. He turned around and nodded to a couple of hunting buddies, who nodded back and then resumed their conversations. He thought it odd that with all the backslapping and fellowshipping going on, nobody other than Preacher Dodge had approached him with questions about that stupid stolen weenie. He had expected that people would be hounding him like crazy. Normally he would be relieved that they were leaving him be, but right now, he wasn't relieved. He felt like he'd been psychologically exiled from his community. He was a wart that had been neatly severed by a scalpel. Had his Elvis bungling embarrassed every Christian in the county? Obviously, since nobody would even give him a howdy-do, his silly plan to pick up a lead at the potluck was not going to pan out. He moved to the back of the fellowship hall and sulked while pretending to read the flyers on the large bulletin board.

Molly skipped by, and Todd reached out and grabbed her. "You find your grandma?"

"No, Daddy, we're playin' hide from the reporters!" She giggled and wiggled out of his grasp.

"Well, don't be runnin' around inside the - hide from the reporters? What kind of game is that?"

Molly twirled back to him. "You know, like you did yesterday."

"I did not hide ... oh, never mind, just go find your grandma," said Todd irritably. "I've got to get back to work." Great, thought Todd. Even my own daughter knows I'm the laughingstock of the televised world. As if she read his thoughts, Molly giggled and skipped off.

Out of the blue, Sikes appeared at Todd's side holding two paper plates of pecan pie. He held up one but Todd turned it down. Sikes eyed him curiously. At a church potluck, pecan pie was always the first dessert to go. If you didn't get a piece as soon as the sweets were set out, you were out of luck. Sikes shrugged, dumped the slice of pie onto his plate, and commenced to devour both pieces. In between bites, he asked, "What you mopin' about now, Cotton - the reporters, or Agent Slaughter?"

"I've only gotten one backslap so far this mornin'," muttered Todd, "not includin' when Tammy saved me from chokin'."

"What the heck you talkin' about?" asked Sikes as he funneled another gooey forkful into his mouth.

"Nobody wants to be around me. I'm a pariah."

"I reckon that's somethin' you ain't never had to deal with before - you bein' the town's fair-haired boy and all. Well, welcome to the underclass, bro."

"Plus, I let Elvis get stolen."

Sikes rolled his eyes. "Oh, here we go again. I've got a violin in the car. I'll get it as soon as I finish my pie."

Todd fastened desperate eyes onto Sikes. "Who could have stolen it, Sikes? Who?"

"Like I said before, when you find that hidden motive, you'll know who took him."

"There you go with that stupid stealth motive of yours."

Sikes finished his last of his pie, wiped his mouth with a paper napkin, and tossed his trash into a nearby bin. "Be seein' you around, Cotton." He took a few steps then turned back and gave the gloomy sheriff a slap on the back. Startled, Todd jumped back, attempting to avoid the inevitable coffee mishap. Sikes snorted. "There, that makes two good-ol'-boy backslaps for the day." Chuckling to himself, he headed for the exit doors.

Todd found a stack of clean paper napkins lying on the deep sill of a nearby window. After he wiped coffee off his cuff, he returned to his brooding while pretending to look outside. He was jerked out of his sour thoughts when he noticed a small man sitting on a swing in the church playground. It was a strange sight. The wind was ripping leaves from trees and a cold drizzle had begun to fall. Todd looked closer and discerned that the man was Sam Lee, LeeLee's husband. The despondent look on his face made him a sad contrast to his brethren inside, who were basking in the warm glow of each other's company. With his diminutive, angular build, Sam fit well in the wooden swing, but his shoulders were slumped and he was studying the ground. His dark-brown hair was matted down by the drizzle. The lenses in his square, black plastic glasses were beaded with tears from the sky.

Walt Higgins and Phil Mills walked up to Sam and immediately got into it with him. Sam's shoulders heaved up and down as he continued to stare at the mud below his feet. Todd almost laughed out loud at the incongruity of what he was seeing. Sam was a soft-spoken, homegrown man with a droll sense of humor. Maybe he was playing a joke on Walt and Phil. But Walt and Phil looked to be in no joking mood. Indeed, the threesome seemed to be acting out a shakedown scene from the Godfather trilogy rather than participating in the usual post Sunday-go-to-meetin' chinwag. Todd looked around the room. There was still a crowd, though a bit smaller than before. He wondered if anyone had noticed the weirdness on the playground, but no one was looking out the windows. They were standing in conversational knots, jabbering off their latest dose of caffeine, while the fatties revisited the remaining desserts. Todd looked back at the playground. Sam was on his feet now. Bearing down on Sam, Walt was actually jabbing the little man so forcefully that Sam stumbled backwards.

Todd set his coffee cup on the windowsill and headed toward the back door, but then stopped when he passed the next window and saw that Walt had backed off. Sam wheeled around and began to leave, but Phil grabbed his arm. Sam threw it off and stormed away. Walt and Phil exchanged a few words, then turned up their collars and departed the scene in the opposite direction. Todd stood rooted to his spot. What the hell was that all about? Perhaps LeeLee knew something. But then, maybe she didn't know anything, and it would upset her if he grilled her about her husband right now. After all, her hormones and tranquilizers had been prescribed only twenty-four hours ago. Given that this strange occurrence had happened in the midst of the Elvis fiasco, Todd wondered if Sam, Walt, and Phil knew something about the whereabouts of Elvis. It seems unlikely.

Todd was so deep into his ruminations that he jumped when Catch Ryder slapped him on the back. "You catch Lorena Bobbitt, yet?" he joked, taking a sip of coffee. Catch had grown up in Yankee Land and therefore lacked the mountain drawl of his adopted home. He was a gangly dentist in his mid-forties who, in Todd's opinion, wore his sandy blonde hair a bit long, especially for a professional. In fact, Todd thought that Catch looked more like a small town college professor in his tweed coat with leather patches at the elbows.

"Elvis ain't talkin' yet," Todd retorted crossly. After less than forty-eight hours on the case, he already hated that particular query. "But Ms. Bobbitt called and said she was goin' after certain county commissioners who denied the sheriff his new radar equipment." That was it! Walt, Phil, and Sam were all county commissioners, along with Catch Ryder. The only commissioner not here was Lymon McMyrtle, but Lymon hadn't been a regular church attendee since his wife died. Also absent was Commissioner Billy Evans, who was very likely that loose collection of bones at the state lab. Todd wondered if Catch had noticed him watching the others through the window. Maybe Catch was trying to distract him by engaging him in conversation. Or maybe I'm paranoid.

Catch rocked in his gently scuffed loafers and said good-naturedly, "Hey, don't blame me. I argued for that expenditure. You're going to need it to track all the drunk drivers after the Liquor-by-the-Drink passes."

Todd caught Catch's meandering baby blues. "Besides the drinkin' thing, are there any more hot issues that I need to be aware of?"

Catch leaned toward Todd and spoke out the side of his mouth. "You know us. We have our knock-down-drag-out fights on just about everything. Whoever's left standin' in the end prevails, and buys the beer. Remember that time Sonny…"

Todd's mind drifted off. He was required by his job to attend county commissioners' meetings, which were painfully boring, given that disagreements were hammered out in a private summit before the official meeting. The commissioners always worked out ahead of time how they were going to vote on each issue, and they always voted unanimously. That way, if they made an unpopular decision, the heat was spread around, and no single one of them was likely to be retaliated against come time to run for office again. From what Todd had read in the papers, it was a common practice in Georgia.

Todd forced himself to concentrate on Catch, who continued to rock on his feet and said in his usual cheerful manner, "If you'd stay at the meetings instead of giving your report and scramming, you'd know more about what's going on around here." Then he tossed his coffee cup in the can and slapped Todd on the back again. Employing his usual corny joke, he said, "Catch you later."

"Wait!" Todd called out. Time to be more direct. He stepped close to Catch. "I just saw Sam Lee being bullied by Phil and Walt on the playground. You have any idea what it could be about?"

"On the playground? Hmm, maybe Sam couldn't get either of them to push him on the swing." Catch's playful eyes danced.

"Phil was pushin' Sam, and they weren't on any swing."

"Sounds like one of Sam's practical jokes." Catch slapped on a haughty face and said through his nose, "In the city, they call it "Performance Art." He chuckled and looked around. "Oh there's my ball and chain, gotta run. Wish Elvis well for me." Catch bumped Todd's arm with a fist then took off across the hall in his characteristic flopsy-mopsy gait.

Where's Elvis?

Todd watched him and Mrs. Ryder move toward the front doors. Catch pulled on the handle, swiveled his head back and gazed at Todd with an inscrutable look that, strangely, sent a shiver down his spine. Then, Catch disappeared through the doorway, leaving Todd to his ruminations. He mentally listed the weird events of the last three days:

*Day One: Elvis appears.
*Day Two: The bones show up.
*Day Three: Two county commissions shake down another commissioner on the playground.

Todd had heard more than one outsider claim that Duckett County, with its backward ways and corpse-strewn wilderness, was about as weird as weird gets. But three bizarre happenings in three straight days was a bit much, even for here. This lent credence to the notion that these events could actually be related. Todd wondered if he would be able to weave together these clues as expertly as he braided Molly's hair. He looked out the window at the swing dancing in the blustery wind. It was as if a silly Halloween poltergeist was perched on it, swinging its ghostly legs in opposite directions. Without realizing it, he asked out loud, "What's the next step, Elvis?"

Molly skipped up to him. "Who's Elvis?"

Chapter Five

"Monday, Monday, Can't Trust That Day..." —The Mamas & the Papas

Jasmine drove her little Honda SUV down the steep, winding mountain road toward the center of Emerald Lake resort. Her first day of work had finally arrived, and she was fuming over the fact that her furniture had yet to make an appearance. Every time she called To Infinity and Beyond International Moving Company, she was placed on hold and forced to listen to Muzak interspersed with insipid self-promoting commercials featuring the theme from Star Wars and ending with the oxymoronic motto, "If we can move you across the universe, we can move you anywhere!"

Jasmine reminded herself that she needed to stop wasting mental energy and focus on her new position. She was now the chief financial officer of the Property Owners Association of Emerald Lake Resort. This was a big jump from being assistant comptroller of the non-profit charity where she had worked since graduating from Harvard four years ago. Beside the fancy title, the other perk that accompanied this job was that she was granted the privilege of living in this mountain paradise. She rounded a hairpin curve and was rewarded with a bird's-eye view of the lake below and the Blue Ridge Mountains above. Seemingly overnight the leaves on the trees had exploded in a palette of saturated ambers, umbers, and a myriad of additional fall hues. Indeed, she felt as if she were driving through a Monet painting. Glancing down at Emerald Lake, she decided it should have been named Mirror Lake because the trees and sky were perfectly reflected in the still, fern-green water. Motorboats weren't allowed on the lake, only battery-powered pontoon boats or canoes, so quiet prevailed everywhere, and that silence allowed the animals to take center stage. The silence was suddenly sliced open by the screech of an osprey that was gracefully circling the sky below. Jasmine drove around another curve and startled a cluster of deer that was loitering on the asphalt. She stopped and waited for them to disperse. Half the group ran across the road and nimbly bounded up the mountainside; the other half turned tail and scampered down the embankment. One young buck sporting two fuzzy antler stubs couldn't make up his mind. He stood in the middle of the road and turned right, then left, then right, then left again. Finally, he darted across the road and quickly scaled the mountain, disappearing in the tree line. The only word Jasmine could use to describe the whole experience of Emerald Lake was seductive.

Despite its obvious beauty, the thirty-year-old resort had gone into receivership eight years prior. It was subsequently purchased for pennies on the dollar by upstart Brad Whitestone, who at the time was all of twenty-seven years old. When the economy took off again, Whitestone managed to turn Emerald Lake into one of the most successful non-coastal upscale resorts in the Southeast. Jasmine had obtained a copy of last January's edition of Atlanta Magazine, which featured the jade-eyed, boyishly handsome developer grinning like a fox that had just raided the hen house. The article reported that Whitestone spent as much time in Atlanta marketing "The Emerald" as he did at the resort managing his stable of builders and real estate agents. Indeed, Whitestone had become a big player in Atlanta society and was considered the city's most eligible bachelor.

Jasmine had met Brad when she was applying for the job. He was indirectly her new boss's boss because he held a controlling interest on the immense Property Owner's Association (POA) board of directors. He had convinced her that he'd work with her to turn the POA's finances around, which everyone admitted were in need of professional therapy. Since Brad's reign began as king of Emerald Lake, the POA's revenues had ballooned, due to an ever-increasing number of luxury homes being built. Oversight, however, had slipped. Jasmine's master's thesis had been on the subject of untangling tangled finances in not-for-profit organizations, so she saw this new position as an opportunity to put her system into practice. She was encouraged by the fact that Whitestone had been keen to get her down here and started on the job.

It was unfortunate that the POA was in its current situation given the heavy responsibilities it carried. The organization ran and maintained the golf course, tennis courts, fitness center, riding stables, and all the rest of the amenities. It provided security, maintained 150 miles of asphalt roads, and enforced a strict code of covenants. According to Jasmine's research, POAs, especially large ones, were frequently problematic. Their board members sometimes morphed into a junta of tyrants, a situation that tended to spawn heated brawls and even legal battles with the homeowners. The situation at Emerald Lake Resort was especially complicated, given the size of the POA and its triangular relationship with the residents and the developer, Brad Whitestone.

Jasmine reached the bottom of the mountain and turned onto Emerald Lake Parkway, the narrow, curvy road that ran around the lake. A few minutes later, she pulled into the POA's parking area. She stepped out of her Honda and walked around the corner of the expansive building, which resembled a large hunting lodge. Entering through the massive wooden door, she saw a fire roaring in the gigantic stone fireplace, even though it was only slightly chilly outside. To her left, she could see Emerald Lake through a span of very tall windows. Monday morning was apparently men's bridge day, because a dozen game-sized tables were occupied by older men, all of them wearing the uniform of the corporate retiree: a light-weight golf sweater vest over plaid shirts, khaki slacks, and high-end loafers. Jasmine realized she was going to have a difficult time telling faces apart because they all looked the same to her. She crossed the room and paused outside the door marked

"Property Owners Association, Administration Office." Inhaling deeply, she reached for the door handle.

The receptionist was sitting on her desk, simultaneously talking on the phone and painting her fingernails. Jasmine remembered her name was Cheryl, and just like the first time she met Cheryl, she was again struck by how young and overweight she was. Cheryl hung up the phone and flipped her long, natural-blonde hair over her shoulders.

Jasmine held out her hand. "Hello. Remember me? I'm the new—"

Cheryl's amber-tinted cat eyes widened. "Oh my God, she's here! It's the gal!" She dropped her nail file, jumped off her desk, and shouted down the hall, "Hey, y'all, it's her!"

Jasmine's hand floated down on its own accord. She wondered if this zeal upon greeting a newcomer was some sort of Southern custom.

No one came running, so Cheryl yelled down the hall again, "Come on, y'all. It's the tallywhacker gal!"

Jasmine's stomach did a three-sixty, and she fought the impulse to turn and run. That option was cut off when two women sprinting from the break room at the end of the hall hemmed her in. The short dark-haired one said, "Hey, I'm Valinda. You met me but probably don't remember. My husband, Phil, is on the county commission. If you ever need—"

Cheryl interrupted her, and nudged the taller woman. "This here is my Aint Alice."

"Hey," said Alice, who was tall and thin. "You saved my Sonny's life. That's my husband. For what it's worth, thanks." Alice patted her short brassy hair. "So what's it like to be on SNN?"

Jasmine gave Alice a confused frown. "But I wasn't on—"

"Oh yes you were," said Cheryl. "Them news people musta shown that clip of you skedaddlin' out of the sheriff's office a hundert times."

Jasmine groaned inwardly. She had been rattled by seeing the doctor and the mayor collapsing like dominos, and consequently forgot to don her baseball cap in her haste to depart. Now the world knew her as the bird who found the wanger. She smiled nervously. "Yes, well, I hope they photographed my good side."

Les Davis, the general manager of the POA, was sitting in his office chinwagging with Junior Tuttle, head of maintenance, and Dan Boggs, head of security. Les was a barrel-chested man, who topped off at an even six feet and sported a gut that was considered modest by Duckett County standards. Except for the army of Confederate-gray soldiers amassed around the borders, his hair was the color of sandalwood. When the trio heard the commotion in the reception area, Les leaned out of his open office door and saw that his new chief financial officer was surrounded.

Turning back to Ed and Junior, he said, "Excuse me, fellas, the squaws have circled the wagon," then he strode briskly down the hall, waving his arms and barking orders. "Break it up now, Sopranos. Give our new CF of O some breathin' room. She's been through a lot this weekend and y'all ain't makin' it no better."

When Les reached the gaggle, he hitched up his pants and said to Jasmine, "Well, I s'pose you've gotten reacquainted with the gals."

"Cheryl, Valinda, and Alice," said Jasmine in her naturally harmonious voice. "But, please, don't ask me their last names."

The ladies edged out Les as if he weren't present. "Les just calls us the Sopranos," said Valinda, "on account of the fact that we all three sing in the First Baptist Church's choir. Oh, by the way, what's your denomination? We got three churches right on Main Street. There's the First Methodist and First Baptist—"

Cheryl broke in. "And then there's Last Hope. That's where you want to go if you're into tongue."

"I ... I beg your pardon. Did you say tongue?" Jasmine had presumed that religious people did not include the use of the tongue among their sexual practices.

"And of course you got your holy rollers down at the Foggy Bottom

Temple. They play with snakes and chug strychnine," Alice chimed in enthusiastically. "So you got your full array." She looked Jasmine up and down. "What kinda church did you grow up in over thar in England?"

Jasmine drew back. She never had anyone she barely knew inquire as to her religious beliefs. She looked at the ceiling and said, "Well ... "

Les was leaning against Alice's desk, his arms folded. He looked at his watch. "Come on, Sopranos, that ain't none of yer business."

The women continued to fixate on Jasmine. "You seem like yore an Emerald Lake Chapel person to me," said Cheryl, eyeing Jasmine. "It's nondenominational."

Valinda said, "That's right. You live in Emerald Lake so you could go to the chapel." She leaned toward Jasmine. "But they're awful watered-down over there, what with their preacher bein' Episcopalian and all."

Jasmine switched her satchel from her right hand to her left and nervously played with her pearl necklace. Hoping to end the discussion, she said, "Ah ... actually, I ... I was raised agnostic."

Alice said, "Oh, I think they got some of them Agnostic Churches down in Lumpkin County, but it's a fer piece to drive."

Les lost his patience and waved off the nosey clerks. "Well, now that we've saved our financial expert's soul, I'm gonna take her back to her new office. Cheryl, could you make us some more cof—"

"Shhh! Todd-the-Bod's on SNN again!" Cheryl exclaimed, turning up the volume on the small TV sitting on her filing cabinet. Indeed, the photogenic-but-befuddled looking Sheriff Todd McPherson was once again standing on the front steps of the jailhouse, flanked on one side by a couple of deputies and on the other by three GBI agents who were wearing crumpled suits and couldn't seem to stop scratching and slapping at themselves, thanks to their stay at the Restful Forest Motel. Alice, Valinda, Les, and Cheryl gathered around the TV just as the cameras zoomed in for a close-up of Todd. Jasmine attempted to edge away just as Ed and Junior joined the party and hemmed her in.

On the screen, Todd thumped several microphones, causing each one to emit a high-pitched squeal that no doubt pained the soundmen. Rather stiffly he said, "I am displeased to report that the male organ which was discovered in Duckett Forest last Friday has still not been recovered. Nor have we found the owner of the appendage. As previously reported, sometime during that night, the organ was taken from where it was being held ... ah ... kept." Junior and Ed snickered. The Sopranos twittered. As if he could hear them, Todd frowned into the cameras. "We here at the Duckett County Sheriff's Department are appealing to the public to contact us with any pertinent information they may have. We're posting the phone numbers below right here on the television screen for y'all to call, and are offering a reward for anyone with information that leads to the recovery of Elvis—I mean, the body male part, the male body part."

Cheryl asked out of one side of her mouth, "Did he just call the tallywhacker Elvis?"

"Don't Fearless look just like Paul Newman in Cat on a Hot Tin Roof?" asked Valinda with a dreamy smile on her face.

"Paul Who-man?" asked Cheryl.

"Quiet!" intoned Les. The group once again tightened around the TV. On the screen, the press burst into an uproar of questions, but Todd held up his hands.

When quiet prevailed, he continued, "As you know, the GBI and the Georgia State Patrol are vigorously lendin' a hand—"

Ed and Junior burst out laughing. The ladies giggled. Les shushed them all.

"I mean lendin' support to this investigation. If anyone out there has any information on the whereabouts of this particular male organ and/or its ... ah ... former owner, please contact the Duckett County Sheriff's Department. And please, do not attempt to handle it. That should only be done by experts."

This time even Les could not hold himself together; he, Junior, and Ed erupted into wild guffaws. The Sopranos shrieked with delight. Jasmine worked her way between Ed and Junior and moved toward the door. She thought it might be better to leave the office now and circle back later when sanity had returned.

On the screen, Todd said, "That's all I've got to say about that. Agent Harwood Slaughter of the GBI will now answer a few questions." Todd stepped away from the microphones, and a blotchy-faced Slaughter stepped forward. The press asked the same questions fifteen different ways over the next five minutes, with Slaughter repeating the same terse answers while vigorously scratching various parts of his body.

Ed snickered. "I know where he slept last night."

Slaughter beat a hasty retreat, and the camera shifted to Ansley Mason, who began to summarize the lawmen's comments. The hilarity in the room was fueled by the fact that she was able to maintain a straight face only through obvious effort. Once the merriment had died down, Les grumbled, "That's what happens when the county elects a baby for sheriff. I voted for Mumper." He looked around and noticed Jasmine had a hand on the door handle. "Okay, that's enough dirty talk for today," he pronounced. "Everbody git to work!" He took Jasmine's elbow and guided her to his office, where he directed her to a guest chair and settled behind his desk.

Alice stuck her head in the door. "I'll be leavin' at lunch to get your brother, a.k.a. Sonny Davis, sprung from the hospital."

Alice's head disappeared and Cheryl flounced in, dropped some papers on Les's desk and said, "I'm gonna be long for lunch. I gotta go take the checkbook over to that good-for-nuttin' son of yorn." She sat on the corner of the desk, looked at Jasmine and said, "We're tradin' in our single-wide for a brand new double-wide." She leaned in and wrinkled her petite nose. "Was it all bloody?"

"That's enough. Out with you." Les motioned for Cheryl to leave.

"I think you gals have chewed on this lost-johnson story long enough fer one day."

"Yeah, like yew don't ever make fun of nobody," said Cheryl. "Watch out Jasmine, he's my daddy-in-. I know the man." Then she flounced out.

Les turned to Jasmine. "How 'bout I give ya a tour of the amenities—"

"Cheryl just said you were her father-in-law," stated Jasmine with disbelief on her face. "And please don't tell me Alice is your sister-in-law."

"Alice is my sister-in-law," Les said levelly. "Lookie here, there ain't a lotta people in this county who are qualified. Besides, Cheryl was just engaged to Conner when she started workin' here." Jasmine winced at this unwelcome news. Les straightened the papers on his desk. "Well, who else can a body count on if not his relatives?"

Jasmine pinched the bridge of her nose in an effort to ward off a headache. "That's an issue we'll have to deal with," she snapped, aware that it was she who sounded like Les's supervisor, not the other way around. "I'd like you to show me my office now, and then I'd like to meet with the staff accountant."

Les escorted Jasmine to the office next door, which was bare save a filing cabinet, a desk, and a lone photo of Emerald Lake's famous waterfall hanging on the wall opposite the desk. Jasmine dropped off her satchel, then she and Les stepped across the hall into the accountant's office. She gasped at what she saw when Les opened the door. Strewn over the floor were messy stacks of printed paper, various pieces of discarded computer equipment, mutilated three-ring binders, computer manuals, empty cardboard boxes, a collection of cheesy coffee mugs, and worst of all - dozens of wadded-up, randomly scattered fast-food wrappers.

Les muttered, "I been tryin' to git maintenance up here to clean this mess up, but they keep puttin' me off. I thank it's cuz they're scart they'll get a disease. I been meanin' to whup up on our chief of maintenance, Junior, seeing as how I'm his boss, but I been covered over with work."

Jasmine stared mutely at Les. She realized that when she had applied for the job, she had been steered away from this office and told that the staff accountant was out of town. How could she have been so naïve? *Because I would have done anything to get out of Boston—including disappearing off the face of the Earth.*

Les chuckled nervously. "Funny thang about Glen Baker—the accountant—he up and run off just after supervisin' payroll last month." He thought a few seconds and added, "Right after I announced the board was hirin' you. Maybe he didn't want to work for a prodigy." He ran his fingers along Glen's dusty desk then wiped them on this pants. "Glen said somethin' about how he'd always wanted to motorcycle his way down Baja. I thank that's in Mexico."

Jasmine searched Les's clear blue eyes. "No, no, no, no," was all she uttered.

"It'll be alright, gal," Les said in a reassuring voice.

Les followed Jasmine back to her office. She sat down heavily and swept a palm over the surface of her new desk, drawing strength from its solidity. Looking up, she said firmly, "Please refrain from calling me 'gal' in the future. You may call me Jasmine or Ms. Roseberry."

Les suddenly looked as if he were desperately trying to hold onto a fart. "Sure," he replied, shuffling his feet. "I thank I'll just leave ya alone to git yourself settled in." He tiptoed out of her office.

Jasmine stared at the serene photo on the opposite wall, which didn't juxtapose well with the cold sensation that was settling in her stomach. She suddenly wished she were ensconced in her childhood home in Cambridge, wearing her favorite pajamas, and drinking chamomile tea with her mum. She inhaled deeply, walked over to the filing cabinet, opened it, and became immediately nauseous.

Les returned to his office, closed the door, and called his older brother, Sonny, on his cell phone. He said, "I let Alice off early to carry you home. Did the docs finally tell ya what made you pass out like that?"

Sonny was partially reclining in his hospital bed. He drew on his dear friend, Mr. Marlboro and said in the phone, "I know what happened. That sorry sheriff of ours gave me a good old-fashioned nervous attack over this hacked-off pee-finger incident. As fortune would have it, the nurses keep bringin' me happy pills, and now I'm as cool as a cuke." He took another satisfying draw on his cigarette.

"Well, I'm not," snapped Les. "This media mess you've got on yer hands ain't a good sign—reporters are crawlin' all over the county. Plus, this little gal accountant has sensed right off that somethin' ain't right with the POA funds. And the way she's actin' ... well, I thank she might be made of stronger mettle than I thought."

"Relax," said Sonny, "we're in play." He placed a pillow behind his head. "You know what the best thing about our little plan is—besides the money, of course?" He sucked on his cigarette, drew it up through his nasal cavity and exhaled through his nose. "We know that they don't know that we know." He snorted and added, "Fer once, the chickens have outsmarted the fox." He picked up the spoon from the breakfast tray and turning it around, examined his pearly whites in its reflection.

"You wanna know what I think, Big Bubba?" snarled Les. "I think this here missin' Cap'n Winkie situation is a bad omen. What if Todd cain't wrap up the case soon? I'm near to panickin'."

Sonny sat straight up in bed, dropped his cigarette in a plastic cup of mixed fruit, and said gruffly, "I don't need ya losin' yer grit right now, Leslie. Hell, I'm the one that nearly got strangled by my own nerves." He softened his tone and added, "I need you to stay cool for me. This lost one-eyed-snake case has got an upside. It's at least keepin' Todd runnin' around like a snoutless hog."

"Well then, lets just hope the owner of the snake don't show up shortly wantin' the damned thang sewed back on." Les hung up, chugged next door to Jasmine's office only to discover that she wasn't there. He stepped across the hall to the accountant's office and spied her perusing the filing cabinet, looking very, very discouraged. He leaned on the doorframe and observed her closely.

She said, "It appears that Glen, for whatever reason, deliberately vandalized the accounting files before he departed."

"Now why would he do a thang like that?" asked Les off-handedly.

"It raises some suspi ... " Jasmine looked up and saw that Les had vanished. She returned her attention to organizing the filing cabinet. Eventually Les returned and insisted she meet more of the employees of the POA. He loaded her into an SUV that sported the resort's logo and drove her to the golf club, tennis club, and to the fitness center. Then it was back to the SUV for a trip around Emerald Lake. As Les negotiated the winding, two-lane Emerald Lake Parkway, Jasmine continued to ruminate on the burden she had accepted. Nothing about the morning had been positive. The POA finances were beginning to look FUBAR—fucked-up beyond all recognition. While normally she relished a challenge, a trait that came from growing up with four older, very competitive brothers, she realized that if she wasn't careful, this job was likely to burn a hole in her resume.

Les pulled the SUV over at an observation point. "Ain't that a pretty site? I never git tarred of it. You got yer mountains and yer lake. And look at all the colored leaves. What more could a body ask for?" He turned to Jasmine. "I know that yer askin' yerself, 'Should I bail now or should I roll up my sleeves and jump into this mess?' " He eyed her for a few beats, while she eyed him back. Then he said, "From what I've seen of ya, ya look like you got the wherewithal to whup up on the POA's lil ol' money problems real speedy-like. We shore are in sore need of ya." He looked back at the lake. "Of course, we can tear up yer contract if ya really don't thank yer up to tacklin' the job."

The remark brought Jasmine up short. Les had just gone anticlockwise on her. With the muddle that the POA finances were in, he should be beseeching her to stay instead of giving her an easy out. She examined his profile out of the corner of her eye: firm chin, abbreviated Irish nose. She said levelly, "I'd like to finish the tour, please."

"Alrighty. You've met the froufrou, now I'm gonna let you meet the real workers that keep this place greased." Les drove to the security office near the main gate and introduced Jasmine to the security personnel in the building. The guards and Les exchanged some genial ribbing and backslapping. Next they drove down and around a hill and stopped at a light blue-gray metal building that was hidden from the rest of the resort. The simple sign out front said "Golf Maintenance." Les escorted Jasmine around the building, where a teenage boy was shoveling sand into a trailer attached to a heavy-duty four-wheeler. He was thin and pasty-faced, with dishwater eyes and matching hair. Les called him Wesley. When Wesley was introduced to Jasmine, she observed that he displayed a cheerless resignation. *How sad.*

Wesley glanced briefly at Jasmine then dropped his gaze to the ground and shifted his feet, which were clad in tattered tennis shoes. Hands in his back pockets, he asked, "Seen any b-buyers yet?"

"I'm not selling anything," stated Jasmine with a puzzled look on her face.

"He wants to know if you've seen any bars," said Les with a chuckle.

Jasmine looked her new boss quizzically.

"Bears."

"My stars, no." Jasmine found that Les's dialect was hard enough to understand, but Wesley's was unintelligible. Apparently, Duckett County's dialect had a dialect.

Les turned back to Wesley, "Did Sonny fix you and Donna up with some wheels?"

"He couldn't find us n-nuttin' we could a-ford. I s'pose I gotta keep on a-hitchin' a ride with Churl."

"I'll talk to Sonny," said Les. "How's them two kids of yorn?"

"The baby took sick over the weekend, but we cain't afford no doc."

Jasmine was shocked by what she had just heard. This man-child apparently had a wife and offspring. Les took Wesley aside, said something to him, and then pulled a white envelope from a pocket inside his windbreaker. Jasmine wondered to which account that money would be charged. Needless to say, she had to admit that while Les Davis may not run a POA with the tidiest financial records, he apparently held the loyalty of his employees.

The last stop on the tour was Emerald Lake Village, a picturesque country square that was tucked away in a peaceful grove of Georgia white pines and set against a backdrop of yet another divine view of the lake. The miniature town consisted of a small stone and wood-faced grocery, a chapel, a conference center/guest hotel, a boutique, a gift shop, and the Emerald Lake Realty office—all reflecting the upscale rustic style of the resort.

The realty office was nestled in the middle of the square, skirted by a soft bed of fragrant pine needles. Les parked the SUV, and as they walked to the entrance, he said with a slight tremor in his voice, "I reckon that I oughta disclose to ya that my daughter, Sherry, is the receptionist here." When Jasmine stopped to look at him, he added, "But Whitestone Development Corporation has nothin' to do with the POA, as you know."

"Except that Mr. Whitestone indirectly controls the board that governs the POA," added Jasmine, just to be precise.

The décor of the spacious reception room was high-end Bob Timberlake. Though Jasmine felt a cool breeze coming from a nearby air-conditioning vent, there was a comforting fire burning in the fireplace. The rustic paneled walls accentuated the wide-plank, heart-of-pine flooring, while roughly hewn cedar beams crossed the vaulted ceiling. It was all very homey, yet upscale at the same time. On a large-screen TV, a promotional DVD featured scenes of Emerald Lake with the words of Henry David Thoreau narrated over a gentle ensemble of banjos and waterfalls. The resulting ambiance was meant to be anything but high pressure. The mood was shattered, however, when the tune of Dixieland emanated from Les's pants pocket. He looked at the caller ID and gestured to Jasmine that he was going out to the porch.

A young, pretty brunette scooted into the room and sat down at the reception desk. "Welcome to Emerald Lake Realty. Can I help you?" said Sherry Davis in a perky drawl. Just then, the meeting-room door flew open and a horde of real estate salespersons burst into the reception area. Jasmine noticed that the agents were wearing a similar uniform as the residents: pressed tan slacks and skirts and forest green knit shirts branded with the Emerald Lake logo over the heart. The only difference, appearance-wise, between the sales agents and the residents was that most of the agents were younger and looked hungry to sell property. Upon spying Jasmine, they gathered around her like flies to honey.

Jasmine backed up against the receptionist's desk and pleaded, "Please, I'm not a customer, I'm—"

"Watch out. They just got outta a sales meetin'," Sherry said under her breath. "Brad always whips 'em up into a feedin' frenzy."

"I see," muttered Jasmine out of the side of her mouth.

"You look like a lake lover to me," said a sporty looking thiry-something woman with heavily highlighted hair. "I just got a listing for a two-acre lot right on the lake that's to die for."

Before Jasmine could respond, a man said, "Hey, I've got a deal on a little three-bedroom on Tecumseh Mountain with a panoramic view. How much can you put down?" He eyed her up and down, quickly sizing up her net worth by the quality of her apparel.

Jasmine stepped back. "No, you don't understand. I have just signed a one-year lease on a cabin. I'm not—"

"Guys, ladies!" said Brad Whitestone as he emerged from the conference room and strode to the middle of the huddle. His face was graced with the same boyish grin he had displayed in his photo on the cover of Atlanta Magazine. He ran his fingers through his golden-brown forelock. "Back off. This is Ms. Jasmine Roseberry, the new CFO for the POA." A few of the disappointed realtors shook her hand limply. Most lost interest and drifted away.

A woman in her mid-forties turned back. "Wait! You're the gal with the winky—I mean, the girl who found the winky!"

Immediately the sticky-beaked flock moved in again, but this time Whitestone raised his voice and said in a jocular tone, "Go sell some real estate, people!" Grinning, he shooed off his agents with a rolled-up sales report. Turning back to Jasmine, he said, "I am sooo glad that you decided to take the job. I intend to do all I can to support you."

Jasmine found herself smiling. "Thank you, Mr. Whitestone. Your words are very comforting."

"Call me Brad," he said, offering her a smile that made him look younger than his thirty-five years. His expression turned sincere. "I'm terribly sorry about that unfortunate business in Duckett Forest." He looked around the room. "I thought Les brought you over."

"He did. He's outside taking a call on his cell phone."

Brad smiled broadly. "In that case ... Will you walk into my parlour?"

"Said the spider to the fly," replied Jasmine, finishing the stanza.

"'Tis the prettiest little parlour that you ever did spy," added Brad as he escorted her down the pine-paneled hall.

"The way into my parlour is up a winding stair," recited Jasmine with a Cheshire cat smile on her face.

"And I've many curious things to shew you when you are there," replied a grinning Brad as he opened his office door. "So you apparently take pleasure in the works of Mary Howitt."

"Doesn't everybody?" asked Jasmine as she crossed the threshold. She discovered that Brad's office had the appearance of a National Geographic explorer's study, rather than the typical Bob Timberlake theme that she already found uninteresting. Instead of Scottish plaids and pillows covered with fake bearskin, the spacious room sported simple but comfortable-looking furniture in distressed chocolate-brown leather and canvas.

A richly toned, distressed table large enough to accommodate a topographical map substituted as Brad's desk. Indeed, it was obvious that he loved maps because a half-dozen of them hung on the walls. Others, in all stages of being either rolled up or unrolled, were lying on nearly every flat surface. Jasmine thought that Ernest Hemingway would find this room to be a comfortable space in which to pen yet another exhilarating adventure novel.

Brad beckoned Jasmine to a model of Emerald Lake sitting on a round table near one of the large, old-fashioned, multi-paned windows. Like a kid who had just found a new playmate, he proudly pointed out the resort's landmarks. Les stuck his head in the door and said he had to go take care of some nuisance bears up at the Collier's house. He asked if Brad would drive Jasmine back to the POA office. Brad replied that he'd be delighted.

After Les left, Jasmine sat on the comfortable couch while Brad, lit up by the bright midday sun streaming through the windows, continued bouncing around his office, throwing map after map onto her lap and excitedly outlining his future plans for his scenic Camelot. Jasmine couldn't stop smiling at his enthusiasm.

Brad finally paused for air. He whirled around to study her, and she saw that his round eyes were glowing with excitement. "So what do you think?"

"Quite impressive," was all she could manage without revealing her own state of breathlessness.

Brad rolled up the maps on her lap. It was a slightly sexy gesture and oddly, Jasmine found herself not minding it. He said, "Listen to me, babbling on about my company. I'm going to drive you to the golf club and we'll have some lunch. I want to know all about you."

* * * * *

The octagonal dining room at the Emerald Lake Golf Club was encased by triple-storied glass walls, allowing for a panoramic view. The requisite rustic beams above, and an unnecessary fire was burning in the giant stone fireplace. Below the clubhouse, there were views up two fairways that ran along the north and west sides of the lake. The scenic course was embraced by the tree-covered North Georgia Mountains, which butted up against the mystical, overlapping ridges of the Blue Ridge Mountains just across the state border.

They were approached by a painfully thin waitress, mid-forties, with nicotine-stained teeth and straw for hair. She scribbled their drink order on a pad. Brad ordered a scotch, but Jasmine insisted on sparkling water with lime, so he agreeably changed his order to iced tea. After the waitress left, Brad said quietly, "We try to employ the locals as much as possible."

"The locals are the only people available to employ," responded Jasmine forthrightly.

Brad changed the subject. "I know the POA finances are in a bad way. You see, thirty years ago, Les Davis was hired as a teenager out of high school to the lowest position of all—the golf course maintenance crew. He eventually worked his way up to head of maintenance. Just before I came here eight years ago, the general manager's post was vacated, and the board appointed him acting GM. None of the subsequent boards got around to appointing a more-qualified individual. And I admit that since I came, I've been too busy with everything on my end of things to deal with Les."

Brad ran his fingers through his golden-brown forelock. "And to his credit, Les is very popular with the POA staff and residents— especially with the right residents. He knows whose back to keep scratched, if you know what I mean." Jasmine only nodded. He added, "Now that we have acquired an extremely qualified CFO," he bowed his head in her direction, "we need to retire Les and obtain a professional

GM for the POA."

Jasmine smiled ruefully. "My, that's a mouthful of letters."

The waitress brought their drinks and took their food orders. When she departed, Jasmine asked, "By your phrase 'the right residents' I take it you mean the old guard? They call Les when they have a problem—say a tree falls across the driveway or a bear wanders on their property—and as sure as Bob's your uncle, he's up there with a crew to solve the problem while he personally supervises."

"Say, you're quick on the uptake," said Brad with surprise and appreciation in his voice. "You sound like you've been here for years."

Jasmine swept her hair to one side. "My parents are university professors. I grew up hearing all the stories about the politics of academia. 'I'll scratch your back if you scratch mine' was a recurring theme." She surreptitiously studied Brad's face as he sipped his tea. While not drop-dead gorgeous, there was a harmony to his straightforward features that was quite appealing, and his gilded locks set off his eyes, which Jasmine decided were the color of the crystalline green found in an Arctic iceberg. Yet, when he turned his peepers on her, she found them playfully engaging rather than cold and remote as one would expect. She realized she was daydreaming. And so soon after Stefan. She cleared her throat. "What do you know about this staff accountant, Glen Baker, who has vacated the premises?"

"I won't snow you. Glen was a slacker. I say good riddance to him. He probably didn't want to deal with yet another CFO. You know the last three haven't lasted more than six months each."

"And they've signed confidentiality agreements, so I'm not going to obtain any information from them," retorted Jasmine disagreeably.

"No matter. The POA has been without one for the last seven months. I'm afraid you're on your own." Their food arrived and Brad dove into a filet mignon while Jasmine picked at a grilled-salmon salad. He leaned toward her and pressed his palms together in supplication. "I'm begging you, Jasmine, please give the job a chance. As I said before, you will have my complete backing."

She exhaled deeply. "It's only my first day. I'm not going to run away."

"That's the spirit!" said Brad, looking visibly relieved. "Now, tell me all about yourself."

Jasmine disliked open-ended questions, but she dutifully took up the task at hand. "Well, I'm a Harvard grad. I have a B.A. in accounting and economics, also minored in French and English lit. I completed my MBA at Brandeis while working at Feed the Little Children and I—"

"Stop." Brad made a time out sign with his hands. "I read your extraordinarily impressive resume. I want to know about you."

Jasmine found herself telling Brad all about her life growing up in a time-honored university town like Cambridge, England. As she spoke, she lifted her hair off her warm neck. The crackling fire in the fireplace gave her cheeks a delicate flush. "After Harvard, I worked in Boston while earning my masters degree. And that brings you up to date on my life thus far." *Except for the part about being jilted the day of my wedding.*

The way that Brad looked at Jasmine made her feel as if she were the only person in the room. He asked, "So what makes a beautiful, overqualified young lady like you venture out into the wilds of Appalachia?"

"Why, pray tell, did you come here?"

"Well, my family owns a string of family restaurants in Indianapolis. After graduating from Northwestern, Pops expected me to work in the family biz, but I disliked the restaurant industry. And I wasn't too keen on working for my old man. Not that he's a bad sort. I just wanted to do my own thing." He gestured toward the view before them. "And this sure beats baked chicken." He grinned broadly, showing off his pearly whites.

Jasmine ended up telling Brad about her missing furniture and admitted to her uncomfortable feelings about moving to the middle of nowhere. She found him easy to talk to, and he didn't ask one question about the Elvis fiasco.

"Look," he said, "you're experiencing culture shock. All newcomers go through it. Take me, for example. After my first week here, I was about ready to jump off Crying Rock."

"Don't put the idea in my head. I drive past it on my way down the mountain." Just the day before, she had stopped at the observation turnout and looked down at the flat outcropping called Crying Rock some seventy feet below the road. From where she sat now, she let her eyes climb 4,000 feet up the sheer vertical face of McLean Mountain until she spied the dramatic outcropping. "The cabin I'm renting is right up there, just a few hairpin curves above the observation turnout."

"That face of the mountain between the turnout and Crying Rock is all shale," replied Brad. "Twice a year, some of the maintenance men rappel down to the ledge and brush off the damn thing. Otherwise, Crying Rock would eventually look like a giant snow cone."

"I suppose the reason they call it Crying Rock is that some unhappy Cherokee lovers, forbidden to marry, threw themselves off of it."

"Isn't that always the story? If it is true, they threw themselves into a gorge, not a lake. All the lakes in Georgia are manmade. Emerald Lake was created when the first developer built an earthen dam on a tributary of the river."

Jasmine was intrigued. "It seems, from what I read, that the resort started out quite modestly."

"Those little cabins like the one you are renting are some of the original weekenders." Brad's expression turned thoughtful. "Say, since you don't yet have your stuff here yet, I have a fully furnished corporate guesthouse you can use until—"

Jasmine held up a hand. Her nails were trimmed and sported sensible, clear polish. "No thanks, I've grown accustomed to sleeping on the floor." The offer underscored Jasmine's impression that Brad really did intend to give her 100 percent of his support.

"So what's the name of this dastardly moving enterprise that has left you high and dry?"

Jasmine picked up her glass and with a dramatic flair proclaimed, "To Infinity and Beyond International Moving Company, LLC."

Brad snapped his fingers. "By jiminy, I've heard of that outfit! It's based in Indianapolis. I'll call Pops, he probably knows the owner." Rewarded with a grateful smile, he reached over and squeezed her hand. "Just give it some time, Jasmine, and you'll fall in love with this place."

He went on to tell her about some of his most embarrassing moments when he first arrived. "I was young and green, never having developed so much as a kiddie playground. Yet here I was, completely under water and juggling incompetent builders, meth-crazed construction workers, demoralized real estate agents, Les Davis, and a weird assortment of moonshine-guzzling POA employees. Not to mention the aforementioned powerful click of well-to-do residents who demanded that I serve them at their beck and call. On top of everything, I couldn't understand the local lingo half the time. I was a truly babe in the woods."

Jasmine was so engrossed in Brad's tale that she hadn't noticed the room, which had been brightly lit by the sun when they had walked in, had grown forebodingly dark. Suddenly, an earsplitting clap of thunder caused her to jump, and rain began to pour out of the sky. A breathtaking atmospheric light show ensued, as jagged bolts of lightning forked their way across the sky and played hide-and-seek among the mountains. On the golf course below, Jasmine spied a party of middle-aged golfers scrambling for their carts.

Another clap of thunder reverberated through the clubhouse. The lights flickered, and then failed. Brad touched Jasmine's arm. "This happens all the time. The backup generator is giving us problems. I can't get anyone to work on it except Darryl and his brother Darryl." He smiled at his joke, his white teeth gleaming in a sudden flash of lightning.

Jasmine looked around and realized they were the only guests in the restaurant. "Oh, crikey! How long have we been here? I must return to the office."

Brad gave her a reassuring smile. "Don't worry about that. You're okay with me."

"But it's my first day at my job, and I'm worming out of work." Jasmine felt like she was back at school and had awakened one morning and realized that half the semester was gone without her having yet to attend one Latin class.

She stood, but Brad placed his hand on her arm. Over the noise of the pelting downpour, he said, "We can't go outside now, it would be dangerous."

His statement was punctuated a series of staccato lightning strikes flashing through the room. Jasmine felt the ensuing bombardment of thunder reverberating through her bones and she melted into her chair, as if the greedy storm had drained her of all her energy.

Into the room traipsed the rain-drenched party of male golfers that she had watched scurry from the downpour a few minutes before. They walked over, brushing off their L.L. Bean ponchos and joking about the trials and tribulations of scratching out a living in the "wilderness." Brad laughed amicably, then introduced the men to Jasmine.

She smiled politely and held out her hand. "Such a pleasure to meet all of you." They look even more identical when wet.

Brad and Jasmine moved to a couch in the bar while they waited for the storm to subside. He ordered coffee for himself and hot tea for her, then turned to her and casually placed an arm on the back of the couch. "There's a charity ball at the Fox Theater in Atlanta on Thursday—"

"Please do not ask me on a date. You sit on the POA board—the board that pays my salary."

"Now, who said anything about a date?" chided Brad. "This will be strictly business. These events are big marketing opportunities, and if I bring you," he touched her shoulder lightly, "people will see a professional with an Ivy League background and think that the management of this resort is on its way up. So what do you say?"

Jasmine pondered his offer, then looked him in the eye. "Perhaps we can strike a deal. You pull your family strings and get that lorry carrying my furniture down here by Thursday and I'll be at your charity event with bells on."

"Deal!" exclaimed Brad without hesitation. They shook hands and Jasmine found herself smiling broadly in response to Brad Whitestone's engaging grin.

Chapter Six
Monday Evening:
Sacked in the Backfield

Todd hung up the phone and slumped back in his chair. Another promising lead had gone south. For three days now, Todd, Rusty, and junior detectives Tawanda Berry and Shawn Higgins had dogged down a dozen hard leads that had been culled from a hundred superfluous phone tips, most of which had been crank calls, naturally. He had hopes that one of the leads would pan out, especially since none of them involved his friends on Main Street. Unfortunately, they all led to dead ends. Harwood Slaughter had been holding his own leads, if indeed he had any, close to his chest. Todd could tell, however, that the crusty agent was having similar luck because for the last two evenings, the scowling curmudgeon and his toadies had trudged from the Checkered Flagg to the crime van, then slammed the door and roared off to a termite-free motel somewhere outside Todd's county. *Wimps.*

Todd repeatedly banged his head on the desk. When the futility of that action dawned on him, he sat up and gazed out the window. "Elvis! You're freakin' drivin' me insane," he said out loud. There was a knock at the open door. Todd's head snapped around and he saw that it was Rusty. He hoped that his second-in-command hadn't heard him talking to a wayward penis.

Rusty closed the door then grasped the back of the guest chair. "We've got to talk." Todd motioned for him to sit. "I don't get the secrecy thing over the bones," said Rusty, settling into the chair. "It's been thirty-six hours since the bones turned up. And while Cody and Tiffany can keep a secret, Virgil and Blaine sure cain't. You know this county. This is all gonna come out anyway pretty quick."

Todd sat back, placed his hands behind his head and propped his

131

feet on the desk. "True, but the news will get out slower if we keep the lid on. This will give us some breathin' room so as we can focus on finding Elvis and the rest of the corpse. And since the Evans/Wells case is in the freezer, puttin' the investigation off for a few days ain't gonna change much." Todd pulled out a wet wipe from the desk drawer and applied it to a spot of Georgia clay on the heel of his boot. "Havin' said that, I want you to check the computer again for Billy's Taurus."

Rusty shot Todd a look of disapproval. He was three years older and had more boots-on-the-ground experience than Todd. This was a situation that guaranteed a certain amount of frustration on both sides. "You know that's just busy work," he said with an uncharacteristic edge to his voice. "That vehicle is in auto heaven."

"I know, but I want to be able to tell the relatives we are working on several leads, one of which is a renewed attempt to locate Billy's car."

Rusty's mouth repositioned itself into a grim line. "Do you realize how that sounds? You ... " Abruptly, he gave up on that line of thought. "You say you don't want to advertise the bones, but surely you have to figure a press briefin' might jog someone's memory. Maybe someone had seen the killer's car on Pirkle Road that night."

Todd folded his arms across his chest—it was the top half of the universal cop stance. "You know how deserted these country roads are, especially after dark. Nobody saw nothin'." He studied his not-too-happy second-in-command. "A few days, Rus. That's all I'm talkin' about." Rusty still looked skeptical, so Todd added, "I promise you I will make an announcement by Friday. We're bound to know whether or not the bones are Billy by then." He snorted. "This is a great time for that skeleton to show up. Friday's Halloween."

"There's gotta be more evidence out there. In the very least, we should be able to find the skull. Don't you think we should call up the search-and-rescue—"

"No, let's just keep Cody and Tiffany on it. I'm bettin' the skull is

132

no further than a gnat's brow from where the bones were found. This crime went down after sunset, which means it would have been pitch black in the Forest, and the perps would have been afraid to stray too far from their vehicles."

Rusty agitatedly ran a hand over his short-shorn, carrot-pigmented hair. "I know, Todd, that you've got a knack for solvin' crimes, while I have more patience for the admin work—but this time you done got me horn-swaggled."

Todd stared at Rusty as if he had suddenly sprouted a third eye. "I've just explained my logic to you," he retorted irritably.

Rusty's eyebrows resembled two furry fire-engines colliding head on. "A press briefin' would be standard procedure at this point. You don't even have to mention Billy and Bonnie. Just say you found some bones."

"Rus, you are the most stubborn lawman I ever met. And that's sayin' a lot. You know everyone would jump to conclusions that the bones were Billy's, and they'd all be buggin' the crapola out of us, wantin' to know every detail of our investigation. Not to mention the fact that we'd never get rid of those vampires camped out on our front steps." Todd swigged his coffee and said gamely. "Who knows? Maybe the bones and Elvis are connected."

"Well, knock me down and steal my choppers!" proclaimed Rusty, who hadn't caught the joke. He didn't bother to hide a look that said, You are out of your ever-lovin' mind. "There's not one friggin' shred of evidence of a relationship between Elvis and those bones. You best—"

"I just said I'll make this public by Friday," said Todd more sharply than he had meant. Rusty regarded the floor for a few beats then stood up heavily. Todd added, "I'm handin' the Elvis investigation over to you for now. I gotta run an errand."

"So, it's to be yet another double shift," grumbled Rusty glumly from the doorway.

"I'll come back later and relieve you as soon as I can."

Rusty snorted. "Yeah, right. You have a way of gettin' yourself waylaid with all your zig-zaggin' around. Heather don't like bein' alone at night with three little kids, you know. She's startin' not to like you." He disappeared before Todd could respond.

Todd pulled out a packet of antiseptic wipes from his desk drawer in preparation for his pre-departure desk-sanitizing routine. The late afternoon sun was slicing through the half-open blinds. Its lazy warmth penetrated his weary bones, making him long for sleep. But, he had to drive up to Emerald Lake. Brandy had called earlier from the limo that was bringing her and "Mr. Golf Bags" from the airport to their residence in Emerald Lake. She had insisted that Molly stay with her until the Elvis situation blew over. Too tired to argue, Todd reluctantly agreed.

Now that the lovely Jasmine had mysteriously appeared in his life, Todd could not think about Emerald Lake without thinking of her. Then he was struck by an idea. Maybe there's still a chance to see her.

Reenergized, Todd hastily called in Shawn and wrapped up his desk-sanitizing duty. He told him to stay late to work the tip line. Shawn promptly produced a pout. Todd felt that, though young and immature, Shawn had the potential to be a good investigator. Shawn's problem was that, like all the other young deputies, he would rather race around in a cruiser chasing down speeders, dope dealers, and wife beaters than tediously dog down every possible lead in an ongoing investigation.

Nevertheless, Todd refreshed Shawn on the art of tip evaluating while he ran one last germicidal wet wipe over the desktop. Before he could scoot out, however, he heard an unsteady step-clop, step-clop across the lobby. From her desk, LeeLee called out, "Fearless, Dwight Beezer has checked himself into Chez McPherson again." Todd groaned and signaled for Shawn to follow him. Dwight was lying on the cot in cell No. 3. His voluminous blubber spilled over the narrow bed; and like yeasty bread dough that had been pricked, half of it hung almost to the floor. Despite the fact that Dwight had his arm slung over his face, Todd could smell his liquid lunch from three feet away. He spied the drunk's prosthetic leg sticking out from under the metal cot, and it made him want to puke. The sight of fake limbs always left him nauseous. He loomed over the self-made prisoner and said sharply, "Dwight! Despite rumors to the contrary, this jail is not a motel."

Dwight's muttered response was irritatingly slurred. "But Tammy gave me about a dozen Budweisers with my cheeseburger."

Todd mulled over this all-too-familiar scenario. Tammy was gaming him again. While she was generally sufferable during church, her smoldering resentment of him tended to surface once she was back in her own greasy territory. Even though he already knew the answer, Todd asked rhetorically, "What the hell is Tammy doin' givin' you so much beer?"

Dwight produced his typical pig-snort. "Because she knows I'm gonna walk right next door and sleep it off in your jailhouse, duh. I cain't drive, since y'all done shredded my license in your mean little paper shredder."

Despite the greasy alcoholic smell wafting off Dwight, Todd bent over his ward and got in his face. "Look at me!" he barked as he shoved Dwight's arm away from the old drunk's face. "I thought we settled all this last week." Dwight's eyes fluttered shut and a snore approaching the volume of a stock car rumbled out of his mouth.

Todd used his considerable strength to yank the obese drunkard into a sitting position. "You wanna be in jail? Then you're gonna go through bookin', just like every other drunken idjit in the county." He shoved the prosthetic leg into Dwight's chest. "Strap on your appendage—now!"

Though he had apparently removed his ambulatory aid with alacrity, Dwight was all thumbs when it came to the task of wrestling it back on. Todd grabbed the leg (with attached sneaker) and tossed it to Shawn, who was standing in the doorway. "Book that," he ordered fiercely. Shawn frowned quizzically, then shrugged and tucked

Dwight's leg under his armpit.

Todd pulled Dwight to his foot, but now that his bladder was upright, Dwight suddenly cried, "I need to pee right now." Since Shawn was far too little for the job, Todd planted his feet, secured hands onto thighs, and stood butt cheek to butt cheek with the one-legged, 300 pounder while he emptied his ocean-sized bladder. Unfortunately, most of the peculiarly malodorous urine landed only in the vicinity of its stainless-steel target. As Todd struggled to keep his unbalanced prisoner vertical, he quoted one of his criminology professors by muttering in a sarcastic falsetto, "You'll always be proud to uphold the law!" Shawn snickered and the fake leg tucked under his arm bobbed along with his skinny shoulders.

Once Dwight and his plastic leg were booked, Todd rushed home to shower and change into his sexiest jeans and a form-fitting T-shirt. He threw on a jeans jacket and hustled over to the farmhouse to get Molly, but found only Jessie sitting at the kitchen table shelling peas. She said, "I told you Molly was goin' over to your sister's from school so she could play with Kylie."

As he inhaled a few bites of meatloaf, Todd said, "You're right, Momma. I'm just a little scattered lately. Thank God I have you to help me with my little darlin'." He kissed her goodbye, jumped into his red Chevy pickup, drove to Katie's place and picked up Molly.

There were two possible routes to Emerald Lake from Todd's sister's farm. One was all asphalt and the other one was a primitive dirt road that cut twenty minutes off the trip, if one were willing to tackle rough terrain and cross a questionable bridge that spanned a narrow stretch of the river. Todd buckled Molly into her booster seat. When they reached the cutoff, he asked her, "You wanna go roughridin'?"

Eager sprite that she was, Molly's sparkling eyes took on a mischievous gleam. "You betcha!"

Todd turned into Duckett Forest. Immediately, the heavy tree cover dimmed the late afternoon sun. The truck followed the nearly nonexistent dirt road that sliced its way through a dense grove of mountain laurel and other foliage. When they reached the antique covered bridge, Molly and Todd high-fived and yelled, "Termites Holding Hands!" It was the local nickname of this particular conduit of questionable integrity.

Once across, the heavily pitted road grew rough. "You like this, Molly?" shouted Todd over the noise as they bounced along.

"Yee haw!" she shouted, throwing her arms in the air.

Out of the corner of his eye, he spotted the fresh tracks of a truck that had circumvented the gate to the Northwest sector. Then he noticed the freshly turned soil on the dirt service road beyond the gate. Abruptly applying the brakes, he stuck his head out the window and scrutinized the scene. This sector was the most pristine wilderness in all of Duckett Forest, open only to hikers and bow hunters if they were willing to drag out their prey on a litter. Broken branches lined the road, which had become little more than a footpath. The vehicle must be sporting a heavy-duty brush guard, because from the looks of the damage to the trees, it had barreled along at a maximum possible speed.

"What is it, Daddy?" asked Molly.

"Fresh tracks—looks like a pickup. See how they went around the gate?"

Molly sat up as straight as she could and peered over the dashboard. "What are you gonna do about it?"

Todd grinned broadly. "Well, golly, Miss Molly, I expect we better go check it out."

Molly's eyes grew two sizes. "You gonna arrest someone?"

"Would you like that?"

She stuck her arm out the window and banged on the door. "Let's do it, Chief!"

Still grinning, Todd looked at her quizzically. "Since when did my little girly-girl get so tough?" Molly displayed a miniature of her father's grin and jabbed a finger forward. "We're wastin' time!"

"Yes, ma'am!" Todd reached over and rolled up her window to protect her from the tree branches, then stepped out, unlocked the gate, and drove through. It was slow going. Tree limbs slapped at the windows, and Todd occasionally heard the screech of a broken-off branch raking the side paneling. Cursing under his breath, he thought about how much the Chevy's recent paint job had cost him.

Molly asked, "Why didn't you just go 'round the gate like the bad guys?"

"Because I didn't want to drive over their tracks. Those tracks are evidence."

"Evidence," Molly repeated slowly.

Todd continued to push the Chevy through the virgin woods. Eventually, he entered a clearing of about three square acres that had been burned by a lightning strike a few summers ago. Conner Davis, Wade Davis, and a Hispanic man were piling surveying equipment into an oversized, black Ford pickup with a slogan on the side that read, "Davis Cousins Surveying."

Todd ordered Molly to stay in the truck, then he stepped out and called, "Conner, Wade! Y'all get up on around here." Wade and Conner moved only as far as the back end of their pickup, one on each side, while the laborer quietly climbed into the bed and settled on top of the built-in metal toolbox. Todd leaned against the front grill of his pickup and crossed his arms. "What's goin' on here, guys? Y'all know this section of the Forest is closed to all unofficial vehicles."

At the age of twenty-eight, Wade Davis, Mayor Sonny Davis's only child, already possessed a fast-food paunch that cascaded heavily over his belt. Once a star nose tackle on Todd's high school football team, Wade seemed destined to become obese like his father. Wade lifted his Braves baseball cap and wiped sweat from his forehead with the sleeve of his work shirt. "We just came up here to practice some surveyin'."

Todd snorted. "Practice surveyin'? Why would y'all do somethin' like that in a wilderness? It ain't like somethin' is gonna be built here."

Conner Davis features resembled a younger version of his father, Les Davis, who was the CEO of the POA at Emerald Lake—Jasmine's new boss. Unlike his cousin, Conner still had his athletic build from his days as a high school tight end. He rested an elbow on top of the rear panel of the pickup and mumbled, "That's what they told us to say."

"Shut up, Conner," hissed Wade.

Todd's penetrating stare switched from one cousin to the other. "Who are *they*?" Wade returned Todd's stare with equal frankness and said nothing. Todd stated emphatically, "You can't survey in Duckett Forest."

Wade moved to the tailgate, leaned on it, and crossed his arms. "Look, it's a job. Times are tough, and we need the work."

Conner stuck a twig between the gap in his front teeth and still managed a bit of clarity as he said, "Cheryl and me just bought a double-wide."

"Bambi's always bustin' my chops over child support," said Wade. "Damn she-male refuses to take up somethin' better payin' than beauty work."

Molly unbuckled her seatbelt and hung out the window. "Bo Davis is in my class!"

"Molly, get inside!" barked Todd, and Molly's blonde head immediately disappeared inside the cab. Todd turned back to the Davis cousins. "What kind of project are you two supposed to be surveyin' for?" He gestured to the woods. "I mean, look around you, this is county-owned wilderness. It will never be developed."

Conner used his twig to flick a dried spatter of orange clay off the truck. "Like I said, they said we couldn't tell." He turned back to the short man in the truck bed. "Right, Franciso?" The man shrugged.

Todd straightened up and crossed his arms again. "Now I'm gettin' peeved. I oughta give you two pissants a ticket for drivin' up here and doin' surveyin' or whatever the fu ... " He remembered that Molly was within earshot. "Whatever you're doin' up here without a permit. The law is the law."

Wade looked at Connor and jerked his head toward Todd. "Man, it's just like we're back on the squad and Mr. Tight-ass Team Captain here is bustin' our chops for somethin'."

Conner crossed his arms and said, "We shoulda known that stick-in-the-mud McPherson would grow up to be the county sheriff, right, Wade?"

"Yep, before it was always..." He raised his voice and said mockingly, " 'The rules are the rules.' Now it's 'The Law is the Law.' Fuck that shit."

Todd felt a little crushed. He had always thought he'd been a popular team captain. "Well guys," he said sternly, "the rules are the rules, and the law is the law."

Wade and Conner laughed derisively. Wade said, "You cain't arrest us. You ain't wearin' your stupid little uniform and your stupid little badge."

"Nor your stupid little popgun," added Conner between peals of laughter.

"Ah, but I do have my stupid little ticket book," retorted Todd, copying their sarcastic tone. He reached into his truck and pulled out a ticket pad and a pen, and started writing. "Look, I'm responsible for every last one of these trees. Now I want the name of this company that hired you and I want to know what you were surveyin' for."

Connor crossed his arms and screwed up his face to where it resembled a chicken's butt. "Well, we ain't a-gonna do that."

Wade held up his hands. "Throw us in your stupid little jailhouse. Waterboard us. We don't care."

Todd rubbed his forehead vigorously. *Surveying in the wilderness?* Another weird event was enfolding before his eyes. That made four weird events in four days. "Let's just shuck this down. I'll let y'all off with a warning as long as y'all don't come back up here. But I need y'all to talk."

Conner spat, "I know my rights."

Wade kicked at a pine sapling. "You cain't push me around, Fearless. My daddy is mayor, and the president of this fuckin' county."

Todd pulled the ticket from the pad. "Y'all asked for it."

Wade looked at Conner and jerked his head toward the cab of their truck. He climbed into the driver's side while Conner scrambled in on the passenger's side.

Todd helplessly watched the big truck circle around. As it roared by, Wade yelled out the window, "Nobody liked you in high school!" Then he flipped Todd the bird and roared off through the tall Georgia pines.

"You forget I was homecoming king!!" Todd yelled after the departing pickup. He threw the ticket pad into his truck, climbed in, and slammed the door. He knew that Conner and Wade knew he wasn't going to pursue them in his private vehicle, especially with his little girl along. He wondered why were they being so secretive. The Davis cousins had never kept a secret in their lives. They'd been huge gossips in high school and were frequently the source of all kinds of interpersonal teenage mayhem.

Molly huffed. "I'm gonna tell Bo that his daddy said the F-word."

As Todd buckled the belt over Molly's booster seat, he said, "No, don't do that, sugar." He added under his breath, "You don't want to grow up to be a stick-in-the-mud like your daddy."

"You didn't give them their ticket," Molly said in a disappointed voice.

"Oh, don't worry darlin'." Todd started the engine. "They're gonna get their ticket."

Todd drove on in silence as he ruminated on the events of the last four days. Just before reaching Emerald Lake, he pulled over, withdrew his memo book from his back jeans pocket, and wrote down his mental list of the recent strange events in chronological order.

Where's Elvis?

Recent Weird Events
* Friday - Elvis discovered
* Saturday - The bones turn up
* Sunday - Schoolyard brawl between commissioners
* Monday - Davis cousins surveying in Duckett Forest

As he was trained to do, Todd looked for any possible relationship among the events. He decided that if the bones were Billy's, then that meant they were the bones of a county commissioner." Wade and Conner were surveying land and most of what the county commissioners did was to zone and rezone land parcels. He rewrote by subject:

Recent Weird Events
Possible land rezoning/development issue?
* The bones - if indeed they belong to Billy Evans (a county commissioner)
* Catch, Walt, and Phil gang up on Sam in church playground. (All are county commissioners)
* Davis cousins surveying in the Forest

Wildcard

* Elvis

Todd was surprised all the events, save Elvis, could be lumped under the topic of "land development." Weird. He pulled back on the road and soon found himself driving up to the main gate to Emerald Lake. Slim, trim senior guard, Betty, warned him that due to a wet afternoon gust-up, the roads were covered with "a gazillion, evil, slippery leaves." Todd smiled and gave her a quick salute. She returned his smile and pushed the button that opened the gate. Todd turned onto Emerald Lake Parkway and drove around the lake at the insufferably slow speed limit. Finally, he turned off the parkway and headed up

Emerald Mountain. Immediately, his middle-aged pickup groaned in protest. As he rounded a sharp turn, Molly rested her chin on the open window and looked down at the expansive lake. The red-orange-, and yellow-leafed trees on the mountains were reflected in the mossy green water below, giving the illusion that there were two resorts instead of one. "It's just like a magic mirror, isn't it Daddy?"

"Just like a magic mirror," said Todd with a trace of irritation. He disliked Emerald Lake, if only for the reason that his ex-wife had left him for a man who lived here. Fortunately, it wasn't often that Duckett County law enforcement was summoned to these mountains. There was virtually no crime in the gated community. The resort was, however, the site of frequent accidents on its twisting mountain roads. Because crashes were so numerous, the Emerald Lake security guards had an understanding with Todd that they would only summon his department in wrecks involving injuries. Otherwise, his little cadre of deputies would be trekking back and forth practically daily.

Todd noticed that Molly was getting a little green around the gills. "You okay, Little Miss?"

"I'm doin' better than last time," she said weakly. "Maybe I'm growin' outta my car sickness." Molly handled rough roads fine, but steep, twisting roads were another story. Sure enough, a little moan escaped from her lips.

"Try not to look down," said Todd.

"Yes, sir."

"Feel any better?"

"No sir." Molly slapped her hands over her mouth. Todd stomped on the emergency brake, jumped out of the truck, and hurried around to the passenger's side. He lifted Molly out of the booster seat, held her horizontally with one hand, and with the other pulled back her hair while she vomited her after-school snack in the wild sumac that grew alongside the road. Then he sat her back in the booster seat, cinched the seatbelt, wiped off her face, and gave her a bottle of water.

Where's Elvis?

By the time they pulled into the faux-cobblestone driveway of the Stanton residence, Molly's carsickness was in the past. The house was a true country manor, its complex façade consisted of elegantly stacked stone and stained cedar shake. Dual stone chimneys rose from an intricate wood-shingled roof, and a tasteful wooden sign out front displayed the name of the house, "High Heaven." Todd had gotten the scoop on Herb Stanton from Bambi, who was Brandy's best friend. After completing a stint in the South African Air Force, Herb had immigrated to the United States and ended up making a ton of greenbacks in manufacturing golf bags. When he was in his mid-forties, he shed his job and his first wife. Now in his early fifties, Herb had it all—a personal fortune, three grown daughters finally off financial support, and a vivacious young wife. Indeed, when it came to Brandy, Herb had a tiger by the tail. Todd wondered how long it would take for that tiger's tail to become a noose around the man's nuts.

He helped Molly out of the truck and then slipped her miniature backpack over her slender shoulders. She bolted to the massive front porch and rang the bell beside the custom glass inlaid door. Todd looked around and decided that, although the view was magnificent, he didn't believe that the top of a mountain was a very practical spot to put a house. The structure's backside was practically hanging off the mountain, just waiting for a stiff wind to claim it. He looked down at Molly, who had grabbed his hand and begun to dance. "Little darlin', are you excited about seeing your momma, or do you have to go to the bathroom?"

"Both." She grimaced, exposing her pearly baby teeth.

The housekeeper, Anna, opened the door. Todd had no idea how this former citizen of Seville, Spain, who appeared to be in her forties, had come to live with the Stantons in the wilds of Georgia. But Todd liked the fact that she had an agreeable temperament, and was fond of Molly. Anna said, "Good evening, Mr. Todd and Miss Molly. It is bery nice to see you this evening." Anna was taking English lessons, and her

144

teacher was fond of formality. "I trust that your treep up the mountain was not bery diffi—"

Todd held up a hand. "Excuse me, Anna, but she needs to go to the little girl's room."

"Of course. I will escort her." Anna took Molly's hand and glided across the expansive marble foyer with the little girl crab-walking beside her.

"Thanks, Anna," Todd called after them. He looked around the two-story foyer and decided that it had to cost a fortune to heat a place like this with propane. Propane was the only way to heat a home in Duckett County, unless you had a stove that burned firewood, corncobs, or pellets.

Brandy glided into the foyer. Her flaming red hair was cut in a short, angular style. When she had been with Todd, it had been long and wild. She was wearing black stretch pants with a fuzzy, deep-pink sweater and Barbie-style clear high heels, each of which was adorned with a pink fuzzy pom-pom. Even in heels, the top of her head barely reached Todd's shoulder. She interlocked her hands palm to palm with his and waved them around, seemingly forgetful of the fact that they were his hands and not hers.

"Todd, Todd, Todd. Ain't it awful?" Brandy's emerald eyes loomed large. "Can you believe that Duckett County was all they was talkin' about in Florence? Duckettville—Florence, it just don't mix. I was soooo discomfited. Herb thinks it's funny, but he has a warped sense of humor." Brandy let go of Todd's hands, but locked onto his elbow and pulled him into the great room, where he immediately freed himself of her grip. Herb was sitting with his back to them across the room on a burgundy and forest-green tapestry sectional sofa done in a golf motif. He was watching a golf game on a gigantic wall-mounted flat-screen TV and talking on the phone at the same time.

Brandy picked up a pillow off a club chair and threw it at Herb's head of neatly groomed, pewter-colored hair. "Don't you have a warped sense of humor, Herbert?" Not waiting for an answer, she turned back to Todd. "Oh, he's on the phone making golf plans for the week. I don't think he minded cuttin' our trip short at all. He's got golf balls for brains."

Todd glanced around the room. The voluminous two-story living room showcased a panoramic view of the Blue Ridge Mountain range. Off to the west, the sun was about to surrender to the mountains. And even though its rays reached through the wall of windows and ignited Brandy's already fiery hair, the cavernous room felt chilly.

Out of habit, Todd glanced at the glass Brandy had picked up from the bar. "Oh stop it," she said. "It's peach flavored reverse-osmosis oxygen-infused water. Keeps me pretty." Brandy turned to Herb, "Todd thinks I'm drinkin' again!" With his ear glued to the phone, Herb turned halfway around, smiled politely, and waved distractedly. Brandy turned back to Todd. "I ain't had no alcohol in over four goddamn years, and that the Lord's truth." She threw up her arms and said theatrically, "I wish somebody would give me some credit for stayin' un-shitfaced all this time!"

Todd rested an elbow on the bar. "You didn't have to come back from your trip so soon. Like I said on the phone, Molly's fine."

"Molly's fine. Molly's fine!" mocked Brandy. She rested her fists on her hips. "How can Molly be fine? If regular mind-your-own-business Tuscanites have heard about the wangdo lost in Duckett Forest, don't you think the story's goin' around Duckett Elementary?"

"She's just in kindergarten." Todd chided. Even though Brandy had begun seeing Molly sixteen months ago, Todd still wasn't used to having to share parental authority.

Brandy folded her arms and frenetically tapped one clear Barbie high heel. "I want her to stay here all week," she stated flatly. Herb abruptly ended his phone conversation, twisted his head around, and sent Brandy a look that said he had raised three daughters already.

Again, Todd was perplexed over Brandy's behavior. Her mothering needs were usually completely satisfied with the two weekend sleepovers a month that their custody agreement allowed. Any more time than that with Molly made her nervous.

Molly bounced into the room and jumped into Herb's lap. She liked Herb a lot. Todd figured it was like the way cats enjoy rubbing up against people who are allergic to them. Brandy knelt down and stretched out her arms. "Molly, sweetie, come here and give Momma a great big hug!"

"Yes, Molly, give your mum a big smootch. Off you go." Herb placed his hand on Molly's back and gave her an almost imperceptible push, all the while not taking his eyes off the TV. Molly scampered over to her mother.

"Mmmm...I love you," purred Brandy.

"I love you more." Mother and daughter hugged and rubbed their matching pixie noses together.

"Now go up to your room and see what Papa Herb and me brung you from Tuscany!"

"Yes Ma'am!" Molly tore off in the direction of the stairs.

"Wait!" yelled Todd. "You forgettin' somethin'?"

With a goofy grin on her face, Molly ran back, jumped into her father's arms and they hugged cheek to cheek. "I love you. Be good," said Todd, giving her a peck on the lips. Molly nodded emphatically. Squealing, she flew up the stairs, ever so curious about her present. Todd wondered what kind of toys they made in Tuscany for five-year-old girls.

"That poor, poor little puss—what she must be going through," moaned Brandy dramatically. She picked up her peachy water and inhaled it just the way she used to swill vodka.

Todd looked at his ex-wife quizzically and wondered what was really in that ozone confluence she was drinking. Then, Garth Brooks, the Stanton's overweight, longhaired Persian, sauntered in from somewhere and rubbed against Todd's leg. Brandy set her glass on the bar, swept up the feline, and stroked its luxurious fur. "God, I'm glad Momma ain't alive to see this…shamefulness." She pointed one of Garth's front paws at Todd. "You fix this tallywhacker mess—now."

Todd suddenly grew irritated with Brandy for treating the Elvis case like it was the most scandalous crime of the century. He put on his suckup face and said, "Yes Ma'am, right away. Anythang you say, Boss Lady."

Herb swiveled his head in their direction and said, "Now, Bran, these things take time."

"Oh, go back to your TV," retorted Brandy, dropping the cat. She shook her head dramatically, just the way she used to do when her hair was long. "I'm so beside myself these days. We've been havin' our share of chaos up here, too. Them three bears. I mean, those three bears—a momma and her half-grown cubs that have been causin' a nuisance all summer have done broke into the Collier's place this morning, and tore up the kitchen." She placed a palm on her chest. "God, that kitchen was to die for. Can you imagine? The Colliers of all people. They're richer than God!"

"I reckon the bears don't have any respect for the social order around here," said Todd as he pulled his keys out of his pocket.

Without taking his eyes off the big-screen TV, Herb snorted and said, "You've got a sense of humor, my man."

Brandy shot back, "Oh, Herb, don't encourage him!" She grabbed Todd by the arm and escorted him to the foyer. "Talk about bears. Do you recall in eleventh grade when we was neckin' in the Forest and that humongous male bear came up and tried to get in yer window?"

Todd couldn't help but smile out of one side of his mouth. "I got the rifle out of the rack but couldn't find any ammo."

"The bear started rockin' the pickup and P.J. and Tammy, who was in P.J.'s truck, saw our truck rockin'." Brandy started giggling. She was practically jumping up and down and all the while that she was gripping Todd's arm. She said, "They thought we'd broken our True Love Waits vows."

Todd's smile widened. He couldn't help but chuckle. Brandy grew quiet. "I am glad we did wait 'til we got married—to go all the way, I mean," she said chastely.

"Shoot, it was wait or go to hell. I was president of Student Athletes for Christ and you were the daughter of an Evangelical preacher." Todd's smile suddenly reversed directions. Sex was a dangerous subject between them. He pulled his arm away. "Of course, somethin' tells me you and Ol' Golf Bags didn't wait," he said sourly.

"You want me to feel guilty about Herb? Well, I don't." Brandy huffed. "You're just like Daddy."

Todd felt a stab of resentment, both for himself and for Molly and even for Brandy's father, Preacher Dodge. "Guilt is beyond your range of emotions," he snarled.

Brandy's eyes shot red-hot molten daggers at him. "Let me tell you somethin', Todd Hoyt McPherson. You left me a long time before I left you. You and your stupid books, always studying with your law school girlfriends and always checkin' up on my drinkin'."

Todd walked toward the door so Brandy wouldn't see his face turning red. Over his shoulder he said, "I hope you never quit AA, cuz you sure got a lot a' meetin's to go to before you give up your—what do they call it?" He turned back to her. "Oh yeah, your stinkin' thinkin'." He yanked open the door and stormed outside.

Brandy moved to the doorway as Todd stomped toward his pickup. She called out, "Be careful drivin' down the mountain. Your pickup might run off the road, go over the edge, hit a rock, burst into flames, and blow up before you ever hit the lake." As Todd yanked open the pickup's door, he turned to glare at Brandy. She faked a big smile, retreated inside, and slammed the door.

Todd stepped in the truck and slammed his door. When it came to Brandy, he had been on a roller coaster ever since he'd met her when they were both four-year-olds attending the Mother's Day Out program at Last Hope. He had stood entranced, gazing at the petite redhead with the upturned nose, who was sitting in the middle of the raised, wooden sandbox, gleefully throwing sand at her terrorized pint-sized peers. That recollection was Todd's first memory in life.

Brandy had been a heavy drinker and partier by the time high school rolled around. Todd, on the other hand, drank the least because he was the designated driver and protector of everyone in their jock/cheerleader click. Late one Saturday night, his pack was drinking while loitering behind the Checkered Flagg when they decided to wander over to the county courthouse where Brandy climbed up on the statue of the horse, Eulalie. Then she climbed on the statue of Stewart R. Duckett, who sat astride Eulalie. She made it to his shoulders before she fell head first, but fortunately, Todd had positioned himself just in time to catch her. It seemed like he had spent a lifetime snatching Brandy from the jaws of disaster.

Although the Todd and Brandy Show legally ended when Molly was a baby, now that his ex-wife was back in his life, she regularly attempted to draw him into her contrivances. Brandy had a fondness for drama, and Todd seemed to provide it to her in spades. He had to admit, however, that part of him still missed her. His feelings for Brandy were as twisted as the treacherous mountain roads of Emerald Lake.

* * * * *

Jasmine heated up a can of soup in the aluminum camping pot, and after eating a few bites, threw the rest away. Then she poured herself some Chardonnay into a plastic cup and headed for the bathroom, where she stuck her head into the cabinet under the sink. She reached into her father's plumber's toolkit and clumsily drew out the giant wrench. Her adjustments, however, only succeeded in making the dripping pipe drip more. Now her white T-shirt was damp.

She pulled her head out from under the sink, leaned back on the cabinet, and sipped her wine. What a roller coaster today had been! Hell, she'd been on a roller coaster ever since she arrived in Duckett County. She felt as if, like Alice, she was free-falling down a rabbit hole to a place where everyone sounded like the Jabberwocky and every event was happening anticlockwise.

Tristan laid his head in her lap and she stroked his silky fur. The only thing nice about today had been lunch with Brad Whitestone. He had proven to be an enthusiastic listener, and in his company she temporarily forgot her woes. But when the thunderstorm had passed and she returned to her office, her frustration resumed. All alone now, she listened to the unfamiliar groans and pops of the empty cabin. A cold knot began to grow in her stomach. Sensing her sadness, Tristan whined softly and thumped his tail. "At least you like it here," she told him. It was quiet now that she'd turned off her cell phone. Her friends and relatives, having seen footage of her running from the sheriff's office, had been calling nonstop. Even Stefan had had the nerve to call and leave a message. That was one call she would not return. "Too bad it hadn't been his wanger on that rock," she confided to Tristan. She fantasized that if she did return the call, she would sound witty and urbane about the whole ridiculous affair. Stefan admired women who were glib conversationalists. His new woman no doubt possessed oodles of élan.

The doorbell rang, and Jasmine remembered that Sheriff McPherson had left a message earlier saying that he had more questions. No need for her to drive all the way to Duckettville, he had explained, because he had an errand to run up at Emerald Lake. Trying to extricate herself from under the cabinet, Jasmine knocked her head. She wasn't in the mood for more probing questions from the gormless sheriff who leaked her name to the media and whose only skill seemed to be holding atrocious press conferences.

She strode up the hall, jerked open the door, and looked up. She had been in too much shock before to notice that he was quite tall. His face was nicely planed. He was dressed in faded jeans and a jeans jacket over a dark blue T-shirt. Jasmine had to admit to herself that the man before her could probably make a lot more money in a week as a male model than he made in a year as a small-time peace officer. Besides, he was too young to be in charge of those imbecilic deputies that worked for him. She placed her hands on her hips. "Well, good evening, Mr. I-Promise-to-Keep-Your-Name-Out-of-This."

Todd shrugged and looked away. "I didn't promise." He stepped into the living room, which was devoid of furnishings except for some items Jasmine had picked up at the local thrift store: a wooden-folding camp chair, two neon-pink, see-through blow-up chairs, some crates, a few butt-ugly thrift-store pillows, and a tipsy pole lamp.

Todd stuck his hands in his back pockets. "Nice blow-up chairs." He glanced at her again and then glanced away.

"I purchased them at the Walmart in the next county, in case you're interested in picking up some for yourself."

"So, I guess your furniture ain't here yet."

Do you see any furniture, numb nuts? "The last update is that the lorry carrying my worldly belongings is circling the Indianapolis 500 Speedway."

Todd looked around the room some more. He seemed to be avoiding looking at her. He said, "I bet this place, even a modest place like this, costs an arm and a leg up here. Funny how property values triple once you drive inside the gilded gates of Emerald Lake."

"Yes, well, it's called relative perceived value," said Jasmine frostily. She wanted this silly tyre-biter to get back in his redneck pickup and depart.

"Well to me, dirt is dirt." Todd removed his jacket and threw it over the camping chair. "Pardon the civvies. I feel like I've been livin' in a uniform since this whole mess started." He looked down and rubbed his neck, then suddenly latched onto her eyes. "So, you doin' okay?"

Jasmine had to admit that the man had a low-key kind of charisma with his unpredictable manner and penetrating eyes. She was beginning to feel both relaxed and self-conscious at the same time. It was an odd sensation. She said, "I'm faring as well as can be expected under the circumstances."

Todd suddenly smiled. "Do you Brits usually take your showers in your clothes?"

"I beg your pardon?" She followed his eyes down and to her horror saw how much her damp T-shirt was revealing. She gasped, quickly crossed her arms over her breasts, and muttered, "I was attempting to repair a leaky pipe in my WC."

"I'm not sure what a WC is, but show me the way."

"No, really, you don't have to. I can call the landlord," Jasmine protested hastily.

"Who knows how long he'll take to get someone up here? I grew up in a 100-year-old house, so I learned to fix damn near anything."

Jasmine led the way down the hall, and with her arms awkwardly entwined over her chest, pointed to the doorway of the bathroom. Todd inspected the pipe under the sink, which was leaking even more after Jasmine's attempts to fix it. Then he inspected Jasmine's plumber's wrench. He stood up and pulled off his T-shirt. "Excuse me, I don't wanna have to drive home in a wet shirt." Jasmine tried not to look at his nicely ripped chest. He lay down on his back and stuck his head inside the cabinet. Jasmine sat down beside him and wrapped a towel around her shoulders to hide her brazen bosom. He pulled out a box of Tampons and waved it around. From inside the cabinet he said, "Sorry, I gotta have more room."

Jasmine felt her cheeks grow warm. She quickly pitched the box into the closet. "Hand me that wrench," said Todd. "How come you have one of these on hand? Not many people do."

Jasmine picked up the cumbersome tool and placed it in his hand. "It's my father's," she replied as she eyed Todd's abs. *If I had a couple of mallets I could play him like a xylophone.*

From inside the cabinet Todd said, "He's a plumber? I don't take you as a plumber's kid. You're much too uptown."

"You don't even know me," protested Jasmine. "My father worked as a pipe fitter while earning his doctorate. Both my parents are professors at Cambridge University." *Too bad this six-pack is wasted on someone who is so not my type.*

"I thought you came from money."

"What? You're wrong there," asserted Jasmine. Does Brad Whitestone have pecs like these? "If my father wanted to make money, he would have remained a plumber." Jasmine stepped into the closet and pulled off her shirt. "All throughout their teaching careers, my parents had to scramble for funding for their respective programs. Trust me, after paying tuition for five kids to attend private schools all the way through their graduate studies, my mum and dad are not wealthy." She donned a bra and pulled a lightweight autumn-red sweater over her head.

Todd yanked the wrench one last time. "Too bad none of your clan took up plumbin.' Plumbin' is steady work." He stood up and turned the faucet on and off. Satisfied the job was done, he pulled the hand towel from its ring and dried off his chest.

"So is crime fighting." Jasmine looked away while he pulled on his shirt, hoping that he didn't notice her blush.

Todd followed Jasmine to the kitchen where she offered him a beer. He asked for coffee instead, so she started a pot in her second-hand coffeemaker. They stood in awkward silence in the cozy kitchen while it brewed. Jasmine finally asked, "Did you grow up in Duckett County, Sheriff?"

Todd rested his nicely shaped buns against the counter. "Oh hell, yes. My people go back a more than a century in these parts. And please call me Todd."

"Well then, you certainly don't fit the stereotype of the restless American."

Todd crossed his arms. "I went to Florida for spring break my senior year of high school."

"Ah, so you do have somewhat of a peripatetic spirit," Jasmine said wryly. Given that this McPherson character was little more than a well-built man with a gun, she found it all too easy to mock him.

Todd gave her a frank look. "I reckon I'm as adventurous as the situation calls for."

Jasmine thought that was an odd answer. She was relieved to see that the coffee was ready. After filling a mug for him, she picked up her plastic cup of wine and they stepped out onto the screened-in back deck, where fortunately, the last tenants had abandoned a round redwood table and four padded chairs. They settled in across from each other, with their chairs turned halfway toward the woods. Tristan padded out, collapsed at Todd's feet, and was rewarded with a vigorous scratch behind the ears.

Todd said, "Damn, this dog smells nice."

Jasmine gazed fondly at her pooch. "He's my surrogate child, I suppose."

"Then you're gonna have some nice smellin' kids someday." Jasmine started to reply when he said, "Shush! You feel it?" He sat perfectly still, except for his eyes, which roved about, taking measure of something. He reminded Jasmine of a lion, its ears swiveling and nose twitching in the breeze.

"Feel what?" she asked.

"There's a shift that always happens right as the sun goes down. Everything in the woods changes."

Jasmine grew still. "Yes, I feel it," she said dreamily. "These aren't the tallest mountains I've ever traipsed around, but there is something uniquely mystical about them."

Todd chuckled. "That's cuz they're older than dirt, which makes them very wise."

They sat quietly for another moment, and then Jasmine turned toward him. She noticed that he held his coffee mug close to his face and was steadily gazing at her over the brim. Instead of observing the woods, now he was sizing up her, and she found it disconcerting. She asked, "So what was the errand for which you drove up to Emerald Lake?"

Todd set his mug on the table. "I brought my daughter up to visit her momma. Molly's her name—my daughter, not her momma. She's five." He reached for his cell phone and produced a picture of Molly. "She's only knee-high to a grasshopper, but I'm sure she'll catch up to the other kids someday," Todd said with a slightly constricted voice.

Jasmine squinted at the photo. "She's quite lovely." It was difficult to make out the child's finer features in the twilight, though she was surprised that a man as young as this sheriff was the father of a school-age child. Then again, from what she'd seen in her short time in Duckett County, the locals married or shacked up right out of high school and popped out a couple of baby rednecks by the time they were twenty. Then they struggled to raise a family on little or no income and with no more than a slight chance of moving up in the world. In fact, to the typical inhabitant of Duckett County, upward mobility meant moving from a single-wide to a double-wide.

Jasmine laid a finger on her lips and studied Todd. "Where in the resort does your former wife live?" She wouldn't have expected that the mother of his child lived in high-toned Emerald Lake. Sheriff Todd McPherson was growing more complex by the minute.

Todd pointed across the lake. All the homes were million-dollar mansions in that area. With a composed voice he said, "She lives on the very top of that mountain over there, along with a middle-aged retired golf-bag millionaire named Herb and a fat cat called Garth Brooks."

As she sipped her wine, Jasmine studied Todd's profile and decided that he was faking an air of insouciance. His wife had obviously chosen money over sex—probably great sex, she thought wickedly. As dispassionate as Todd sounded, losing her to another man must have hurt.

Todd pulled his black memo book from his back pocket. "A few more questions have come to me."

"Sheriff, quite honestly, I've already told you and those uncouth GBI agents everything I can. I really don't understand why you bothered to come up here tonight."

"Elvis brung me," Todd mumbled.

"What?" The question was delivered on the crest of an incredulous laugh.

Todd ducked his head and studied his memo book. "Nothin'. Sometimes I blurt out stupid stuff." He made the situation worse by adding, "I've gotta bit of that Tar-ettes syndrome."

"I see—I mean hear," Jasmine said amusedly.

Todd shifted his weight, then pressed on. "Now in your statement you said you'd met with the owner of this cabin on the previous Friday, a whole week before you discovered the...ah—"

"Penis. Are we having trouble with that particular noun again?" Jasmine's lips curled up into a Cheshire-cat smile.

"Yeah, no, uh, anyways, that means you'd been in Duckett County seven days before you found the...ah—"

"Penis. Actually I arrived in Georgia on the Thursday prior to the Thursday before the fateful Friday. That would make it eight days before P.S."

"P.S.?"

"Penis Sighting."

"So you left Boston on ..."

"The Sunday before. I took my time driving down and camped in some state parks. I told you I know how to take care of myself."

"Okay, Calamity Jane, where did you stay the night you got into the area?"

"At the Wingate in Buckhead."

"Buckhead! Lordy, that's uptown. And it's way down in Atlanta, which is a long, long way from here—in more ways than one."

"That's where the owner of the cabin lives. Besides, other than the Emerald Lake Lodge, which requires reservations far in advance, there are no overnight facilities in this county."

"Except for the Restful Forest Motel," rejoined Todd as he suddenly grinned for some reason unknown to Jasmine. His grin soon faded and he returned to the business at hand. "Does the Wingate have a restaurant and bar? Did you go down there to eat? Have a drink? If so, did you hookup with anybody?"

Jasmine could see where this was going. He had no leads, so she had become the prime suspect. "See here, I've already waded through this with the GBI. Nevertheless, apparently, you think I plopped that poor pitiful penis on that rock." She heard her words turn flinty, though her tone had no effect on the sheriff's expression. He continued to watch her with those wide-open eyes that missed nothing. "In the first place," continued Jasmine, "you've jumped to the conclusion that the perpetrator was female. Maybe it was a gay lover's quarrel. Don't you have gays down here, or do you routinely dispose of them in Emerald Lake?" She knew she sounded ridiculous.

"Are you telling me you're a lesbian?"

Jasmine rolled her eyes dramatically. "Whatever the case, I don't partake in the hookup scene."

Todd held up his hands. "Hey, I have no reason to suspect you, okay?"

"You've a bloody check is what you have." Jasmine couldn't help but bristle. So what if he'd fixed her sink? She noticed that now he was back to that damn sincere expression. He was his own good, bad-cop routine. Slowly, as if she were speaking to an errant schoolboy, she said, "When I arrived in Atlanta, I checked into my hotel straightaway. I skipped dinner, indulged in a long, hot shower, and went to bed. The next morning, I picked up the key from the owner and drove up here."

Narrowing his eyes, Todd leaned toward Jasmine. He reminded her of a sadistic dentist probing for a live nerve in a particularly deep cavity.

"What about the weekend," he asked, "or the next week, when you weren't hiking all over hell and back? Did you go out honky-tonkin'? Did you meet any men?" The sincere expression surfaced again. "I'm sorry to have to ask these questions."

"Like hell you are." Jasmine leaned toward him and said conspiratorially, "There's something I must confess, Sheriff. I did go out the night before I called your office about the wanger. I went slumming at the dance hall on Route 84, the Running Cow—"

"The Buckin' Bull."

"I met a rather pleasant-looking local bloke at the bar and brought him back to my cabin, only he couldn't perform because he was quite blotto. I was so utterly furious that I sliced off his penis with my camping knife, and the next day drove out to the woods and laid it neatly on that nice, flat rock. Oh, and then I called your office." She punctuated her confession with a defiant toss of her hair.

Todd's expression was unreadable. "So where's the poor fella now?"

She stood up, walked to the railing, and with her back to him, said, "I stabbed him fifty times, and now he's down there in that body of water." She gazed down at the lake, which in the twilight looked like a photographic negative of an empty skating rink. The October fog was settling in, and along with it a wistful loneliness was creeping into Jasmine's soul. She turned to Todd. "See here. I did not venture out in the evening any day last week. I was alone in a new place and not a soul knew of whence I came. And this county grows disconcerting at night—it's darker than…" She searched for an illustrative metaphor but couldn't find one. "It's darker than dark out there." She gazed out at the motionless, ebony-on-ebony woods, then looked back at him. "There is not a situation where I would go out honky-tonking, as you so grossly put it." She gave him her best "I'm-better-than-you" look. "Besides, the hillbilly social scene is really not my idea of a good time," she added smugly.

159

Todd's expression hardened. "Well, this is turnin' out to be a great evenin' for not gettin' along with anybody, especially the female sex." He unfolded his long legs. "Maybe you should meet my ex-wife— seems like y'all got a lot in common. I'll let myself out—don't want to contrary you no more." As he stood up, his cell phone rang. He answered the phone, listened, and then said to whoever was on the other end that he would arrive on site in twenty minutes.

Out of curiosity, Jasmine followed him and stood on the front porch, listening as he talked over his two-way radio in his truck. Most of the radio communication was an unintelligible combination of code words and numbers. She did, however, hear a male voice say something about a fire. She walked over and leaned in the window on the passenger side. Todd started up the engine, but she didn't move away.

"Relax," he said brusquely, "you're no longer a person of interest."

"So you're not going to bother to dredge Emerald Lake?" asked Jasmine with a coy smile. Suddenly, she didn't want Todd to leave. She didn't want to be alone in this spooky cabin clinging to the side of a shadowy mountain on this moody October night.

Todd's expression remained unchanged. "Get inside your house. There's hungry bears on the prowl." He slammed the truck in gear.

Jasmine jumped back as he pulled out of the driveway. He drove down and around the steep curve below, and his truck was eaten by the dark. She said to the listening woods, "I hope I never see that man again!"

Chapter Seven
The Fire God Cometh

Virgil and Blaine had rotated to swing shift as of Sunday, and both were glad to be in a time zone with more action. Whatever bad was going to happen in Duckett County, it was usually going to happen during the swing and graveyard shifts. Both men agreed, though, that graveyard was a pain because staying awake all night was a form of torture even more hideous than sitting through one of Todd's safety lectures. During swing shift, however, there were enough calls to keep a deputy from being bored, and yet there was also sufficient down time to relax here and there. So, in between running down meth dealers, bagging wife beaters, and smoking out burglars, Blaine and Virgil would pull into a speed-trap hideout and catch a few winks. This usually happened at some point in every shift.

Afterward, they usually rendezvoused at the Checkered Flagg for free coffee, and when the Flagg closed, they would hit up the Bucking Bull on Duckett Mountain Highway and sip more free coffee while girl watching. Most of all, both men agreed that the best thing about swing shift was that they didn't have Baby Chief breathing down their necks, unless, that is, something heavy went down, in which case they didn't hesitate to request the dispatcher to summon him. Their definition of "bad" was loosely defined as anything that was likely to end up involving lawyers, guns, and money—in other words, anything that would result in a mountain of tedious paperwork.

Right now, both deputies were parked in identical Broncos in a speed-trap hideout on Whitey Arnold Road, just off State Road 81, next to a seldom-used, chained-off entrance to Duckett Forest. Their duties were to bag speeders traveling on the deserted road and to scare off lusty teens looking to circumvent the entry to the Forest for an opportunity to make out. Virgil's truck was facing in and Blaine's truck was facing out so that they could pass a reefer between them. They had never smoked dope on duty before, but Virgil had been feeling reckless since he's been partnered with the much younger Blaine. Virgil suggested that they needed a means to celebrate their move to swing shift. Blaine was reluctant, but Virgil, "curly-hair, yellow-bear, double-dog" dared him, so naturally Blaine felt obliged. To hide the smell of pot on his clothes, Virgil sprayed his uniform liberally with a cheap cologne called Ripped that he had purchased at the Piggly Wiggly. Satisfied that he was duly scented, he passed the bottle to Blaine, who followed suit. Their second trick was to administer eye drops to prevent reefer-induced red-eye syndrome. Lastly, they rolled down the windows to dispel the smell of marijuana from inside their Broncos. Virgil pulled a joint out of his pocket, lit it, and handed it to Blaine, who asked, "Where do you git this shit?"

"In another county. That way, I'm legal, since I didn't buy it here."

Blaine took a toke and passed the reefer back to his partner. "This is the life, ain't it, Virg? No bein' at Todd's beck and call."

"Well, they say hard work won't kill ya, but why take the chance?" Virgil snickered at his own joke, took a toke, and passed the reefer back to Blaine.

Blaine was beginning to feel the effects of the pot. He sat back and watched the shape-shifting mist on the bog on the other side of the road. "Just look at that mist comin' up over there," he said dreamily. He took a toke and handed the clip to Virgil.

Virgil looked at the bog through his side view mirror and took a quick, hard draw on the joint. When he exhaled, he said, "October's a spooky month. I was on the internet lookin' at "Eye in the Sky" today, seein' if there was somethin' about a tallywhacker conspiracy goin' on. But, I couldn't find no reports of any other run-amuck Elvises. Or is it Elvii?" He yuck-yucked and passed the joint back to Blaine.

Blaine took a toke and when he exhaled said, "You don't really believe all that conspiracy crap about the jet contrails bein' full of

162

cyanide or the UN puttin' Super glue in ex-lax, do you, Virg?"

Virgil narrowed his eyes. "The comet thang is the thang to watch. Antex says we're gonna get hit by a giant meteor the size of the Atlantic Ocean on Tuesday, November fourth, and it will be the end of the world as we know it."

Blaine passed the clip to Virgil. "Don't ya think it would be on the news if a giant comet was headin' our way?"

"Blaine, you big bubble butt, don't you ever listen to me? The aliens have put a cloakin' device on the meteor so we cain't detect it." He took a toke and handed the clip back to Blaine.

Blaine was still skeptical. "Yeah, but you've been talkin' about the end-of-the-world thang for a year now. Last spring you said that Antex said the meteor was gonna hit on April 24th and nothin' happened." Blaine took a toke and handed it back to Virgil.

"God Almighty, how many times do I have to tell you?" Virgil sometimes grew as exasperated with the stubbornness of Todd's second cousin as he did with Todd. The whole clan was a bunch of pigheaded Scotsmen— porridge wogs—through and through. Virgil said, "Antex apologized about that. It seems there was a glitch in his software, but he swears he's right this time. A lotta people—millions of people—are gettin' ready for the end of the world as we know it." He inserted the dwindling reefer in a clip and handed it to Blaine.

"I ain't heard from none of 'em besides you," retorted Blaine, while wondering if he should stock up on canned refried beans and beer, just in case. He was pretty good at surviving disasters. His father had wandered off when he was a baby and left him and his alcoholic momma in a dilapidated single-wide on his Grandma Colleen's front pasture. Then when he was twelve, his momma staggered off to Tennessee with a copper miner from Duck Town. Since Blaine didn't get on with Grandma Colleen and Grandpa Monk, he had moved in with his Great Aunt Jessie and Great Uncle H.T. But his cousins Todd and Katie were off at college during the week, which made life boring. Plus Uncle H.T.

was down with the cancer, all of which meant that Blaine was saddled with extra chores. So when he turned seventeen, he chopped the kudzu vines from the doorway of his mother's old single-wide and moved in.

Blaine thought that a single-wide was no shelter against a tornado, much less a giant meteorite. Even a medium-sized meteorite would crush a single-wide. He decided that when he got off probation and got his first pay raise, he'd move into a real house. *But if the end of the world does come, then there won't be a pay increase anyway ...*

"Hey, don't bogart that joint," complained Virgil.

Blaine handed Virgil the clip. Virgil took a toke. "I been stockin' up for months—dried beans, water, beer, weed, girly magazines—in case I wanna stroke my muskrat, you know." Virgil winked.

Tendrils of fear snaked up Blaine's spine. "Come on, Virg. You don't really believe Antex, do ya?"

Virgil shifted his gaze around the deserted area, as if he were afraid someone or something might overhear. He said in a stage whisper, "I think this whole tallywhacker-slashing job is a sign that the comet's comin'." He passed back the clip.

"Now that makes perfect Virgil Pilch sense," retorted Blaine. "You are a piece of work. How in the world could those two thangs be related?" The weed was beginning to make him feel almost as paranoid tonight as Virgil always was. He surmised that the only way to keep the fear down was to argue.

"Do I have to spell everything out to you, numb nuts?" Virgil said irritably. "The link is obvious. Antex said there'd be signs of natural disasters and such."

"I got news for ya—a man gettin' his bush-whacker hacked off ain't exactly the end of the world," said Blaine with a smirk etched on his face.

"I bet to him it was," replied Virgil. Both men snickered. "Okay, you just wait and see," said Virgil. "I'll be sittin' pretty on my mountaintop." He pointed a boney finger at Blaine. "You all, includin'

164

Baby Chief, will be wanderin' around in the rubble, blind from the radioactive dust and starvin' to death. Just don't come a-beatin' a path up to my door wantin' grub and toilet paper and such."

Blaine couldn't imagine a hoard of desperate people racing up to Virgil's place for anything, much less salvation from the end of the world. For one thing, they'd have to dodge all his irate fighting cocks, each one standing on top of its own little doghouse in the front yard. (According to Virgil, it was illegal to fight cocks in Georgia, but it wasn't illegal to raise them.) Secondly, Virgil lived on top of a sharp peak, named, appropriately, Sharp Peak. While not excessively tall, it was one of the more inhospitable mountains around. Since Virgil believed the Red Chinese were secretly beaming fertility-damaging infrared particles into the electric supply, he ran every appliance off of a generator that had been altered to run on alcohol or rooster poop, or some such thing. So, any refugees expecting to take shelter with Virgil would have to hide their booze or put up with an unpredictable supply of electricity, since Virgil's shack was off the grid. But then Virgil himself was off the grid—way off the grid.

Blaine watched the darkness in the woods deepen as a genteel dusk surrendered to a troubled evening. A waxing moon hung below a bank of eerily lit clouds, whose palette shaded from granite gray to cobalt blue. For the first time, he noticed that the pond across the road lay under a blanket of silence. It seemed to him that just last week the crickets' rhythmic rasping and the pond frogs' croaking had been so loud that Virgil and he had to shout to each other to keep the conversation going. Apparently, Sunday's fierce norther' had silenced the pond creatures until next summer.

Blaine peered up and down the road. Not one speeder had flashed by tonight. Likewise, no romantically inclined teenage couples had chosen to spark in this sector of the Forest. Blaine was getting tired of the tedium, so he did what he usually did when he was bored: he played on Virgil's paranoia. "I betcha Loretta Bobbitt's out there tonight lookin' for another victim."

"Oh, suck a fart out of my butt!" growled Virgil as he nervously swiveled his head around in search of signs of an imminent attack by a knife-wielding banshee. Blaine hyena-laughed and passed the clip to Virgil.

Virgil took the clip, drew on the joint, and passed it back. "Today when I was tryin' to get some sleep, you know what I dreamed about? Dancin' chopped-off willies—all in a chorus line—gyratin' to the tune of Oklahoma."

Blaine was holding his breath from the toke he had just taken, but the image Virgil had painted caused him to explode with laughter, which promptly turned into a paroxysm of coughing. When he could talk again, he said in a constricted voice, "We ought not'a be doin' this on duty. Besides, it ain't healthy." He passed the clip back to Virgil.

"Hell, I been smokin' weed for thirty years," Virgil retorted. "A little grass tunes up them nervous receptacles in the ol' gray matter." He tapped his narrow, deeply lined forehead. "Makes ya smarter. All that crap you hear about weed messin' with your brain is just another conspiracy concocted by that so-called disease research place in Atlanta, the CDC, which stands for the Communist Department of Collusion." He took a toke and passed the clip back to Blaine.

Blaine thought about this for a moment. He had intended to take one last toke, but instead opened the clip and the reefer fell on the asphalt between the two Broncos. "You mean before you started smokin' dope, you were even more stupider?" he asked.

Before Virgil could answer, his radio crackled to life. It was Scratch, the swing shift 911 operator, dispatching them to investigate a fire at the Meriwether homestead.

* * * * *

As Todd approached the cutoff that eventually led to the Meriwether's property, he could see an ominous orange glow above the treetops to the north. A fire truck was parked along the side of the road, but the only person in it was the driver, Butch Foxworthy. The remaining firemen had hopped rides with Virgil and Blaine, who had beat Todd to the scene. Todd waved to Butch, headed in, and abused his Chevy truck mercilessly on the deeply rutted dirt road. Visiting Meriwether Holler involved fording two streams (nicknamed Bubba and Sissy), climbing steep embankments, and otherwise crossing terrain so rough it was barely passable with even the toughest of off-road vehicles. And to make matters worse, the afternoon thunderstorm had created some seemingly bottomless mud holes along the trail, which is why nobody lived back here—except Alex and Sunbeam Meriwether. For days after bad weather, if they wanted to get out of the hollow, Alex had to fire up one of his old army trucks with an attached winch. He would wrap the cable around a stout oak at the top of the embankment and pull the jeep up to the dirt road.

Todd lurched down the embankment and drove under the open high gate from which a simple wooden sign that read "Happy Hippie Holler" dangled by a single tether. He could see that the entire house was engulfed in towering flames that were dancing on the rooftop and licking at low, dark-gray galloping clouds—the kind of clouds Todd's mother called ghost riders.

Six defeated firemen stood in a ragged line and watched the conflagration. One fire jockey was zig-zagging around the yard in pursuit of a grunting three-hundred-pound pig. Another one was attempting to round up Alex's collection of prized narcoleptic goats, but their random stop, drop, and snooze antics made the job more chaotic.

A slack-jawed Virgil Pilch stood riveted to a spot in front of the house. Todd approached him and noticed that Virgil was exuding the scent of a French poodle fresh out of Polly's Pet Palace. Todd waved his hand in front of the old deputy's face, but received no reaction. Virgil was oblivious to everything, including the panicked chickens and ducks that were scurrying helter-skelter around and between his legs. Vince

Verona was the only one who appeared to be accomplishing anything, as he busily captured the scene with his Nikon, moving deftly through the befuddled poultry and stepping over snoring goats.

The prototypes of Alex Meriwether's inventions were scattered everywhere, giving the property the appearance of a sci-fi junkyard. Twenty old jeeps and army trucks stood off to the left side of the house. On the opposite side, Sunbeam Meriwether was seated in a peeling, fluted, fifties-style green metal chair. She was facing away from the fire and looking toward the woods. Blaine was pulling on her skinny arm in an attempt to dislodge her from the chair while she fussed and slapped at him with her free hand. Todd tried Alex's cell phone and heard one of his trademark messages: "If we aren't here, does that mean we're somewhere?"

Todd walked with trepidation toward the blaze and tapped Vince on the shoulder, startling him. Vince apparently hadn't heard Todd's arrival over the amplified snap, crackle, and pop of the conflagration. Todd could feel the hot blast on his face. "I hate fires!" he shouted. He had had nightmares about fires ever since he'd accidentally burned down the barn when he was five while playing with matches near the hay. The entrancing flames had paralyzed him, but his father had run in, wrapped him in a wet blanket, and carried him out to safety.

"I hate fires!" Todd shouted again. He grabbed Vince's arm, moved him a few yards back, and then headed toward Sunbeam. Vince called after him. Todd turned around and Vince pointed to the deep front porch where a completely blackened body was lying on the sofa. It looked like it had been wrapped in cloth, but now the fabric was turning into black flakes that were separating and being drawn upwards by the draft created by the intense heat. Incandescent blue flames were performing a victory dance of death along the length of the corpse, while undulating amber flames cradled the scene. Todd fell to one knee and stuffed his fist in his mouth. His stomach roiled. "Alex. Oh, Alex," he said. He pulled himself together and stood on shaky legs.

Vince held up his camera. "I hate to say it right now, but this could be a Pulitzer Prize-winning photo."

Todd shook his head slowly. "You are a real hard case, Vincent. I can't figure out why I almost like you."

Todd hated to think it, but he wished that the body was someone else, and not his friend Alex. The odds were, however, that it was him. Todd peered into the dark woods surrounding the compound, hoping against hope that Alex-the-Hippie-Sorcerer would magically appear in the knee-high fog, which driven by the heat, was moving speedily across the yard. The flames' dancing shadows penetrated deep into the woods and turned the trees into an angry hoard struggling to pull up their roots in order to advance menacingly on the careless humans who had dared to taunt The Fire God. Todd thought that a rousing, dramatic classical music score like one of those on the old-timey Disney cartoons would complete the scenario. Then maybe Alex-the-Hippie-Sorcerer really would show up.

Todd walked over to Sunbeam, where an exasperated Blaine sputtered, "I've worked up a sweat tryin' to get her outta this chair."

Todd pulled him aside. "Was everything alright when you checked on them Saturday night?"

Blaine shrugged his shoulders. "Sure, they was fine."

Todd studied the probie. Something wasn't right about him. He smelled of too much cologne. This scent combined with Blaine's usual *eau de gym locker* threatened to make Todd queasy again. He ordered, "Go put some—"

"Crime tape around the scene," muttered Blaine. "I wish I could get a different task for once, Cuz," he said over his shoulder as he trudged toward the truck.

"And don't call me cousin on duty," Todd shot back. He grabbed the other green metal lawn chair and placed it in front of Sunbeam. Even this far away from the fire, the chair was warm to his touch. He sat down and leaned forward on his elbows so he could get a good look at Mrs.

Meriwether. "You okay, Sunbeam?"

She bobbed and weaved her head. "Move, Fearless, you're blocking my view. Alex will be home soon," she said in her faint New England inflection. Sunbeam was maybe fifty-five, but years of mental illness and homesteading in a remote hollow next door to a wilderness had aged her to where she looked a decade older. Her thin face was deeply lined and her body held on to little flesh. Her stringy, long, gray hair was filthy. She was wearing a dirty white gown, a tattered pink terry-cloth bathrobe, and rubber flip-flops on her feet. Todd kept his chair close to her, but moved it at an angle so she could see the woods. Vince appeared and prepared to take a photo of Sunbeam, but Todd gave him a look. He lowered his camera and stood next to Blaine, who had returned and was ever so slowly unrolling the crime-scene tape. Both men knew that Todd's interview of Sunbeam promised to be entertaining.

"I love you Alex!" Sunbeam suddenly called out and blew a kiss toward Duckett Forest.

"Oh, is Alex here now? Should I say 'Hey' to him?" asked Todd as he pretended to watch the woods, when in reality he was watching her carefully.

Sunbeam gave him a withering look. "McPherson, are you a complete imbecile? Of course Alex isn't here. Not yet."

Todd was totally confused now. "Sunbeam, are you expectin' Alex to walk out of the Forest?"

Exasperated, Sunbeam sighed loudly. "Mon Dieu! Of course I am!"

Just then, one of Alex's prized goats ran up to them. His silly goat-ears flapped as he quickly swiveled his head to study Sunbeam with his peculiar alien eyes. Then he hastily swiveled his head to peer at Todd. Suddenly, he fainted dead away and lay at their feet, stiff as a corpse with all four legs extended straight out. Sunbeam and Todd watched him idly, each lost in their own thoughts. After ten seconds, the goat raised his head, bleated, jumped up, and ran off.

Todd laid a hand on Sunbeam's arm. "Why did Alex go off into the Forest?"

She rolled her eyes. "He didn't go off into the Forest, you dope. He's back there on the porch burnt to a crisp." Abruptly, she reached out and slapped Todd across the face. Blaine dropped his tape, and he and Vince simultaneously moved towards her, but Todd waved them off. Vince returned to the front yard and began to take more photos, but Blaine remained rooted in his spot a yard behind Sunbeam's chair.

"Now why'd you go and slap me?" asked Todd, rubbing his cheekbone.

"Because you are one ridiculous twit, McPherson! Reee-dick-cue-lous! Now leave me be, I have to concentrate. The arch-angel said I have to concentrate."

Sunbeam leaned forward and focused again on the edge of the woods, where the malevolent trees were amassing their armies. Then she sat up and stared intently at one spot. After a few seconds she snorted, then muttered, "Just a shadow." She wrapped her tattered robe tighter around her thin body and resumed staring into the woods.

Once again, Todd attempted to wade into the nutty hippie's convoluted mind. "Excuse me, Sunbeam. I don't have much experience with arch-angels. Could you please tell me what else it said to you?"

Sunbeam pursed her thin, wrinkled lips. "Man, you are one dumb potty-head. He's not an it. He's a he. And he said what all arch-angels say: 'If a female cuts off the organ of regeneration of her beloved and lays it out nicely in a secret place in the enchanted woods, then her beloved will regenerate and return to her in three days.' The arch-angel is a Shambala priest, you know. Didn't you ever watch Kung Fu? Best TV show ever. Kung Fu knows magic and he is a chum of the arch-angel. Alex will come striding out of those woods any minute. Now shut up so I can concentrate."

Todd sat back and rubbed his chin. Then he leaned over and spoke softly in Sunbeam's ear. "Did you burn down the house, Sunbeam?"

171

"Of course I burned down the house! The arch-angel and I did it together. Grasshopper, don't you know anything? Hellooo?" She knocked on Todd's forehead. "You have to give your beloved a Viking funeral first or else the spell won't work. The arch-angel and Kung Fu told me that."

Todd nodded solemnly. "Oh, I see. And can you tell me just where you put the…ah…organ of regeneration?"

"Of course not! That is a secret to be held tightly in my bosom." She folded her skeletal arms over her caved-in chest. "If I talk, all is lost—you should know these things, being in the lost-and-found business and all."

Todd stood and walked over to Virgil, who was still standing in the same spot, still slack-jawed, and still utterly mesmerized by the triumphant flames. Todd grabbed his arm, pulled him over to Sunbeam, and sat him down in the chair he had just vacated. Without a word, Virgil craned his neck around and stared back at the fire. Todd placed a hand on top of Virgil's head and turned it towards Sunbeam, then ordered him to watch her.

Sunbeam patted the deputy on the arm. "Hello, Virg," she said cheerfully. "You can help me watch the woods."

Virgil craned his head to gaze back at the blaze. "Watch the woods for what?" he asked absently.

Todd returned to the front yard and was surprised by the site of Mayor Sonny Davis's old Land Rover lurching down the embankment. The mayor pried himself out of the SUV, followed by his wife, Alice, and three mud-covered EMT technicians, who informed Todd that their EMS unit was stranded in the mud back at Bubba's Creek. At that moment, with loud cracking pops and groaning protestations, the blackened timbers of the Meriwether home surrendered to The Fire God. Everyone ducked reflexively and covered their heads. The frustrated firemen, including the one that had by now given up on the animal round-up, sat on the embankment and watched the flames devour the remains of the Meriwether abode. The on-and-off drizzle powered up to a light rain, as if the Lord's sprinkler system had belatedly switched on.

Todd strode toward the barn, desperately hoping that Alex was in there. Perhaps Alex had been tied up by an intruder, and Sunbeam had somehow subdued said intruder and set him on fire on the porch. Todd knew it was a ridiculous scenario. Sonny followed Todd, peppering him with questions. Todd mostly ignored Sonny as he checked the barn then circled the compound. Alice, in a see-through, hot-pink, plastic raincoat thrown over a flowery muumuu, followed her tottering husband on unsteady tiptoes as she struggled to hold a University of Georgia Bulldog's red-and-white striped umbrella over his head. The pig tagged along and the goat followed the pig so that the obese man, the tall, thin woman, and the curious animals formed a comical little parade.

The paramedics paced back and forth between Sunbeam and the police radio, conversing with the emergency-room resident at Blue Ridge Regional Hospital. The doctor there was hesitant to prescribe a sedative sight unseen to a psychotic woman. In addition, neither the paramedics nor Todd could persuade Sunbeam to give up her vigil. Finally, it was Virgil who simply asked her if she'd take a ride with him, because after all, a watched pot never boils. She agreed, so he stood up and offered his elbow, which she took amiably. Todd was dumbfounded, and a little irritated. He had applied his usually successful approach at extracting cooperation from a female, and had been soundly rebuffed. In fact, if he included his performances with Brandy and Jasmine, he had batted zero-for-three tonight. And before that, Molly had witnessed him getting sacked in the backfield by the Davis cousins. So actually he was zip-for-four when it came to extracting cooperation from anybody tonight.

Virgil helped Sunbeam into the backseat of his Bronco, and then climbed into the driver's seat. Sensing Virgil wasn't quite right, Todd pulled Virgil out of the front seat and shoved him in the backseat with Sunbeam. Todd sat behind the wheel and cranked the engine. Just as he was about to pull out, the mayor stepped in front of the Bronco and then tottered around to the driver's side. "Sorry, Sonny," Todd said, "we gotta carry Sunbeam to the hospital."

Sonny fastened two ham-hock fists over the open window. "That's what the EMTs are fer. You gotta—"

"Gotta run," interjected Todd as he stepped on the accelerator.

When he reached Sissy's Creek, Todd came across the GBI crime-lab van stuck in the mud. The van had forded Bubba's Creek—and thus made it past the EMS truck—but it had been captured by the ever-conniving Sissy's Creek. Harwood Slaughter's mud-caked assistants were attempting to push the van out of the muck, while Slaughter sat behind the wheel cursing and gunning the engine, an act which slung even more mud onto his protégés.

Todd shouted, "Go back, Harwood! There's nothin' you can do—the site is too hot." He hit the gas, and Virgil's Bronco spewed mud inside the driver's side of Slaughter's van. Glancing back into the rear-view mirror, the last body part Todd saw that night was Special Agent Harwood Slaughter's middle finger sticking out of the window.

* * * * *

On the way to the hospital, Todd racked his brain to remember everything he knew about Alex and Sunbeam Meriwether. Alex made—or had made—a good living keeping the computers in Duckett County running. In his spare time, he whiled away the hours at the Checkered Flagg, upending longnecks and hustling at the pool table. He carried a leather string in his pocket that he used to secure his shoulder-length, snow-white hair while he played. Tied back, his hair looked a little neater, but in Todd's estimation, Alex could have stood to pay a visit to Sike's Barber/Gun Repair Shop, if only to get his scruffy beard professionally trimmed.

As if to make up for his poor grooming, Alex was great company. He was widely read and loved to swap ideas on just about any topic, and he was the only one that could carry on a conversation with Virgil about the current hot conspiracy theories. Todd enjoyed hearing about Alex's many wacky experiences in his sixty-nine years. Born and raised in Oakland, California, he came into a small trust fund as a young man in the late-1950s. He then fell into "disuse," as he liked to put it, getting involved with the beatnik scene and motorcycling around the country while smoking acres of weed. When the sixties rolled around, Alex rolled around in them, drifting from commune to commune, political cause to political cause, and drug scene to drug scene.

He met Sunbeam at Woodstock. She was an eighteen-year-old freshman from a private New England college, and Alex immediately fell for her winsome personality and lithe body. Sunbeam hooked up with him and they tripped through the seventies together. When she was in her late-twenties, Sunbeam experienced a psychotic break and was diagnosed with schizophrenia. From the day she became ill, Alex made taking care of her his life's purpose. Twenty years ago, he bought land adjacent to Duckett Forest and designed and built an ingenious off-the-grid passive solar home.

Todd liked Alex immensely, though he thought the brilliant hippie was a little off. But, Alex's eccentricities were understandable, considering all the illegal drugs he consumed, as well as a number of Sunbeam's legal drugs that he had probably sampled. Still, Alex was the rock of Gibraltar compared to Sunbeam.

As Todd had witnessed tonight, Sunbeam's demeanor would change dramatically when she was off her meds. Even on her meds, she said and did some very strange things, but basically, she functioned adequately within the confines of the small, insular society of Duckett County. Indeed, her childlike sweetness and whimsical ways made her a popular figure. However, she periodically discontinued her sanity pills because she grew irritated with the lethargy that accompanied them. Unfortunately, when she was un-medicated, she became the village crazy person.

Where's Elvis?

By the time they arrived at the hospital, Sunbeam's fragile grip on reality had further deteriorated. She now believed she was in a giant bowl and the emergency room staff was about to apply a huge electric mixer to whip up a Sunbeam-Jesus-Paul McCartney soufflé. The ER resident was forced to order restraints because of his new patient's growing agitation.

The intake clerk wanted to know Sunbeam's legal name, Social Security number, and the name of her psychiatrist. It was information that Todd didn't have. The resident physician stated flatly that he would not treat Sunbeam without knowing her medical history. Todd called Dr. Mahmondi, but Gorov said he had never seen Sunbeam as a patient and knew nothing about her case. Alex had been secretive about certain things, one of them being his and Sunbeam's health.

Sunbeam's ranting finally exhausted the patience of the sleep-deprived resident and he administered a shot of a powerful sedative. Soon, the peacefully slumbering patient was loaded into the ambulance for a ride to Grady Hospital, which was located in downtown Atlanta. Todd had objected to sending her to all the way to Grady because it was a two-and-a-half-hour drive from Duckett County, but the resident said there was no facility in the mountains that could and would accommodate a psychotic Jane Doe. For all intents and purposes, Sunbeam Meriwether was now a ward of the state.

Todd and Virgil watched the ambulance pull out, and then they headed to the parking lot. When they reached the truck, Todd abruptly grabbed Virgil by the lapels and roughly shoved him up against the hard metal of the Bronco. Virgil's knees buckled. Todd yanked him up, got in his face, and snarled, "If you ever smoke dope on my watch again I will personally Lorena Bobbitt you. And I guarantee you nobody will ever find your Elvis because I'll grind it up and feed it to the catfish in my pond! Then I'll throw you in the slammer for so long you'll forget you ever had a buddy named Elvis in the first place cuz your cellmates will be too busy corn-holing you until your tiny little balls fall off! You got that?" Todd slammed Virgil against the Bronco again to punctuate his threat. Virgil's Adam's apple bobbed spastically up and down, and the only sound he made was a pathetic whimper as he slid down the side of the truck.

Chapter Eight
Tuesday Morning: Nailing Jell-O to the Wall

It was still dark when Todd's cell phone jarred him awake. He forced one eye open and saw that the clock said 5 a.m. A feeling of déjà vu crept over him as he fumbled for the phone.

"Hello, Sheriff McPherson? This is Ansley Mason from SNN news. What can you tell me about the fire at the Meriwether homestead last night?" Before Todd could open his mouth, Ansley followed up with, "Was the body on the porch indeed that of Mr. Alex Meriwether?"

"It's too soon to ascertain that," snapped Todd. *How did this vulture get my cell phone number?*

"Is it true," asked Ansley, "that his mentally ill wife claims that she cut off her husband's penis, hid it in Duckett Forest, and then burned down the house?"

Todd growled and clicked off, resisting the urge to flush the phone down the toilet.

* * * * *

At 6:30 a.m., Jasmine called security, then drove from her cabin to meet the guard in the parking lot at the POA lodge. The guard was hesitant about letting her into the building, so she gave him a song and dance about Valinda forgetting to give her a key yesterday, and threw in a little eyelash-batting and hair-tossing until he relented.

Once inside, Jasmine walked directly to the file cabinet in the Glen Baker's office and spent the next hour pouring over accounting documents and taking notes. She found a plastic container stuffed with nearly hundreds of cancelled checks dating from the period of time

178

between seven to three years ago, when the bank presumably stopped including checks in their monthly statements. Seven years struck a chord. Then she remembered that was when Les Davis was promoted to the job of acting general manager. She grabbed a handful and began to lay them out numerically. None of the checks had two signatures, as was generally required for amounts over $400. In the bottom right-hand corner, each check had only Les's tidy school insignia.

Jasmine returned to the file cabinet and began to pull invoices. She noticed that Les stuck with the same contractors year after year, especially for big-ticket projects. For instance, there were numerous invoices from a F.L. Restaurant Supply that stocked the golf club's bar. (Since the amenities at Emerald Lake were privately owned, the Liquor-by-the-Drink controversy didn't apply.) Jasmine noted that, although F.L.'s invoices were marked paid, no check numbers had been referenced on the invoices. Similarly, there were numerous invoices from a company named Bilkey Resurfacing and Road Repair. Mr. Bilkey had been paid $194,000 to resurface the roads in Emerald Lake the year before, but Jasmine found no evidence that the job had ever been bid out, or that any independent inspections were performed. She wondered if, like the mayor, Mr. F.L. and Mr. Bilkey were related to Les Davis.

Jasmine knew that with majority control of the POA board, Brad Whitestone had the power to fire or retire Les. She was not sure she bought Brad's excuse that he had been too busy developing Emerald Lake to deal with Les. Maybe he hadn't taken the issue head-on because he felt too inexperienced to go up against the old guard, who valued Les as their personal servant. Perhaps Brad was waiting for a CFO foolish enough to run the gamut for him, and if the CFO's move against Les failed, said CFO could be sacrificed. *That would be me.*

From what she gathered, Les did keep things running. Roads were kept in reasonably good repair, considering that the weather was always conspiring against them. Tennis courts were regularly resurfaced.

Where's Elvis?

Liquor flowed at the golf clubhouse. Perhaps nobody cared that much if the POA functioned in a less-than-professional manner as long the good times kept rolling. The problem, however, with tolerating minor financial sloppiness was that over time it led to major financial sloppiness, and major sloppiness provided the perfect environment for embezzlement. In short, negligence to this degree was ... criminal. Jasmine realized that she was dealing with a situation above her level of professional experience.

She looked over at the shelves behind Glen's desk and frowned at the chaotic jumble of papers, technical manuals, and office supplies. Amongst them, a number of plastic actions figures were battling for control of the rugged terrain. She spotted a plain cardboard box on a shelf in the middle of a large, messy collection of plastic Star Wars figures. Carrying the box to her desk, she rummaged through it and found an audit from three years earlier. The cover letter gave the auditor's name and address, which was in Duckettville. Is he yet another one from the Davis clan? Looking the report over, she found that only a bare minimum required inspection of the books had been performed. When she picked up the flimsy cardboard box to return it to the shelf, the bottom fell open and the contents scattered on the floor. Groaning loudly, she set the box back on her desk and turned it upside down in order to tape the bottom. There, taped to the inside of one flap, was an envelope.

Jasmine's heart began to hammer out a warning message. Yet, the building was still and quiet, as if the very walls were watching to see what she would do next. Suddenly the humongous furnace rattled on and, startled, Jasmine cried out. She clapped her hand over her mouth, hoping that no one else had entered the admin office to begin their workday. She glanced at her watch. Seven-fifty. She had only ten minutes to get this material back in the accountant's office before anyone else arrived. Why was she afraid of being caught doing her job? She quickly opened the envelope and found that it contained only one item: a key. It looked like a key to a file cabinet. She pocketed it and taped up the bottom of the box.

After hastily refilling it, she carried it back to Glen's office. She picked her way through his junk and placed it back on the shelf. She poked around the disordered room, wishing she could get her hands on the incompetent Mr. Baker. She wondered if he had applied for the job of CFO, was incensed that he hadn't been chosen, and had deliberately messed with the files before exiting stage right. She sat in Glen's chair and studied the black computer screen. Turning on the computer, she stared at the password screen. She tried Glen's first name, then his last name, and then both names, none of which proved to be the magic mantra. She typed "accountant" and then "idiot," both without success. She let out a frustrated, "Arrrrgh," then took a deep breath, stepped out of Glen's office, and paced the hall. She remembered seeing a file cabinet in Les's office. Stopping in front of his door, she reached out and tried the knob. It was not locked. She had opened the door only few inches when just like a bomb going off, Les burst through the entry door, followed by Cheryl. Jasmine quickly closed the door and wheeled around.

"Hey, caught ya!" called out Les as he pointed at her.

Jasmine's knees threatened to fold, but she noticed that Les was grinning. He appeared to be one of those male employers that liked to tease his female subordinates. Cheryl turned on the television as Valinda and Alice hurried in. They immediately gathered around the TV, hoping to hear the details about last night's fire. Cheryl switched the channels back and forth between SNN and the other twenty-four-hour news programs. Jasmine hadn't heard about Duckett County's latest disaster, and thought they were looking for another installment of the hijacked-penis story. Since she had no desire to listen to any such news, she returned to her office, sat at her desk, and unloaded her briefcase. In a few minutes, Les leaned against the doorframe. He held a cup of coffee in one hand and an unlit cigar in the other.

Jasmine said, "Tell me that you're not going to smoke that in here—"

"Ha, the Sopranos would string me up. This little baby is for later," Les said genially. "I'm tryin' to quit cigarettes." He sniffed the cigar, stowed it in his breast pocket, and patted the pocket gently. "Sometimes, I just like to pull it out and play with it."

Jasmine shot him a questioning look. She cleared her throat. "We need to have a meeting with the clerks immediately. With what I've seen of the financial records, I don't expect that Mr. Baker will ever return from Baja."

"Just as well. Glen weren't much of a bean counter—couldn't add and subtract worth his left leg. But he's a good boy, and a lot of fun to be around." He suddenly looked disappointed. Jasmine guessed that he didn't care much for her sour mood.

"Please don't tell me that Glen is your cousin."

Les snorted. "Don't you know by now that everbody in Duckett County is related? That's why we're all a little tetched."

"Tetched?"

"Touched, darlin'." Les tapped his temple. "See, the reason we're all related is, we don't got a lot of population cuz half the county's made up of the Duckett Wildlife Management Area. We just call it Duckett Forest. And we're tetched because that's what happens when your DNAs don't come from a biggie-sized gene pool. Instead, we get our DNA from a kiddie blow-up wader."

"Have you even tried to contact Glen?"

"No, but I got a postcard from him. He said that he's off the grid— no cell phone—nothin', so it's no use tryin' to get ahold of him. He wrote that he's movin' all around and campin' out under the stars. Got a senorita ridin' on the back of his hog." Les pulled out his cigar and smelled it. From his expression, Jasmine guessed that he was picturing himself Harley-surfing up and down Baja alongside Glen. Les returned his attention to the present and stowed the cigar. "Like I said, Glen's a good kid. I'm sure he didn't do nothin' wrong on purpose. His daddy's a buddy of mine. He saved my youngest boy, Scratch, from drownin' in the river wonst. He had to creel Scratch out from under a submerged log—"

"Creel?"

"Pry—he pried him out. You gotta learn the way the old folks talk if'n you wanna get along in Duckett County, darlin'. Anyways, it was real chancy thar for a while—for both Scratch and Glen's daddy." For a few beats, Les wore a solemn expression on his open face, but then he shrugged and became his happy-go-lucky self again. "By the way, besides bein' the swing shift dispatcher for the sheriff's office, my youngest boy, Scratch, is internin' with my brother and mayor, Sonny, at the Moonshine Runners Gently Used Autos. So if you ever need a new used car, Scratch can get you a deal. And if you ever need any surveyin' done, my middle boy, Conner, will be glad of it."

Jasmine frowned. "So, the fact that Glen's father saved your son's life qualified Glen for the job of accountant?"

Les's look said, 'Well, duh.'

"I think Glen Baker may have embezzled money from the POA."

Before Les could answer, Cheryl yelled down the hall that Duckett County was once again on SNN.

"Showtime," said Les as he jerked his head in the direction of the reception area. He chugged down the hall and joined Valinda and Alice around the TV, while Jasmine followed reluctantly.

On the screen, a petite blonde reporter was standing by, pressing on her earpiece, and waiting for her cue. The blackened ruins of the Meriwether dwelling could be seen in the background. She received her cue and said, "Behind me are what is left of a devastating fire that took place last night at a remote homestead next to the Duckett County Wildlife Management Area. This event makes for the second time in less than a week that a bizarre tragedy has struck this remote North Georgia county. Sheriff Todd McPherson held a short on-site press briefing early this morning for those reporters who managed to slog through the muddy, rough backwoods terrain in order to cover the story." In her most authoritative voice, Ansley added, "Naturally, I was one of those resourceful adventurers." She displayed a smug face, then returned to the story. "The sheriff stated that the victim of the fire was most likely Alexander P. Meriwether, owner of the property."

"Sheriff McPherson went on to state that Alexander Meriwether was an eccentric inventor and computer repairman who lived here with his common-law wife, known by everybody as Sunbeam. He stated that Sunbeam suffers from schizophrenia and is in protective custody at Grady Hospital in Atlanta. He pleaded for her regular psychiatrist to step forward so that she can be treated properly. The sheriff brushed off the rumors that this tragedy has anything to do with the penis found on a nearby rock, and its subsequent disappearance."

"Excuse me, Ansley," broke in a pleasant-faced African-American anchorman as the TV switched to a split screen. "We are getting word that the mayor of Duckettville is leaving his home. As you just stated, the sheriff has refused to comment on a possible link to the Elvis case but perhaps the mayor can clarify the situation." The TV screen switched to Sonny Davis's front yard.

"That's my front yard," said Alice.

On the screen, Sonny was stuffing his gelatinous body into an oversized SUV as a semicircle of reporters fired questions at him. Rather than being perturbed, Sonny was beaming. He closed the door, rested an elbow on the open window and said, "Yes, two weird events in less than a week are very unusual for our sleepy lil ol' co-munity; and yes, the two events are related. The fire is a major dee-velopment in the case of the missin'…pee finger." Sonny held up his index finger, which for some reason was bent ninety degrees at the first joint. "We're gonna have us a press conference in a couple of hours, so stay tuned." With that he gave the camera a smart salute and backed out of his driveway.

"Did he just call Elvis a pee finger?" asked Cheryl.

"Well that's what we called it when our boys was little," retorted Alice.

Valinda piped up. "I don't see why they went to Sonny for a statement about somethin' that happened up by Duckett Forest. He's just the mayor of Duckettville, not king of the county. They shoulda talked to my husband. After all, Phil's a county commissioner."

Alice said, "Oh don't get biggity, Valinda. Sonny is the COO of the county too. Plus, the press came to Sonny cuz him and me was thar. You see, after Jasmine found the pee finger, Sonny told Scratch to contact him if the sheriff's department got any more bizarre calls, since Todd sure ain't keepin' him informed. So, we hightailed it out thar after Scratch called us."

"That's my boy," interjected Les. "He's learnin' how thangs work."

Cheryl wrinkled up her petite nose and drew near Jasmine. "What did Alex's body look like? Was it all gooey?"

"Not to change the subject," said Jasmine, "but I very much need to meet with all of you ASAP."

The phone rang and Cheryl answered. When she hung up she said, "Les, that was John Collier. The bars is back."

Jasmine looked at Les. "Bars ... Bears?"

"That's what I said," said Cheryl. "They's three of 'em sniffin' around their front door. And the workers who are s'posed to be fixin' up their messed-up kitchen are scared shitless."

Les set down his coffee mug and threw on his windbreaker. "Guess I better run up thar and shoo 'em off again."

"Can't security do that?" asked Jasmine. "We really must address some of these bloody financial issues."

"But it's the Colliers," replied Les, "Anyway, I'll be back soon. If I just go wave my arms around, the big lugs run off—usually run off. Even the bars know who is general manager of this place. Wish me luck, Sopranos," he called out as he slipped out the door.

"I don't see why he couldn't let security handle it," complained

Jasmine.

Alice rolled her eyes. "Because, it's the Colliers."

Jasmine frowned. That's exactly the way the incompetent do their jobs. Instead of planning and delegating, they spend their time scratching backs and culling favors. As she mulled over these thoughts, the Sopranos continued speculating about the fire. She realized this was the fire that the sheriff had headed off to last night. She thought that if that dotty hippie lady was indeed the one who left the penis on that rock, then at least the story would be concluded and she could put the whole incident behind her.

Jasmine turned her attention to the task at hand. She asked Cheryl to turn off the TV and called an impromptu meeting. Alice and Valinda settled in at their desks, and Cheryl made herself at home on top of hers. Jasmine stood where they could all see her and said, "First of all, can any of you enlighten me as to why the financial files are in such a ghastly condition? They are completely out of order, and dozens of statements aren't even filed; instead, they were just thrown in drawers or boxes."

Alice said, "Oh, that was Glen's doin'. He got real sloppy toward the end, and we wasn't allowed to touch any of his accountin' files."

Valinda added, "I think maybe he sabotaged those files on purpose, though I don't know why."

"Why is the operable interrogative," said Jasmine. "Does anyone know the password to his computer?" All three shook their heads.

Cheryl said, "We each have our little bookkeepin' programs that he made up. We'd turn them in wonst a month and he would incorporate what we done into the big picture."

Jasmine gasped. She couldn't believe Glen had succeeded in locking everyone out of the POA's accounting program. She decided that since she had the Sopranos attention, it was best to move on for now. "Our challenge is that we don't currently have a dedicated bookkeeping staff. In fact, none of you has those duties written in your job descriptions."

"Thangs are kinda catch-as-catch can 'round here," muttered Valinda, who was looking resentful over the possibility that new job duties would be piled on her.

"Such casualness could very well lead to fraud," said Jasmine bluntly.

Cheryl drew back. "You mean you don't trust us?"

"What I mean is… The POA has been entrusted to manage the fourteen million dollars it receives annually. The monthly dues are mandatory, and they're not inconsequential—not even to an affluent household—and not every resident up here is wealthy. We owe the property owners the best stewardship of their money that we can offer, and—"

"Just what you gettin' at, Missy?" sniffed Alice.

"My name is not Missy," Jasmine snapped. "As I was saying, our mission is a gravely important one, and we—"

"Maybe her name's Preachy," added the usually taciturn Valinda. Cheryl and Alice snickered.

Jasmine studied the recalcitrant trio. Valinda was inspecting her nails and Alice was gazing out the window, while Cheryl was clearly sulking. Jasmine attempted to appear more positive. "Okay, now, who accepts the mail?"

"I do," said Cheryl offhandedly as she inspected the ends of her hair for the presence of split-ends.

"Who records the receivables?"

"Me do," said Cheryl. Looking cross-eyed, she slowly split a splayed end of a hair.

Jasmine frowned. Wrong answer. "Who deposits the receivables in the bank?"

"Yo," said Cheryl, turning her attention to her nails.

"You will no longer be taking in the mail, recording receivables, and making bank deposits. You need to just take in the mail." Jasmine took in a big breath and exhaled deeply. "Now, who balances the bank statements?"

"I ain't never been called untrustworthy," pouted Cheryl, her catlike eyes narrowing in her fleshy face.

Jasmine said forthrightly, "It's not that I don't trust you. This is for your protection also—for all of you."

"I didn't never think I needed no protection," countered Cheryl.

Jasmine looked at the ceiling and sighed audibly. "That statement has so many double-negatives, I can't begin to unwind it. Now, back to the subject. Who balances the bank statements?"

Alice piped up. "I used to do it, but it got to where I couldn't figure out Glen's complicated program, so Cheryl volunteered to—"

"That's right," said Cheryl. "I do 'em—when I can get around to it."

"When you can get around to it!" blurted Jasmine. "Statements need to be balanced promptly."

Cheryl huffed, "Well, it's kind of tough when the phone's a-ringin' and residents are a-sashayin' in and out wantin' to know where they are on the boat slip waitin' list, or some such thing."

Jasmine stated, "You should not be balancing statements in the first place. The same person should not be taking in mail, recording receivables, depositing the funds, and balancing the accounts."

"Don't look at me," said Valinda. I've got my hands full with payroll and payin' the subs." A smile played about her lips. "'Course there ain't been much to do, what with Glen leavin' and all. I done got a nice break."

"Which means," responded Jasmine, "you may not receive a paycheck on the first of next month."

"I ain't worried 'bout that. Les takes care of his people, come hell or high water."

Alice returned to the subject at hand. "Well, I cain't take on any more bookkeepin' cuz I got my hands full managin' the subs and handlin' residents' complaints."

Jasmine rubbed her temple as she asked rhetorically, "How could such basic GAAP principles have been ignored?"

"What kinda of principles does a jeans store got that we don't got?" asked Alice belligerently.

"Phil says Gap jeans make my butt look big," pouted Valinda.

"Not Gap. Gee-A-A-Pee—Generally Accepted Accounting Procedures," said Jasmine irritably. "It appears to be a subject about which that tosser Glen, or any of your previous dithering CFOs, apparently never got around to teaching you."

"Your butt is too big," said Alice to Valinda.

Cheryl fixed a hard, accusatory eyes on Jasmine. "You think I'm filchin' funds."

"No, I'm not accusing anyone of anything." Jasmine began to pace the reception area while thinking out loud. "First, I will hire a computer expert to hack into our financial operating program. Second, I intend to set up some basic internal controls and standard operating procedures. She stopped and looked each clerk in the eye. "And I will be rewriting your job duties." *So get used to it.* She managed a perky smile. "That way when we hire our new staff accountant, we will be ready to forge ahead. So ladies, 'keep calm and carry on,'" she quoted her father, who favored the slogan on the World War II poster that hung in his office at Cambridge University.

"I don't think my butt's too big," said Valinda to Alice.

Cheryl continued to stare at Jasmine with those hostile, feline eyes. "Well, you English people up thar in London may need some of that Gee-double A-Pee, but down here in Duckett County we got such a thang as personal integrity and we don't need no G-double A-Pee." The phone rang and she answered crossly, EmeraldLakePropertyOwnersAssociation." She pressed the hold button, dangled the phone casually, and looked blankly at Jasmine. "It's yore movin' company."

Jasmine signaled that she'd take it in her office, then sprinted down

189

the hall and picked up the phone. "Hello, this is Jasmine Roseberry speaking," she said with breathless anticipation.

"Ms. Rosybottom?"

"Ms. Roseberry. Please tell me that a moving van carrying all my earthly belongings is sitting at the main entrance."

"Ms. Rosybottom, this is Jack Spoon with To Infinity and Beyond International Moving Company. I'm afraid there's been another…ah…" To Jasmine's dismay she heard Jack Spoon snicker nervously. "There's been another computer glitch."

Jasmine's response was to the point. She yelled "Fuck!" She heard the Sopranos twittering down the hall. Jasmine slammed her office door shut and said into the phone fiercely, "I am so not hearing this!"

"Now there's no need to get ugly, young lady," retorted the man with the flat As of a Midwesterner. "It's just that the satellite navigational system sent the truckers to … well … to Emerald Lake, Maine."

"Let me get this straight. You have transported all my furniture from Boston to Emerald Lake, Montana and then all the way to Emerald Lake, Maine?"

"That's right, Missy. Your stuff's gettin' a whirlwind tour. Oh, and the gas is on us."

Jasmine set the phone down on her desk, and grabbing her hair with both hands, bent over and screamed silently. Then she stood up, took a deep, cleansing breath, and picked up the phone. "Fine, just drop it off and I'll move up there—as long as Emerald Lake, Maine does not have a Property Owners Association."

"Well, I can check and see—"

Jasmine clicked off the phone and dropped it in the wastebasket.

* * * * *

After his brief, early morning press conference in front of the remnants of Happy Hippie Hollow, Todd had remained on the site to confer with the GBI arson expert, while mostly avoiding the three blind mice and those reporters, including Ansley Mason, who had obtained a lift from a four-wheel-drive vehicle to the site.

Now, he was sitting in the Bronco in the back parking lot of his office, ignoring questions shouted to him by a throng of those reporters who had followed him from Happy Hippie Hollow. Todd stepped out of the truck and bulldozed his way to the stoop. Lurching across the threshold, he shook off one tenacious reporter, then locked the door behind him. He cruised down perp walk and ended up in the lobby, where LeeLee was typing. Without stopping, she grumbled, "In the twenty-five years I've done worked here, I don't never recall us havin' to lock ourselves in with the bad guys. I've got the heebie-jeebies just thinkin' about it." She shuddered. "By the way, Sonny wants to talk to you about the press conference you're gonna conduct at lunchtime."

"I'm gonna—well don't that knock the lips off a moose." Todd stomped into his office. He plopped down behind his desk and stewed over the fact that Sonny was now presuming to arrange his press conferences. Fatso didn't know shit from Shinola when it came to running an investigation. He used to know that.

Todd suddenly remembered the ticket he'd written to the Davis cousins yesterday afternoon. He pulled it out of his pocket and looked at it. His gut told him that this ticket was the piece of some puzzle. He slipped it back in his pocket and headed out. Ten minutes later, he was pulling up to the little office with the sign above the door that said "Davis Cousins Surveyors." He tried the front door and found that it was locked, so he shaded his eyes and peered through the glass. Where was the receptionist? Wade had said that hard times were affecting the business, so perhaps they had to let her go. Just as Todd turned back, he saw Wade pull into the degraded parking lot in the company's monstrous, black Ford pickup. When Wade saw Todd he turned the truck around and peeled out of the lot, spewing gravel in his wake. Todd jumped into the Bronco and activated the lights and siren. Wade didn't go over the speed limit, but he didn't pull over either. This went on for a mile. They passed by a bored Dillon, who was parked in a speed trap in cruiser No. 9. He immediately radioed Todd and eagerly offered to assist in the chase.

Todd said reluctantly, "Negative, we're about to hit Duckett Mountain, and the offense is minor." As much fun as chases were for the deputies, they were dangerous for civilians, especially when they took place on Duckett Highway, the treacherous two-lane road that zig-zagged over Duckett Mountain. It was the only gateway in and out of the county on its eastern border, thanks to the smothering presence of Duckett Forest. Todd flipped off his lights and siren and turned the Bronco around. He wondered why Wade would go to such lengths to evade him. It made him all the more curious as to what the Davis cousins had been up to in the Northwest sector of Duckett Forrest. Perhaps Wade's father, Sonny, could shed some light on the subject.

Todd's mind returned to his list.

Land Development
* Bones, assuming they are Billy's. He is a commissioner.
* Commissioners brawling in the church playground-Phil and
  Walt ganged up on Sam
* Davis cousins surveying in Duckett Forest

Wild card(s)
* Elvis
* Alex's death before or during the fire at his homestead

As Todd drove back to his office, he mulled over last night's events. Now there were two wild cards. Were they related to each other? If indeed Sunbeam was the person who had deposited Elvis on that rock, who had removed him? Todd pulled into the lot behind the jail. Although the doc wasn't high on Todd's list of suspects, just to be thorough, he strode with long, reaching strides up the street to the

Duckett County Family Clinic. As he expected, a half-dozen reporters clattered along behind him like cans tied to a "just-married" pickup. After a fifteen-minute interview with Gorov, which revealed no new clues, Todd walked next door to the office of the Duckettville Weekly and questioned Vince Verona. In keeping with his tough-guy image, Vince was amused at the idea that he was a suspect in the theft of Elvis; but, like Gorov, he said nothing to incriminate himself. Vince rented half his house to Gorov, and both men had reported being exhausted after the search Friday night. Each had revealed that after having a beer together, they retreated to their respective bedrooms and sacked out. Neither could vouch for the other's location until Saturday morning.

As Todd returned to his office, he utilized his long-reaching stride to outdistance himself from the pursuing reporters. Once he was safely ensconced at his desk, he called the GBI lab in Atlanta and asked to speak with Angie Brooks. When she came on the phone, he said, "Hey, it's the sheriff with the penis problem. I mean the missing penis problem. I mean—"

"Todd, everybody here at the state crime lab is very concerned about your ... ah ... sticky situation," Angie said with exaggerated solemnity.

"Everybody's a comedian," muttered Todd as he doodled on the desk pad.

"Sorry. I couldn't help myself."

Todd smiled into the phone. Angie was Todd's contact at the state lab, and though he had spoken with her often on the phone, he had only been in her physical presence a few times. He had found her light auburn hair and luminous eyes complemented her keen intelligence. Indeed, Todd thought of Angie as his fantasy girl, and had wanted to ask her out for a long time. Unfortunately, the two-and-a-half-hour drive between them made a relationship prohibitive. He realized he hadn't had one thought about Angie since he met Jasmine. Now he had a new fantasy girl, although so far she was proving to be a prickly pear. Of course, treating her like a suspect last night hadn't helped. That had been a reckless play.

He said, "It's alright, Ange. You're not the only one that's been givin' me grief since this whole mess blew up in my face."

"Well, down to business. We utilized the blood on the skin swabs you sent down, and are in the process of working up a DNA profile to feed CODUS. That way we can see if the owner of this penis has a record. We should know something by tomorrow."

"Is there anything you can do to speed things up?"

"Computers can't be bribed, Todd." He didn't reply, so she added, "Listen to this. We picked up some seminal cells off the swabs from the penis. We also recovered some vaginal epithelial cells."

Todd sat up. "So the penis had sex with a vagina—"

"Elvis probably did the funky monkey sometime in the twenty-four hours prior to getting separated from his owner. Trace seminal fluid on a penis can sometimes be detected after one shower, maybe two, but that's it."

"Can you run the vagina's DNA through CODUS?"

"No, the sample is too degraded."

"Is there anything else you can find out from those samples?"

"That's it. Of course, if we had the actual specimen here, we could do more."

"What about the bones?"

"We're attempting to test for a DNA match between the insurance salesman's son and the bones. We've taken shavings off a variety of areas on several bones, but are having difficulty getting a usable sample."

"I have to know by Friday. That's when I promised Rusty I'd announce the discovery of the bones."

"Never fear. Angie's here."

"What about the cause of death? Can you tell me anything?"

"We have placed the vic's T.O.D. around nine months to a year ago." Todd whistled. She asked, "Does that match up to the salesman?"

"Evans and his secretary disappeared ten months ago."

"Do you know if he wore a built-up left shoe?"

Todd thought that was something he would have noticed since he knew Billy fairly well. "Don't know, but I can find out. Why do you ask?"

"The right femur is an inch longer than the left, but there was only a tiny amount of wear on the right hip socket, which means that Evans wore orthotics or special shoes to balance his gait."

"That's good to know." Todd wrote a note on his blotter.

"I've sent the bones over to Trace. They might be able to tell if this vic was poisoned. But this doesn't seem like that kind of crime."

"He was shot in the head, and so was his secretary. I know it in my… bones."

"I'm sorry I can't tell you more right now."

"You've told me enough that I may be able to make a tentative ID. I'm much obliged." Todd smiled once again into the phone. "By the way, you're still my favorite criminologist, darlin'."

"And you're still my favorite sheriff, darlin'."

Todd hung up, and Blaine shuffled into the office. Though he was on swing shift, he was apparently subbing for someone on dayshift because he was in uniform. Todd indicated for him to close the door, and he did so with the speed of a sloth. Then he stood in the middle of the room and cast his eyes downward. Since he hadn't gotten yelled at yet, he looked up and was surprised to see his boss/second cousin leaning back, hands behind his head, grinning.

Todd said genially, "As I recall, Blaine, when you were picked to go to the deputy academy, you were as happy as a dog with two dicks. Weren't cha?"

Relieved that Todd was in a good mood, Blaine smiled broadly. "Oh, I was happier than a horny toad at a porn convention!"

Happy Todd morphed into a furious demon. He leaned over his

desk, glared at Blaine and growled, "You were lyin' last night when you said you had checked on the Meriwether's homestead on Saturday night, weren't you?" Blaine looked down and shuffled his feet. "It's important that you tell me the truth, Blaine. I'm tryin' to pin down Alex's time of death."

Blaine shrugged. "Okay, I lied. I didn't go out there. It was dark and I was tired."

"Look at me. I have another bone to pick with you and I'm even madder about this one."

Blaine shrugged and shifted his facial features to resemble those of a lost bush-baby. "I thank I know what yer all burnt up about. How'd you know it was me?"

"It had to be you or Virgil. And Virgil may be one fry short of a Happy Meal, but he knows when it's important to keep his trap shut." Todd rubbed his forehead frenetically. "Blaine, everyone is entitled to make a mistake once in awhile, but lately you are runnin' a franchise on stupid." The doughy deputy grimaced and reflexively pulled at the too-tight shirt that squished his man-boobs, under which he was sweating. Todd wondered if his second cousin ever not sweated.

Blaine slapped on his most sincere face. "Here's the lowdown. I was tryin' to deal with Sunbeam and get her in the truck and she kept talkin' about cuttin' off Alex's happy stick and pitchin' it in the woods—"

Todd picked up a pencil and rapped it on his desktop, staccato fashion. "I know that part," he snapped. "Let's get to the part where the press gets ahold of the happy stick story."

Just like Bambi, when Blaine told a story he tended to go up on the end of each sentence. "It's like this? I carried the mayor and Mrs. Mayor home last night cuz they was too scart to drive back over that muddy road? I told 'em what Sunbeam said. I thought it'd be okay cuz Sonny's also the County CEO? So, I 'spect the mayor told some of the press about what I said Sunbeam said?" He rounded off his confession by returning his features to his bewildered bush-baby expression.

With one hand, Todd snapped the pencil that was threaded through his fingers. He stood and walked around the slouching deputy. Todd squared off and his sharp eyes drilled Blaine down. "Rule No. 5, Blaine. What's rule No. 5?"

Blaine came to attention and snapped his heels together. "A deputy must never repeat to a civilian what he sees or hears at the scene of a crime during an ongoing investigation."

Todd's jaw clenched then unclenched. "Alright, I'll give you one get-out-of-jail-free card on account of your youth and innate stupidity." Just as Blaine sighed with relief, Todd thrust his nose in Blaine's face. "Last, but most important, have you been smokin' dope on duty?"

"No way, I swear." Blaine's big brown eyes traversed the ceiling in order to avoid Todd's stony stare.

As quickly as if he were catching a fly with one hand, Todd grabbed Blaine's pudgy face and, squeezing his cheeks, forced the young probie to look at him. "If I find out you're lyin', or if you see someone smokin' grass on duty and don't report it to me, your ass is grass!"

Blaine's sloping shoulders bobbed up and down. Sounding as if he were underwater, he said through squished lips, "Ha—you just made a pun. Smokin' grass, yer ass—"

Todd growled and released Blaine's face. "Attention, Deputy!"

Instantly, Blaine resumed an at attention posture. "Yes, sir!"

"Startin' next week all deputies will have to submit to random drug testing. Anyone who tests positive will be fired on the spot, as well as prosecuted to the fullest extent of the law. Understand?" Blaine nodded emphatically. Todd backed up two steps and looked him up and down. "Also, you need to lose some weight. You're too damn fat. Don't think I'm gonna be easier on you because we are related. I will, in fact, be harder on you. And if you don't think that's fair, you can go back to your old job baggin' groceries at the Piggly Wiggly."

Blaine swallowed hard. "I never done no drugs at work," he lied.

He raised his right hand and said, "I swear on Great-Great Granny's grave."

Todd jabbed a finger into Blaine's shoulder. "You better straighten up and fly right or I swear you will be sharing Great-Great Granny's grave."

From the reception area, LeeLee yelled, "Todd, the mayor's standin' on the front steps gettin' ready for the press conference!"

Todd and Blaine scrambled to the reception area and peered through the window, bobbing and weaving for the best view around the backwards "Duckett County Sheriff's Office" letters. Sure enough, Mayor Sonny P. Davis and GBI Agent Harwood Slaughter were standing on the steps in front of a dozen cameras.

"Well, ain't this a titty-twister," muttered Todd.

LeeLee said, "Y'all come over this a-ways and watch it on my tube cuz y'all look dopey on TV starin' out the window."

Todd and Blaine scrambled over to LeeLee's desk and squinted at the small television sitting on her credenza.

Sonny spoke first. "Ladies and gentlemen, as you know we had a terrible fire last night at the home of two Duckett County citizens. We believe that a person who lived thar, Alexander Meriwether, was the victim of the dismemberment that occurred last Friday." Todd gasped. He couldn't believe what he was hearing. The mayor continued, "Detective Harwood Slaughter of the GBI and I have concluded that Sunbeam Meriwether committed the crime of severance on Mr. Meriwether's ... ah... man thing, probably after he had already died of unknown causes. Mrs. Meriwether, who is mentally tetched and is currently residin' in the nervous ward at Grady hospital, caused the fire that burned down thar house. The sheriff is busy workin' hard to tie up all the loose ends and will get back to y'all as soon as more details are available." The gaggle of impatient reporters broke in with a barrage of questions, but the mayor promptly held up his hands. "That's all I've got to say right now. Here's Agent Slaughter."

Slaughter's red-polka-dotted face appeared on the screen. In between bouts of furious scratching, he explained that an arson investigator had been sent to the site, and an active investigation was ongoing as to the cause of the fire. The main suspect, he stated, was Sunbeam Meriwether, who was also the most likely perpetrator in the dismemberment case. He wrapped up by urging the public to be a little more patient, and promised that the whole affair would be sorted out soon.

By now, Todd's blood was boiling. That idjit mayor was standing on his jail steps conducting this premature, ill-conceived press conference. And Slaughter knew nothing about Alex and Sunbeam. Nothing! He just wanted a quick end to this affair so he could sleep in his own bed tonight.

On the TV screen, Sonny nudged his way back in front of the microphones and slapped on a broad grin. "I just wanna remind folks to come on out to the Moonshine Festival this weekend. Duckettville has the super-est fall festival in all of the tri-state area. Oh, and next Tuesday we're gonna be votin' for the Liquor-by-the-Drink referendum, so we're gonna be havin' our restaurants servin' alkeyhol soon and—"

Sonny blithered on and Slaughter rolled his eyes, then slipped off the steps and disappeared into his crime van. The reporters turned their backs on Sonny and began delivering their summations to their cameras. They were obviously uninterested in the upcoming Liquor-by-the-Drink vote. Todd figured they had probably lived their entire lives in places where one could buy hard alcohol by the drink. Sonny received the message, and after giving a stupid little wave to the reporters' backs, he tried the locked door to the sheriff's office. Then he banged on it. Todd reluctantly unlocked the door and let him in, then relocked it.

Despite being dismissed by the press, Sonny was elated. "Whew, I'm sooo glad we won't have Elvis hangin' over the Moonshine Festival." He rubbed his palms together. "Now we can get back on track—with everthang." He ceased his hand-rubbing and rested his fists in the vicinity of his hips. "Say, Fearless, why didn't you think of Sunbeam? Their homestead is close to Elvis's rock, and seein' as how Sunbeam's got multiple personalities. You should of went straight out to thar place."

Todd assumed the universal cop stance: arms crossed and feet slightly apart. "It just so happens that I sent Blaine to check on them, but it seems he got lost." Todd looked around for Blaine to glare at, but he was nowhere to be seen, having wisely slipped out the back door. Todd turned his attention back to Sonny. "Look, there are more reasons why Sunbeam may not be the penis-poacher than there are legs on a pill bug. And tryin' to prove that Sunbeam sawed off Alex's dingdong and laid it on that rock is like tryin' to nail Jell-O to the wall. First off, Sunbeam is a schizophrenic, which is not the same thing as havin' multiple personality disorder. What it means is that we cain't believe any confessions she makes when she's off her meds. Second off, Sunbeam has never shown any violent tendencies, on or off her meds. And thirdly, since poor Alex's body is now ashes, we don't have any physical evidence to prove that anyone sawed off his pickle."

Sonny threw up his arms. "Thar you go again, tryin' to confuse me with yer so-called facts! What you need to be thinkin' about, son, is your som-bitch attitude, which is so piss-poor that I decided not to even include you in that press briefin'!" Sonny stomped toward the door, and then turned back. "The Elvis case is settled in my book," he pointed his finger at Todd, "and that means in your book too, Fearless."

Just then Harwood Slaughter banged on the door and Sonny let him in. Slaughter grumbled, "We just got a call about a homicide in South Georgia—in another shit-kicking sewage dump of a county." He scratched his splotchy neck vigorously. "Up here, I gotta put up with all you clueless crackers and down there, I got the ignoramus coons to fool with."

"I'll thank you not to use those labels in my office," growled Todd. "And there will be no more slip-shod press conferences held on my front steps!"

Sonny shouted, "Tell him, Harwood. This case is closed!"

Todd shouted heatedly, "Wake up and smell your own farts, Sonny! The case is not solved!" He ran a hand over his hair and paused it at the back of his neck. "Need I remind you two that Elvis is still missin'?"

Slaughter sneered. "Elvis could be in Timbuk-fucking-tu for all I care. The case isn't solved, but I consider it hopeless due to it being so fucked-up from the beginning by you, Baby Chief. Next time, call me pronto, and just maybe I'll save your ass—if, that is, your ass is still on the payroll. Until then, A.M.F." Slaughter opened the door. "That's short for 'Adios, Mother Fucker.'" He exited and slammed the door behind him. LeeLee, who had been watching the scene from her desk, slapped her hands over her eyes, afraid the glass would shatter.

Todd walked over, opened the door and yelled lamely, "Yeah, well ... up your butt with a coconut!" He too slammed the door, and LeeLee jumped in her seat.

Shawn was standing at the opening to the hallway containing the jail cells. "Good comeback, Chief!" he exclaimed sincerely, but when he saw the smoke coming from Todd's ears, he stepped back into the darkness of "perp walk" where it was safer.

Having regrouped, Sonny enjoined, "Todd, your job is to take Sunbeam at her word. It's for the judge to decide if her confession is coming from a sane or insane person." Sonny rubbed his pate vigorously, then pointed at Todd. "Keep in mind, she could very well have killed Alex before dismemberin' him."

"I've known Sunbeam since I was a kid," countered Todd, pacing the lobby. "I believe that, medicated or not, she doesn't have it in her to harm another human being."

Sonny began to pace in the opposite direction from Todd. LeeLee nervously chewed on her nails, her eyes darting from one frustrated, stomping man to the other. She felt a hot flash coming on, so she began to fan her face frenetically with the paper fan that featured Jesus soulfully gazing upward on one side. On the other side were the words "Courtesy of Grimes Funeral Home" in shimmering gold letters.

"Well, I still thank Sunbeam is the slasher," said Sonny. "Tetched is tetched." He wheeled around to face Todd. "Don't you see? We've found the perfect out. Everbody wins."

Todd stopped pacing and fixed a hard stare on Sonny. "I'm not lookin' for an out, I'm lookin' for the truth. Or don't the truth mean anything to you anymore?"

"But you heard her confess! She cut off Alex's wing-ding cuz she was told to do so by the fart-angel—"

"Arch-angel." Todd folded his arms across his chest. "Arch-angel," he said again. Obviously Blaine had mistranslated when he'd relayed the story to Sonny.

"Yeah, whatever. The point is she heard the fart-angel tellin' her to chop it off and put it in the," he raised his pitch and wiggled his fingers, "enchanted woods."

"I interviewed some of Alex and Sunbeam's homesteader friends," said Todd. "The Wilsons were out at Happy Hippie Hollow until midnight on Thursday. Which means the earliest Alex probably died was Friday. So Sunbeam could have lived with a dead body on her front porch for three days expectin' Alex to resurrect himself."

Sonny shrugged. "Yeah, so? It worked for Christ, and he was sane. Sunbeam's schizoo…schizoo—what you said. So a whole day could be like five minutes to her. Case closed, as far as I can see. Look, why would she be a-blabbin' about cuttin' it off if she didn't do it?"

Sonny could bring out Todd-the-Sarcastic faster than anybody. "Well, hmmm, let me think. Maybe because there's been this weird news story about a chopped-off prick that's been plastered all over the boob tube, and a schizophrenic off her meds can't tell the difference between what's on TV and what's inside her scrambled-up brains!"

"Christ, almighty. Are we back to that? Alright, smartass, I don't see you comin' up with any other suspects."

"I can't disclose the details of my investigation."

The remark reignited Sonny's ire. "Fearless, you make everthang so goddamn complicated when it's really as plain as the wart on yer granny's fanny. I want the Elvis case wrapped up—now!" He made a fist with his pudgy right hand and slammed it into his pudgy left hand. Then he adjusted the collar on his sports coat and grumbled, "Stupid little, cow patty kickin' know-it-all ..." He continued to grouse under his breath while stomping out of the office.

Todd opened the door and called out, "Obviously, you've forgotten that I saved your stupid little life on Saturday!" He slammed the front door, causing the glass to shake ominously. LeeLee grimaced and slapped her hands over her eyes again.

"You've done gone too far with Sonny," she chided. "If thar ever was a time to do some serious butt-smoochin', this is it."

Todd gave her the stink eye, stomped into his office, and plopped behind his desk. Through his open door, he could hear her trying to get the press off the phone lines. He leaned back and attempted to concentrate on the Meriwether case. "Jasmine," he whispered. A wave of embarrassment rolled over him when he realized he'd said her exotic name out loud. By God, he was infatuated. He had shut out the sight, scent, and feel of females for two interminable years. And now, through the worst of circumstances, he had come face to face with the one woman who could transform his life. Indeed, every time he thought of Jasmine, a devilish cyclone of desires threatened to engulf him. His loins ached for her softness and his skin itched for the salve of her touch.

He shook his head to rid himself of the vision of her angelic face. There was too much to think about right now. Would Jasmine have liked Alex Meriwether? Todd thought that Alex definitely would have liked her. Alex would have called her Feisty Feline Furriner. Alex had a nickname for everyone, including Todd—as if Todd needed another nickname. Alex's nickname for him was Flying Fearless Farmer Boy. Todd sat silently for a few minutes, recalling his friend Alex

Where's Elvis?

Meriwether. Despite having burnt out a few brain cells in the fifties, a lot more in the sixties, and drastically thinned out his nasal septum in the seventies, Alex Meriwether had ended up a decent guy who'd found an unselfish purpose in life—the care and feeding of his lady love. Who was going to take care of Sunbeam now? Todd reached for the phone.

Chapter Nine
Tuesday Afternoon
at the Loony Bin

It seemed to Todd that the traffic in Atlanta was perpetually snarled. Every time that he drove in this slow motion catastrophe, he wondered why people would purposely live in this city—in any city, for that matter. His destination was Grady Hospital; but before going there, he decided on the spur of the moment to make a stop at the state courthouse. Once inside the courthouse, he asked for directions to the records department and was directed to the basement. When he found the door marked "Records," he entered a cavernous room, deserted except for a lone clerk sealed off behind a high counter and a Plexiglas window.

Todd bent down to speak through the mouse hole to the attractive but heavyset, fortyish African-American lady. "Excuse me, ma'am, my name is Sheriff—"

"Sir, get back behind the line and wait your turn," she said perfunctorily.

Todd looked around the empty room. "But I—"

"Please, sir, step behind the line and wait until you're called."

Todd looked down on the floor and found a flaking black line painted on the faded linoleum. With one big toy-soldier step, he positioned himself behind it. He fidgeted for a few minutes while the clerk busied herself with whatever it was she was busying herself with. Finally, without looking up she said, "Step forward, please."

Once again, Todd toy-soldier-stepped to the Plexiglas widow and bent down to speak into the mouse hole. "My name is Sheriff Todd McPherson of the Duckett—"

"What is it I can do for you today?"

The clerk spoke so quickly that it took a few seconds for Todd to decipher what she said. "Ma'am, if it don't discomfit you any, I am in sore need of a trial transcript."

The clerk shoved a form under the Plexiglas. "Write down the information and the date." Todd didn't know the exact date, but he wrote down what he knew and pushed the paper back under the window.

The clerk looked at the form, and then at him. "This trial was forty years ago."

"Yes, ma'am. Do you still have it?"

"The only transcripts we keep after twenty years are the capital cases."

"And this is that."

"Hold on, I'll check." She returned in a few minutes. "You're in luck. We just finished scannin' that year into our computer. We can give you the transcript on a CD if you pay for the CD, plus a processin' fee."

"Thank you, ma'am!" said Todd enthusiastically. He had expected he would be here for hours staring at microfiche until his eyeballs shriveled up and fell out of their sockets. "When can I pick it up?"

"Can you come back in a few hours?"

Todd grinned and replied even more enthusiastically, "Yes, ma'am!" He dug a credit card out of his wallet.

"Oh, you can't pay here. You have to take this invoice to the cashier's office on the second floor."

Todd returned his wallet to his back pocket. "Much obliged."

After finishing his business at the courthouse, Todd drove to Grady Hospital. Just as he pulled into the visitor's parking area, his cell phone rang. It was Duckett County's AWOL prosecutor, Delray Hamilton, who said jovially, "Fearless, I've been watchin' you on the idiot box, and I think you have the makin's of a hit reality show. You could name it Lost...in Duckett Forest."

"Devilray, I only like sarcasm when I get to be sarcastic." Todd squeezed the bridge of his nose in an effort to distract himself from thinking about what a pain the in the ass Delray could be.

"What a lineup of characters! There's one good-lookin' cornball kid for a sheriff, a bubble-butt blowhard for a mayor, and that luscious lass that tripped over the dipstick."

"We were scheduled to be in court yesterday. Or have you forgotten about the Kenny Pete Brooks case?"

"Kenny Pete, the sticky-fingered redneck Rastafarian? He's nothin' considerin' what you've had served on your plate these last four days." Delray hyena-snickered. He enjoyed amusing himself with his own cleverness. "Relax, I've talked with our majestic magistrate, and we are rescheduled for next Wednesday. As a matter of fact, that's why I called you."

"God, Delray, that's about the tenth time you've rescheduled Kenny Pete's hearin'. I'm surprised Judge Tibbit hasn't ground you up into mash and fed you to that pretentious pot-bellied pig of his. Seriously, you're gonna aggravate him so much that he's gonna take it out on Kenny Pete."

"No chance. Tibbit has been treating me with kid gloves ever since he developed a monstrous crush on my widowed mother-in-law. Besides, Kenny Pete doesn't understand what delays mean to his case. He's one cracker who's not the sharpest cheese on the…ah…cracker. Oh, I just made a double entendre!" No appreciative remark came from Todd, so Delray continued, "Anyway, my little tummy tumult has developed into the flue. Kathy has been afflicted too." He hesitated then added, "In fact, Kathy's had a bit of a…spell."

"Yeah, well, I'm gonna put a spell on you if you don't get your apathetic ass down here."

"Have you no sympathy for your fellow crime fighter whose apathetic ass has spent the last four days in the crapper?"

"We found some bones in Duckett Forest. They came from a man who was about five-foot-ten."

Delray whistled. "Billy Evans. I thought he ran off with his secretary."

"I never thought that. After I find out who murdered and mutilated Big Elvis, I'm gonna get the killer of those bones. Then you get to prosecute him."

After a pause, Delray said, "I'd rather not. State can have that job."

Todd could have predicted that answer, but there was a weird un-Delray-like edginess in his voice that pricked Todd's interest. "You should be elated to get the opportunity to try a murder case. Where's the fire in your belly, man?"

Just like that, Delray reverted to his typical glib, carefree persona. "Well, Hot Toddy, I'm not takin' odds that you'll catch this bones killer anyway."

Were it possible, Todd would have reached across the state line and slugged Delray in the stomach so hard that those devilishly handsome dimples would have popped off his devilishly handsome face. However, Todd's anger was quickly replaced by puzzlement. *Why does he think I won't be able to solve the case?* Todd attempted to think of something clever to say. Nothing came to mind, so he retorted lamely, "Yeah, well, me and Elvis still need you."

Delray laughed wickedly. "Oh, Toddy, I'm gettin' all hot and gooey!" He paused then added, "From what I've been seein' on TV, you've been havin' such a good time. I couldn't bear to take any of your fun away."

Todd pictured Delray's face with his trademark shit-eating, Rhett Butler grin plastered on it. He was still lounging around that comfy lodge playing poker, drinking his fine Kentucky bourbon, and puffing on Monte Carlos. "I'm on my way to question Sunbeam. I could have used you to come along." It was only a halfhearted statement since Delray's company would have been of little help. Still, Todd suddenly realized how isolated and alone he felt.

"Holy hushpuppies! Buddy, you are wastin' your time. You know that Sunbeam Meriwether is several washin' machines short of a fully functional front porch."

"I've known Sunbeam since I was a kid, and when her meds kick in, she sort of makes sense."

"Sort of doesn't cut it in court. Still, I'd have loved to come along for the pure entertainment value. Don't worry, Cowpoke, when you really need me, I'll be there—pinky promise. Bye for now."

Todd reluctantly clicked off his cell phone and locked his duty belt with his Glock in the back of the Bronco. After a few false starts, he located the entrance to the enormous old hospital. Eventually, he found the elevator that took him to the correct floor. The steel double-doors to the loony bin were locked. He peered through the thick glass windows and saw two African-American nurses working behind a counter. He realized that the hospital seemed to be mostly staffed by black people. Todd decided that the difference between Atlanta and the mountains of North Georgia was…well…black and white.

He rang the bell, held his credentials to the glass, and the heavyset nurse pushed a button that electronically unlocked the door. As soon as he stepped in, the door closed and electronically locked behind him with a loud clunk. He looked around at the shiny floor and hospital's pea green walls. On the other side of the hall, a half-dozen zombies sat staring blankly at Judge Judy in a sitting area. She was haranguing a woman who had assaulted an argumentative neighbor by whipping out a breast and spraying him in the face with breast milk.

An eerie sense of déjà vu swept over Todd and he was flooded with unpleasant sights, sounds, and smells from the time when Brandy bottomed out on booze and pills. He walked up to the desk. The attractive younger nurse was talking on the phone, and Burnt Orange was entering data into a computer. She glanced up at him over her reading glasses. He told her who he was and that he was here to interview Sunbeam Meriwether. Without taking her attention off of her computer, the nurse slapped some forms on the counter. Todd leaned down and applied pen to paper. From the corner of his eye he saw a tall, nice-looking African-American man in a white coat smoothly moving toward him.

The man said loudly, "Oh hell, Fleet, just run eighty yards down the middle and look for the bomb!"

Todd snapped up. With a wide grin on his face, he exclaimed, "Well, get out of here! If it ain't Fleet Street, you son of a gun!" The two men glad-clapped each other and commenced to perform their team handshake, which concluded with a jiggy step. Burnt Orange smirked, and the pretty young nurse giggled.

Dr. Street said, "Fearless, look at you, sheriff of Duckett County. I ain't seen your pretty mug since...well...high school graduation."

"And look at you, Doctor Andrew Street!" The two men grunted, chest-butted, and clapped each other on the back again.

"Velma, Chaniqua," said Andrew, "this is my high school quarterback that I've told you about—Todd Fearless McPherson. We called him Fearless because our offensive line had some weakness and he got sacked a lot, but he always managed to stand back up." Todd smiled sheepishly. The younger nurse smiled shyly. Burnt Orange looked bored. Andrew grinned mischievously, then hunkered down and said in a low, intense voice, "Nine seconds to go in the game for the state championship and the Duckett Bucks were down by five points. We had the ball, but we were on the opponent's fifteen yard line and it was ... " He looked at his old teammate.

"Third down and nine to go," said Todd excitedly. The patients who were sitting on the couch craned their necks to watch the outcome of the imaginary game.

Dr. Street laid his arm around his old teammate's shoulders. "We were huddled up and Coach Flagg sent out the call for Todd to run a bootleg screen pass to the other running back, Travis Lee, in hopes that he could move the ball down the field."

Todd interjected, "But what Coach didn't know was that Travis was so wiped that he was bawlin.' Travis had a bawlin' problem."

Street continued, "So Fearless here looks at me and says—"

"Oh hell, Fleet, just run eighty yards down the middle and look for the bomb!" Andrew ran a few steps and Todd pretended to pass an imaginary football. Andrew looked over his shoulder, turned around suddenly, jumped up, pretended to bobble the football, and then reeled it in. He raised his arms in victory. "Touchdown!" yelled Todd softly, and he hummed the Duckett High fight song. Andrew performed a few jiggy steps and spiked the pretend ball.

"Well whoop-ti-do," said Velma, but Chaniqua clapped delightedly.

"Most beautiful pass I've ever seen," said Dr. Street.

Todd's grin widened. Some of the adrenaline that he had felt that night years ago was rushing through him now. He looked at the ladies and said, "Street plucked that ball right out of the hands of two defenders." He reached over and clapped Andrew on the shoulder. "So, what are you doin' in Atlanta? I thought you were in medical school up north somewhere."

"I was," he said as he accepted Sunbeam's metal-clad file from Chaniqua. "But they finally got tired of seeing my ugly mug around so they graduated me. I'm a psych resident here."

"God Almighty!" Todd stepped back and took a new look at Andrew. "Fleet Street is a shrink!"

"It beats slicing and dicing."

Todd realized that his childhood friend had dropped the Southern Appalachian drawl that was characteristic of Duckett County. While Andrew escorted him down the hall, Todd avoided looking at any patients because it seemed rude—plus, they brought back painful Brandy memories.

As they ambled along, Andrew said, "Anyway, how's your momma?"

"Healthy as a horse. How's yours?"

"Hanging in there." Andrew stopped outside a small room with a large glass observation window. "How's Brandy and the baby?"

Todd smiled crookedly. "My baby is now in kindergarten. I've had custody of her since she was nine months old. Brandy left me for a ka-zillionaire that she met at an AA meetin' up at Emerald Lake. How's that for a kick in the teeth?"

"Somehow, that seems so Brandy," admitted Andrew with a rueful smile. "Anyway, when I saw that Sunbeam had been admitted, I asked for her case." He exhaled deeply. "I'm so sorry about Alex, man."

"Yeah, me too." Todd dropped his gaze to the shiny floor.

As Andrew opened the door to the visiting room, he said, "Alex got me through high school calculus."

"He was one of the good guys," said Todd soberly as he followed his old teammate into the room.

Andrew stood by the simple table that almost filled the small rectangular room. Flipping through the chart, he said, "They'll bring Sunbeam in a few minutes. Have a seat."

Todd sat down, stretched out his long legs, leaned back, and laced his fingers behind his head. "Man, oh man, I ain't thought about that game in so long."

Andrew remained standing. "Really? I think about it every day." There was an un-Andrew-like tension in his voice. He bobbled the file and it clattered on the table. He laid his hands on both sides of it and leaned forward. "Man, I'm sorry I missed your daddy's funeral."

"Well hey, dude, you were away at med school."

"No, I wasn't. It was summer. I was home on break."

Todd shrugged. "You missed a great keg party afterwards. The rest of the team was there, so you don't have to apologize."

"Yes I do. You came to my daddy's funeral."

There was a solemnity about Fleet that Todd didn't remember. "Hey! Would you quit apologizin'? Shrinks don't believe in guilt, right?" Andrew shrugged noncommittally. Eager to change the subject, Todd sat up and laid his hands on the table. "That Sunbeam's chart?"

The heavy look on Andrew's face did not change. "I heard about your baby being born with fetal alcohol syndrome. I'm sor—"

Todd sat back and crossed his arms over his chest. "Hey, cut the crap before I slam you, dude-dette."

Andrew held up his hands in surrender. He returned to inspecting the contents of the chart, then suddenly snapped it shut. "I've got a monkey on my back and I've been wanting to wrestle it off for a long time." Todd gave him a puzzled look. Andrew inhaled deeply. "Ten years we played ball together, from peewee though twelfth grade. You always got the glory, you know that, don't you?" His voice was suddenly constricted with long-held resentment.

Todd frowned. *Where in the hell did this crap come from?* "Now wait a minute there, Fleet," he said good-naturedly. "Those cheer-leaders made as many banners for you as they did for me."

"But you were Duckett High's fair-haired boy." Andrew ran a hand over his own close-shorn, coal-black hair. "Class president, homecoming king—you were the 'it' boy."

"Hey, Coach Flagg always said that you were the best runnin' back he'd ever—"

"I'm talking about the undercurrents, Todd. Undercurrents."

Todd's confusion grew. He could hear down the hall some crazy woman cursing the staff in between her chilling screams. "Hope that's not Sunbeam," he quipped. More yelling, muffled now. He lowered his hands to the arms of his chair and studied the heavily fortified, fifties-style windows. Finally he shrugged and said, "Hey, you're the one who got the football scholarship to Bowling Green." It sounded more defensive than he had meant.

"That means nothing. You could have gone—

"What's this all got to do with now?"

Andrew placed his hands on the table again and stared at them. Todd looked down at his own hands—his twenty-seven-year-old hands, which suddenly appeared so different from the way he remembered his baby-smooth seventeen-year-old hands. In a few seconds, scenes of his growing-up years blew through his mind. Ever since they were in peewee, Fleet had always been there, ready to catch any ball Todd threw at him, even a high wobbler or a fluffy throwaway girlie pass. And Fleet had always been ready to take the hand-off with his large, sure hands. He had the hands of a concert pianist.

Todd knew that Andrew came from one of only a handful of African-Americans living in Duckett County. They were mostly the descendants of the slaves that the Duckett family had brought in to work on their estate. Even today, most of them dwelled in one cranny of the county, preferring to live under the radar. After the race riots that had taken place in the cities back in the sixties, the county turned a cold tit to the African-American community. For the overwhelmingly white mountain counties like Duckett, the prejudice that erupted grew more from the fear of the unknown than anything else. The hysteria escalated to the point where the fledgling Klan added an addendum underneath the Welcome to Duckett County sign that read, "Don't Let the Sun Set on Your Black Ass Here." Each time the sign was swiped, some members of the Klan replaced it. Eventually the game was abandoned and the Klan dwindled away, as there was really nothing for it to protest locally. All that had happened long before Todd and Andrew were born.

Todd looked Andrew in the eye. "I think what your sayin' is that me personally should have given you more credit."

Andrew laid the file down, rested his hands on the table, and leaned forward. "You could have said somethin'. You were, after all, the mighty team captain. You were the goddamned team captain on every goddamn team that we played on—be it baseball, basketball or bad-fucking-mitten."

Todd leaned back and laced his fingers behind his head. "My only excuse was that I was a stupid cow-pie kickin' teenager, totally wrapped up in sports and Brandy and oblivious to everyone else around me." He gave Andrew a wry smile. "Wonst I was yer buddy and I done ya wrong." Andrew rolled his eyes dismissively. He straightened up and

214

looked away.

Todd thought about what to say next. He realized that his and Fleet's childhoods culminated in that touchdown in the last few seconds of the state championship game their senior year. Shrugging, he lowered his hands and grasped the chair's arms. "Ah, forget the crowds, Fleet. Forget who got what glory. That's all in the past. The truth is you and me shared a moment when I threw an eighty-yard bomb, and you plucked that baby from thin air and scored the winning touchdown." He took a deep breath and looked Andrew in the eye. "We shared a perfect moment, probably one of a very few perfect moments either one of us will ever have in our entire lives. And you know what? It was the same perfect for you as it was for me. The same perfect."

Andrew's drawn-down, totem-like mouth remained carved in wood. He was quiet for what seemed like a month, and then, slowly, his eyes lit up and one corner of his lips rose. "Yeah, yeah, the same perfect." He looked away and sniffed.

"So, we cool?"

"We done made a right smart start." Andrew cleared his throat and said crisply, "Well, down to business." He settled into a chair and perused the file again. Todd laid a hand on his chest and exhaled. Heavy personal business like this was taxing when it happened out of the blue, especially in the middle of a damned loony bin where no manly lager was available to take the edge off.

Andrew said, "When I came on duty early this morning I couldn't believe that Sunbeam Meriwether was a guest—and man, she was a mess. Despite the advances in treating mental illness, Schizophrenia is still damned difficult to handle. And not knowing what meds she had been on, it was basically a clean-up-in-aisle-two situation. It would sure help if I could speak to whoever has been treating her."

"Can you find out?" asked Todd.

"We're hoping her regular shrink will catch the plea you made on TV this morning. Anyway, as far as pulling her together, I got lucky.

The first combination of drugs I tried have somewhat stabilized her. But she has a way to go. I'm not sure if talking to her today will be of much help."

"Last night she told me she sliced off Alex's penis. Do you think she is capable of that?"

"Again, that's something we need to ask the doctor who's been treating her—if we can find him." Andrew's pager beeped. After looking at it, he said that he had to go. He instructed Todd to wait and an attendant would bring Sunbeam to him. And so, Fearless McPherson and Fleet Street awkwardly attempted another execution of the Fighting Bucks team handshake—this time without success. They ended up just shaking hands and smiling self-consciously. Todd stood in the doorway and watched as Andrew tucked the file under his arm, lowered his head, and hustled down the hall, expertly dodging patients and staff alike.

In a few moments, a young, muscular black man escorted Sunbeam into the room. "Sir Fearless," Sunbeam exclaimed brightly, "this is Sir Terrell, my manservant."

"Pleased to meet ya." Todd shook the orderly's hand.

Terrell said, "I'll be just outside, Mr. Fearless, watchin' through the glass." In a lower voice he added, "All her spinners aren't exactly back on her wheels yet."

Sunbeam waved dismissively at Terrell. "Oh, pshaw. Me thinks my manservant maligns me." She began to waltz around the table, holding out an oversized hospital robe as if she were holding up the hem of a ball gown. Todd thought it looked like she didn't have anything on underneath. Finally, she daintily sat in a chair. Todd sat across from her. Terrell signaled military style for Todd to keep his eyes on the patient, then he backed out of the room, leaving Todd alone in this stuffy coffin with a lunatic.

Todd laid his hands on the table, forced a smile, and said, "Well, Sunbeam, you're lookin' a lot better today." She rocked back and forth, quietly humming Will the Circle Be Unbroken. Todd caught her

216

wandering gaze. "Sunbeam, what was your name before you met Alex?"

Sunbeam adopted a dead-on Southern slave accent. "Well, I don't rightly know, Mr. Butler. I don't remember nothin' before Master Alexander won me in a poker contest." She dropped the accent and in her typical New England clip asked, "You're coming to take me home, correct? I've apple preserves to put up, and Alex will want to sup on the porch tonight."

Todd hunched over the table. "Don't you remember? Your house is burned down, and Alex is ... dead." He watched Sunbeam's face carefully.

Tears welled up in her honest gray eyes. "That's right, silly me. I forgot about Alex being burnt up. Alex is a crispy critter." Then she looked around the room and started to sing softly while she absently fingered the collar of her robe. "I want to go to the spirit in the sky. That's where I want to go when I die. Gonna take me up—"

"Sunbeam ... "

"He always wanted that song sung at his farewell service, even though he wasn't a believer. His beliefs were full of contradictions. You are full of contradictions too, Fearless, and that's not a good way for a lawman to be." She tsk-tsked him a few times. "Anyway, can you make that song happen at Alex's service?"

"I surely will."

Sunbeam sat quietly for a moment and twirled her hair, which thankfully had been washed.

Todd cleared his throat. "Sunbeam, I have to ask you, did you kill Alex?"

She gasped. "Todd Hoyt McPherson, are you mad? Do you really think that I could murder the love of my life?" She paused and smiled gamely. "You know, when I first met my old man at Woodstock, I balled him every day for a hundred days." Through the observation glass, Todd saw Sir Terrell slap a hand over his mouth and bend over, struggling to contain his laughter. Obviously, the glass provided little in the way of sound insulation.

Todd covered Sunbeam's small, weathered hand with his large, square one. "I didn't think you killed Alex, but my job requires me to ask. Can you tell me what happened to him?"

Sunbeam shrugged her shoulders. "He had just eaten some apple pie and said he wasn't feeling well. He gave me a juicy smooch and a fierce hug and said, 'See ya, Bouncing Betty Boop,' and then he went out and lay on the sofa on the front porch. I was putting up the last of the green beans—you know the pole beans—that's the only kind one should grow in my book. Those bush beans don't have a smidgen of flavor—"

"Alex. What happened to Alex?" asked Todd, no longer able to hide his impatience.

"Alex loves his green beans."

"Yes, I know Alex loves green beans. What happened after Alex went out on the porch to take a nap?"

"No, you don't know how Alex likes his green beans," insisted Sunbeam. "How could you? You've never, ever, put up beans for Alex. He likes a couple of thick slices of bacon cooked in with them, and a pinch of sea salt with some Herbal Bouquet and ... We slaughtered a pig just last month, did you know?"

"What happened when you finished with the green beans?"

"Well, I didn't finish them. I just received an intuitive thought to go check on Alex. You ever get a feeling? How could you? You're a football player. We used to watch you get tackled in the backfield. It's amazing that you won state because your front five were actually narcoleptic goats and your running back was my psychiatrist."

Todd laid his hands over Sunbeam's again and gently squeezed. "You went out on the front porch to check on Alex, and what did you see?"

Sunbeam pulled her hands back. "His chest moving is what I didn't see, snoring is what I didn't hear, and a pulse is what I didn't feel." She played with the lapel of her robe then said mournfully, "I'm grieving, Fearless." There was more playing with the lapels. Todd feared she might yank open her robe and expose her wrinkled hangy-downs in front of him. A sight like that could permanently damage a young man's libido.

Sunbeam sighed mournfully. "My Alex was gone, gone I tell you!"

"I'm so sorry, Sunbeam," said Todd sincerely.

"I'm so sorry, Sunbeam," mocked Sunbeam.

"Do you remember what you did after you discovered that Alex was dead?" asked Todd gently.

Sunbeam laid a finger on her chin while her eyes scanned the ceiling. "Let's see, I ate dinner while I watched the news. After that, I watched American Idol, and Lost, then went to bed."

"What day was it?"

"I don't know. They're all the same to me."

"How did Alex's body get all wrapped up?"

"I tried to wrap him, but I couldn't. I ended up just tucking some quilts around him. It's been getting nippy at night. I hope my chickens are alright."

"This mornin' some of your homesteader friends rounded up your animals and took them away for safe keepin'." Todd was struck with the thought that the arch-angel Sunbeam had been babbling about the night of the fire could have been a real person. He leaned toward her and attempted to corral her wandering eyes. "Now who's this arch-angel that you told me about?"

Sunbeam replied matter-of-factly, "The arch-angel came and helped me, and told me about how to get Alex back. Only he was wrong. Alex hasn't regenerated. If he had, he would have come and checked me out of this rubber hotel." She sighed audibly. "The arch-angel lied, lied, lied—peed in the pie."

"So, is the arch-angel a man or a woman?"

Sunbeam answered with a noncommittal shrug. She looked around, and putting her hand beside her mouth, whispered, "Who can know these things?"

"Did the arch-angel tell you to cut off Alex's penis and put it in the woods?"

Sunbeam suddenly jumped up and cried, "Fearless, take me home or rape me!" In the next instant, she was on Todd's side of the table, looming over him and shouting nonsense. Todd shrank back in his chair, unsure of what to do. Sunbeam grasped his cheeks. Pulling and pushing on them, she caused his face to morph into a series of ghoulish expressions. Then she threw her arms in the air and shouted grandly, "I'm going to become a swan and dive into the inkwell of divine blueberry muffins!"

Todd looked out the window and to his dismay saw that Sir Terrell had abandoned his listening post. Thankfully, though, he appeared in the next instant, dashed into the meeting room, and muscled Sunbeam out. Over her shoulder she called out, "Say hello to Virgil for me!"

Todd sat for a moment. Was it possible to extricate the truth from Sunbeam's delusions? He felt as if he were trying to separate an egg yolk from the white using only his fingers. From down the hall, he heard Sunbeam singing at the top of her lungs:

"Goin' up to the spirit in the sky,
That's where I wanna go when I die.
When I die and they lay me down to rest,
Gonna go to the place that's the best."

Chapter Ten

Tuesday Twilight: Cornbread Scryin' with The Wart Taker

Once Todd broke free of the Atlanta traffic, he slipped on his earpiece, called LeeLee and asked her to search the TV Guide to find out what night Lost and American Idol aired. Since only one satellite company provided TV service to the county, Todd hoped that those shows would pinpoint the day that Alex had died.

Todd then called Jeanie Evans's cell phone number. School had just let out and he hoped that she would be available to talk. He asked her if Billy wore a built-up left shoe and she said yes, that all of his nicer shoes had built-up lefties. But for his sneakers, he just put several liners in the lefty. She said a car wreck when he was a teen had shortened that leg. Todd told her that he believed the bones were Billy's, based on three pieces of circumstantial evidence: the time of death, the estimated height of the skeleton, and the shorter left femur. Jeanie said goodbye in a choked voice and abruptly hung up. Todd immediately felt sorry that he hadn't spoken to her in person.

Next, he called his mother and asked her once again if she remembered anything more about Sunbeam that would be helpful. Jessie said that Sunbeam was tight with the town psychic, Marvalena LeJeune. Maybe she would be able to answer his questions.

Todd realized that he had not yet interviewed Marvalena, also known as the wart taker, concerning her whereabouts after she left the search-and-rescue team on Friday. According to Slaughter's sparse notes, she had received only a cursory questioning by one of his two clones. When Todd arrived back in Duckettville, he parked the Bronco behind the office, and to his relief discovered that the reporters had left to badger someone else for a change. He began to walk up Main Street toward Marvalena's house, but was accosted by Pastor Ed and Preacher Dodge as they stepped out of the Checkered Flagg. Without a howdy-do, they asked in unison if he'd found Elvis. He brushed them off with a cursory nod and kept walking. Pastor Ed caught his arm and squared up. "You know, Kiddo, I christened you, so I feel like I can say this. One of these days you're gonna have to decide if you're gonna get back on the path or just select the tenets of the faith that you want to follow."

Todd pulled his arm away. "I don't know what I believe anymore." He continued past the Main Street storefronts until he reached the residence and business establishment of the mysterious wart taker. Marking the transition point between commercial and residential Main Street, it was a whitewashed clapboard house with a Carolina Tar Heel blue front door. The front yard was defined by a wobbly whitewashed picket fence that corralled a chaotic mix of perennials, weeds, and summer herbs, all of which were in some stage of drying up and bending over in submission to autumn. Dozens of trolls, fairies, and unicorns were scattered among the dying vegetation. From out of this botanical chaos grew a faded white wooden sign that read, "Palms R Us: Psychic Readings for You."

To Todd, Marvalena LeJeune wielded the kind of mystical feminine power that he as a man knew nothing about, and therefore instinctively feared. This was probably why he had unconsciously delayed questioning her. His feet suddenly fused to the cracked, uneven sidewalk, and he was seized by a desire to turn heel and retreat to the masculine familiarity of his office, even if perp walk did smell of pee. He girded his loins, willed himself through the gate, and strode up the stone walkway.

As he reached the first step of the porch, Mrs. Street, Dr. Andrew Street's mother, walked out the front door. Just like Todd remembered from his childhood, her tall wiry frame was clothed in a dress with a small-print pattern cinched in with a wide, black-patent-leather belt. In the crook of elbow hung her trademark humongous, sixties-style black-patent-leather purse. The only differences that Todd saw between the lady he remembered as a kid and the one now before him was that her once black hair was now gray and her glasses had grown thicker. Also, she favored her right side, probably because for the past half-century she had lugged around a succession of those shiny, monstrous purses. Todd remembered that one time Mrs. Street had hauled off and whacked Andrew over the head with that seemingly rock-filled bludgeon. He couldn't remember what Fleet had done to get thunked like that. Fortunately, at this moment Mrs. Street was peaceably slipping a little brown paper bag into her glossy weapon of choice.

Todd reached out and helped her down the fickle wooden steps. "I can't believe this, I just can't believe this. I just ran into your son today in Atlanta and now I'm runnin' into you, Miz Street. What are the chances of that?"

"That's October for you. They's always strange goin's on under a harvest moon." Mrs. Street pushed up her thick glasses and adjusted her head to get a better look at him. "Speakin' of which, have you found Elvis yet? Alex Meriwether deserves that, don't he?"

Todd sighed loudly. "I'm not sure that Elvis was Alex's... um...Elvis. But whoever does own or did own him sure does deserve to get him back, yes ma'am."

"But on TV the mayor said—"

"It was nice seein' you again, Miz Street." Todd turned toward the house but she grabbed his arm.

"I never said nothin' before, but you could have been better to Andrew in high school. Y'all was such good buddies in peewee football and Little League. Everybody always gave you all the glory, and you let them. You could have gave Andrew a few nods." She shifted the patent-leather purse from her elbow to her hand and Todd feared she was going to start flailing away at him.

"That's funny you mentioned that," he said, "because I already ate crow with your son over that very subject this afternoon. You're right, and I'm sorry."

Mrs. Street looked him up and down again, harrumphed, and headed toward the gate. Over her shoulder she called out, "Come by the house sometime and I'll give ya some of my put-up mincemeat to take to your momma."

"Thanks, Miz Street," called out Todd as he topped the stairs. Mumbling under his breath he added, "Come by so you can give me a concussion with that patent-leather-covered club."

Now that he was on the porch, Todd grew a second set of cold feet. It didn't help that the dozens of dream catchers hanging from the ceiling brushed the top of his head. It felt like spiders were crawling through his hair. Standing between him and the doorbell was a gargoyle so tall that it eyed his duty belt. Todd was not one who understood or particularly liked gargoyles. He hoped that it was only a Halloween decoration like the black cauldron that sat by the other side of the door. He rang the doorbell, stepped back, and leaned on the railing. Suddenly, he swung around, attempting in vain to catch the falling ceramic troll that had been sitting on the rail.

Todd swung back as Marvalena opened the door, hoping that she wouldn't spot the missing statue. She was clad in a red University of Georgia Bulldogs T-shirt and a pair of jeans. Todd had half-expected a black robe and matching hat. On her face was a pleasantly distracted smile, as if she were listening to the deep, rich tones of the long wind chimes hanging at each end of the porch. Marvalena was in her mid-fifties, which put her at about the same age as Sunbeam Meriwether. But, where Sunbeam was all knobby knees and sharp elbows, Marvalena was padded around the middle and rounded off at the corners. Where Sunbeam's translucent skin was as withered as dried tobacco leaves, Marvalena's complexion glowed with the secrets of life; and even though her face showed an excess of sun-induced wrinkles, there was a youthful alertness in her bright, aquamarine eyes.

Todd said, "You know, the mayor hates this blue door. He thinks you're a Carolina Tar Heels fan."

"This color is haint blue—it keeps the haints away," she said. "I can't help it if the Tar Heels adopted it as their color."

"What are haints?"

"You young people don't know nothin' from nothin'," she chided. "Haints are evil spirits."

Marvalena's long, frizzy hair—top half gray, bottom half blonde—stirred in the warm, moist breeze. It was pulled back loosely in an oversized barrette, but a good quantity of the strands had liberated themselves and were flying free about her head. As if she knew what Todd was thinking, Marvalena reached up, found the barrette, and freed the remainder of her hair. As she smoothed it, she said, "It always goes haywire when I'm doin' a readin'." She led Todd back to the cozy kitchen, grabbed a potholder, and pulled a skillet of cornbread out of the chipped enameled stove.

Then she turned to him and asked, "You hollowed out?" Todd's head bobbed involuntarily. He realized he hadn't had anything to eat since this morning when he'd stuffed a couple of leftover biscuits into his mouth as he left the apartment. The pungent aroma of cornbread unmercifully seduced him. If the wart taker was going to put some kind of potion in his food and steal his Methodist-raised soul, he was helpless to resist it. He saw his tombstone: "Here lay Todd Hoyt 'Fearless' McPherson, done in by the wart taker's homemade cornbread."

Marvalena spooned some pinto beans onto two dishes and laid a large slice of cornbread on one plate and a smaller one on the other. "I had to put this in the oven in the middle of Miz Street's readin'," she said. "Nowadays, even granny witches have to multitask." She took a bowl of leftover collard greens out of the microwave and added them to both plates. She then handed the plates to her unexpected guest, who set them on the little table next to a half-open window.

Todd cleared his throat. "How long have you been practicing ... ah ... what do you call it ... granny magic?"

"Well, I moved away from here after high school." With a dismissive wave, she added, "I couldn't wait to get out of this stifling, self-righteous, Gulag work camp called Duckett County. I ended up in New Orleans, where I married a nice Cajun boy. That's how I came to have the last name LeJeune." Her face grew luminescent. "Oh, Rhemy was my sweet, sweet lover boy." The light in her eyes faded. "But he died in a shrimpin' boat accident a month before I bore our daughter. So I brought my baby back here and apprenticed with my momma. Momma made her transition last May, you know," she added as she handed Todd the cutlery. "Momma was the soul of this house. Place feels so vacant now."

Todd set the table and stood waiting for her. She poured two glasses of buttermilk and set them on the table. Todd pulled out her chair and waited for her to sit down. After they were seated, Marvalena held her hands over her food and looked at Todd expectantly. Despite feeling silly, he followed suit. She said a prayer that sounded like it was in the Cherokee language. Then she pinched off a corner of her cornbread and tossed it out the window. "Have to keep the fae happy."

"The fae?"

"You know, the little people—fairies." She looked at him expectantly.

"Oh, the fae." Todd nodded soberly, then pinched off a corner of his cornbread and threw it out the window. While Marvalena rewarded Todd with an approving smile, he noted to himself that she hadn't asked him if he'd found Elvis yet. Was it because she knew where Elvis was? Maybe she was planning on brewing up some fertility potion in her cauldron with poor little ol' Elvis as the main ingredient.

Todd dropped his cogitations and ate greedily for a few minutes. He asked permission to take more cornbread; in fact, he ended up eating seconds of everything. Then he took an extended swallow of buttermilk and wiped his mouth with a paper napkin plucked from the clear plastic holder by the window. He asked, "Friday after the doc and I put Elvis in the clinic—did you hear anything unusual in the middle of the night? You're only a few doors up from the clinic, so I'm thinkin' you might have heard a car in the alley or—"

"I wasn't here. As is my habit, I drove to my daughter's place in Atlanta on Friday night. She's an ob/gyn resident at Grady Hospital."

Todd sat straight up. "I can't believe this. I was just down at Grady today and I ran into Andrew Street. And just now on your front steps there was his momma ... and now you say your daughter works at Grady."

Marvalena placed a finger on her pursed lips. "Hmmm, three coincidences between sunrise and sunset. When you go home, turn around thrice before you go in the front door. I'll give you a fern, but you'll have to keep it inside by the door until spring, then you need to move it to your porch. Ferns are good for keepin' bad luck from crossin' your threshold. If you want, I can do some scryin' in a bowl of cornbread crumbs for you. I'd do it for free as a community service, since you're workin' on a difficult case. Scryin' is usually done in dirt, but I've developed a new method using cornbread crumbs. It's my contribution to the profession. I gave a talk on it up in North Carolina at a folk gatherin'," she added with a hint of pride in her voice.

"What did you do on Saturday?" asked Todd, uninterested in the topic of cornbread crumbs.

"Went shoppin' with my daughter, and then returned home late that afternoon." Marvalena squirmed and rubbed her lower back. Much to Todd's alarm, she reached over to the counter drawer, pulled out a butcher knife and laid it under her chair. "Cuts the pain of my rheumatism," she mumbled. She drained her glass and wiped her mouth. "I enjoy spendin' time with Daisy, but I try to give her space. You remember my Daisy, don't you? She graduated from Duckett High the same year as you."

Where's Elvis?

Todd rubbed his chin and let his thoughts drift back in time. In his mind's eye, he scanned the faces of the seventy-three kids in his senior class and settled on the image of a slightly built, pale-skinned girl with long, blonde hair. "Did she wear clear plastic glasses?" Marvalena nodded. The image sharpened. He pictured a thin-faced, humorless girl always lurking in the shadows and loaded down with library books. To make matters worse, she wore weird outfits that looked like they were partly homemade and partly came from the county thrift store.

"You jocks were kind of hard on her," said Marvalena. "And Todd, you were their leader. You could have set a better example." She leaned on her elbows and gave him a frank stare.

Todd suddenly recalled long-forgotten pranks he and his buddies played on Daisy LeJeune, mainly on account of the fact that her mother and grandmother were witch doctors. Around Halloween time, they became especially naughty. They would leave a broom leaned up against her locker. Once, Todd had even set a stuffed black cat on Daisy's seat in his mother's English class, and he'd had to clean out the hen house later for it. Over four years of high school, Todd and his gang of jocks stole several dozen ceramic trolls and elf statues from the LeJeune's front yard, hauled them off to their hangout shack in the Duckett Forest, and shot them up with their 22s.

He squirmed in the chair that was suddenly too small for him. For the third time this day, he was being forced to realize what a creep of an adolescent he'd been. The nice, clean-cut young man who was president of the Student Athletes for Christ had been two-faced. But hey, it wasn't entirely his fault. There was the peer pressure thing. And also, did Marvalena have to go and name her daughter Daisy and dress her in costumes? That hadn't helped any.

He exhaled loudly. "I'm sorry, Marvalena. Please accept my apology on behalf of every ignorant jock that has gone through Duckett High School. I will write a letter for you to give to Daisy. Also, I apologize for all those trolls and fairies that me and my buddies stole from your front yard. I will replace them."

Marvalena looked at him thoughtfully. Finally she said, "I've been waitin' a long time to hear those words." She wiped the cornbread crumbs off the table into her hand and dumped them on her plate. Picking up both their plates, she carried them to the sink, then returned to the table. She looked into Todd's eyes. "Let me see your palm." Todd drew back. "Come on. I don't bite." She reached out and pulled his manly hand to her side of the table. She turned it over and slowly ran her palm across his palm. Slipping on reading glasses, she intensely examined the lines. Suddenly, she looked up at him with surprise on her face. Then she looked back at his hand.

She finally said, "You might go places you never dreamed of. There are amazin' untapped abilities in you. You're waitin' for someone to come along who has the key to unlock your hidden strengths. But she may never show up. And in her absence, you've chosen the easier path."

Todd looked at Marvalena as if a boiled egg had just dropped out of one of her nostrils. *Chosen the easier path, my ass!* He pulled his hand back and said evenly, "You were sayin' that you usually come back from Atlanta on Saturday evenin'."

"Yes, Daisy spends the rest of the weekend with her fiancé, Andrew Street. Right now, they both have Sundays off."

Todd's eyes nearly popped out of his head. "Fleet!?" He attempted to picture the handsome, dark-skinned former halfback paired with the spindly, pale-blonde egghead from his memory.

As if Marvalena could read his mind, she said, "I know they'd look funny walkin' together down Main Street in Duckettville, but all kinds of people pair up in Atlanta."

"How's his momma takin' it?" asked Todd, wondering if Fleet had faced the patent leather club upon giving her the news.

"She's comin' around." Marvalena changed the subject. "Now it's my turn to ask a question. You said you were at Grady today. How's Sunbeam?" There was deep concern in her eyes.

"Still mostly out of it." Todd abruptly returned to his own line of questioning. "What did you do after you returned from Atlanta?"

"I called everybody that evenin'. Told them I wasn't feelin' well and I wouldn't be holdin' service on Sunday. Nobody answered at the Meriwether place, so I left a message."

Todd rubbed his chin as he pondered this information. Maybe by Saturday, Alex was already dead. Without Alex there to supervise, Sunbeam had probably skipped her meds. By the time the firemen arrived Monday night, her thoughts were as tangled as a nest of water moccasins. Still, maybe she hadn't been alone. Maybe Sunbeam's "arch-angel" was a real person. Todd filed the thought and returned to his line of questioning. "Do you know the name of Sunbeam's doctor?"

"No, Alex kept that to himself. He was funny about some things."

"Did Alex ever come to you for medical advice?"

Marvalena pulled her hair off her neck and picked up a paper plate to fan her face. "Sorry—hot flash. What were you sayin'?"

"Did Alex ever come here for some kind of treatment?"

"He'd come by here once in awhile to talk about metaphysics. Only one time did he take a medical consultation for himself. I gave him an adapatagen."

"An adapatawhat?"

"A tincture of herbs to help his beat-up body cope with what he'd put it through."

"Did you ever treat Sunbeam?"

"That poor woman. It would be too risky combining herbs with the drugs she was on. My magic ain't that strong," she said, fanning herself faster.

Todd leaned in a little closer and locked onto her eyes. "You ever practice black magic?"

"Todd McPherson!" Marvalena jabbed a finger into his forearm. "Black magic always boomerangs, remember that." She pushed her unruly hair off her face then smiled the faintest of smiles. "However,

230

sometimes a little gray magic can be in order…"

Like a fidgety teenager, Todd balanced the back of his fork on his finger and pretended to put all his attention on it. "Would gray magic involve slicin' off a man's penis and puttin' it on a rock in the woods?" He suddenly shifted his attention to Marvalena.

"I see where you're goin' with this. And to think I just fed you." Marvalena stood up and snatched Todd's fork.

"I didn't mean you, personally, Marvalena. I just meant, you know, in theory. You're the witch expert. Maybe there's a cloven around here that—"

"The word is coven." She glared at Todd, but he held her eyes. Then she added thoughtfully, "The male organ is a very powerful symbol of fertility." She lit a small bundle of dried sage and waved it around the kitchen. "The vortexes in the Forest have been fluctuating wildly lately, and Mars is in retrograde, which may be what's causin' all this foolishness."

Todd suddenly wanted to exit this strange-smelling house. He wanted to put a good distance between himself and the gargoyles, trolls, and the stupid little fae. And he wanted to put distance between himself and his guilt over being such an ass of a teenager. He thanked Marvalena for supper and untangled his long legs from the little table and chair.

As he headed to the front door, Marvalena followed, still waving the bundle of smoking sage and prattling on. " … Need to ask Spider Grandmother for guidance … " Todd ignored her. He had only one thought on his mind—escape. But Marvalena continued her jabbering. "…Strange vibes…like last month when I got a call from somebody offering twice what this house is worth."

Todd turned back. "Huh, that's weird. Who was it?"

"Said he was with some property investment company out of Indianapolis. Anyway, I didn't care for his energy. He called again last week, but I hung up on him."

"If he calls again, could you please get the name, number, and address of the company?" Todd's list of Recent Weird Events flashed through his mind. He had grouped three of the events under the heading of Land Development – the bones (if they were Billy's), the commissioner's brawl, and the surveying by the Davis cousins. Now someone wanted to pay way too much for Marvalena's house. Was this another item to put under that heading?

"Sure," replied Marvalena. She followed him out into the front garden, and handing him the smoking bundle of sage, picked out a potted fern. Then she gave the plant to him and he returned the burning herbs to her. She said, "I'm gonna study a spider web for you one of these mornings. October's a good month for web watchin'. And Todd, make sure you cross the river on the way to your farm. You don't want Alex Meriwether's ghost followin' you home."

Todd closed the little white gate then turned back and watched the wart taker, silhouetted against the deepening sunset, offer the smoking bundle of sage to the four directions.

Holding his fern unceremoniously in one hand, he strode quickly back to the familiar masculinity of his jailhouse. He entered through the back door and walked down perp walk, where he noticed that Chez McPherson had a new prisoner, who was at this moment drooling on his Confederate flag tattoo. Todd continued down the hall toward the reception room. Rusty had gone home to take a break from the exhausting and frustrating job of chasing down another unproductive lead on the Elvis case. Virgil, tonight's duty officer, was standing in the middle of the reception room, attempting to teach himself to moonwalk. Scratch, Todd's neophyte dispatcher and snitch to his uncle Sonny, was playing paper football on his desk. Todd snapped his fingers and pointed to the game pieces. Scratch jerked his head up, and noticing Todd, swept them into the drawer.

"Why is Beaver Bailey in a cell?" asked Todd. "Don't tell me he was drivin' with a suspended license again."

Virgil said, "I brought him in about an hour ago. Seems we had a high-speed chase."

Todd's face turned crimson. "Why am I hearing about this just now!? I am to be informed of high-speed chases immediately!" His piercing stare shifted between the green dispatcher and the tetched deputy.

Virgil tugged upwards on his duty belt and said, "Well, Todd, it wasn't really all that fast of a chase. You see, Beaver was ridin' a one-horsepower vehicle—a pretty lil ol' Quarter Horse. It seems he was on his way home from the liquor store across the county line when he made a left turn without yieldin' to oncomin' traffic. Dillon witnessed the violation and started out after him, but the Beav - he just plain ol' refused to pull that mare over. In fact, he threw her in high gear and tore out down Route 78. Blaine, Forrest, Bo, and Wyatt joined the chase and tried to block him in, but you know how well a Quarter Horse can cut on a dime. So, they all dogged ol' Beaver until his mount finally ran out of gas. 'Course, that took a while. For a sprinter, that lil' gal went the distance."

"A horse?" asked Todd quizzically.

"Yep," said Virgil and Scratch in unison.

"A horse."

"Yep," responded Virgil and Scratch again.

Todd rubbed his eyes. He didn't need any more weirdness today. "So where's this law-flaunting beast now?"

Virgil looked at Scratch. Scratch ducked his head and pretended to study the police codes.

"Well?"

Virgil finally said, "All this happened over nearbouts that farm of yours, so Blaine impounded the lil' gal off in one of your pastures."

Todd grinned ghoulishly. "Another hay burner. My prayers have been answered." He gave Virgil and Scratch a look, then retreated to his man-cave where he pulled the compact disc from his brief case and printed the first hundred pages off the transcript of Sike's murder trial.

He stuffed the papers in his satchel, and after plowing though a half-dozen phone messages, called it a day. Or so he thought.

* * * * *

    After work, Jasmine ran the six-mile trail that stretched around Emerald Lake. She returned to her SUV, and as she tackled McLean Mountain, she encountered a descending fog bank. Once home, she showered, dressed in a comfy pair of pajamas, fed Tristan, and ate a light dinner of lentil soup, crackers, and feta cheese. After pouring a glass of wine, she flopped on her air mattress, which she had moved to the living room in front of the wall of windows. She had discovered that when the first light of morning touched these primeval mountains, a kind of mystical transcendence took place. She relished practicing her tai chi routine in the midst of such magic.

    Tristan flopped down next to her, and she idly stroked him while ruminating over her problems with her new job. This was only her second day at work, yet there was already tension between her and her so-called boss. She believed the POA's fiscal fiasco was a ticking time bomb that needed everyone's immediate attention, whereas Les saw the situation as a nuisance that was getting in the way of his bear-shooing activities. Clearly, he was a people person and not a numbers man. Jasmine, on the other hand, was not doing so well in the people department, as she hadn't exactly won over the hearts and minds of the Sopranos. She gazed out the wall of windows. The setting sun appeared to be lounging on top of the fog bank. Jasmine longed to build a comforting fire in the fireplace, but it was far too warm outside to achieve a proper draft. The unfamiliar chime of the doorbell startled her. She cautiously opened the door.

    "Hey, I'm Brandy Stanton," said the young woman with short, stylishly angled red hair. She was dressed in tight black stretch pants and a belted blouse that was bursting with the colors of a Pollock painting. From each of her earlobes dangled a shiny red globe that was too large for her small face. Her feet were nestled in a pair of red calf-suede boots. She was a shade over five-feet and had a curvaceous figure. A bundt cake was cradled in her hands.

She said, "Herb—that's my worse half—he was on the golf course this afternoon with Les Davis, who told him all about you bein' our new chief bean counter and how you moved from… Austin?"

"Boston."

"And how your movin' van had given you the slip. Well, tonight I'm a poker widow. They're all over at my house smokin' those nasty cigars. It'll take a week to get the smell out. Anyways, welcome." She handed Jasmine the heavy cake. "This was made by my housekeeper, Anna. She's from Madrid. It's a long story."

"Please come in," said Jasmine, "Would you care for some wine?"

"No, I brought some raspberry ginseng-flavored water." She opened the chilled bottle and Jasmine handed her a tin cup. Without losing a beat, Brandy continued, "Cute place. Herb and I, we have that house right across the lake from you. You should come over some time. I left my first husband for Herb. My first husband drove me to drink, that's why I have to drink flavored water now. Oh, I think you met my first husband, Todd, on account of that hideous thing-a-ma-whop you found in Duckett Forest. That was horrible. What'd it look like? No never mind, I'm bein' rude. I am just so glad it's all done with. I guess he gave you the third degree. He used to give me the third degree—about my drinkin' that is. I've known him all my life. He's a hunk, but I had to trade him in. He got on my last nerve, you know what I mean? Do you like facials? You look like you could use one. You look stressed about the eyes. And if you need a massage, Hans at the spa gives the best Swedish rubdown. I had a baby by him. Not the massage guy—by Todd. She's at home watchin' TV with Anna. Molly's her name, named after my late momma, who died of the dropsy and menopause and —"

"Thank you so much for popping over." *Does this woman ever come up for air?*

"Listen to me, jabberin' like a jaybird. Anyways, it's nice to meet someone close to my own age. Most people up here in Emerald Lake are kinda long in the tooth, and they look at me sorta funny—especially wonst I open my mouth. I got a bit of the local inflection, which I'm tryin' to lose. In fact, I'm takin' elocution lessons."

"I feel a bit out of place around here, also," confessed Jasmine. She set the cake on the bar. "Would you care for some?"

"No thanks, I need to drop five pounds." Brandy plopped on one of the neon-pink, blow-up air chairs and wobbled around in it. "Whoa, this is kinda sinful! You sound like you're from farther away than Boston."

Jasmine sat Indian-style on the air mattress. "Right you are. I hail from Great Britain, but I've lived in Beantown for the past seven years. I moved there when I was sixteen to attend Harvard."

Brandy's eyes popped open. "Wow, you must be some sort of prodigy! I ain't—I mean, I haven't—been to Boston, but last spring Herb and me—I mean Herb and I—went to New York. So what in Jesus's name caused you to move down to Fuck-it County—excuse my French?"

Jasmine sighed deeply. "It's a long, sordid wedding-gone-wrong sort of tale." By the way that Brandy perked up, Jasmine realized she had already said too much.

Brandy stretched out her short, shapely legs. "Tell Momma all about it. I ain't got nothin' else to do."

"Maybe some other time." *No way in hell, you silly gadfly.*

The bell rang again. Jasmine opened the door and two young men pushed a rack of evening dresses into the living room. They shuffled out and returned with boxes of shoes and clutch purses. The taller of the pair said, "I'm Dwayne and this here's Jimmy. We run errands for Brad—Mr. Whitestone, I mean."

"Hurry it up, Jimmy," said Dwayne, "we've got more shit—stuff to do."

Jimmy handed a clipboard to Jasmine and said, "Brad—I mean, Mr.

Whitestone—said for you to pick out one of these outfits to wear Thursday night to the thing y'all are goin' to." Jasmine was not surprised. Brad's secretary had emailed her after her chat with Brad on Monday. The secretary had asked for her dress and shoe size. Jimmy added, "His company is gonna pay for it. We'll be back Friday night to pick all this shi ... stuff up." Jasmine signed the paper on the clipboard, handed it back, and opened the door for the lads, who disappeared into the fog.

By now, Brandy had grown two saucer-sized peepers. "Jasmine, you been on your job less than a week and you've landed a date with Golden Boy—Georgia's most eligible bachelor. Man, you English gals work fast!"

"Oh no, it's not a date. It's a charity event," replied Jasmine flipping through the gowns.

Brandy joined her on the other side of the rack. "The question is," she said impishly, "what kinda charity is Brad gonna get?"

Jasmine paused and peered through the clothes rack at Brandy, then resumed inspecting the gowns. For the next hour, she tried them on while Brandy critiqued. They decided on a dress called Sea Foam by Vera Wang. It was an iridescent, pale-green number that left one bare shoulder.

After Brandy finally left, a curious restlessness fell over Jasmine. All day, she had been thinking about the key she had found taped to the underside of the box from Glen Baker's office. She looked at her watch. Nine p.m. She wheeled the party dresses and boxes into the bedroom and threw on her comfy pair of jean shorts and a Harvard T-shirt. Rummaging through her purse, she found the key and slid it into her pocket. Then she grabbed her wallet and jumped into her Honda.

* * * * *

Despite the fact that he felt sheepish about it, Todd altered his route so that he drove over the river as Marvalena had instructed. He had liked

Alex immensely, but that didn't mean he wanted the old fart sharing his bed, especially if he ever got Jasmine in said bed.

By the time he approached the McPherson farm, a low cloud cover had moved in, obscuring the stars and the waxing harvest moon. Gusts of wind were whipping up mini-cyclones of leaves, and yet the atmosphere was unusually warm. Hooty and the other dogs barked Todd through the open gate. When he stepped out of the truck they sniffed him, and ID confirmed, returned to their posts. The compound was utterly dark. The days were growing shorter, and the pole lamp had yet to come on. Todd made a mental note to adjust the timer on the light. Fern in one hand and satchel in the other, he started up the long, steep stairs to his apartment. He noticed that the lights were off in the farmhouse. That was funny. It was a little early to be in bed, even for Jessie McPherson. Todd set down his satchel. He needed to check this out. He decided the fern had a better chance of surviving if he gave it to his mother. He crossed the compound to the front porch of his mother's farmhouse. Left hand curled around the fern, he reached for the doorknob with the right hand, but it froze in midair. Cursing under this breath, he turned around three times as quickly as he could, and then reached for the doorknob again.

"I see you been hangin' out with the wart taker," came a voice from the porch swing.

"Jesus, Sikes! You 'bout scared the pee-waddin' outta me!" Todd was grateful for the darkness because he could feel his face growing warm.

"I was fixin' your front gate until it got too dark to see. Of course, I was wastin' my time in the first place since y'all don't ever actually shut the dang thang. Your momma told me to tell you that she's gone line dancin' at the Buckin' Bull."

"Did you say Momma's gone dancin'? Now I know the world has flipped upside down."

"She went with LeeLee and some other ladies. By the way, have you found Elvis yet?"

"You so don't want to go there," growled Todd.

"You hungry? Come on back to town and we'll grab a bite at the Flagg."

"Marvalena already fed me and I've had a long day."

"Oh well, suit yourself, but I'll be sleepin' on your couch since I don't have any way to get back to town."

* * * * *

The walls of the Checkered Flagg were covered with autographed posters and photographs of famous NASCAR drivers. The dining area consisted of eight booths and an equal number of tables. An old pool table sat off in a side room, which was open to the restaurant. Billy Rae Cyrus was singing Achy Breaky Heart on a juke box that had been kicked so many times it could no longer play anything louder than medium. Tammy liked it that way. The diner was vacant except for four men barely out of high school in work boots playing pool and Todd's retired high school math teacher, Mr. Moon, and his wife, who were eating a late supper at a table near the front window. All the early dinner guests had gone home to get ready for bed and rest up for another day of work. Before returning to town, Todd had showered and dressed in jeans and a black T-shirt and an unbuttoned light blue work shirt. He said 'Hey' to the Moons and passed on by before they could ask him about Elvis. The pool player tried to get his attention, but he cut them off with a look and they returned to their game.

All the tabletops were done up like shadow boxes, and underneath each piece of Plexiglas lay mementos of a particular NASCAR driver. Sikes and Todd sat at the "Bill Elliott" booth near the back. Tammy plodded up. As usual, her deep chestnut hair was pulled into a severe ponytail, except for her too-long bangs. She was wearing her fall uniform, which consisted of her usual too-tight-across-the-thighs jeans and too-tight-across-the-bust Dale Earnhardt Jr. T-shirt. It was the same

239

shirt she wore in the spring. In hot weather she wore a short-sleeve Dale Earnhardt Jr. T-shirt, and in winter she wore a Dale Earnhardt Jr. sweatshirt. When anyone remarked on Tammy's monotonous wardrobe, she retorted, "They ain't no use dressin' up as long as my husband, Jimmy Flagg, is in the pen." She always referred to him as "My husband, Jimmy Flagg," not as "Jimmy" or "my husband." Tammy plopped down two flimsy, laminated menus and both Sikes and Todd looked up at her with surprise on their faces.

"I know y'all know the offerin's by heart," said Tammy, "but I got a new item. See, it's right chere." With a chewed-down fingernail, she pointed to the menu. Both men scrutinized the item, which was written in pencil on a little square of ruled paper and scotch-taped to the menu.

Sikes pulled his reading glasses out of his pocket, read the new entry, then looked up at Tammy. "Buffalo chips?"

"You know how Sonny and Les are always tryin' out new business schemes? Well, they been raisin' a couple of buffalos on Les's brother-in-law's farm, and Les carried one to the slaughterhouse the other day. He wants me to try it out on the customers, so he brought me a bunch of these little patties." She made a circle with her thumb and forefinger. "He said they come back from the slaughterhouse that way. So, I named them buffalo chips."

"I'll just take a Bud Light," said Todd promptly, hoping to steer the conversation away from edible feces. Sikes ordered an iced tea. His choice of beverage didn't surprise Todd, who had never seen Sikes take a drop of alcohol.

Tammy plodded back to the bar and returned with their drinks. "So, Sikes, do you think buffalo chips is a good name?"

Sikes ran his thumb under the piece of paper and looked at Tammy. With a slightly distasteful look on his face, he said, "I wouldn't use the word chips."

Todd swigged his beer. "How about buffalo medallions?"

Tammy's normally slightly pissed-off expression abruptly turned dark. "I'm not speakin' to you, McPherson. You run them GBI agents back over here yesterday. That's just what I'd expect from the man who sent my husband, Jimmy Flagg, to the pen." She swept her bangs away from her face with a beefy forearm. "Those GBI creeps acted like I broke the law."

Todd locked eyes with Tammy. "That reminds me, you better quit sellin' so many beers to Dwight Pickens or I'm gonna charge you with contributin' to the drunkenness of a drunk, or somethin' like that. Which means you will be sharin' a cell with that stinky boozer."

Tammy snorted. "Well, that would make you happy, wouldn't it? To have put two Flaggs behind bars."

The boys at the pool table were getting rowdy, so Todd had to raise his voice to be heard. "As far as the three blind mice are concerned, for your information, I didn't run them over here. Anyway, I've been drug through the mud enough already today. Knowin' that should make you feel better."

Tammy rolled her eyes then looked at Sikes. "Scooch over."

Sikes rolled *his* eyes. "Why is it always me that has to scooch over?" he asked grumpily as he made room for her.

Tammy sat down and pulled a cigarette out of the pack in Sike's breast pocket. He lit it for her. She raised her voice in order to be heard over the din. "Now, y'all know I'm the only one allowed to smoke in here." She took a draw and as she exhaled said, "That Agent Slaughter's a jackass. He acted like I'm the one that stole that Lil Orphan Andy from Gorov's clinic."

Todd said, "The GBI always acts like you're guilty when they question you. And they'll keep on questionin' you over and over until you trip up on your story, or until they get somebody else to pin the crime on. Anyway, they left today and they're not comin' back anytime soon."

"Well, what have you been doin' all day?" asked Tammy as she flicked ashes into Todd's beer bottle. "Did you find Elvis yet?"

Clamoring to his feet, Todd inserted fingers in his mouth and whistled. The raucous boys at the pool table immediately grew quiet. "Attention everybody! Just for everybody's edification, I have not yet found Elvis. As soon as I find Elvis, I will personally let each and every one of you give him a big smooch!" He glared at the foursome around the pool table. "And will y'all quiet down over there!? I can't hear myself drink." The men around the pool table broke into wild guffaws. Mr. and Mrs. Moon, who were diligently masticating their buffalo chips, stared at their normally normal sheriff. Todd flopped down into the booth, knocking the green vinyl-padded bench back a good six inches.

"You don't have to act like a damn fool," said Sikes severely. "Don't forget, you are the law herebouts."

Todd stretched out his legs, grabbed Tammy's cigarette, and drew in smoke. She rose, snatched up the menus, and thunked them over his head. He flinched reflexively. She said, "Yeah, you don't have to act like a damned fool in my establishment." Then she stomped off.

Todd dropped the cigarette into his beer bottle. "There goes somebody with biggy-sized problems. I don't know why her wrath is always focused on me. It seems to be growing the longer this Elvis case goes on."

Sikes chuckled. "Maybe your height makes you a lightning rod."

In a minute Tammy returned and refilled Sikes's glass of tea. Biting her bottom lip, she asked, "Anyways, will you try the buffalo?"

"Okay, okay, I'll try it," said Sikes.

"I'll take another Bud Light when you bring his food," said Todd.

Tammy frowned. "Ain't you gonna eat somethin'?"

Sikes said, "He don't need nothin' to eat—the wart taker fed him. He was consultin' with her on the case."

Tammy snorted. "Man, you are gettin' desperate." She snickered as she tromped back behind the counter and gave the order to the cook.

Todd's expression turned morose. "You know what I saw today? Bunch of shit-eatin' teenaged idjits hung a banner out of a second story window of the high school that read, 'Where's Elvis?'"

Sike's shoulders bobbed along with his laughter. "Now, how'd they get away with that?"

"It ain't funny."

"Oh, here we go again with the pity party." Todd just shrugged, so Sikes changed directions. "Too bad about Alex. I'm sure gonna miss him. But at least you solved where Elvis came from, right?"

Todd rolled the beer bottle between his palms. "Most of me doesn't think that Elvis came from Alex. What I do think is that Elvis gettin' himself stolen had somethin' to do with where he came from in the first place."

"But apparently the GBI thinks Elvis came from Alex," said Sikes, "else they wouldn't have left town so soon."

Todd placed his forearms on the table and leaned forward. "You know, when Slaughter was interviewin' you, I was expectin' him to go diggin' more into your past. All I ever knew about you was that you were my daddy's employee. But there were rumors. Daddy wouldn't discuss the matter. I've never asked you about ..."

Sikes studied the miniature Bill Elliott stock car under the Plexiglas with the same intensity that Marvalena had demonstrated while studying Todd's palm. "You're askin' about the murder." He lifted his gaze to Todd.

"Now I'm askin'."

"When I was young and stupid I got in a fight in a bar with a young white man – a redneck to be precise. I'd had a couple of prior run-ins with him over my girl. I ended up shootin' the man, and he died on the spot. I gave up twenty years for my crime." Sikes sighed deeply. "As I told Agent Slaughter, after I got out of the pen, I landed up here because your church had a program that found jobs for parolees, and bein' a religious man, your daddy offered to hire me." Sikes paused to sip his iced tea. "I only wanted two things—to work outside and to keep a low profile."

Todd snorted. "Could you have found a whiter place to lay low? I mean, other than my deputy, Tawanda, weeks go by before I see another African-American person in this county. Don't you miss hangin' with your people?"

"I don't like the way you put that, Cotton."

"Huh?"

"Hangin'."

"Oh, ah ... sorry."

"I was thrown in with all kinds of people in prison, people I hoped were not my kind. When I got out I didn't particularly feel drawn to any one group or another. My momma was dead and she was the only person I cared about." Sikes pushed with his hands against the table, pressing himself into the seatback. "I was wonderin' when you was gonna get around to runnin' a background check on me. But you never did, else you would have asked me these questions already."

Todd shrugged one shoulder. "You never broke any laws on my watch. More importantly, my daddy trusted you. Oh, y'all tangled from time to time, but it was all in jest." Todd tipped up his beer bottle, took yet another generous swallow, and looked in the direction of the men playing pool. Sikes sucked on his straw and studied the little model of Bill Elliott's Chevy below the Plexiglas. Finally Todd spoke. "Man, that's heavy—killin' somebody ... dead and all. Ninety-nine percent of lawmen never even have to do that to a criminal."

A heavy shroud of sadness settled over Sikes. "There's not a day gone by since that night that I don't think about that young man whose future I stole."

"What about your gun repairin' gig? You're a convicted felon. You're not supposed to be around guns."

"Aw, that parole board done forgot about me a long time ago. Half of them's probably dead by now."

Tammy walked up, and noticing Todd's legs were stretched out beyond the table, kicked the bottoms of his boots. When he drew in his legs, she plunked a steaming platter in front of Sikes. It contained half a dozen buffalo chips, a giant scoop of mashed potatoes, and a gob of sweet peas, all of it smothered with gravy. She pulled a long neck and a bottle opener out of her apron pocket. Opening the bottle, she handed it to Todd. Then hands on hips, she waited for the verdict on the new menu item.

Sikes cut off a bite and chewed—and chewed some more. "A little tough, but otherwise palatable," he offered up.

Tammy almost smiled, laid the check on the table, and returned to the counter, leaving the young man sitting in silence while the older man methodically ate his supper. Though Todd never planned to bring the up Sikes's crime, he was relieved they'd had this talk. How weird, he thought, that for most of his growing up years, a convicted murderer lived in the apartment over the garage while he and Katie played nearby. Just then, he glimpsed the depth of his parent's faith in the Almighty.

After Todd finished his beer, he reached in his pocket and slapped some bills on the table, then drew in his legs and stood. "I am done in. You best get home pretty soon, too. The weather's lookin' precarious. It's too damn warm. Bad moon on the rise." Fortunately, Sikes lived over his shop, which was next door. Just before Todd was about to turn away, he turned back to Sikes. "By the way, have you had anybody callin' you up and offerin' you a lotta cash for your shop?"

Sikes wiped his mouth with a paper napkin. "Why you ask?"

"Some company out of Indianapolis offered Marvalena double what she figures her house would normally go for."

"Now that you mention it, I've had a guy from some company leavin' me a few messages about wantin' to buy my place. He sounded like he had a Midwestern accent. What's up? Why would anyone wanna throw so much money at the wart taker's house?"

Todd pulled his keys out of his jeans pocket. "Well, duh—because it's October and Mars is in retrograde."

Chapter Eleven
Tuesday Night:
The Girl, the Tub, and the Forces of Nature

Jasmine began to tackle the hairpin turns on her way down McLean Mountain road. She had learned since her arrival that after dark the creatures of Emerald Lake turned into party animals, and of course, since the resort was a wildlife preserve, they had the right of way. Sure enough, she soon had to stop for a raccoon family ambling across the road. Further down, she waited for a meandering possum to discern the location of tonight's festivities. She finally reached the bottom of the mountain and turned onto Emerald Lake Parkway.

It had been foggy up at her cabin, but now that she was lower, a light drizzle was falling, and the road felt slippery. Hunched over the steering wheel, Jasmine searched for the entrance to the POA lodge. When she found it, she turned into the asphalt parking lot, which was lit only by some low-voltage ground lamps. The lot was difficult to navigate, not only because of the darkness, but also because it was irregularly shaped, having been designed to preserve the most number of trees possible. She parked between two pines near the back corner of the building. It was the farthest space from the parkway. She still had no key to the lodge. She had asked for one this morning, but Valinda said not to worry, that there was always a key under the carved wooden bear statue by the back service door. Jasmine grabbed the flashlight from the glove compartment and followed the stone walkway around the corner of the building. She passed by the main entrance, turned another corner, and walked past the wall of glass. The sudden splash of a trout cut through the silence, startling her. The sound made it seem like the edge of the lake was only a few yards away.

As she turned the third corner, Jasmine saw that the sidewalk ended. There was only a path of stepping-stones. Given the unseasonably warm weather, she doubted if the snakes had begun to hibernate. This meant that any minute she might cross paths with a timber rattler warming itself on one of the stones or an ill-tempered copperhead venomously guarding its territory. She quickly negotiated the stone pathway and stepped onto a concrete doorstep. A four-foot bear statue carved from a the trunk of a tree guarded a plain metal door. She shined the flashlight on it and saw that it was covered with spider webs. Picking up a stick, she removed the larger webs, then attempted to wipe off the rest of the webs with the hem of her T-shirt. The more she wiped, the more the damp, diaphanous threads clung to the wooden bear. Giving up, she grasped the slippery statue with her forearms, and despite its heaviness, managed to rock it back and forth until she had moved it a foot. Sure enough, a key lay on the cement.

She regarded the metal door, so unlike the fashionably rustic design of the rest of the lodge. She wiped the key on her shorts and shoved it into the bolt lock. After a few 'open sesames' and some determined key wiggling, the door gave way. She found that she was in the storage room in the back of the administration offices. She shined her flashlight on the various boxes, but found nothing of interest. Next, she walked into Glen's office and shined her light here and there, looking for a hidden compartment. Nothing interesting. She left the office and found herself standing outside Les's office. This was the point of no return. She glanced around for security cameras. Of course there were none. This was not a sophisticated operation.

Jasmine knew the proper way to go about all of this was to request a forensic audit, not to creep around in the dark snooping for evidence. However, she feared that whatever it was that the little key opened could very well disappear before she could hire an auditor. Not wanting to leave fingerprints, she used her T-shirt to turn the doorknob to Les's office then. Still holding her shirt, she tried the top drawer of the filing cabinet. The unlocked drawer contained personnel files, and the lower drawer held contractor information. She pulled from her pocket the little key that she had found taped to the underside of Glen's box. She attempted to insert it in the lock of the filing cabinet. Not a fit. Exiting Les's office, she walked back down the hall toward the storage area. An invading wind rattled through the air vent above the tiled ceiling, and Jasmine found herself cringing. She was beginning to feel quite silly. All she wanted to do now was retreat to the cabin and cozy up with Tristan, Robert Frost, and a cup of chamomile tea. Enough with the Nancy Drew impersonation.

She backed out of the service door and relocked it. Laying the building key on the concrete slab, she rocked the bear statue back over it, then retraced her steps past the wall of windows and the main entrance. Just as she rounded the corner to the parking lot, she found she was staring into a pair of headlights. She jumped back, praying she had not been seen. The vehicle turned and its headlights tracked away. She peeked around the corner and was able to make out a white truck with the Emerald Lake logo on the side. Her heart began to pound so violently that she feared it would simply explode. Obviously, the security guard had seen her car and was no doubt calling in her plates. She tried to think up a plausible excuse to be skulking around the POA lodge this time of night with spider webs clinging to her shirt. Maybe he would just assume she was working late. In a completely dark building? The truck circled the lot again, then crossed Emerald Lake Parkway and entered the parking lot across the street that serviced some condos. It came to a halt facing the POA lodge, and then the headlights were extinguished.

Jasmine turned and walked the other way around the building. The far corner was no more than a few feet from the parking lot and her little SUV. She planned to slip into her vehicle and be gone before Bubba the Guard could start his engine. Once again, she passed the front entrance.

She turned the corner and walked past the wall of windows. She rounded the third corner and when she reached the metal service door again, she saw that the stepping-stones stopped. Shining her flashlight into the darkness ahead, she saw that twenty feet of open ground stood between her and a dense grove of pine trees that lightly kissed the building.

After drawing in a deep breath, she stepped onto the open ground. Halfway to the trees, the unmistakable rattling of a timber rattler brought her up short. Why hadn't she seen him? She shined her flashlight on the ground and saw that the snake was about three feet in front of her, coiled and ready to strike. The blinding light of the flashlight was apparently the last straw, because with one explosive movement, the rattler launched itself. From Jasmine's perspective, the hellish fiend looked ten feet long as it uncoiled and flew through the air toward her exposed calf. It took a few seconds for her to realize that the rattler had brushed by, its deadly fangs missing their mark by a hair's breath. Apparently, the light from the flashlight had confused it. Having struck out, the embarrassed Grumpy Gus hastily slithered off into the woods. True to the timber rattler's comparatively mild disposition, it had apparently decided that discretion was the better part of valor.

Jasmine's legs turned rubbery, but she managed to stay vertical. She pulled herself together, knelt down, and felt around for the flashlight. She found it and shined it forward. Keep calm and carry on. Soon, the open ground was behind her. Slowly, she groped her way along the building while pine branches slapped her face. Just as she came out of the copse of trees, she stumbled over something and fell on all fours. Upon righting herself, she shined her flashlight downward and discovered a cellar door. Her cursory inspection inside the building had not turned up an entrance to a cellar or basement. It was not surprising, though, since the POA lodge, once a mansion that belonged to someone in the Duckett family, had been originally constructed when cellars were dug separately from the main building. Jasmine examined the door and discovered that it was secured with a slightly rusty padlock. She pulled on it, but it refused to give.

She resumed feeling her way along the wall toward the parking lot, then stopped abruptly and slapped her forehead. The key! Retracing her steps, she slipped the little key into the padlock. After some maneuvering, it sprang open. Throwing her back into it, she pulled the heavy door open and shined her flashlight down into the abyss. All she saw at first was inky blackness, but as her eyes adjusted, she spied hundreds of gossamer spider webs crisscrossing the cellar entrance. Even more ominously, wherever she shined the flashlight, skittering and scratching sounds emanated from deep within the cavity. She shuddered involuntarily, but then stiffened her resolve by recalling that she had spent her childhood ridding herself of every conceivable kind of icky insect that her four older brothers dropped down her shirt collar. She broke a branch off a pine tree and used it to brush away the cobwebs as she descended the cellar's rickety stairs.

The space, approximately eight-by-ten, appeared to be a mausoleum for a number of cardboard boxes and castoff office equipment. Jasmine gasped when her little shaft of light fell on an enormous rat sitting on top of an obsolete printer. Unfazed, he stood perched on his hindquarters, rubbing his front paws together as if he were the conniving mayor of this subterranean shantytown. Mr. Mayor rudely stared at Jasmine with his protruding black eyes, no doubt mulling over how he could benefit from the presence of this gigantic, pale-faced stranger. Jasmine stuck her tongue out at him.

She aimed her flashlight at the closest stack of boxes, and once again heard the skittering sound of what seemed like thousands of little legs scrambling over cardboard. She spied the source: a disorganized column of cockroaches poured from the boxes, no doubt on a reconnaissance mission to discover the origin of the strange lights. She was seized with equal amounts of panic and a morbid curiosity. The confusion generated by the confluence of the two emotions fused her feet to the concrete floor. Most of the roaches were very large—larger than any she had ever seen. She recalled she'd read something about roaches being able to digest paper and withstand nuclear fallout. Apparently, evolution's gift to the post-apocalyptic world would be the cockroach.

Jasmine moved forward and bumped into a stack of old computer monitors. She thought that perhaps the blackness of the cellar had confused her, because she no longer remembered exactly why she happened to be in this beastly oubliette of horrors. Turning around, she spied a thigh-high pile of unmarked cardboard boxes. She tentatively opened the flap of the top box and jumped back as a garrison of cowardly roaches abandoned their makeshift fort. Then, horror of horrors, one panicked roach flew at her and ran up her arm. She shrieked involuntarily and flung out her conquered limb repeatedly in a desperate attempt to dispel the dastardly devil, but the little bastard apparently had suction cups for feet. A wild dance ensued as Jasmine struggled to brush it off with her flashlight. Not surprisingly, she lost her balance and landed on her bum on the stack of boxes. This event caused a legion of roaches to abandon their cardboard headquarters, some of which chose Jasmine's body as a path to safety. Shrieking involuntarily, she attempted to attain her feet, but her efforts were complicated by the constant shifting of the boxes beneath her. After what seemed like an eternity, she managed to stand just as the stack of boxes fell over sideways.

She frantically shook her long curls, fearful that the reckless roaches were clinging to her scalp as if they were hanging onto a tilt-a-whirl at the fair. A wave of nausea washed over her as she brushed several dead squished roach foot soldiers off her thighs. She thought she'd go mad just from the feel on her skin of the pecan-pie filling oozing from their hard-chocolate shells. The impulse to run was almost overwhelming, but she concentrated on steadying her breathing and visualizing clean bed sheets, of all things.

Looking down at the toppled tower of boxes, Jasmine noticed that her squirming bottom had caused them to burst open and regurgitate some of their contents. One box drew her attention because the partially spilled documents included an old-fashioned three-ring binder style checkbook. It was the kind bookkeepers used before the advent of computers. There were computer papers also. All of them had ragged edges, a telltale sign that the low-life roach soldiers had been snacking on the contents of their cardboard fortresses. Grimacing, she forced herself inspect some of them. Spreadsheets. This messy juxtaposition of old and new technology reminded Jasmine of someone – Glen Baker. She picked up the nasty papers and the checkbook and returned them to their raggedy box. Then, she carefully picked up the box, and holding it as far away from her body as possible, carried it up the stairs. Somehow, she forced herself to descend once again into the dank tomb, where she hastily shined her flashlight on the contents of the other boxes. None of them looked promising. She said good riddance to the smirking Mayor Rat.

She quickly climbed the stairs, closed and locked the cellar door, and resumed moving along the backside of the building until she reached the parking area. Squinting through the darkness, she observed that the security truck was still parked in the lot across the street, its driver no doubt laying in wait to accost the recently hired, radically mental CFO. Thankfully, her Honda was only a few steps away. She opened the tailgate, deposited the box, and then opened the driver's side door. She pulled out a container of wet wipes and vigorously scrubbed every exposed bit of skin until she had exhausted the entire supply. Once inside the safety of her little SUV, she rested her head on the steering wheel and added up the risks she had just taken. There could easily have been a colony of venomous vipers or barbarous black widows in that demonic mausoleum. What an abhorrent place in which to depart this world! She had just risked her precious life for a raggedy, roach-infested cardboard box full of vaguely suspicious papers.

Turning onto the parkway, she noticed that the road had become even more treacherous. The drizzling rain, combined with the fallen leaves and the ubiquitous thin layer of oil that over time had dripped from various engines, promised to make the twisting two-lane road a possible accessory to homicide. As if it were in collusion with the road, the fog on the mountains had descended into the valley. Jasmine estimated her visibility to be no more than one car length ahead. Though she could not see the lake below the road, she sensed it. As she rounded a sharp curve, she was nearly blinded by the headlights of an oncoming vehicle with an unmistakable silver peace sign on its front grill. The dark, heavy sedan had borrowed her side of the road in order to conquer the curve more expeditiously. The thought flashed through Jasmine's mind that after all she'd been through tonight, including narrowly escaping death by serpentine, the cause of her untimely expiration was apparently going to be murder by Mercedes. She yanked the steering wheel to the right, narrowly avoiding a head-on collision. Now she was off the road and angling down the slope toward a towering pine tree. Never one who was particularly interested in the laws of physics, she yanked the wheel hard to the left. The Honda, being an object of mass, was obligated to follow the laws of physics. It flipped several times and slid down the embankment toward the patiently waiting black water.

* * * * *

Todd parked his pickup in front of the stairs leading to his apartment. Before stepping out, he called LeeLee on his cell phone. She said there wasn't one night when the news, Lost, and American Idol aired sequentially on TV. Sunbeam had confused her nights or programs. There goes another lead. As he opened the door, the radio crackled to life. He heard Scratch asking if any units were near Emerald Lake because there had been a single-car accident with injuries to the occupant. He commented that the vehicle belonged to the new CFO, and went on to opine that all they needed up at Emerald Lake was another female driver. Grabbing the mic, Todd told Scratch that he would drive up there personally since he was close by, and to leave the gender-related commentary off the radio. He spun the truck around and tore out of the compound, spewing gravel, perplexed dogs, and flummoxed chickens in his wake.

As he drove up on the scene of the accident, Todd could just make out through the fog Booger Boggs and his nephew attempting to attach a cable to Jasmine's Honda, which was lodged sideways against two trees some fifteen yards below the road. Just below her overturned vehicle lay the promise of a cold, silent, watery grave. The top of the Honda was bashed in to such an extent that Todd was surprised the firemen hadn't had to use the Jaws of Life to extract his precious fantasy girl. He screeched to a halt and ran to the EMS unit, where he spied Jasmine sitting sideways on a gurney and clutching a white blanket around her shoulders. Todd exhaled with relief, sprang into the truck, and sat down next to the EMT, Mark Cantrell. Both men gazed wondrously at one fortunate girl who had not one scratch on her.

Jasmine said, "Sheriff McPherson, would you please inform this gentleman that I do not require a visit to the hospital, as I merely bumped my head."

Mark pursed his lips. "Todd, she oughta let us take her in so she can get a CAT scan. She's gotta big ol' bump a-comin' up." Mark pulled Jasmine's head down and parted her hair at the crown so Todd could feel the bump.

"Yep, you gotta nasty ol' knot, Ms. Roseberry," Todd said.

Jasmine raised her head and flipped her hair out of her face. "Please, I'm fine, thanks to the air bags. I just want to go home. If I feel bad tomorrow, I'll check myself into the hospital."

Todd said to Mark, "How about I take her home and watch her for a while?"

Mark exhaled loudly, "It's against my better judgment. But I s'pose I can trust you." He looked at Jasmine, "Todd's my cousin." He removed his plastic gloves and looked Todd in the eye. "Just don't let her go to sleep for four hours." He looked at Jasmine and held up four fingers. "Four hours, Jasmine. And if at any time you feel nauseated or dizzy, get to the hospital ASAP. You got that?"

Jasmine nodded, and Todd helped her out of the truck. Together they watched Booger haul up her Honda, which had been transformed into modern-art metal sculpture.

Over the noise of the winch and the grinding metal, Todd asked her, "Can you tell me what happened?"

Jasmine gestured to the road. "A black, maliciously marauding Mercedes of titanic proportions sped around this curve and commandeered my lane just as I was coming from the opposite direction. Consequently, I was forced to deploy evasive maneuvers to avoid a head-on collision. And then I rolled approximately one dozen times—at least it seemed like a dozen times—until the rotations were abruptly halted by several of those Georgia pines."

They both looked again at Jasmine's Honda, which was now on the road but lying on its side. Booger's nephew repositioned the cables and Booger engaged the winch. Jasmine shuddered as, with the sudden screeching and crashing sounds of metal-on-metal, her mangled vehicle fell into an upright position.

After Todd helped Jasmine into his pickup, she remembered her wallet and the box of papers. With turns and twists worthy of a yoga master, Todd and Booger's nephew managed to retrieve from the wreckage the beat-up box, the numerous pieces of paper, the checkbook, and Jasmine's wallet. Todd tossed everything but the wallet back into the box and stashed it behind his driver's seat. He handed the wallet to his ward.

Jasmine sat in gloomy silence as the pickup grudgingly climbed McLean Mountain. Only the whine of the protesting transmission broke the quiet.

"I won't lie to you," stated Todd. "It's gonna be tough finding that Mercedes since it didn't have any contact with your car. And maliciously marauding isn't a commonly recognized descriptive term for a wanted vehicle. Nonetheless, I'll have a couple of my deputies process the scene as soon as it gets light tomorrow, while the guards search the vehicle records of the residents and guests."

When Jasmine didn't respond, Todd stole a peak at her. Though the temperature had remained balmy all evening, she was shivering, and she looked to be on the verge of tears. When Todd finally pulled into the cabin's asphalt driveway, though, he was relieved to see that she was no longer shaking. Perhaps the shock was wearing off already.

He jotted his cell phone number on a piece of paper. "Before I forget, I want you to have this. Call me any time, and I'll fill you in on the investigation into your wreck."

Jasmine tucked the paper in her wallet. After stepping out of the truck, Todd pulled his cell phone out of his pocket and tossed it on the seat. He didn't want anyone calling while he was with Miss Fantasy.

Once inside, Jasmine offered Todd wine, but he requested beer. She opened a bottle of Budweiser for him, then glass of wine in hand, she carefully wiggled her way into one of the neon-pink, blow-up air chairs. Todd wrestled his way into the other one, but as much as he squirmed, he couldn't seem to get his knees below his ears. Over the rim of his beer bottle, he studied the goddess before him while she unglamorously guzzled her wine.

She set the empty glass on the floor and said mournfully, "All my belongings have been hauled off to Emerald Lake, Siberia, and now I don't even have my little Honda." She picked up the bottle of wine and tipped it up.

"Maybe you oughta stop drinkin' until your head feels better," warned Todd.

She harrumphed and said testily, "Quand les poules auront des dents."

"What's that mean?"

Jasmine looked at him scornfully, as if to say that everyone knew

256

that particular phrase, duh. "It's French for When Pigs Fly," she retorted and gulped more wine. Then she opened her throat and out from it escaped a police car's wail that in sheer decibels rivaled one of Molly's howls when she was in one of her states.

Jasmine blurted, "I simply cannot believe that I actually signed a year's contract to work under a boss for whom after a mere two days in his company, I haven't a shred of respect! And as far as my subordinates are concerned, they're a trio of inbred, imbecilic ignoramuses! I'm stuck in Bum Fuck, Egypt, a thousand miles from my mates and three thousand from Mummy and Dad. And, yes, I'm famous all over the planet for having found a wastrel of a wanger on a rock!"

Jasmine hiccupped once then said on hitched breath, "A rattlesnake tried to gank me, a supercilious rat scorned me, and I have the remnants of squished roach custard all over my legs ..." She wept woefully for a moment, then settled into a sappy sobbing with her head between her knees. She lifted her head and wailed, "And now I have a bump on my head!"

Todd clumsily bounced his see-through chair next to hers and patted her on the back. "There, there," was all he could think of to say. "There, there." He tucked a lock of hair behind her ear. Even disheveled, she still looked adorable.

Jasmine's weeping gave way to spastic hitches, and Todd took that as a sign that the situation was improving. Just then, a moan escaped her lips. "What is it?" Todd asked, eying her for signs of an impending brain fart. He did not want to drive her to the hospital. He wanted her here, with him. On the other hand, he knew that head injuries were nothing to monkey around with.

Jasmine ratcheted herself into a standing position and said weakly, "Me thinks me needs to worship at the porcelain throne," and scuttled down the hall.

Todd gave her a few minutes and followed her path, sniffing for barf and listening at doors for a moaning noise. It didn't take long. He knocked on the back of the door with one knuckle.

"You alright?" he asked. There was no answer, so holding his breath, he opened the door and saw her sitting on the floor pressing a damp washrag to her neck.

He placed his fists on his hips, and in his most authoritative voice said, "I'm gonna carry you to the hospital right now."

Jasmine waved him off. "No, no. I'm sure this was the lentil, feta cheese, and red wine mishmash that I imbibed earlier. Now that I no longer harbor that particular amalgamation in my stomach, I feel as fit as a butcher's dog." She managed a weak smile.

Todd noted that her face was the color of onion paper, and her body was as limp as celery that had been out left out of the fridge overnight. "You don't look as fit as a butcher's dog," he pronounced.

Jasmine weakly raised her arms and Todd pulled her to her feet. She let go of him and grabbed the towel rack for support, then looked down at her bare legs. "I'm totally skanky and absolutely must scrub every inch of myself in a near-scorching shower." She looked at Todd and made a shooing motion with her hand.

But he stood his ground and crossed his arms over his chest. "It's too soon to take a shower."

Still gripping the towel rack, Jasmine backed into the corner between the shower and the wall. "Who are you, Robocop? I rent this stall, you know." She gripped the chrome bar on the shower door with her free hand. "Quite honestly, you are annoyingly fetching in a trashy romance novel sort of way. And I am seriously alarmed by the fact that you wear your pelt so ludicrously neat that one could very well call you Helmet Hair."

"You can take a shower," barked Todd, "but I'm stayin' here. Don't worry, me and my helmet hair are harmless, and anyway, I won't be able to see your privates through that fuzzy shower glass. He ratcheted his tone down to an even-more-commanding level. "But if you pass out in there, I'm haulin' your skinny, nekkid ass down to the emergency

258

room."

Jasmine looked as if she'd just had a bucket of ice thrown over her head. She stood perfectly still. Only her eyes moved as she mentally weighed her options. Finally, with a facetious smile, she opened the shower door, stepped in, and closed it firmly behind her. Todd lowered the lid to the porcelain throne and sat down. He watched as the jean shorts flew over the door, followed by the Harvard T-shirt. Next, her panties and bra were catapulted over. The panties landed at Todd's feet. The bra ended up on his lap and he dropped it on the floor, but not before surreptitiously checking its size on the label.

As she adjusted the water temperature, Jasmine said over the sound of the shower, "I have to warn you, Sheriff, I enjoy practicing my Italian arias in the shower."

Forty minutes and seventy-five attempted operatic high notes later, Todd sloshed into the living room in very, very damp boots. He had just sat on a hard toilet seat through what had to have been the longest shower in the history of showers. He surmised that this cabin had to contain at least four hot-water heaters for someone to be able to sustain that amount of prolonged hot, moist pleasure. His clothes were just this side of dripping, and his suede chukka boots would probably become a couple of chewies over which his dogs would fight. The only constructive thing he had done during his extended Turkish bath besides lose ten pounds of water weight was to clean the porcelain throne of Jasmine's regurgitated lentil, feta cheese, and red-wine mishmash while trying not to vomit.

Todd passed up the neon-pink blow-up chair, settled into the short-legged canvas camping chair that sat opposite the air mattress, and peeled off his socks and boots. While he waited for Jasmine to dress, he brooded over the fact that she was not behaving like the ideal woman of his dreams. Her pre-puke moaning had not exactly been the kind that he had been fantasizing about for the last four days.

After a few minutes, a barefooted Jasmine entered the living room wearing white pajamas stamped with colorful likenesses from the Harry Potter series. A towel was wrapped around her head and she clutched a big-toothed comb in her hand.

"Nice p.j.'s," remarked Todd.

"Thank you. My mum sent them to me. Being a writer of children's books, she's a mate of Jo Rowling." When Todd looked at her blankly, she said, "The author of the Harry Potter series. She's quite nice."

"Huh." Somehow the revelation didn't surprise Todd.

Jasmine sat Indian-style on the air mattress, with her back to the wall of windows. She leaned forward and squinted at him through the dim amber light of her weepy thrift-store pole lamp. "Your clothes look wet. There's a dryer in the laundry room off the kitchen."

"I've spent many a night soppin' wet, freezin' cold, and dog tired whilst huntin' in Duckett Forest."

Jasmine gave him a suit-yourself-shrug. "There's bundt cake in the kitchen if you're hungry."

"No thanks, but I hope you don't mind that I helped myself to another beer." Todd stretched out his legs and crossed them at the ankles. Jasmine stared into the middle distance, and whatever she was seeing caused her to take on the expression of a lost kitten.

"If it makes you feel any better," Todd said, his voice oddly even, almost wary. "I got cut down to size three times today, and my favorite mentor told me how he used to be a murderer."

"Somehow that doesn't make me feel any better," muttered Jasmine as she pulled the towel off her head, shook out her damp hair, and began to tame it with the comb.

Todd was spellbound. Everything about this lovely young woman was enchanting: her rosy lips, her glowing skin, her delicate, fluttering hands.

"Seriously, Sheriff, I just do not fathom this land that time forgot. It's just that everybody is somebody's cousin or brother-in-law or ex-something. For example, earlier this evening your former spouse showed up at my doorstep."

Todd pressed his elbows into the camp chair's armrests and pushed himself upright. All he could say was, "No kiddin'?" Brandy never ceased to astound him. This had to be more than a coincidence.

"She brought the cake."

Todd slouched down and watched Jasmine from over the rim of his beer bottle. "Just don't believe a word she says about me," he said in the same watchful voice.

"She said you drove her to drink."

"Ha, that would have been in middle school, since that's when she started imbibing." Then, more thoughtfully, he added, "Right after her momma died."

Jasmine was quiet for a minute. The look on her face said that she wasn't getting off her pity-pot anytime soon. "Oh, it's all so hopeless," she moaned. Lowering her head, she threw her damp locks forward and began to comb. "My problems are simply insurmountable." A loud sigh emanated from behind the dark curtain of hair.

Todd snorted. "So you think you're the only one with troubles? According to Brandy, I'm the laughing stock of Tuscany, Italy."

"Pardon?" Jasmine parted the curtain of hair and peaked at him.

"And the mayor wants to fire me because I won't say for sure that the Elvis you found was Alex Meriwether's Elvis."

Raising her head, Jasmine flipped back her hair. "What? Now there are two Elvis's?"

"Yes ... no ... I don't know. Anyway, People Magazine called the office today. They want to put me on the cover of next week's issue sitting on the rock next to Elvis's outline with the headline, 'Sheriff looses penis.' Newsweek and Time are sending reporters and photographers. The Tonight Show wants me, so of course, Letterman called. And the high school kids are settin' out 'Where's Elvis?' signs all over town. So you're not the only one with a crappy life right now." He upended the bottle again.

Jasmine pulled in her knees and rested her chin on them in an effort to hide a smile. Her attempt at suppressing her mirth resulted in a few strangled coughs.

After the moment of humor passed, she tentatively explored the knot on her head. "How much longer do we have before I can go to sleep?"

Todd looked at his watch. "About three and a half hours."

Surprisingly, Jasmine began to cry again, this time quietly. When she was finished, she looked around. "I have a box of tissues around here somewhere."

Todd pulled out his handkerchief and handed it to her. "It's clean. I'm not the allergic type."

"Of course not, you're Robocop." Jasmine wiped her face and blew her nose. "What do we do now?"

"Let's keep on talkin'."

"About what, pray tell?" She sounded bored. She tilted her head and ran her manicured nails through her long locks.

"Well, what were you doin' tonight that caused you to have a run-in with snakes, roaches, and rats?"

Jasmine quickly pulled herself together. "That is proprietary information," she said firmly.

"What could be proprietary about some bugs and varmits?" asked Todd. Jasmine remained mute, so he offered, "I think somethin' beside gettin' roach custard on your legs has gotten you down in the dumps. You may as well tell me your violin story."

"My, we're striking rock bottom, aren't we?"

Todd only shrugged.

Jasmine inhaled deeply. "His name is Stefan and we crossed paths at an art gallery. We grew a friendship, then fell in love. We became engaged and lived together for a year. We were to be married last August seventh." Her words grew unsteady. "And just before the ceremony, he corralled me in the dressing room and said," She deepened

262

her voice, "'Jasmine, you know how I've always told you it didn't matter that you weren't Greek Orthodox? Well, imagine my surprise when I realized it does matter. I've secretly been seeing a Greek woman for the past six weeks and want to call off our wedding.' " She straightened her robe. "So we did." She tried to keep a stiff upper lip, but her mouth melted into a pitiful pout. "How many violins does that confession rate?"

Todd stroked Tristan absentmindedly as he assessed her level of misery. "I give you three out of five violins."

Jasmine straightened her back and resumed her cross-legged position. Todd could see the outline of her breasts against the soft white cotton and had to force himself to concentrate on her words as she said, "So, now you have to tell me your violin story. I rather doubt that you can beat my score." She gave him an ironic smile.

Todd returned to peering at her over the rim of his beer bottle. "I'm sure my ex has told you."

"Not really. Anyway, I want to hear your rendition. Wait!" She hopped up, scurried to her bedroom, and returned with a black violin case. Plopping down on the mattress, she resumed her cross-legged position, opened the case, and pulled out the instrument. "Fortunately, I packed this in the car when I drove down from Boston," she said, positioning the instrument. She began playing a slow, melancholy tune.

Todd laced his fingers on top of his head and sat back. "Nice touch. What is it?"

Jasmine paused at the end of a musical phrase. "Chopin's Etude Opus 10 No. 11 in E-flat minor. Now, go ahead."

Todd uncrossed his legs, re-crossed them then uncrossed them. "I met Brandy when we were four, and by kindergarten, we already had a history. Nonetheless, I was hooked. I even made her a wedding ring at the Play-Doh station. The summer before eleventh grade, she finally decided I was cool enough to be her sweetheart. She was wild as a March hare, and sometimes when she drank, she got crazy. But I was always there to catch her when she fell."

Todd paused, and Jasmine embellished his story with a swelling of the expressive music. After a few more stanzas, she halted. Todd continued, "We married right after I graduated from college. I started law school, but she wasn't happy and her drinkin' worsened. Then she accidentally got pregnant, which really pissed her off. She swore to me that she had quit drinkin', but she sneaked vodka the whole nine months and Molly was born with F.A.S.—fetal alcohol syndrome."

Jasmine positioned the violin, plunged into a dramatic interlude. When she stopped, Todd said, "I gave up law school, and we moved back to Duckett County. After six months, Brandy bottomed out and went through the thirty day rehab thing. Since she was sober, I thought our marriage was gonna get a new start. But, she left me for a multimillionaire, and now they live on Millionaire Mountain in a—"

"Castle in the air."

"Yeah, that's it. Castle in the air. So that is that." Todd emptied the beer bottle. "And two days after she left me, my daddy died. End of story." He looked straight at Jasmine. "So how many violins do I get?"

Jasmine grimaced as she carefully returned the violin to its case. "Ouch, I would have to award you at least four and a half violins for that narrative. Someone could compose a truly maudlin country ballad from such a tortured tale." She stretched her right leg until her bare foot touched his bare foot and he curled his toes over hers. "I suppose we are two of the most miserable, wretched, sad arses on the globe."

"I reckon we are," lied Todd. Right now, in this poorly lit mish-mash of a room, he was playing footsy with Jasmine Olivia Roseberry. And he was happy.

Jasmine yawned. "How much time do we have left now?"

Todd looked at his watch. "Two hours and forty-five minutes." He also yawned. "I shouldn't have drunk those beers."

Jasmine rubbed her eyes. "I'm knackered. I just want to go to Bedfordshire."

Todd didn't understand exactly what she said, but hoped it meant, I'm horny and I want to go to bed with you. But, he assumed that wasn't the case.

* * * * *

Todd's head snapped forward and he woke with a start, realizing that somehow he had managed to doze off in damp clothes in a cramped camping chair. He looked at his watch and gasped. Apparently, they had both fallen asleep far sooner than Mark had said was safe. Todd looked at Jasmine, who was lying on her back on the mattress. His heart began to hammer as he scurried over to see if she was dead. Her hands were folded over her abdomen, which was alarming, but he was encouraged when he saw her take a breath. What if she's in a coma? He tickled her nose lightly with his finger. She reached up, scratched it and rolled on her side.

Todd sighed with relief and tucked her blanket around her. Then he tiptoed through the kitchen to the laundry room, stripped completely, and tossed his damp clothes in the dryer. He removed a folded towel from the overfilled laundry basket sitting on the floor. Laying it on the floor, he sat on it and leaned his back against the dryer. He propped his elbow on the laundry basket of folded laundry and rested his head on the heel of his hand. He dozed off until he was jolted awake when his head dropped off his hand. He reached into the dryer and found that the only dry item of apparel was his boxers. He pulled them on, restarted the dryer, and tiptoed back into the living room, where he wrapped himself up in the other blanket and lay down on the floor next to Jasmine's mattress.

* * * * *

Though it was still pitch black outside, dawn was not far away. Jasmine was sleeping on her stomach with the blanket spread over her bottom half, and Todd was sprawled half on the mattress. His right hand was holding his wadded-up blanket under his head and his left hand was lying protectively on Jasmine's back. Suddenly, an explosion caused Jasmine to sit bolt upright. "What was that!?" she cried, clutching her blanket to her bosom.

Todd attempted fruitlessly to switch on the weepy floor lamp. Over the racket outside, he yelled, "Thunder! Looks like a gutter-buster!"

Just then a rash of lightning strikes lit up the troubled sky outside the wall of windows. More explosive blasts followed. Almost immediately a neon-white light penetrated the room. An ear-deafening blast resounded through the shuddering cabin. Even Todd flinched. The wind began to howl ferociously. Heavy rain lashed at the windows.

"I've never been in a thunderstorm like this before!" shouted Jasmine over the din.

Todd yelled back, "You've never been in one at 4,000 feet before!"

Jasmine threw back her head and laughed heartily. "This is too cool!" Electrified by the raw energy coursing through the room, she jumped up and ran barefooted onto the back deck, where she raised her arms and twirled madly.

From the open patio door, Todd watched appreciatively as Jasmine's pajamas became soaked through and clung provocatively to her body.

"Yahoooo! What a ride!" she shouted.

Todd thought that the driving rain must be stinging her face, but she continued to hold it up to the sky while laughing ecstatically. Fearful for his mistress's life, Tristan leaned against Todd's leg and barked incessantly. The rapid lightning strikes lent Jasmine's movements a strobe-like effect, and her white teeth shone like a string of pearls against the ashy black background of the storm.

"Come on, McPherson, dance with me!" shouted Jasmine, just as another flash of lightening brought her lithe body into relief. Suddenly, she slammed on the brakes and stared at him. "Are you in your undies!?"

"It's not what you think!" Todd was grateful for the darkness that hid the blush that burned his cheeks and pricked his entire scalp.

Fortunately, she only laughed and commenced to skip around the deck. Todd presumed that after this foolishness was over, he would be cleaning the porcelain throne again, as well as fishing for foot splinters.

Jasmine extended a hand and yelled, "Come out here and dance in your bloody boxers, you twit!"

Todd heard the unmistakable sound of a freight train bearing down on them.

"Come on, before it's over!" Jasmine grabbed his hand.

He in turn grabbed her arm and yanked her into the cabin. With her in tow, he ran down the hall to the little tiled room that had already been the place of enough human pathos tonight.

"What the bloody hell are you doing?!" shouted Jasmine over the cacophony outside.

Tristan shadowed them, still barking continuously. Once the three of them were inside the bathroom, the door slammed shut with a horrific bang as if some ill-tempered, herculean poltergeist had been rudely awakened by the wailing wind and was taking his annoyance out on them.

Todd shoved Tristan in the shower stall, but the dog immediately pushed the door open and jumped up on Jasmine. Todd turned to the linen closet door. Using both arms, he pulled mightily against the sudden force created by the unnatural vacuum. After several precious seconds, he wrested the door open, shoved the dog inside, and then let the door slam shut of its own accord.

Jasmine yelled, "What are you doing to my—?" Then she heard the sound of the wind as it wound itself into a conical frenzy, its pitch rising from a low moaning to an insane shrieking. She immediately looked up as if she possessed the power to peer through the ceiling. The portentous shrieking was now being punctuated by numerous exploding land mines—dozens of tall Georgia trees were being ripped up by their roots and thrown down like the storm was playing a game of pick-up sticks. The cabin began to shimmy and shake, and Jasmine, still staring at the ceiling, reached out and grabbed Todd's arm.

Her humble abode groaned so loudly that Todd feared it would come unmoored from its foundation and slide down the mountain into Emerald Lake. He dropped into the Jacuzzi tub and pulled Jasmine in so that she was sitting with her back to him. Just then, the noises morphed once again. The insane shrieking bore down on them, leaving no doubt that some marauding malignancy was now hovering over the roof. Todd realized this banshee was no wimpy EF1, or even an EF2. This bitch was the real deal. He bent over Jasmine, pushed her as low as possible, and covered her head and neck with his hands and arms. The twister ratcheted up the pressure in the room just for the hell of it and Todd's ears were struck with a horrible pain. He thought that, were the cabin a person, it would be immensely relieved to simply explode. The beast settled on the roof, and with terrifying ripping sounds, perfunctorily stripped away the cedar shingles.

"There goes the roof!" shouted Todd. But as soon as the words left his mouth, they were snatched away, so that not even Jasmine, whose delicate ear was so near his lips, could have heard him. Now they were being pelted with rain and debris from all directions. The bathtub began to make weird little screaming noises like lobsters being dropped in boiling water. The tub lifted a few inches and Todd tightened his grip on Jasmine.

Resisting the tornado's efforts to claim it, the tub settled back down. But not to be denied, the ravenous phantom then did her best to suck Jasmine and Todd from their porcelain cradle. Todd pressed his buttocks hard into the back of the tub and, wrapping his legs over Jasmine's, pushed his feet against the other end of the tub. A ferocious 'Arrgghhhh!' involuntarily escaped him as all the muscles of his body knotted and trembled while he fought to keep the two of them in place. Jasmine gripped his forearms, as if such an action would help the physics of the situation.

After an eternity, the sucking eased. The banshee had not taken all she wanted, but she had taken all that she could, so she lifted and spun off to play with other people's lives. A curious stillness descended in her wake. Jasmine, sapped of any strength, was capable of doing nothing but leaning back on Todd. He crossed his arms over her chest, willing strength back into her body. He could feel her heart pounding—always a good sign.

He spit out a leaf that was entangled in Jasmine's wildly arranged hair. "You okay?"

Jasmine replied weakly, "I believe so."

Slowly, they shucked off the debris and climbed unsteadily out of the tub. Mouths agape and eyes blinking in wonder, they gazed at the amazing decorating job wrought by Mother Nature. The tile floor was carpeted with small branches. The mirrors and walls displayed an interesting decoupage of festively colored leaves, mangled twigs, and other bits of nature's wreckage, along with someone's jock strap, and an Emerald Lakes Golf Club scorecard. Curiously, a steering wheel with the Mercedes symbol in the center sat on top the toilet, leaning against the wall.

Todd and Jasmine turned to searching themselves for bodily damage. Jasmine had only a few superficial scratches, but Todd had a gash on the back of his head that was trickling blood steadily. In addition, a wooden shingle had been driven into his upper arm. Other than that, there were only some superficial scrapes on his back and arms, an amazing fact considering that the only flesh of his that had not been exposed to the whims of the banshee had been inside his boxers.

Jasmine pulled open the narrow drawer beside the sink and discovered that the scissors she had placed in it several days ago were gone, along with everything else she had stowed there. The tornado had cleverly opened the drawer, stolen the implements, and then re-closed it. Jasmine looked around and gasped when she spied the scissors driven into the window frame. She yanked them out and Todd helped her cut a piece of fabric from the hem of her pajama top.

While he held a folded washrag to the wound, she tied the strip of cloth around his head. Then she pulled the shingle out of his upper arm, and immediately blood began to pour from the deep puncture wound. She dressed it with two more pieces of fabric from her pajama top, while Todd, no longer cognizant of any pain, surreptitiously admired her bare midriff.

Whimpering and scratching noises emanated from the linen closet. With a mighty two-armed tug, Todd yanked open the mangled door and Tristan staggered out, dazed but otherwise unharmed.

Todd spied some flip-flops in the closet and handed them to Jasmine. He exhaled loudly, and with a voice that faltered on ragged breath, said, "Well, that was a boredom-buster."

Jasmine peeled a festively tinted leaf from his cheek. "And not all that dreadful, actually," she replied in an equally shaky voice.

Todd raised an eyebrow and then looked up. Jasmine followed his eyes and saw that instead of a white ceiling, the first light of dawn was invading the murky moonscape. She said cheerfully, "I rather thought this water closet would be benefited by a skylight." Wrenching her gaze from the vertical view, she tried the faucet, which issued forth a thin stream of water. She searched for her toothbrush and toothpaste and deduced that they were now somewhere over the rainbow.

Looking in the linen closet, Todd pulled an extra tube of toothpaste off a shelf and was amazed to see that all the shelves' contents were still neatly arranged. He handed a new tube of toothpaste to Jasmine. She ran a line of toothpaste down her index finger, followed suit on his finger, and then smiled broadly.

With her characteristic British aplomb, she pronounced, "The world may be crashing down around our ears, Sheriff, but as long as morning breath is kept at bay, civilization marches on."

Todd couldn't help but grin. "You may not like my helmet hair, Roseberry, but I sure do like your spirit." He touched his fingertip to hers.

Chapter Twelve
Meditating on the Porcelain Throne

The bathroom door was concaved inward, as if someone had tried to break it down from the outside with a battering ram. Todd braced his foot on the doorframe and pulled. Finally it opened. He reached up and touched the thin bandage on the back of his head. It was already soaked through with blood. He began to feel as though he might have to worship at the porcelain throne himself. Hoping to stave off that eventuality, he closed the toilet lid, sat down heavily and, elbow on knee, rested his chin on his fist.

Jasmine noticed a long lady's slip wound around the doorknob on the outside of the bathroom door. Inspecting it, she said, "I don't believe this is mine, but I suppose someone somewhere is contemplating what use they might have for my polka dot knickers." She laid the slip on the counter and cut it lengthwise. After removing the bandage from the back of Todd's head, she placed another scrounged washrag over the gash and secured it with a new a strip of cloth from the slip. She fiddled with it until he said, "Enough!"

Jasmine stepped back and looked him up and down. "Where in bloody hell are your garments, pray tell?"

Todd looked up sheepishly. "In the bloody-ass dryer."

She placed her hands on her hips, and with a smile playing about her lips said, "I see. So the Great White Hunter had indeed surrendered to the forces of nature, eh?" Todd shrugged. "Well, no matter," she said cheerfully, "since I have footwear, I shall retrieve your clothes." She picked her way to the laundry room, then returned after a few minutes and said, "Your garments, Sheriff, may very well be in the dryer, but alas, the dryer, like Elvis, has left the building, along with just about everything else, including my violin and most of the walls."

Todd drug a hand down his face. "Oh ... my...God."

With Jasmine following, he picked his way to the wrecked living room, where they hunted fruitlessly for his chukka boots. Suddenly overwhelmed, Jasmine returned to the safety of the bathroom to spend some quality time meditating on the porcelain throne. Todd stepped outside into a post-apocalyptic world. Fortunately, he found his reliable "Like-a-rock" Chevy pickup intact and more or less in the same spot where he had parked it. He pulled his gym bag from the backseat, unzipped it, and slapped his forehead. The compulsive cleanliness thing that had plagued him all his life had directed him to wash his jogging clothes the day before, even though he had not used them. Unfortunately, because of the forgetfulness thing he'd also had all his life, he had failed to repack the bag. Also, he had set his running shoes outside on the deck to air out, and there was no telling to what state the twister had airmailed them. How much bigger could this pickle get? Before he could orchestrate a proper countywide cleanup operation, he was going to have to drive home in his boxers, slap on something to wear to the clinic, fire up his Sheriff's Bronco (if the twister had left it fire-able), get stitched up, then sneak on the back door of the jail, mostly for the purpose of avoiding LeeLee. Next, he would shower in the locker room - keeping the stiches as dry as possible - then dress in his spare uniform that he kept in his locker. Only after all that could he go out and do his job. He realized that if the road home was blocked by fallen trees, he might have to face his deputies wearing his underwear and a lady's slip on his head. This pickle was so big now it was in contention for a blue ribbon at the state fair. Todd rummaged around underneath the back seat and found an old pair of black cowboy boots. As he pulled them on, he noticed that a light rain was descending, so he grabbed his black Stetson hanging from the gun rack. Might as well complete the outfit. He prayed that if Jasmine owned a camera, said camera had been creatively relocated somewhere.

Todd hiked up the road to the next cabin and discovered that the front porch had been surgically removed. That was the extent of the banshee-induced havoc, other than the abundance of small branches plastered about and the sporty red Mercedes convertible standing nearly straight up against an oak tree. Calling out, Todd pounded on the front door. There was no response. He surmised that the dwelling must be owned by a weekender, which meant that the Mercedes was probably just visiting, having been dropped in unannounced.

Todd trudged back down to Jasmine's yard, and then climbed over the half-dozen tree trunks blocking the road. The cabin below, like Jasmine's, was practically demolished. Todd stepped carefully through the rubble and shouted, "Anyone here?" God help them if they are "Gone with the Wind." He heard nothing. Not even the wind.

When he returned, Jasmine was standing in the doorway of her cabin, the driest spot in the house. She had a hand on each side of the doorframe as if she were holding up what was left of her rented dwelling. Gaping at Todd's sexy costume, she whistled, and then squinted at his boxers, which were black with white signatures all over them. She crossed her arms and gave him a simpering smile. "And who, pray tell, is Dale Earnhardt, Jr.?"

Todd crossed his arms. "Some fella who sings Italian opera way better than you," he retorted irritably. He didn't care for Jasmine's teasing at the moment. In fact, it seemed that their camaraderie of a short while ago had left as abruptly as the banshee herself.

Jasmine leaned on the doorframe. "Did you know that you have a definite case of ghastly pallid farmer's legs?"

Todd looked down at his legs, which he had to admit appeared pale against the background of the asphalt driveway.

She added, "There are places where you can get a tan sprayed on, you know. It's just like going through a car wash."

Todd placed his fists on his hips. Despite the fact that he mostly grew cotton and hay, he said, "I'm real proud of the fact that my ghastly white legs help feed the nation, thank you very much." He growled and added, "Besides, they complement my red neck."

Jasmine tossed him his wallet and keys. "Somehow they ended up wedged behind the washing machine. How badly are the other homes damaged?"

Todd held the keys and wallet in one hand and adjusted his boxers with the other. "The cabin above is okay, except for an inconvenienced but sturdy oak tree and a Mercedes in sore need of its steering wheel."

"Ah, but the wheel is busy right now meditating on the back of my porcelain throne."

"The cabin below looks like this one. But everybody's gone." *One way or the other.*

Jasmine lifted her damp locks off her neck. "That miserable tornado stole my pink blow-up air chairs."

"Too bad. They were growin' on me." Todd stepped into the pickup, found his cell phone, and called High Heaven. Herb answered, and Todd asked if Molly was alright.

In his soft, South African accent Herb said, "Oh yeah, mother and daughter are fine, but I've got a backache because I was put out of my bed and ended up on the guest bed. Molly wanted to snuggle with her mum. Those two have come a long way," he added thoughtfully. "Anyway, the storm was damn loud, but we didn't get the tornado. It seems to have skipped our mountain. Your mum okay?" Before Todd could answer, Herb said, "Wait—she wants to talk to you."

Todd thought he meant Molly, but instead Brandy's high-pitched voice came over the phone.

"You okay?" she asked nervously. Before Todd could respond, she said, "Molly's fine. The thunder 'bout scared the pee-waddin' out of her, but you cain't talk to her right now cuz she's sleepin'. How's things over to your place?"

"Fine, I hope." From where he sat, Todd could see Jasmine wandering around the cabin sifting through the ruins. He surmised that

Jasmine's fiddle had played its final tune last night.

"Whatcha mean? Ain't ya at home?"

"I gotta go. Give Molly my love." Todd clicked off and called his mother.

"Son, where were you last night?"

"I got hung up somewhere."

"Is Molly okay? Our phones are down and I cain't charge my cell cuz we ain't got no electricity."

"Molly's fine. Did the twister get us?"

"It come up just before dawn and skimmed right over us. Hail from all directions—golf-ball sized, too. It done just about finished off the old barn. We might have to replace the roof on the house, the garage, and the new barn."

Todd didn't respond. He knew that in any crises his mother always jumped to the worst-case scenario. Their tin roofs could take a lot more punishment than those dumbass asphalt shingles that they put on roofs these days.

"Cattle's skittish," Jessie said, "and you'd think that crazy stallion of yorn would be wilder than a March hare with all the goin's on, but he's too busy nuzzlin' a smart lookin' Quarter Horse mare that the tornado dropped right inta his pasture."

Todd had to smile at that remark. His mother must not have seen Virgil depositing the mare in their pasture yesterday.

Jessie continued, "Anyway, LeeLee has done called here four times. So where are you? "

"I'll catch you later. I gotta call the office now. Bye."

"But you didn't answer my ques—"

Todd clicked off and radioed dispatch.

LeeLee responded. "Where the hell are you? We got damaged buildings and downed power lines. I done called your place and yore momma didn't even know where you was at. And your cell just kept—"

"What are you doin' on dispatch this early?"

"Duh, we're all followin' your dumb Disaster Preparedness Plan, the one you drove us all crazy with when you was schemin' it up. I come in early so we could have two dispatchers on duty, just like your plan calls for."

Todd gingerly touched his bandaged head. The bandage was a bit wetter. He had to admit to himself that he was a bit addled.

LeeLee asked pointedly, "For the third time, what's your 20 and how soon can you get here?"

"I'm stuck on a mountain in Emerald Lake. There are downed trees across the road so I gotta wait 'til a crew gets up here with some chainsaws."

"What the hell are you doin' up at Emerald Lake at six in the—oooh, Fearless," LeeLee cooed, "was you with that limey gal last night? Did you *lay* with her?"

LeeLee was an expert at laying it on, and Todd thanked God she couldn't see his state of nakedness right now. He said gruffly, "It ain't what you think. I was doin' my duty."

"Right…duty. So that's what you youngin's call it these days. Well, Rusty has just walked in. I'll let him brief you." Todd started to say something, but LeeLee kept the mic open and he heard her yell, "RUSTEEE! I've found Sheriff Lover Boy!"

Jasmine opened the back gate of Todd's pickup and directed Tristan to jump in. Then she climbed in on the passenger's side. It was the only place with protection from the drizzle. She attempted to follow the jabbering on the radio as Todd took command of the tornado rescue and cleanup in his unconventional outfit. Jasmine self-consciously pulled her damp pajama top away from her body. She watched him out of the corner of her eye and thought it odd that he didn't even speak to her or acknowledge her presence. Perhaps the experience of coming so near death together held too much intimacy, and just like a one-night stand, the morning after was painfully embarrassing.

The awkwardness continued for an hour while Todd talked nonstop over the radio, often in code words and numbers that were meaningless to Jasmine. At one point, she borrowed his cell and called the Emerald Lake Pet Lodge to make arrangements for Tristan. Eventually a crew reached the roadblock of trees that had fallen across the steeply pitched road. They promptly fired up their chainsaws and went to work. The noise was deafening. Since the drizzle had abated for the moment, Todd and Jasmine climbed out of the truck to watch. She spied a grinning, chainsaw-brandishing Les standing on top of the tangle of fallen tree trunks. He waved and gave her the thumbs up. To Jasmine, he looked quite happy, definitely in his element. Les raised a hand to shade his eyes from the sun that was cresting the ridge and did a double take when he saw Todd's Chippendales costume. He corralled the attention of the crew, and one-by-one the chainsaws quieted as they began to point and guffaw. Les wore a facetiously befuddled expression as he called out, "That you, Sheriff?"

Todd answered by crossing his arms. He had by now resigned himself to the fact that for many years to come, he would be the subject of a story that was going to be passed around Duckett County like a tall fishing tale. The deafening buzz of the chainsaws started up again. Over Jasmine's mimed protestations, Todd picked up an extra chainsaw and helped the crew finish off the trees.

Finally, the attack of the rapacious chainsaws wound down. Todd rejoined Jasmine and she helped him shuck the numerous pieces of bark plastered to his flesh. As the last of the logs were cut and drug out of the road, Les walked up and said to Jasmine, "Brad wanted you liberated first." He grinned and shifted his gaze to Todd. "Looks like we freed your fella here as a bonus."

"Let me explain," said Todd quickly. "Well, it was like this ..."

Jasmine jumped in. "I was waiting for the sheriff's bump to go down—I mean, he was waiting for me to go down—"

"And this twister come along and sucked our clothes right off of our backs!" exclaimed Todd, eyes wide with sincerity.

"Hey, I'm a modern guy," said Les with a barely disguised grin.

Todd and Jasmine retreated to the truck and waited for the crew to move up the road. He turned to her. "Where do you want me to take you?"

"To work," she stated curtly.

Todd studied her, wondering if she had come down with posttraumatic stress syndrome. "But you're wearin' torn, wet pajamas and flip-flops. That's a little too casual even for the POA's standards."

"I don't care, I need to work."

"How about I carry you to my farm and you let my momma fix you up? I gotta go by the farm, so it wouldn't discomfit me any to carry you there."

"Don't try and be polite," snapped Jasmine, her irritation with him boiling over. "You embarrassed the hell out of me in front of my supervisor." She angrily gathered her damp locks and attempted to arrange them into some kind of order.

Todd snickered, "But you're the one who said you went down——"

Jasmine's venomous stare cut him off. "And you're the idiot who said the tornado disrobed us! Next time you are caught up in a major meteorological malfunction, Sheriff, I should think you would bloody well remember to actually remain inside your bloody clothes!"

Todd ate a smile. Even when madder than a wet hen, Jasmine was adorable. "Yes ma'am," he exclaimed, throwing the truck in gear. Still, he wondered what had happened to last night's carefree girl who danced ecstatically in the rain?

As he pulled out of the driveway, Jasmine cried, "Stop! I have to lock the door!"

Todd laughed devilishly. "Take a look at your house, Miz Scarlett. There ain't no lockin' out the Yankees today."

Jasmine swiveled her head and saw that the house looked like it had suffered through a WWII air raid. Other than a few half-demolished walls, the doorframe was the only structure still vertical. Jasmine promptly exclaimed, "Oh fiddle-de-dee!"

On the ride down McLean Mountain, Todd took measure of the damage done by the tornado while Jasmine fixed her eyes straight ahead. He reluctantly dropped her and her pooch off at the POA lodge parking lot. A staffer from the Emerald Lake Pet Lodge was waiting to pick up Tristan, so Jasmine handed over her damp, dirty, and disheveled dog. Then just as damp, dirty, and disheveled herself - she reported for duty.

* * * * *

Ansley Mason stood at attention in front of Mayor Sonny Davis's house. When she received her cue she said, "That's right, John, I'm still in the tiny town of Duckettville, Georgia, which has been besieged by the media since last Friday evening when a human penis was found on a rock in a vast wilderness area formally named The Duckett County Wildlife Management Area. The penis had been handed over to the medical examiner for safekeeping, but it was later stolen some time during the night. Then Monday evening, firefighters were called to a major fire at the home of Alex Meriwether, whose corpse was devoured by flames."

Ansley drew in oxygen. "As if the stolen penis and the fire hadn't wreaked enough havoc, a twister skipped through the county just before dawn. The tornado—an EF3 on the Enhanced Fujita scale—appears to have hit hard in Emerald Lake Resort, where four homes were completely destroyed. Fortunately, no fatalities have been reported. The tornado skipped through the tiny town of Duckettville, damaging dozens of buildings. As you can see behind me, the mayor, who lives on residential Main Street, has lost his front porch." She spied Sonny stepping through his front door, and said, "Here he comes now. Perhaps we can get an interview."

Sonny stepped awkwardly down and around the remnants of his porch. When his feet found solid ground, he tottered confidently towards Ansley. She asked, "Mayor Davis, first there was the penis problem, then the fire, and now a tornado. Do you feel that Duckett County is under some kind of Halloween curse?"

Laughing heartily, Sonny said, "No way, Ansley. The case of the missin' man-part has been cleared up to my satisfaction, and as far as this mornin's little dustup, we'll have to hustle, but all the mess is gonna be cleaned up in time for the Moonshine Festival this weekend." Under his breath he muttered, "If'n I can get my hands on that night-prowlin' tomcat of a sheriff." Then he grinned, wrapped his arm around Ansley and looked into the camera. "Ya'll come out now, hear?"

Being petite, Ansley's head was practically buried in Sonny's fleshy armpit, but as her job required, she managed to control her nausea and give the camera a smile, however stilted.

Sonny released her. "Well, I gotta go check in with the cleanup crews. Bye now." Over Ansley's shoulder, the mayor could be seen tottering toward his Suburban.

Ansley said, "As you've just seen, it takes a lot more than a twister to crush the spirit of this small-town mayor." She paused to listen to the question put to her by the anchorman through her earpiece then said, "That's right, John. There is still no consensus if the penis, which has become known affectionately as Elvis, belonged to Alex Meriwether. In a noontime press conference yesterday, the mayor stated that Mr. Meriwether was indeed the victim of the dismemberment, and the GBI said there was a strong possibility that was the situation. But when Sheriff McPherson was asked about the matter earlier, he refused to concur, and stated that the Elvis case was still under investigation. I had planned to ask the sheriff this morning if he had changed his opinion since yesterday, but oddly, nobody seems to be able to locate the young man who the locals call Baby Chief." She allowed a slight smile. "Understandably, Mayor Davis is not very happy with the sheriff right now. One thing is certain: the residents of this sparsely populated county want a resolution to this case. All around town we are seeing signs like this." Ansley held up a poster that said, "Where's Elvis?" in bright-red magic marker. "The signs started as a teenage prank, but now they're popping up all over the place. This county has an election coming up next Tuesday, but as we drove around, it was apparent that the "Where's Elvis" signs far outnumber the political signs. Someone's printing up T-shirts too."

The camera zoomed into Ansley's bust while she opened up her jacket and displayed a green T-shirt with "Where's Elvis?" emblazoned in gold lettering.

* * * * *

Jasmine sat motionless at her desk, her hands clasped and resting on its surface. She was wearing a gray sweatshirt that was three sizes too wide and gray baggy sweatpants that were three sizes too short. The clothes had been loaned to her by Valinda, who had fished them out of her gym bag. Jasmine had slipped into them after taking a spit bath in the restroom. Since Valinda's sneakers were too small, Jasmine was still wearing her flip-flops. Now that she was semi-clean and mostly dry, she decided it was time to assess her situation. She had no clothes, no home, no furnishings, and no car. She possessed neither a credit card nor a driver's license—not even a library card. Worst of all, she had lost her lifeline to the outside world: her cell phone. In fact, she had nothing to her name except her beloved Tristan.

Even more alarming, she was grappling with the indisputable fact that nature had attempted to recycle her. Though she had grown up being a lover of the outdoors, life in Duckett County had already taught her a new lesson: that her relationship with the natural world in this wilderness promised to be filled with occasional bouts of terror.

Valinda Mills was the only other person in the admin office at the time. Her sole duty seemed to be flipping through the channels on Cheryl's TV, looking for news about the tornado. Alice had stayed at home to deal with insurance adjusters, and Cheryl's absence was due to the fact that she had lost her brand new double-wide to the maelstrom. Fortunately, her husband and land surveyor, Connor Davis, had previously dug a storm shelter on their property. Otherwise, Cheryl and Connor would have been more tribute for the banshee. Les, of course, was still out coordinating the cleanup in Emerald Lake.

There was a knock at her open door. Jasmine looked up and saw Brad Whitestone leaning on the doorframe, looking rustically dapper in neatly creased tan slacks, soft brown loafers, and a high-end L.L. Bean leather jacket.

"Well, look at you," he said with genuine sympathy beaming from his eyes. "I heard about your car accident from Les this morning. I'm going to have to fine you for denting up several of my trees." He applied a mischievous grin, which Jasmine answered with a peeved look. He cleared his throat. "So, the sheriff, he helped you out with the accident?"

"His function was to keep me awake," said Jasmine glumly, "and he failed miserably at that. However, he did keep me alive during the tornado. I suppose that counts for something."

"Todd's good for some things," said Brad, looking away. He returned his gaze to Jasmine and broke into a broad smile. "I have great news! Right after our lunch on Monday, I called Pops. He belongs to the same country club as the top dog at To Infinity and Beyond International Moving Company, and Pops convinced the old boy to order an emergency run. Your furniture will be here around noon today."

Jasmine stared at him blankly, then suddenly threw her head back and burst out laughing. "That's the funniest thing I've ever heard," she managed to say between peals of hilarity. "My furnishings are finally here, but the twister has whisked my house over the rainbow."

Brad laughed heartily, collapsing into the guest chair. Jasmine's guffaws approached hysteria as she pounded the desk, tears rolling down her face. Valinda stuck her head in, shrugged, and left them alone.

The conviviality subsided and the two fell into a companionable silence. Finally, Brad said sincerely, "I took in all I could bear to see of my mangled resort, returned home, cleaned up, and drove down here to provide you with any service you might require. I am here, Milady, to take you anywhere you need to go—to acquire a loaner car, some new clothes," he raised his eyebrows," which you are so desperately in need of at this moment. Nourishment—you probably need something in your tum-tum. In that outfit we'd better do the drive-thru at the Dairy Queen. On second thought, maybe not. This is Duckett County, after all. You'll fit right in."

Jasmine abandoned any effort to follow Brad's words. She heard only the insane shrieking of the tornado inside her head.

Brad stood and walked around the desk and cupped her chin. With true concern in his eyes, he said, "I seem to be losing you. You're getting that haunted look again." Jasmine's gaze drifted out the window. Brad snapped his fingers. "Hey, I almost forgot." He extracted her leather wallet from the pocket of his jacket. "A retired orthopedist who lives over on Tecumseh Mountain found it in her bird bath."

The soggy wallet looked like a shark had chewed it up, and finding it indigestible, had regurgitated it. Brad pushed a wavy lock of golden brown hair off his forehead. "So you see, Ms. Roseberry, things are looking up." He laid the wallet on her desk, stood back proudly, and gestured to it as if he were a caveman presenting a fresh kill to his cave woman.

Jasmine observed the object, but couldn't connect with it. Why would her wallet be in some eye doctor's birdbath? Her thinking was becoming as tangled as the debris in her cabin. Maybe it was because of the bump she'd received on her head when her car overturned last night. Was it last night? She picked up the wallet, opened it, and touched her Massachusetts driver's license. She pulled out her green card and studied it as if it were a specimen from Mars. As she returned it to its slot, a slip of paper fell out. There were blue letters and numbers on it. They were fat and bloated from the dampness, making them look like a colony of caterpillars. Jasmine saw that the first group of letters spelled out "Todd."

"I don't mean to be rude, Brad," she said. "It's just that I'm attempting to process what has happened to me in the last sixteen hours."

The look of sympathy on Brad's face deepened. "I can understand that." He clamped his hands over the back of the guest chair, leaned forward a bit, and watched her.

Jasmine slipped the little piece of paper back into her wallet then looked at Brad. "It was so much...bigger than us...words fail." She stood and slowly walked toward him. "It was like...some monster was trying to...devour us." Close now, she probed his eyes. "Do you understand what I'm saying?" She took in his cologne. It smelled of brandy and dark wood paneling—and safety.

"Hey, I'm from the Midwest," Brad replied softly. "I've lived through a few twisters." Jasmine parted her lips, but no sound escaped. Brad reached out and pulled her in.

Then the tears came.

* * * * *

Once he arrived at the clinic, Todd was escorted promptly back to an examining room. Such treatment was one of the perks of being in law enforcement. Gorov appeared, inspected Todd's wounds and asked how he got them. Todd merely growled under his breath, so Gorov held his tongue and began to apply iodine to the head wound. Todd silently pondered the Elvis case.

As Gorov placed the final stitch to the back of his head, Todd said, "We know that Elvis's blood is type A positive."

"A common type."

"But we don't know Alex Meriwether's blood type. Are you sure he never came in here for anything?"

"Like I said yesterday, he never came here or discussed his health

285

with me."

Todd reached up to scratch the new stitches inside the shaved rectangle on his scalp. He received a slap from Gorov and obediently dropped his hand. Todd asked, "Can the techs at the state crime lab tell Alex's blood type from those bone fragments?"

"Not unless they can conjure up a spell to turn bones into blood. Now let me see your arm."

Todd removed his shirt, pulled up his T-shirt sleeve. Gorov untied the blood-soaked makeshift bandage on his upper arm, then painted iodine over the wound.

"You need only two stitches here. I'm not going to put any anesthetic on this, okay?"

"Yeah, whatever...OUCH! WHAT THE HELL ARE YOU DOIN'?" Todd looked at his arm, saw a needle being shoved into his skin, and sensing an impending dizzy spell, quickly looked away.

"Ha! Big Baby Hunk. That needle was the anesthetic. I was just trick-or-treating you."

"I knew that," muttered Todd sheepishly.

Gorov deftly placed the stitches, then wrote Todd a prescription for an antibiotic. He headed toward the door while Todd pulled on his sweatshirt. At the last second, Todd called him back. He turned around and Todd flipped him a nickel. "There's your treat. Happy Halloween."

Todd sprinted to the office, showered and dressed. Thankfully, Lee-Lee was too busy to give him any more grief over his alleged tomcatting. He hurriedly drove out to supervise the storm cleanup in person. After five hours of darting back and forth between blocked road sites and damaged buildings, he decided the whole process was on the downhill side. Except for Duckett Forest. It would take years to clear all the dirt roads and primitive trails. With most of the work done, it was time to return to the business at hand.

He entered through the back door of the office and cruised down perp walk. Moving to LeeLee's desk in the lobby, he browsed through the mail. "I've turned the last of the storm cleanup over to Rusty," he said, studying an envelope. "I'll be in my office. I want you to hold all my calls."

"Fearless! This is an emergency day! It's important for you to be seen at times like this."

Todd tapped the handful of the envelopes on her desk. "Rusty can handle it."

LeeLee pulled her chair all the way up to her desk and looked up at him. "That ain't what I mean. You have an image to uphold. Election time will come sooner than you realize."

"Have no fear, Lady LeeLee. By then, they will love me again." He tapped her head with the letters, and then turned toward the hall.

LeeLee rose partway and called out, "Ah...before you have a conniption, I didn't do it."

"What are you talkin' about?" asked Todd over his shoulder as he headed round the corner to his office. LeeLee jumped when she heard him curse. Todd regarded the banner strung across the door that read, "Where were you last night, Lover Boy?" It was signed by everyone on dayshift—everyone except LeeLee. Cursing under his breath, Todd stuck the mail between his lips, tore down the banner and crumpled it into a tight ball. He stormed back to the reception area, wound up and pitched it at LeeLee, who with a slight smile on her face, batted it away with the nightstick that she kept beside the little TV just in case a criminal escaped.

Todd entered his lair and brooded about the fact that every deputy now believed that he had sex with the finder of Elvis. Besides feeling humiliated, he winced at the thought that this development could mess with a trial, if this case ever came to one. He could see the headline: "Sheriff tampers with witness." He shuddered, then called the state crime lab and asked to speak to Angie.

"Hey, I heard Duckett County was visited by an EF-3 this morning," said Angie. "So, everybody still alive up there?"

"All fingers and toes have been accounted for."

"Good. Now down to business. We have finished running your penis's [giggle] the penis's DNA through CODIS. It's good you took those blood samples before the thing was mishandled—I mean mislaid—I mean—"

"Just get to the results, please, ma'am."

"There were no hits. The man who lived at the back end of this particular penis had no record."

"Well, that narrows things down a might bit. Probably 98% of the men in this county don't have a record."

"Do you have any idea where the penis could be?"

"Nope. I just hope it's in well-trained hands." That was a stupid remark. Angie must have thought so too because she giggled again, and Todd thought about how disgusted he was with this ridiculous case and its juvenile bathroom humor. He changed the subject. "How about the bones that we found in the Forest? Has trace come up with a DNA match to Billy's son?"

"Like I said yesterday, we were delayed with trying to get a good sample. Things are on track now, and we'll be able to make your Friday deadline." She sighed into the phone. "What you've got on your hands up there is a big stinky mess, huh?"

"If it ain't a mess, it'll do until the mess gets here." Todd opened a letter, saw that it was a complaint and tossed it in the trash.

Angie cleared her throat, an act that told Todd she was about to say something significant. "So I hear you ticked off Special Agent Slaughter. Now I know he screwed you over on that last big case, but he actually has a decent crime-solving record overall." Todd horse-snorted into the phone. Angie continued, "I've heard that when he's turned loose in the boondocks, Harwood is disgustingly racist, sexist, and just plain uncouth. But when he's here at GBI headquarters, he keeps his turd polished just enough to be someone who carries a lot of weight."

Todd opened a bill. "Is that so? Well, I say it's about time the High Muckety Monks down there at HQ put Special Agent Slaughter on a starvation diet before he creates one hell of a PR catastrophe." He tossed the bill into the tray marked "Rusty."

"Todd, please don't burn your bridges with the Bureau."

"Ha! If they keep sending me that low life, I say burn, baby, burn." Todd dumped the remaining mail in the wastebasket.

Angie was quiet for a few heartbeats. Then she replied softly, "I care about you. I'm worried."

"Oh now, Angie, don't I always land on my feet?"

"Bye, Todd," she replied wistfully and abruptly clicked off.

Todd looked at the phone thoughtfully, then shrugged and hung up slowly. He wondered if Angie thought of him as her fantasy man the way he had thought of her as his fantasy woman before Jasmine had arrived on the scene. Maybe it would be more realistic to work out a relationship with Angie. After all, she had grown up in the county next door. She was folk. At the moment she lived in Atlanta, but maybe she could find a criminologist position closer to Duckett County. And even if Angie could not move closer, there was dewy-eyed Bambi, his life-long best female friend. She wanted him, adored him, and she would have his back until his dying day, come what may. That kind of loyalty counted for a lot. Heck, he had been divorced for four years, and it was time to quit dreaming for a dazzling star like Jasmine Olivia Roseberry. Perhaps, thought Todd, his mother was right. He should be fishing in the local pond rather than thrashing about in a dark, roiling ocean of uncertainty. He needed to get on with his life. Jasmine was turning out to be too complicated to remain the flawless goddess of his dreams. But just then, a vision of her fine-boned face materialized in front of him. Damn those light-chocolate eyes and to hell with those dark-chocolate curls! Would her countenance haunt him for the rest of his days?

Todd rubbed his eyes, leaned back in his creaky chair, and stretched out his legs. Like distant thunder, a headache threatened. He decided that he needed to wrap up the Elvis case ASAP, if only for the sake of his career. The discovery of Billy Evans's bones had distracted him, but the Evans-Wells case was a cold case. Elvis was the hot case, and Todd knew he needed to keep his eye on the ball.

He played out a possible murder scene in his mind. Elvis's owner had sex with somebody who was not his wife. Upon discovering some evidence of her husband's infidelity, the wife flew into a jealous rage. Meanwhile, the husband was sleeping off his drunken night of illicit carnal knowledge, and so it had been easy for the wife to stab him to death. She then severed his penis, pulled on a pair of man-sized Georgia Boots, and drove to Duckett Forest. She hiked to the clearing and left Bad Elvis on that rock. She had intended that Elvis would be lunchmeat for the turkey vultures. However, shortly thereafter Jasmine had hiked into the clearing. Jasmine might not have noticed Elvis lying on that rock, but she had been accompanied by her dog, Tristan. Dogs never fail to sniff out private parts.

But something about this scenario didn't sit right with Todd. If the woman had flown into a homicidal rage, then the killing was unpremeditated. He couldn't envision her having the where-with-all to follow-up with an action so ritualistic as to hike into the woods and neatly dispose of one particular body part. Maybe this wasn't a murder case. Maybe all she did was sever Elvis, and then leave Elvis in the woods as further punishment for her husband. In that event, the victim could still be alive. After all, no Caucasian males had turned up missing in the tristate area, and no additional body parts had been found.

In a flash, Todd realized what should have dawned on him days ago. He chided himself for allowing his preoccupation with Ms. Roseberry to distract him. Raging hormones had muddled his deductive reasoning. Indeed, since meeting Jasmine he had been bouncing around inside a churning testosterone-laced thundercloud. This maelstrom had laid waste to his mental faculties the same way that banshee of a tornado had recklessly dismantled Jasmine's rental cabin. The most likely scenario was as obvious as the wart on Granny Quin's chin. He was now certain of the reason Elvis had been stolen—so it could be sewed back on! He looked out the window at the mountains just beyond town. Yes, this case really was looking more and more like a Lorena Bobbitt scenario. Elvis's owner had not been murdered. Instead, he had been Bobbitted.

But who stole the damn thing? Todd ran a hand over his hair, pausing at his neck. The so-called phone tips had dwindled considerably because the jokesters were finally growing bored. Since there were no other leads, Todd had no choice but to return his attention to his loony lineup of suspects—the Main Street merchants who had served on the search and rescue team in the quest to locate the rest of the body. Yet, he still couldn't see any of them swiping Elvis. They were not the type of people to be mixed up in this kind of mess. These hard-working, upstanding citizens of Duckett County were his friends.

Todd deliberated for a few more minutes while the clock on the wall matter-of-factly ticked off the seconds. To him, the noise sounded like a tiny coal miner was hammering inside his skull. The murders of Billy Evans and Bonnie Wells would have to wait. The the owner of Elvis had to be found, and the person who had severed Elvis had to be apprehended. The way to find them both was to catch the thief who had stolen Elvis. If Todd arrested the thief, he was sure he would solve the case. Rising, he settled his hat on his head. He strapped on his weapon and squared his shoulders. He had made a decision. There really was only one possible thief among the Main Street merchants, and of them, that person was the one he loved the most.

To Be Continued

Cast of Characters

Note: This Cast of Characters includes all characters in Book I, II, and III.

The Families

McPherson

Todd Hoyt 'Fearless' McPherson – Young sheriff of Duckett County, Georgia. Son of Hoyt McPherson and Jessie Quin McPherson.

Jessie McPherson - Todd's mother. A tall, raw-boned woman with a deep voice.

Hoyt McPherson – Todd's father (deceased three years prior). Farmer, and beloved member of the community.

Molly McPherson – age five. Todd's daughter with his x-wife, Brandy Stanton.

Katie McPherson Brown – age 30. Todd's older sister. Mother of Kylie, age five, and Will (six months). High school music teacher.

Bobby Brown – age 27. Katie's husband. Assistant football coach at Duckett High School.

Colleen Stewart – age 58. Jessie's sister.

Blaine Hensley – age 20. Todd's second cousin. Probie at the sheriff's department.

Hamilton

Delray Hamilton – age 35. Duckett County's district attorney. Comes from a family of famous defense attorneys. Grew up in Atlanta. Attended Vanderbilt University and Tulane Law School.

Carter 'Pitbull' Hamilton – Delray's father. Lives in Emerald Lake Retired ultra-successful defense attorney. From Atlanta

Kathy Hamilton – age 35. Delray's wife. Met Delray at Vanderbilt. She is a state representative in the Georgia General Assembly.

Judge Garland – (deceased) Kathy's father. Moved to Duckett County upon retirement from the bench.

Mrs. Garland – Kathy Hamilton's mother.

Stanton

Brandy Dodge McPherson Stanton – age 28. Married to Herb Stanton. Daughter of Preacher Dodge. Mother of Molly. Divorced from high school sweetheart, Todd McPherson.

Herb Stanton – age 50. Married to Brandy. Grew up in South Africa. Made a fortune in the USA. Lives in Emerald Lake Resort.

Davis

Sonny Davis – Age 52. Mayor of Duckettville, Chief operating officer of the county, and owner of a used car lot. Grew up in Foggy Bottom, the poorest part of the county.

Wade Davis –Age 27. Surveyor. Former husband of Bambi Davis and son of Mayor Sonny Davis. Played football with Todd in high school.

Les Davis – Late forties. Younger brother of Sonny and General Manager of the Property Owners Association (POA) of Emerald Lake Resort. Brother to Sonny Davis.

Conner Davis – Surveyor. Son of Les Davis. Also played football with Todd in high school.

Scratch Davis – Youngest son of Les Davis. Used car intern and night dispatcher at the Sheriff's Office.

Lee

LeeLee – Late forties. The Sheriff's department day dispatcher and secretary to Todd. Married to Sam Lee.

Sam Lee – 50. Husband of LeeLee. Todd's former scout leader. Retired early from the carpet mill due to allergies to industrial glues.

Travis Lee – 28. Oldest of the three Lee boys. Played sports with Todd in school.

Meriwether

Alex Meriwether – Age 70. Eccentric homesteader and computer repairman. Friend of the McPhersons.

Sunshine Meriwether – Age 58. Common Law wife to Alex. Originally from New England. Suffers from Schizophrenia.

Street

Andrew 'Fleet' Street –Star running back in high school. African American. Now an MD doing an internship in Psychiatry in Atlanta. Engaged to Daisy LeJuene.

Mrs. Street – Andrew Street's mother. African-American.

LeJuene

Marvalena LeJuene –The local granny witch or wart taker.

Daisy LeJuene – Daughter of Marvalena LeJuene. Intern at Grady Hospital in Atlanta. Engaged to Dr. Street.

Flagg

Coach Elvin Flagg – Football, basketball and baseball coach at Duckett High. Father of Jimmy Flagg who is in prison for drug trafficking.

Tammy Flagg – Operates the Checkered Flagg Grill and Pool Hall. Daughter-in-law of Coach Flagg.

The Sheriff's office

Todd McPherson –Sheriff of Duckett County for the past two years.

LeeLee – Dispatcher and secretary for Todd.

Rusty Moore – Todd's red-headed, mild mannered second-in-command.

Deputy Virgil Pilch – Mid-forties. The only deputy on the force over age thirty-one.

Deputy Blaine Hensley – Heavy-set second Cousin to Todd. A probie deputy.

Deputy Shawn Wiggins – Diminutive junior detective in training.

Where's Elvis?

Scratch Davis – Son of Les. Swing-shift dispatcher.
Deputy Forrest Green
Deputy Cody Culpepper
Deputy Tiffany Youst - female deputy.
Tawanda female African American deputy

The Main Street Businesses

Bambi Davis – Hairdresser. Owner of Curl Up & Dye. Bambi grew up with Todd, Brandy Stanton, and Tammy Flagg. She was married to Wade Davis, which makes her Sonny Davis's ex-daughter-in-law.
Tammy Flagg – Age 27. Owns the Checkered Flagg Grill and Pool Hall. Is married to Coach Flagg's son, Jimmy, who is in prison.
Sikes Freeman – Age 60. African-American who owns Freeman's Gun Repair and Barbershop. Close friend of the McPhersons.
Vince Verona – Age 45. Owner of the Duckettville Weekly and volunteer police photographer. Native of Chicago.
Gorov Mahmondi – Age 34. Owner of Duckett County Family Clinic. Native of Mumbai, India. Is working off a federal loan by running the county family clinic. Was also pressed into the job of part-time medical examiner.
Marvalena LeJuene – Age 55. Owner of Palms Are Us: Psychic Healing for You.

County commissioners

Walt Wiggins
Catch Ryder
Harold Mills
Sam Lee
Lymon McMyrtle
Billy Evans (missing)

Emerald Lake Resort

Brad Whitestone – Age 35. Whiz kid developer of Emerald Lake.

Les Davis – Age 50. General Manager of the Property Owners Association of Emerald Lake Resort. Brother of Sonny Davis.

Jasmine Roseberry – Hired to be the CFO for the Property Owners Association (POA) at Emerald Lake Resort.

Alice Davis – Age 52. Clerk at the POA Admin. office. Wife of Sonny Davis.

Valinda Mills – Age 49. Clerk at the POA Admin office. Wife of Phil Mills, a county   commissioner.

Cheryl Davis – Young clerk at the POA Office. Married to Les Davis' son, Conner.

Glen Baker – Mid-thirties. Former staff accountant for the POA.

Property Owners Association (POA) board members

Brad Whitestone – President of Whitestone Development Corporation

John Collier – Wealthy retired businessman who lives in Emerald Lake. Represents the interests of the residents.

Jane the Tennis Lady – Also represents the residents.

There are two unnamed members of the board who work for Brad Whitestone.

Media

Ansley Mason – Early thirties. Television news reporter.

Barry – Young Cameraman

Malcolm – Young soundman

The Churches on Main Street:

First Methodist: Pastor Ed Fowler

Second Baptist: Pastor Jake Jeffords

Evangelical Church of the Last Hope: Pastor J.T. Dodge

Miscellaneous

Where's Elvis?

GBI Special Agent Harwood Slaughter – mid-40s. Agent at the Georgia Department of Investigation.
Fuller – Mischievous Eight-year-old, red headed friend and next door neighbor to Molly McPherson (Todd's daughter).
Misty McMyrtle – Age 28. Oversexed real estate agent who attended high school with Todd. Daughter of Lymon McMyrtle who is on the county commission.
Gil Pirkle – County clerk.
Bunny Pirkle – Court reporter and mother of Gil.
Jeanie Evans – Wife of missing county commissioner Billy Evans.
Shane Evans – Son of missing country commissioner Billy Evans.
Bonnie Wells – Secretary to Billy Evans. She is also missing.
Mark Cantrell – Emergency Medical Technician. Todd's cousin.
Dwayne and Jimmy – 19-year-old college-dodgers who work for Brad Whitestone.
Judge Tibbett – County judge.

Acknowledgements

I would like to thank the following people:

My husband, Dr. Richard A. Lemen, former Assistant Surgeon General of the United States, for believing in me through three decades of marriage, and for doing everything short of super-gluing my fingers to the keyboard. And also for demonstrating great courage and dogged persistence in his efforts to ban the manufacture of asbestos worldwide. These are some of the qualities that make up the character of Todd McPherson (the book's main character).

Sue Ann Taylor for every few years looking me in the eye and asking me how "that novel" was coming.

My editor, Joan Phelps, without whose experience and qualifications I would be lost. Also, she has the patience of Job.

Ms. Denese Clancy, for providing her expert help with plot design and for taking time out of her busy career to review my manuscript.

Thomas and Jean Puett, and Linda Higgins, for providing invaluable information on the history, phraseology, and pronunciation regarding the linguistics of Southern Appalachia.

Dawson County Sheriff's Department, especially Sgt. Cantrell, for giving me a tour of the jail and the administrative offices.

Capt. Craig Cass of the Fulton County Sheriff's office for answering many of my technical questions about what it's like to be a cop.

Larry Fletcher, Viet Nam veteran and author of Shadows over Saigon, for editing the flying sequences.

Genevieve Rupley, who provided humorous church slogans.

I give thanks to my readers: Vivian Varner (my mom) who read through this twice while it was a work in progress; and Harold Varner (my dad), who has an eye for inauthentic details (even though this work is an over-the-top satire); Elizabeth and Rene Bottern; Thomas and Jean

Where's Elvis?

Puett; Lynn Dunagan; Monica Dobbins, Jim Welke; and Teya Shearing and Jim Welke.

CPSIA information can be obtained
at www.ICGtesting.com
Printed in the USA
LVOW03s0300220317
528026LV00001B/1/P